"It wasn't our work on cancer that led to the regeneration experiments," Arthur said to the examiner. "That came later."

"You just suddenly got the idea of how to regenerate organs?" Rosen asked.

Arthur suppressed an urge to smile. "Like all ideas, it was the result of many different stimuli, most of them subconscious until the big 'Aha!' hits."

"The big 'Aha?'" Rosen asked.

"The final realization of the idea in all its splendor," Arthur said. "What you might call the inspiration."

"Inspiration? That sounds like an artist's word, Dr. Marshak. We're talking about scientific research here, aren't we?"

"Albert Einstein said, 'Imagination is more important than knowledge.' He did a fair amount of scientific research."

Rosen huffed. "Very well, you were . . . inspired to think about the possibilities of regenerating organs and limbs. What did you do then?"

"I consulted with my brother, Dr. Jesse Marshak," said Arthur.

"That was the first thing you did when you got the idea that it would be possible to regenerate human organs?" Rosen asked.

Arthur shifted slightly in the witness chair. "The idea hadn't gotten that far yet. I was thinking then in terms of helping paraplegics."

The examiner stroked his mustache for a moment as he slowly walked across the front of the room, eclipsing the judges, one by one, from Arthur's view. "Paraplegics. Was this application vigorously pursued?"

"Not per se. It became part of the larger effort to pursue tissue regeneration in general."

"In other words, you forgot about helping paraplegics once you hit upon the possibility of regenerating organs such as the heart or kidneys. Is that correct?"

"More or less."

"And this would require the use of stem cells?" Rosen asked.

"At first we examined the possibility that—"

"You want to play God!" someone screamed from the audience.

Arthur turned in his chair. A florid-faced woman was on her feet glaring angrily at him.

"Using stem cells is killing babies! Smite this ungodly murderer, this false Antichrist! He's trying to play God!"

"Silence!" Graves banged his gavel on the tabletop. Arthur had thought the gavel was strictly symbolic. "Anyone who makes a disturbance will be removed from this hearing room. Is that clear?"

The woman sat down, muttering to the people next to her.

This isn't a trial, Arthur thought. It's an inquisition.

TOR BOOKS BY BEN BOVA

THE IMMORTALITY FACTOR

BEN BOVA

 TOR® A TOM DOHERTY ASSOCIATES BOOK NEW YORK

This is a work of fiction. All of the characters, organizations, and events portrayed in this novel are either products of the author's imagination or are used fictitiously.

THE IMMORTALITY FACTOR

Copyright © 2009 by Ben Bova

A Tor Book
Published by Tom Doherty Associates, LLC
175 Fifth Avenue
New York, NY 10010

www.tor-forge.com

Tor® is a registered trademark of Tom Doherty Associates, LLC.

ISBN 978-0-7653-4436-6

First Edition: April 2009
First Mass Market Edition: January 2010

Printed in the United States of America

0 9 8 7 6 5 4 3 2 1

In memory of James Blish,
who had faith in me

When a conjecture inspires new hopes or creates new fears, action is indicated. There is an important asymmetry between hope, which leads to actions which will test its basis, and fear, which leads to restriction of options frequently preventing any attempt at [testing]. As we know only too well, many of our hopes do not survive their tests. *However, fears accumulate untested.* Our inventory of untested fears has always made humanity disastrously vulnerable to thought control. Independent science's greatest triumph was the reduction of that vulnerability. [Italics added]

—ARTHUR KANTROWITZ
DARTMOUTH COLLEGE, 1994

Now it is a characteristic of such intellectuals that they see no incongruity in moving from their own discipline, where they are acknowledged masters, to public affairs, where they might be supposed to have no more right to a hearing than anyone else. Indeed they always claim that their special knowledge gives them valuable insights.

—PAUL JOHNSON
INTELLECTUALS

PREFACE

This is not a science fiction novel, let that be understood from the outset.

Although I am known primarily as a science fiction author, the book you hold in your hands is a contemporary novel. It is set in the here and now. Its major characters are scientists, the kind of men and women who are working today in laboratories around the world. It is the entire novel as I originally wrote it more than a decade ago.

When this novel was first published, in 1996 under the title *Brothers,* a major section of the story was excised at the rather insistent suggestion of the book's editor. This edition has restored that deletion, so that now the entire story is available for you to read.

In the mid-1990s, the scientific research being done by this novel's leading characters was futuristic. The idea of regenerating the cells of your body so that you could repair organs damaged by disease or injury, regrow a heart or kidney or limb, seemed little short of fantastic. But in the intervening dozen years such research has progressed to the point where it is the stuff of news headlines.

Much of this research involves stem cells, those human cells that can develop into any and all the other hundred trillion cells of the human body. Many objections have been raised against using fetal stem cells on the religious or moral grounds that a human fetus is destroyed in order to harvest its stem cells. Even the President of the United States has expressed qualms about "destroying life to create life."

But as one of the characters in this novel expresses, scientists are smart enough to find ways to produce stem cells without using fetuses. Yet the objections—religious, moral, political—still continue. It will take time, and a great deal of patience, before the fears generated by this striking new capability in the minds of the ignorant and intolerant are eased or forgotten altogether.

Even in this age of striking scientific advances and ever-accelerating technological breakthroughs, there are remarkably few novels about scientists. Most of the literary community—writers, editors, academics, critics—are sadly ignorant of modern science. And almost always, ignorance breeds fear and even contempt.

Yet science and its offspring technologies are the driving forces in our modern world. There is hardly an issue before us—be it stem cell research, energy, the environment, the economy, education, war—that does not involve science and technology at its very heart. To be ignorant of science is dangerous in today's world. It means that others are making the crucial decisions in your life, and the lives of your children.

Thus this novel. I am trying to depict scientists as I have known them, after spending most of my adult life working with them in one capacity or another. But this novel is about far more than scientific research. It is, at heart, a novel that deals with the human reactions to new knowledge, new understandings, new capabilities.

To me, scientific research is the most human thing that humans do. The drive to understand the world in which we live, and to change it to better suit our needs, is uniquely human. Yet there are dark forces of fear and ignorance that oppose this search for understanding.

Such conflict offers the novelist a truly fascinating setting for examining the human experience. Whether this novel does so successfully is for you to determine.

THE CONCEPT of a science court was originated by Dr. Arthur Kantrowitz, of Dartmouth College, a man with whom I was privileged to work for many years when he was director of the Avco Everett Research Laboratory in Massachusetts.

Much of the technical information in this novel has been

graciously provided by Dr. Kenneth Jon Rose, Dr. Martha Davila-Rose, Dr. Glen P. Wilson, William Cuthbert, and Lionel Berson. I have, of course, taken a novelist's liberties with the information they so kindly provided, so any shortcomings or mistakes of fact are my fault, not theirs.

BEN BOVA
Naples, Florida
December 2007

THE
IMMORTALITY
FACTOR

WASHINGTON:
THE CAPITOL

The crowd surging along the barriers that blocked off the Capitol steps was on the verge of turning ugly. It was much larger than the Capitol Police had anticipated and growing bigger by the minute. At first it had been orderly, well organized, mostly women of various ages led by earnest young men in dark suits and narrow ties who shouted their directions through electric bullhorns. Their permits were all in order and they patiently submitted to searches by the special antiterrorism squad and their bomb-sniffing dogs.

The placards they carried were professionally printed in red, white, and blue.

NO MONSTERS!
DON'T INTERFERE WITH GOD'S WORK
STEM CELL RESEARCH KILLS BABIES
MARSHAK IS A BABY KILLER

But now a different sort of crowd was pouring in, men and women, older for the most part, lots of gray hair and bald heads, many in wheelchairs. They were being searched, too, before being allowed across the broad parking area in front of the Capitol building. They had only a few placards among them, many of them hand-lettered.

DON'T CONDEMN ME FOR LIFE TO THIS WHEELCHAIR
I NEED A NEW HEART
MY BABY IS DYING. PLEASE HELP ME!

The demonstrators marched up and down the parking area outside the Capitol steps, chanting slogans and counterslogans.

"Marshak does the devil's work!"

"Marshak is a gift from God!"

"Marshak . . . Marshak . . . Mar-*shak* . . . Mar-*shak*!"

Now TV news vans were pulling up, like sharks drawn to blood, camera crews focusing on the placards and the marching, chanting, shouting, red-faced demonstrators.

The sky overhead was a clear summer blue, although the morning traffic had already raised a smoggy haze on the streets. Security choppers buzzed overhead; no news media helicopters were allowed near the Capitol. A hot, muggy July morning in the nation's capital; it would have been a slow Monday, news-wise, except for the demonstration. Knots of picketers began to cluster around each of the camera crews, yelling out their slogans and waggling their placards.

Captain Wally Lewis watched it all from the top of the Capitol steps with a sour frown on his dark fleshy face.

"Better call the Army," he said into his handheld radio.

The little speaker crackled. "You mean you can't handle a few yahoos?"

Lewis grimaced. "There's more'n a few." Squinting through the pollution haze past the Supreme Court building up toward the roadblock on Maryland Avenue where incoming buses were stopped and searched, he added, "And more busloads heading this way."

"How many more?"

"Six . . . eight . . . must be a dozen I can see from here. Plenty of nuts in with them." Then Lewis added, "Some terrorist outfit could use 'em for cover."

"You see any A-rabs among 'em?"

"Like they're gonna wear turbans and bushy beards," Lewis grumbled.

"You're overreacting, Wally."

With the weary head shake of a veteran, Lewis said into his radio, "These people are gonna turn nasty, I tell you. I can feel it in my bones."

"The hearing's over at the Rayburn Building, ain't it? Dumb shits don't even know where it's happening."

"Don't matter where the hearings are," said Lewis. "If there's a riot it's gonna be right here."

"Who in hell would've thought people'd get this worked up over some science stuff?" In the tiny radio speaker his supervisor sounded more surprised than annoyed.

"Yeah," said Lewis. Then he added silently, Who in hell?

THE TRIAL:

DAY ONE, MORNING

The noise of the demonstrators was barely audible across Independence Avenue, where the Rayburn House Office Building seemed quiet and calm, little different from any other summer Monday morning.

People were streaming into Room 2318, though, where the House Committee on Science normally holds its hearings. Four uniformed guards at the door carefully eyed the arriving men and women. Although this was an open hearing, every visitor had been searched at the security station in the building's lobby.

There was an electrical crackle of tense expectation in the air inside the hearing room. News reporters jammed the two long tables provided for them and spilled over into the first few rows of benches just behind the prospective witnesses. Their camera crews lined both sides of the unpretentious room, training their glaring lights on the three tiers of long desks lining the front wall of the chamber, where the committee members and their aides normally sat, and the smaller witness table facing it.

"State your name, please, and your affiliation."

"Arthur Marshak, director of Grenford Laboratory."

"Be seated."

As he took the witness chair, Arthur Marshak gave the impression of a handsomely distinguished, hugely successful man of the world. His hair had turned silver in his thirties. The Silver Fox, they called him—behind his back. Poised, self-assured, he worked hard to keep himself in shape. He wore a lightweight suit of deep blue with a carefully knotted maroon tie. He placed a black leather-bound PowerBook computer on the table before him, then sat. The green-baize-covered table also held a single pencil-thin microphone and a stainless steel pitcher of water on a tray with several plain drinking glasses.

Facing him from the bottom tier of desks where congressional committee members usually sat were three unsmiling elderly men, the judges, sitting in the green leather padded chairs. The chief judge, in the center, was president of the National Academy of Sciences, Milton Graves: balding, bespectacled, round-faced, he looked like a harmless old man, yet he was a wily veteran of Washington political infighting. On Graves's left sat a tanned professor of biochemistry from Caltech; on his right, a sad-eyed professor of jurisprudence from Yale. The examiner sat at the end of the row, next to the impromptu gallery that had been set up for the jury.

The chief judge peered at Arthur from over the rims of his bifocals. "Dr. Marshak," he said, as if he had not known Arthur for more than ten years, "I want to point out that although this is not a court of law, you are bound to reply fully and truthfully to all the questions asked of you, under penalty of contempt of Congress."

Arthur nodded. "I understand." Beneath his calm exterior Arthur felt slightly troubled. *Should I call him Your Honor? Or Dr. Graves? Milton Graves had helped Arthur to set up this trial, but now he was acting as if they were strangers.*

The men and women of the jury, a dozen carefully picked scientists, sat in their makeshift gallery along the plain white wall that held portraits of former committee chairmen.

"The point of this science court," Graves said, raising his voice to address the spectators, "is to determine the scientific validity of organ regeneration in human beings. This court has the responsibility of making a recommendation of public policy to the highest levels of government. To make that recommendation, we must ascertain the scientific facts. We will deal strictly with science in this hearing, nothing more." Then he added, "And nothing less."

This would be laughable if it weren't so deadly serious, Arthur thought. We're here to make a sober, calculated decision of scientific fact with half of Washington's news media breathing down our necks. Waiting for me to say that I can grow a new heart for you when your original heart is failing or regenerate an amputated limb. It's going to be a circus.

His brother Jesse was sitting in the front row, off to one side. Arthur turned slightly in his chair to see him, but Jesse avoided his eyes. Julia was not with him. Just as well; she shouldn't risk another miscarriage, Arthur thought. Better that she stays home.

"Dr. Marshak."

Arthur snapped his attention to the examiner. He was a lawyer from a Washington firm, young and tall and utterly serious. Dark brush of a mustache. He looked completely humorless. Slowly he rose to his feet and stood at the end of the table, rigid and upright, posed like a young Abe Lincoln. He held a doctorate in biology, but Arthur wondered how long it had been since this lawyer had seen the inside of a lab.

"Dr. Rosen," said Arthur coolly.

"Grenford Laboratory is a division of Omnitech Corporation, isn't it?"

Arthur's brows went up. "I don't see what that's got to do with the matter at hand."

"Please answer the question, sir."

Arthur shot a glance at Jesse. His brother gave him the slightest of smiles. So this is the way they're going to play the game, he thought. A fencing match. Very well, he told himself. En garde. He knew all about fencing.

"You must answer the question," said the judge on Arthur's left, the law professor.

"Yes," Arthur said warily, "Grenford Lab is a division of Omnitech."

"Omnitech is a multinational corporation?" asked the examiner, stepping slowly toward the witness table. "With extensive operations in Europe, Asia, and Latin America as well as here in the States."

"And in Canada, too," said Arthur. "We mustn't take our good neighbor to the north for granted."

A few of the spectators giggled. Rosen nodded solemnly. Out of the corner of his eye Arthur could see a trio of TV cameras following the lawyer's purposeful strides across the front of the room. The jury was focused on him, too.

"And just what is your position vis-à-vis Omnitech Corporation?"

"I am a corporate vice president. One of twenty."

"And a member of their board of directors?"

"Yes."

"You founded Grenford Laboratory, did you not?"

"Yes. Eight years ago."

"For what purpose?"

"To engage in cancer research."

"Did you do so on government research grants?"

"We received a few grants from NCI—"

"The National Cancer Institute?"

"Yes."

"NCI is part of the National Institutes of Health, is it not?"

"NIH, yes." Arthur could not help frowning. Everyone here knew the jargon, even the reporters.

"Any other government support?"

"No. The overwhelming majority of our support came from the corporation's internal funding."

"I see." Rosen walked away from the witness table a few steps, slowly, as if mulling over what he had just heard.

Then he turned. "And when did your work on cancer research turn toward the objective of regenerating organs?"

ARTHUR

I almost laughed at his question. Like most of my really great ideas, it came to me during sex. Not that I'd tell him that.

It was one of those delightfully unplanned, unanticipated moments. They don't happen often, but when they do they have a momentum of their own. I had shaken hands with Elise Hauser while I was going through the reception line at the Humanitarian of the Year dinner at the Waldorf. She was virtually a giantess, a couple of inches taller than I. Straw-blond hair spilling down to her bare shoulders. She looked splendidly regal. The other women at the dinner were either dowdy white-haired old ladies loaded with jewelry or over-dressed young bubbleheads in the latest flamboyant styles. Elise wore a simple white gown that clung to her like a famished lover, strapless and cut deliciously low.

As the brother of the guest of honor, I was placed at the head table. As a ranking representative of the United Nations, Elise was, too. I got the waiter to shuffle the place cards so I could sit beside her instead of between Jesse and Julia. I hadn't seen either of them since their wedding, and I felt terribly awkward about seeing them now. No, not just awkward. I felt hurt. Pained. At first I thought I'd stay away from this dinner, but Momma convinced me that it would look awful if Jesse's only brother didn't show up for his big night.

Once we were seated next to each other, Elise asked me, "You are the brother of the award recipient?" Her accent was Viennese, her voice was low, throaty. A smoker's voice, I thought. It sounded sexy.

The ballroom was buzzing with two hundred conversations while waiters dashed among the tables with heavy trays laden with banquet fare. The male guests and the waiters were all in tuxedos; the room looked like a collection of penguins accompanying gaudily plumed peacocks. I filtered all of that out to concentrate on her.

"Yes," I said, smiling my best smile for her. "He's my baby brother."

"He is a great man. You must be very proud of him."

"Oh, I am." Then I figured I'd see if she had a sense of humor. "Of course, I taught him everything he knows."

Her brows arched. "You are joking."

"A little."

"You are a physician also?"

"No, I'm a scientist."

"A physician is not a scientist?"

That made me laugh. "They think of themselves as scientists, but real scientists think of them as pill-pushers or butchers."

"You don't have a high opinion of your brother."

"But I do!" I said. And I almost meant it. "Jesse's a fine man. An ornament to his profession. He deserves the award very much." I didn't tell her that he had stolen Julia away from me.

"I see." She turned her attention to the fruit cup in front of her.

I turned and glanced down the row of dignitaries sitting at the head table to take a peek at Julia. Her eyes seemed to look slightly puffy, as if she had been crying. Is she really happy with Jess? He can't possibly be taking care of her the way I could. What a fool she was to throw me over for him. My baby brother. Humanitarian of the Year. What a joke.

A waiter took away my fruit cocktail before I had the chance to do more than stick a spoon into it. Another waiter slapped a plate of soggy salad in front of me.

I returned my attention to the blond Amazon next to me. "Did you say you worked at the United Nations?"

"Yes," she answered, a forkful of wilted lettuce in midair between her plate and her lips. "In the secretary-general's office."

"And what do you do there?"

"Mostly I move paperwork from my desk to someone else's desk," she said with a sigh deep enough to raise my pulse rate. "Once in a while, however, I am able to do something useful."

"Such as?"

"Increase the budget for UNESCO, so that some of the poorer countries can gain the benefits of medical research."

"I see." I made a stab at my own salad. The dinner's sponsors were obviously not spending much of their money on the food.

"What kind of a scientist are you?" she asked.

I was tempted to say that I was the best kind, the kind that deserved a Nobel Prize but would never receive one. But that would have sounded too bitter. So I simply replied, "Molecular biology."

"Ah. Genetic engineering."

She knew quite a bit about molecular biology, it turned out. And she was good at getting me talking. Before I realized it, I found myself telling her how Jesse and I had engineered a microbe that ate toxic wastes and reduced them to harmless natural elements. I patented that microbe and then licensed Omnitech Corporation to produce it. Jesse and I became pretty well off on the royalties; wealthy enough for Jesse to devote his medical practice to the poor and become Humanitarian of the Year. Wealthy enough for my department head at Columbia to get so envious that he drummed me out of the university.

Elise seemed very impressed. I was certainly very impressed with her. I was staying at the Waldorf overnight and we ended up in my suite, in bed. She had a skier's supple muscular body, strong and lithe, and she was used to getting her own way. She wanted to be dominant, but I wouldn't let her. We both enjoyed every instant of our tussle.

It was right after that, while we lay sweaty and spent on the rumpled bed, that the idea hit me. We were already working on the genes that control the suppressor factor that stops cells from multiplying. That was one of our approaches to dealing with cancer. But what if we could find the genes that produce the activating factors that make the cells mature and differentiate? If we could control both the suppressor and activating factors, we could control cell regeneration.

"We could cure paraplegics," I said out loud.

"Huh?" Elise mumbled drowsily.

I don't get many flashes of inspiration like that. Usually Jesse's the intuitive one; I tend to be more methodical. A plodder, in Jesse's estimation.

I sat up in the bed. "That's the great thing about sex. It dissolves the barriers in your mind. It's the most creative act a person can do."

"Thank you."

I was so excited that I got up from the bed and padded naked into the sitting room of the suite. I closed the door so I wouldn't disturb Elise. The room was lit only by the street glow coming through the window. A siren wailed past out there, its pitch Dopplering down as it yodeled along the avenue. Two in the morning and still the city growled and hummed. New York, New York: the town so big they had to name it twice.

I fumbled around in the semidarkness, banged my shin against the damned coffee table before I found the lamp on the end table beside the sofa and clicked it on. The sofa felt cold and a little rough on my bare bottom, but I ignored that, looked up Jesse's number in my notebook, then grabbed the phone and punched it out.

I heard the phone ring once, twice . . .

"Hullo?" Julia's voice. Even after all these months her voice stabbed straight into my heart. I hadn't expected her to answer. I guess I hadn't wanted to think of her in bed with my brother.

"Um, sorry to wake you, Julia. I need to talk to Jess."

"Arthur? Lord, I thought it was the hospital."

"No, it's just me."

"We haven't heard a word from you in a year and you phone at two a.m.?"

"It's important," I said.

"Can't you wait until morning?"

I wanted to apologize to her, I wanted to tell her how much I still loved her and missed her and how deeply she had hurt me, but instead I only said, "By morning he'll be off and running and it'll take me another two days to track him down. Let me talk to him now, will you?"

Something muffled, then Jesse's voice. "Arby? What's the matter? What's wrong?"

"I've got an idea."

"An idea? You're calling about an idea at two in the morning?"

"I know where you are at two in the morning," I snapped. "Most mornings, anyway."

"I don't believe this."

"It's an important idea," I insisted.

"Great. Go back to sleep and maybe it'll go away."

"Dammit, Jess, this is serious! We can repair the spinal damage that causes paraplegia."

"Sure we can."

"How soon can you get up to my lab?"

"Arby, it's two in the morning, for Chrissakes!"

"I know what time it is, dammit! Are you interested in curing paraplegics or not?"

Despite himself, Jesse was interested. I started explaining my idea and Jesse stayed on the phone, listening. Soon he was commenting, making suggestions, adding his own ideas. I heard my brother's voice go from irritation to reluctance to enthusiasm as we batted concepts back and forth just the way we used to do in the old days, before Julia.

"You thinking of using stem cells?" Jesse asked. "That's asking for trouble, Arby."

"Adult stem cells, Jess, not fetal cells. And maybe we won't even need that if—"

Elise swept past, fully dressed, her hair glistening from the shower. She gave me a pitying smile and blew me a kiss. I barely waved to her while I continued to talk with my brother.

JESSE

Humanitarian of the Year. And you know what? I deserved it. As much as anybody in the city, I guess.

I wouldn't have thought so before I met Julia. Never even would have thought about it at all, really. I just did the work I wanted to do and never gave a hoot about awards and honors. That was my brother's kick. Arby always took himself very importantly. Hell, he was talking about winning the Nobel Prize back when I was still in high school and he was a sophomore at Columbia.

Must have hurt him like hell when they threw him out of Columbia. But he landed on his feet, no bruises. Started up the lab in Connecticut and started making tons of money. Me, I just plugged away at med school and then went into practice.

It was Julia who saw the importance of honors and awards. "It will bring more attention to the hospital," she told me. "It will help to attract more donations. And larger ones, too."

She was right, of course. The bigger my name got, the easier it was to raise big bucks for the hospital. And the medical center. Julia saw to it that when we went to Brazil we got plenty of media coverage. Translated into several million in donations.

Arby was as uptight as a Mormon in a cocktail lounge all through the dinner at the Waldorf. We hadn't seen him since our wedding. I'm sure he didn't want to come to the dinner but Ma made him. She's tough. Too bad she couldn't come herself. I had wanted her to, but her doctors said she couldn't travel and Arby sided with them.

Anyway, he was stiff as a totem pole with us. Shook my hand, of course, and took Julia's. Mumbled a couple of words. And then he got as far away from us as possible. Even rearranged the seating at the head table so he wouldn't have to be between Julia and me. Sat himself next to some big blond dish. That's my brother Arby: no matter what happens he comes out okay.

I was awfully uncomfortable in that damned tux. I don't even own a tie. Julia had to do the bow tie for me, and I went all through dinner with it strangling me but when it came time for my little speech I just had to undo it. Got my picture in the *Times* that way, with the tie hanging loose and my collar undone. They didn't see that I was wearing nice comfortable running shoes. They were black and if anybody noticed they didn't say anything.

Anyway, we get through the dinner and the speech and Arby disappears with the blonde on his arm. Julia and I taxi back to our apartment.

"Do you realize," she said as we were undressing, "that this is the first time this month that you've been home before midnight?"

I hadn't realized it.

"Have I been neglecting you?" I asked her.

"You most certainly have." She had that mischievous grin on her face, the kind that said fun and games.

So I gave her my utmost attention. And she did likewise for me. It was terrific.

We're drifting off to sleep, around two or so, when the phone rings. Julia grabs it because she wound up on that side of the bed. I'm thinking it's some kind of disaster at the hospital, who the hell else would call me at two in the morning?

It's Arby. He's got some big cockamamie idea about regenerating spinal neurons in paraplegics. I can't believe it. He hasn't said a word to me in a year, and now he's bubbling over with enthusiasm, just as if he had never been sore at me at all.

And he just wouldn't let me off the phone. I mean, the idea was interesting enough, but he kept rattling on and on about it and telling me he wanted me to help him with it, just like we worked together years ago before he founded his big-time lab, before Julia came into our lives.

Julia sat there in the bed beside me, pressing close so she

could hear what Arby was talking about. I got maybe six words in every fifteen minutes or so. Arby kept yakking and yakking. About science. About us working together to cure paraplegics and allow them to walk again.

After more than an hour of this, Julia gets up from the bed and starts rummaging in the night table on her side. She looked like she was posing for *Playboy* or something, in the nude like that. I started thinking that I ought to hang up on Arby and grab her again.

But she pulls out a pad and ballpoint pen and scribbles a note for me.

He wants to make up with you, her note said.

I looked up at her, Arby's voice still chattering in my telephone ear. Julia sat beside me again and nodded, with a really happy smile on her face. Then she wrote some more on the pad.

This is Arthur's way of getting together with you again, it said. *Don't brush him off.*

Like she was a mind reader, at that precise instant Arby asked, "Can you make it over here tomorrow for lunch?"

"You mean have lunch at your lab?" I asked.

Julia nodded so vigorously it made her breasts bob up and down. I damn near dropped the phone.

"Yes," Arby was saying. "At the lab, tomorrow. Well, later today, actually."

I grinned at my wife and said into the phone, "Okay, Arby. I'll be there around twelve-thirty. How's that?"

"Wonderful!" he said. And at last he hung up.

I put the phone back in its cradle and then pulled Julia to me.

"He wants to get together with you again," she said, all smiles. "He wants to end this separation."

JULIA

had never intended to come between Arthur and Jesse. I had
never meant to cause hurt or pain.

As a matter of fact, I had never intended to fall in love or
get married or live in America. I had a very nice career going
with British Airways, thank you, and I was quite the self-
possessed modern woman, making ready to shatter the glass
ceiling of corporate chauvinism to become the first woman
chairman of BA's board, eventually. I had it all planned out,
you see.

In the meantime I was having great fun, traveling the world
and advancing my career. I had a few flings here and there,
always very cautiously, of course. It wouldn't do for an ambitious woman executive to get the wrong kind of reputation.
And there was always AIDS to worry about.

But Arthur simply swept me off my feet. Here was this
handsome silver-haired man with an absolutely deadly smile,
intelligent as the devil, successful, quite well-off financially,
who just happened to sit beside me on the Airbus flight I was
making to New York. And he exuded this kind of animal heat
without even realizing it.

This was something I hadn't planned on; not at all. In fact,
within two weeks my plans were completely demolished and
I was suddenly living in a different world. Truth to tell, I allowed Arthur to sweep me off my feet. It was enormous fun
and tremendously exciting. I transferred to the New York office and told myself that the glass ceiling could remain un-
shattered a while longer because I was going to add romance
and marriage to my life plan.

Looking back on it, I realize that I never actually loved
Arthur. I was in a whirl and we certainly shared wildly passionate times in bed, and when he asked me to marry him I
said yes without hesitation. I was living life in the fast lane,
the kind of life I could only dream about before meeting

Arthur, and I never even thought of what could happen to us in the long run. It was foolish of me; vain and selfish and foolish. That's what happens when one acts without thinking.

Arthur introduced me to his younger brother, whom he obviously felt very proud of and protective toward. Jesse seemed at first disdainful, aloof, and rather surprised that Arthur could fall so hard for a woman so quickly. At first I thought Jesse suspected me of being an opportunist, an English adventuress who was taking advantage of his big brother. I began to fear that he was right. I told myself that he was jealous of Arthur. And I found that he was, but not in a mean, selfish way.

Jesse was in love with me! Beneath that rigid New Yorkish shell he kept around himself he was a sensitive, vulnerable man who loved me. And I was shocked to realize that I had fallen in love with him. Deeply, truly in love. The calculating part of my mind told me that I was going to ruin everything. But my heart overwhelmed my head; I fell in love with Jesse and there was no remedy for it.

You see, Jesse needed me and Arthur didn't. It was almost as simple as that. There wasn't very much that I could give to Arthur that he didn't already have. I began to realize that I would be a sort of trophy for him, a wife to show off after board meetings. But Jesse and I could share a life together. I could help him become the man he wouldn't even dream of being without me. Jesse would make a fine father, too, I was sure of that.

Once I realized that I was thinking about children, there was no turning back. The smug career woman who had allowed herself to be swept into the fast lane disappeared. Jesse was my life. His career became my prime focus.

It was the most difficult thing I had ever done in my life to break that news to Arthur. I didn't want to hurt him, and I knew that Jesse didn't want to, either. I dreaded the thought of coming between them. I even asked their mother what I should do, a very painful and draining afternoon in her room at the nursing home where she lay waiting for death to overtake her.

There was nothing for it except to tell Arthur the unvarnished truth. It was my own fault, of course. I should never have agreed to marry Arthur so quickly.

His reaction stunned me. He said absolutely nothing. He went rigidly silent and walked out of my life—and Jesse's. Literally. He simply walked away. I felt miserable about it. But Jesse and I were in love and we got married soon afterward. Arthur came to the wedding but said not a word to anyone, certainly not to either of us. In fact, the first words I heard from his mouth came at the Humanitarian of the Year dinner, when he more or less had to say hello as he came through the reception line and took my hand briefly.

That's why I was so glad that Arthur had broken the ice at last and invited Jesse to work with him on this scientific idea of his. I had asked Jesse, now and then, to make some overture to his brother, but Jess wouldn't do it.

"You don't know him as well as I do," he would tell me. "I could stand on my head and turn blue and he'd just stare right past me."

So that night—or that morning, rather—when Arthur called I was overjoyed. Perhaps the two men could start behaving like brothers again. It would be an enormous burden of guilt lifted from my shoulders.

THE TRIAL:

DAY ONE, MORNING

It wasn't our work on cancer that led to the regeneration experiments," Arthur said to the examiner. "That came later."

Rosen seemed to think that over for several long moments. The hearing chamber was absolutely silent, not even a cough or a shuffle of feet. With his back to the spectators, Arthur realized that every eye in the chamber was focused on the lawyer, including the television cameras. He glanced at the

TV monitor set up against the side wall. It showed Rosen's dark-haired, somber face in a tight close-up.

"You just suddenly got the idea of how to regenerate organs?" Rosen asked.

"Yes."

"Such as the heart?"

"Yes."

"And limbs? Legs, arms, fingers?"

"Or toes."

"This idea just suddenly sprang into your mind?"

Arthur suppressed an urge to smile. "Like all ideas, it was the result of many different stimuli, most of them subconscious until the big 'Aha!' hits."

The audience behind him stirred slightly. He heard a couple of small laughs.

"The big 'Aha'?" Rosen asked.

"The final realization of the idea in all its splendor," Arthur said. "What you might call the inspiration."

"Inspiration? That sounds like an artist's word, Dr. Marshak. We're talking about scientific research here, aren't we?"

"Albert Einstein said, 'Imagination is more important than knowledge.' He did a fair amount of scientific research."

Rosen huffed. "Very well, you were . . . inspired to think about the possibilities of regenerating organs and limbs. What did you do then?"

Arthur looked past the lawyer to the panel of judges. "I thought this court was to be a scientific inquiry. What's all this questioning of my personal behavior got to do with it? We're here to settle the scientific issue!"

Before Graves or either of the other judges could respond, Rosen said, "I am attempting to set the background against which this research was conducted. Science does not happen in a vacuum. *People* do science, and their motivations can be as important to the outcome of their research as any other factor."

"That's nonsense and—"

"A young woman died as a result of this work," Rosen said coldly.

Arthur felt his words like a blow to the pit of his stomach. "Her death had nothing to do with this research and you know it," he snapped.

Rosen turned to the judges.

Graves pushed at his bifocals and cleared his throat, tactics Arthur recognized as a way of stalling for time while he thought. At last the chief judge said, "Since this is the first time the science court has been convened, I am willing to allow the examiner a certain degree of latitude. There is the question of wrongful death involved, whether we like it or not."

"This court shouldn't be concerned with that matter," Arthur insisted. "We're here to examine the scientific evidence and nothing more. You said that yourself."

Looking pained, Graves replied, "We would all be grateful, Dr. Marshak, if you would indulge us and answer the examiner's questions to the best of your ability."

He called me Dr. Marshak, Arthur said to himself. Two nights ago we were drinking together at the Cosmos Club and now he acts as if we're strangers.

"Please answer the question," Graves repeated.

"What was the question?" Arthur grumbled.

The clerk pecked at his digital recorder. Rosen's voice droned, "Very well, you were inspired to think about the possibilities of regenerating organs and limbs. What did you do then?"

"I consulted with my brother, Dr. Jesse Marshak," said Arthur.

"That was the first thing you did when you got the idea that it would be possible to regenerate human organs?" Rosen asked.

Arthur shifted slightly in the witness chair. "The idea hadn't gotten that far yet. I was thinking then in terms of helping paraplegics."

The examiner stroked his mustache for a moment as he slowly walked across the front of the room, eclipsing the judges, one by one, from Arthur's view.

"Paraplegics."

Impatiently, Arthur replied, "This is all in the written documentation I've provided the court. If you've read the material—"

"There is nothing in the documentation about paraplegics," said Rosen.

"Yes, there is," Arthur insisted. "In the note I published in *Biophysics Letters* I discussed nerve regeneration in vivo as a means of reversing paraplegia."

"Was this application vigorously pursued?"

"Not per se."

"And what does that mean?"

"It became part of the larger effort to pursue tissue regeneration in general."

"In other words, you forgot about helping paraplegics once you hit upon the possibility of regenerating organs such as the heart or kidneys. Is that correct?"

"More or less."

"There's much more money in organ regeneration, isn't there?" Rosen said. "A bigger market than paraplegics."

He's intentionally trying to make me lose my temper, Arthur told himself. With deliberate calm he replied, "Let me correct myself. We did not forget about helping paraplegics. We simply realized that regenerating nerve growth is a part of the more general problem of regenerating tissue, all kinds of tissue."

"Human tissue?"

"Yes."

"And this regeneration would take place inside the human patient?"

"Whenever possible, yes. That was our goal."

"Grow a new heart inside the patient's chest?"

"Yes, if necessary. In most cases I think it would be sufficient to repair the damaged sections of the heart and make it as good as new. You see, heart muscle cells have differentiated, specialized; they lack the ability to multiply. When the muscle is damaged by a heart attack, the damaged area can't repair itself."

"And your technique would repair the heart?"

"Or grow a whole new one, if necessary."

"This would require the use of stem cells?" Rosen asked.

"At first we examined the possibility that—"

"You want to play God!" someone screamed from the audience.

Arthur turned in his chair. A florid-faced woman was on her feet glaring angrily at him.

"Using stem cells is killing babies! Smite this ungodly murderer, this false Antichrist! He's trying to play God!"

"Silence!" Graves banged his gavel on the tabletop. Arthur had thought the gavel was strictly symbolic. "Anyone who makes a disturbance will be removed from this hearing room. Is that clear?"

The woman sat down, muttering to the people next to her.

This isn't a trial, Arthur thought. It's an inquisition.

ARTHUR

The morning after Jesse's Humanitarian of the Year dinner I drove straight from the Waldorf out to my lab. It was a sunny April morning, the first really warm weather after the long gray winter. Forsythia bushes bloomed bright happy yellow all along the busy parkway. I almost imagined I could hear birds singing.

We had put the Grenford Research Laboratory just over the state line in Connecticut mainly to satisfy Omnitech's corporate tax accountants. Of course, within a year of the lab's opening, Connecticut's taxes rose to meet New York's. But the location was a good one anyway: close enough to New York City for me to feel at home yet far enough into the countryside to enjoy some trees and fresh air. We could attract top talent for the staff and they didn't have to worry about parking or muggers at night.

The building was a low, modern structure of brown brick

with curved corners and wide sweeping windows. It hugged a green landscaped hillside that dropped off to a wooded stream behind the building. A beautiful site, really. Originally it had been the headquarters of an independent computer software corporation. But they had gone out of business in the economic doldrums after 9/11 and Omnitech had bought the building for little more than the back taxes owed on it. Interstate 95 and the more scenic Merritt Parkway were only minutes away; you could hear the muted buzz from the highways coming through the trees surrounding the lab's parking lot.

It was almost ten a.m. by the time I eased my Infiniti over the speed bumps at the entrance to the parking lot and pulled to a stop in my reserved space at the lab's front entrance. The lot was almost full. Usually I got to work among the earliest arrivals, but I had stayed up until dawn talking with Jesse. So I didn't bother going home; I just stuffed my tuxedo into my overnight bag, pulled on the slacks and sports jacket I had brought with me, and checked out of the Waldorf. I felt a flash of relief that my car hadn't been stolen from the parking garage overnight; it's a silver Infiniti Q45, and even though the corporation leases it for me, I wouldn't want to lose it.

I waved hello to Helen, the receptionist, as I went through the lobby. I had deliberately placed my office suite far back in the building, so that I have to walk past most of the staff offices to get to my own. And it was only a few steps away from the working labs, as well.

As I made my way down the carpeted corridors, the staffers nodded or smiled or called their good-mornings to me. Several tried to talk to me, falling into step alongside, but I was already behind schedule, so I put them off with a "Not now, please. I'm running late."

But Darrell Walters, one of the oldest men on the scientific staff, wouldn't be brushed off so easily.

"This'll only take as long as the distance to your office," he said. He looked worried; a frown creased his normally cheerful face.

"Okay," I said, "I'm listening."

I kept the lab's organization pretty loose, but Darrell was closer to being my second-in-command than anybody else. With his long horsy face and the craggy wrinkles at the corners of his eyes, he looked more like a canny old backwoods guide than a biochemist, especially in his chambray work shirt and faded Levi's. But he was one of the sharpest men on the staff. And I knew how much it cost·him to look so unpretentious; the story around the lab was, if Walters ever dressed up, L. L. Bean would go out of business.

"Cassie's run into a real roadblock," Darrell told me. "Blasted NIH won't give their okay for the clinical test."

Cassie Ianetta was one of my bright young cell biologists. She was working on an antibody that had been developed by a university team up in Boston that could stop viruses from reproducing inside human cells. Cassie did absolutely brilliant work, directed mainly to using the antibody as a tumor suppressant. It stopped cancer cells from reproducing; killed the tumor, if the treatment was applied early enough. She had tried it out on laboratory rats and monkeys and even chimpanzees. Now she needed to test the treatment in humans. Volunteers had been easy to come by: terminal cancer patients have little to lose.

I wasn't surprised by the government's refusal for human trials, though. "They're just protecting their asses," I said.

"And then some," Darrell agreed fervently. He was matching me stride for stride down the corridor without running out of breath, as many of the younger staffers would.

"Talk to Lowenstein up in corporate. Tell him what you need. He'll set Cassie up overseas someplace, maybe Mexico."

"She doesn't want to travel. Max and all that."

We had reached the door to my outer office. It was wide open, as always.

"Well," I asked him, "is she more interested in Max than her work?"

Darrell shrugged. "Hard to say."

"You're closer to her than anybody else on the staff. How's it look to you?"

"I don't think Cassie knows herself what she wants to do. She's all tied up in knots over this."

I knew what he was after. "Okay, tell her to come see me," I said. "Let me talk some sense to her."

That was what Darrell had wanted to hear. He broke into a toothy grin. "Right. I'll send her over right away."

"No. This afternoon. After lunch."

Darrell looked slightly disappointed, but he reluctantly agreed. "After lunch. Okay."

"Set it up with Phyllis."

"Will do."

Phyllis Terhune had been my secretary since my days at Columbia. She was black, plump, a youngish grandmother who brooked no nonsense, not even from her boss. She ran my office with cool efficiency, the only barrier between me and the staff people who constantly streamed through that always-open door. And she took pride in making the lab's best coffee.

"Kinda late for you," she said from behind her white-lacquered desk.

"I was up most of the night," I replied. I must have grinned smugly.

She cast me a disapproving look. "I bet."

I went past her to my inner office, peeled off my sports jacket, and hung it in the closet next to the lavatory. Phyllis stood at the doorway to the outer office as I slid into my big comfortable swivel chair.

"Your schedule's on the screen," she said. "Coffee's in the warmer."

"Good."

"You need orange juice?"

"Vitamin E, I think."

She frowned again. Grandma Phyllis. "Better put some citrus scent in the room," she said, half to herself.

That was Phyllis's one quirk. She was into aromatherapy. She was convinced that subliminal odors could alter a person's moods. I teased her about it being voodoo science, but she stuck to her guns. It was a small price to pay for the best secretary I had ever known. And who knows, maybe she was right.

I booted up my desktop computer, checked the morning's commitments, then said, "Jesse's coming in for lunch around twelve-thirty, one o'clock."

"Jesse?" Her smile radiated approval. "'Bout time you two started acting like brothers again."

"Clear everything from twelve-thirty until three."

"The board chairman's secretary wants to discuss the agenda for the next meeting. He's down for two-thirty."

"You handle it, Phyl. If there's anything you're in doubt about, pop in and ask me."

"You want to eat in here?"

"I think that's best. No interruptions."

She nodded once and returned to her desk. I dug into my morning appointments, already behind schedule, but for once in my life I hardly cared. Jesse was coming over to thrash out this hot new idea. I felt an excitement I hadn't known for more than a year, like an adrenaline rush. Despite everything, Jesse was taking the time to come and see me.

Yes, Jesse had stolen Julia from me. She was going to marry me and Jesse had just smiled that boyish smile of his and she had run off with him. The memory still cut me like a knife in my guts. But it was over and done with and there was nothing I could do about it. Time to start over again, time to renew my bond with my brother. I tried to put the painful memories aside. I wanted to forget how agonizing it had been; how furious my brother's betrayal had made me. And I did forget it.

Almost.

DARRELL WALTERS

I knew we would have trouble with Cassie Ianetta.

She was about as big as a minute. At first glance she looked like a child, a nervous little sparrow with skinny arms and legs and a wild mop of unruly dark brown hair that was always flopping stubbornly down over her eyes. But one look into those burning brown eyes and you knew that this was a grown-up, an intense, driven adult with a mind as keen as they come.

But she was an emotional mess. I imagine she had good reason to be, what with her bouts with cancer and all. And she had never had any luck with guys, always picked jerks who hurt her. She looked like a forlorn waif as she slowly shuffled through the cafeteria line, a skinny kid in faded old blue jeans that hung on her like they were hand-me-downs from a bigger sister. I was right behind her in the line. I could look down and see how thin her hair had gotten from the chemotherapy. I kind of felt like an uncle to Cassie; I wanted to help her, protect her, as much as I could. She was really a nice kid, no matter how tangled up she was emotionally.

We slid our trays along the counter, past the steam tables and the sandwich display, stopping briefly at the salads and then at the juice machine. I had my usual brown bag on my tray; no respectable Connecticut Yankee would pay cafeteria prices when he could pack his own lunch. Cassie picked the first salad she could reach.

The tables by the windows, with their view of the wooded hill, were already taken. We weren't interested in the view anyway, so we sat at a table for two in a corner where nobody would interrupt us.

"How're you feeling these days?" I asked as we sat down.

"Okay," said Cassie. She perched on her chair like a little bird, tired and scared at the same time. Her skin was sallow, her face drawn.

"No reversion from the therapy?"

She shook her head, but I saw that her lips were pressed into a thin bloodless line.

"No reversion," she said at last. "It's gone. They got it all."

That made me smile. "Then you'll be okay to go to Mexico, right?"

Cassie looked as if she had known what was coming. "There's no *physical* reason for me not to go to Mexico. Or Timbuktu, for that matter."

I could feel my smile fade away. I knew what was coming next.

"I don't want to be away from Max that long," she said.

"It'll only be six months or so," I told her. "And you don't have to stay down there the whole time. Six months, at most, and then a couple months when the results start coming in."

Cassie shook her head. "You don't understand, Darrell."

"Yes, I do. You love him and you can't stand the thought of being away from him."

"Don't try to be funny."

"You're afraid to be away from him."

She bit her lower lip. Then she admitted, "Yes. I'm scared to death, Darrell. For his sake."

It was nonsense, of course, but she sure didn't see it that way.

"He can't get along without me," Cassie said. "I know he can't."

"That's not true and you know it."

"It *is* true."

She looked sad when she should have looked happy.

I said, "Hey, you can hop back here every couple of weeks, spend a weekend, and then go back."

But Cassie shook her head again. "That wouldn't work," she said, pushing back that tangle of hair that flopped across her eyes.

I hunched forward and grabbed her wrist. It felt as thin and fragile as a soda straw. "You can't give away two years of your work to somebody else, kid! You've got to do the clinical trials, get the results, and publish. Otherwise you'll be going nowhere."

Her face twisted up into a frown. "If only we could do the trials here. New York, Boston even . . ."

"Arthur wants to see you this afternoon," I said. "At three."

"I know. Phyllis told me."

"He's got to know whether you're going to do the clinical trials or somebody else is."

"Yes," she sighed.

"You've got to make a decision, Cassie. It's crucial to your career. Your whole life."

She glanced down at her salad, pushed it away. She looked miserable.

I tried to lighten the mood a little. "Golly, if Arthur wanted to give *me* six months in Mexico, I'd jump at it. Six whole months away from my wife? Heaven!"

Cassie didn't laugh. She didn't even smile.

ARTHUR

I kept one eye on my digital desk clock while I talked on the phone with the corporation's comptroller. "Sid, you're making a mountain out of a molehill."

Sidney Lowenstein's voice was usually silky smooth, but now it had a rasping edge to it. "It's not a molehill, Arthur. Two million dollars is no molehill."

"I told the executive committee about it three weeks ago, at our last meeting. You were there—"

"You didn't tell us you were running two million over budget." As Omnitech's comptroller, Lowenstein was the man who worried most about the money.

I sat up straight in my chair, planted both feet firmly on the carpeted floor. "Listen to me, Sid. When the report comes out it's going to be worth *twenty* million in publicity for Omnitech. You know that!"

"All I know," Lowenstein's voice grated, "is that your people are two million over budget on this one project, with no end in sight."

"But the end *is* in sight, Sid," I said. "That's why we want to start the human trials. All the years of animal tests are finished."

"And you have to go to Mexico for the human trials?"

"Yes. Otherwise we'll have to wait for god knows how long to get NIH approval. In Mexico we can start the trials right away, and the sooner we start, the sooner we finish."

"How soon?" Lowenstein demanded. "And how much more?"

I made a mental calculation and answered, "A few months . . . six, at the outside. And that two million you're frantic about will cover the rest of the program to its conclusion."

"Really?"

"And think of it, Sid. Omnitech can announce a new technique for making antibodies work *inside* a cell. It can stop viruses from reproducing, Sid. It can stop the production of oncoproteins!"

"Onco-what?"

"The proteins that grow uncontrolled in cancerous cells. We'll be able to prevent cancerous cells from multiplying!"

Lowenstein went quiet briefly. Then he asked, "Can it be used against AIDS?"

I had him hooked. "That will take more research, Sid. A lot more research."

"When will this final report be ready?"

"Six months, something like that."

"Maybe we should send one of our PR people down to talk to you about this. We'll want to time the announcement to make the maximum impact on the stock."

I grinned. "Yes, this would be a good time to pick up a few more shares, wouldn't it?"

"I'll clue the PR department in on this. Talk to you later, Art."

If there is one thing that I hate, it's being called Art. Or even worse, Artie. But I said nothing about it as I bid a gracious good-bye to the corporation's comptroller. I gently replaced the phone in its cradle and took a deep breath. I couldn't smell any citrus odor. Maybe Phyllis had forgotten about it. Or maybe it was too faint to detect even when I consciously tried to.

I knew damned well that the final work on Cassie's intracellular targeting project would take more than six months. We hadn't even started the human trials yet. And we'd have to tabulate the experimental results and write all the reports. Why do scientists hate to write? I asked myself. I looked up at the quotation from Michael Faraday that hung on my office wall:

Physics is to make experiments and to publish them.

Publish or perish, I thought. Worse yet, publish or languish in obscurity. How can the world learn about what a scientist has accomplished if the scientist doesn't publish?

The digital clock said 12:30.

Jesse should be here soon. I tried to read one of the reports stacked on the corner of my desk, but it was impossible to concentrate. Jesse was never on time, of course; it was only a question of how late he would be.

My intercom chirped softly.

"Yes?"

Phyllis's voice replied, "Your brother's here; on his way in from the lobby."

"Great!"

Jesse is what you would call a natural. He was born with charm and grace, and he learned how to use his gifts when he was still a baby. I work hard at everything I do; things just seem to fall into place for Jesse. I can spend half an hour fretting over which tie goes best with the suit I'm wearing; Jesse just tosses on whatever's closest to hand and he always looks like he stepped out of an advertisement for men's styles. Even at the previous night's banquet in his honor he had ostentatiously undone his bow tie while giving his acceptance speech. And looked completely elegant and relaxed all the while.

But now he looked nervous as he stepped into my office, his usual boyish grin diminished into an anxious expression of uncertainty. He wore a Western-style suede jacket over an open-collar pale yellow sports shirt and faded rumpled blue jeans.

I got to my feet and came around the desk. Jesse stuck out his hand awkwardly.

"I guess this isn't any easier for you than it is for me," he said as I reached for his hand.

And then we grabbed at each other, clasped each other's shoulders and pounded each other's backs and held ourselves as close as brothers should be.

"It's good to see you again, Arby," Jesse whispered huskily. He still used his childhood name for me.

"Jess." I was on the verge of tears. All I could say was, "Jess. Jess."

The moment passed. We released one another and took a step back.

"You look great, Arby."

I took a breath and decided to plunge ahead. "You, too. Married life agrees with you."

Something flickered in Jesse's brown eyes. "Yeah. I guess it does."

"Julia's fine?" I asked, retreating back behind my desk.

"Wonderful," said Jesse as he sat in the upholstered chair in front of the desk.

"That's good."

"You . . ." Jesse seemed to be studying my face. "You're not mad at us anymore?"

I forced a smile. "No. That's over with. I wish the two of you every happiness. Really I do."

Jesse beamed. "That's great! Maybe you can come into the city and have dinner with us one night. There's a great little Italian restaurant just a block and a half from our apartment and . . ."

It's done, I thought as I listened to my brother with only half my attention. We've broken the ice and we're talking to each other just like we used to do. Maybe I ought to go into the city and have dinner with them. Show them both that there's no hard feelings. Sooner or later they'll invite me to their apartment. But not at first. Not just yet.

Phyllis buzzed on the intercom to ask if we were ready for lunch. Jesse nodded as I said yes and she came in a moment later with a tray of sandwiches, a pot of coffee, and two frosted bottles of juice. I thought I caught a whiff of lavender, her aromatherapy for reducing stress. She deposited the tray on my desk and left the office, closing the door softly behind her.

"You remembered my grapefruit juice," Jesse said as he unscrewed one of the bottles.

"Phyllis did. I can't take credit for it. She's a wonder."

"You still drinking that black poison?"

I nodded as I poured a cup of coffee from the insulated pot. "I keep it down to two or three cups a day."

"Decaffeinated?"

"No. From what I read in the literature, that's just as bad for you in the long run as regular."

"How's your blood pressure?"

"Okay the last time I had a checkup."

"What were the numbers?" Jesse insisted.

I waved a hand in the air. "Oh, I don't remember. Ask Phyllis. She keeps all the records."

"Who's your doctor?"

"The corporation sends us to the Lahey Clinic for an annual physical. They're very thorough."

"Us? Everybody in the lab?"

"Us, the corporate executives. The lab's employees have their own health plan. It's a damned good one, too."

"I'll bet," Jesse said. Then he added, "But the corporate executives have a better one."

"Why not?"

"Because the employees are just as human as the executives, that's why not. They should get the same level of care."

"Have a sandwich," I said, pointing to the tray. "I've heard all your blather before."

He smiled, almost sheepishly. "Yeah, you have, haven't you?"

I picked up one of the neatly cut triangular little sandwiches, thinking how different these were from the thick slabs of bread that Momma used for our lunches when we were both schoolkids.

"Well," Jesse said, nibbling daintily, "my blather got me named Humanitarian of the Year."

"A richly deserved honor," I said. We both laughed at my sarcastic tone.

"You make the money and I get the honors," said Jesse. "I think it's a damned neat system."

"It is, isn't it?"

"Have you seen Ma lately?" Jesse asked.

The question caught me slightly off guard. "Two weeks ago."

"I wanted to take her to the banquet but she wouldn't go."

"She can't travel in her condition. You know that."

"I could have gotten an ambulance. A paramedic van. I would have taken care of her."

"She's got more brains than you do," I muttered.

"It would've been nice to have her there."

I felt some of the old irritation coming up again. "Jess, you just don't think about anybody but yourself, do you? How many strokes has Mom had? Four? That we know of. And there's always the ministrokes that they can't even detect."

Almost petulantly Jesse said, "She would have enjoyed seeing her son honored."

I stared at him for a long moment, fighting down the anger welling up inside me. At last I admitted, "Yeah, I suppose she would have. It's a damned shame she couldn't."

Jesse's expression brightened. "I'm going to bring her the DVD of the ceremonies. She'll enjoy that."

"I'm sure she will."

Our father had been killed in an auto crash on the Deegan Expressway when we had been twelve and ten, respectively. Momma was crippled in the accident, both legs had to be amputated. Now she was dying, slowly, painfully, ravaged by cancer that was eating its way through her organs and a series of strokes that had taken her ability to speak. Sometimes I found myself hoping that the next stroke would kill her, put an end to her suffering. But she was a strong old woman and she would not surrender easily.

From the night of that terrible accident I had taken on the responsibility of raising Jesse.

"You're the practical one, Arthur," Momma told me. "You're my helper. You've got to look after little Jesse for me."

I suppose a psychologist would talk about the older son and the baby son. I just did what Momma told me. I loved Jesse. I wanted to help him and protect him.

We both won scholarships to college, but when Jesse announced he wanted to go on to medical school I paid the bills by working nights as a computer repair technician. Daytime I attended graduate school, heading for a doctorate in molecular biology, paying my own bills with whatever fellowships I could get and tutoring fees.

When Jesse was in his first year of medical school we started tinkering with ideas of genetic engineering. Together we produced a microbe that ingested crude oil and broke it down into methane and carbon dioxide. Others had "invented" similar microbes, but ours was slightly more efficient in gobbling oil spills. We were thrilled speechless with our success. We published our results in the scientific literature—and saw our oil-eating "bug" make fortunes of profits for several bioremediation companies. But not a penny for ourselves.

When we produced a microbe that digested wastes from landfills I patented the invention. I was an assistant professor then. That's when all the trouble at Columbia started. Jesse took the school's side of the argument. He didn't want his name on the patent. He insisted that we should publish in the scientific literature again and give the benefit of our discovery to the world. Instead, I insisted on taking out the patent and then I licensed Omnitech Corporation to produce and sell the microbe. Our royalties made Jesse's humanitarianism possible.

I made the money and Jesse got the awards. It was just as well that way, I thought. Just as well.

"So what about this idea of yours about spinal cord regeneration?" Jesse asked as he reached for another of the little sandwiches. "Still think it's hot stuff now that the light of day is with us?"

"I most emphatically do. I mean, if we can develop agents to block transcription and stop tumors from growing, why can't we develop agents to initiate nerve regrowth?"

Jesse gave me a pitying look. "Tumor cells are *always* multiplying, Arby. They're out of control. That's what makes them so damned deadly, they don't know when to stop multiplying and start differentiating, the way ordinary cells do."

"So they must have a growth factor—"

"Somatic cells," Jesse went on, cutting me short, "especially nerve cells, have already differentiated. They won't multiply anymore."

"Nerve cells regenerate," I countered. "I've seen dozens of papers on the subject. Hundreds."

"Only under very special conditions, Arby. Once those neurons are cut you can't just paste them back together again. It's like Humpty Dumpty."

"Why not? What about the work they're doing at Berkeley with neural growth inducers? Or the work Cephalon's doing on neurotrophic factors?"

Jess made a sour face. "Berkeley's work is with rats, for god's sake. Rat embryos, at that: stem cells, before the cells start to differentiate."

"But they can induce growth of new neurons with stem cells."

Jesse's eyes widened. "Stem cells! Wow."

"Don't tell me you're against stem cell work," I grumbled.

"I'm not, but the government is."

"We won't use government money, then. I can fund this without government backing."

"But they're writing laws, Arby. Against cloning, too."

"Reproductive cloning," I corrected him. "We're not going

to be making babies. The old-fashioned way is good enough for me."

Jesse grinned, but said, "They want to outlaw therapeutic cloning, too."

"Not even Congress is that stupid."

"Wanna bet?"

"Then we'd better get busy and do what we have to do before they outlaw it."

"I don't know . . ."

"Come on, Jess. All I'm talking about is regenerating nerve cells. Not cloning, unless we have to clone some stem cells here and there."

"Here and there?" He raised his eyebrows dubiously.

"While it's still legal."

Jesse shook his head. "Arby, you can't regrow mature neurons that have been completely severed. The damage is too severe. They won't regenerate."

He was still doubtful, but at least he was back to talking science instead of politics. I said, "Under natural conditions, you mean."

"Well, yeah. But it's worse than that, really."

"How?"

"The problem with spinal neurons isn't just making them regenerate, it's getting them to grow to the right target area. The trauma to the spinal cord produces scarring and debris; it's a mess, and the nerves can't just reconnect themselves even if you can make them grow again."

I hadn't thought about that.

"The neurons need a path to follow," Jesse went on. "They need to know *where* they have to grow to reconnect with the severed neurons on the other side of the cut. How're they going to reach their targets?"

I didn't reply. I was thinking.

"I mean, even if you could force some regeneration among the neurons the damned cells would just start proliferating like a bunch of weeds. What the hell good would that do?"

"Suppose you could provide a plan? A blueprint for them to follow?"

"How the hell could you do that?"

I could see that Jess was getting emotional. That was a good sign. That meant he was interested. Even though he was negative about the idea, it had hit him hard enough to shake him up.

I got up from my chair. "Come on out back with me. I want to show you some of the latest imaging systems we've been using."

Jesse looked perplexed. "Imaging systems? What's that got to do with it?"

"You want a blueprint, a map for the growing nerves to follow? Let's take a look at what the mapmakers can do for us."

VINCENT ANDRIOTTI looked more like a Turkish wrestler than an optical-electronics engineer. He was short, thickly built, sparse of hair, swarthy of complexion, and his nose had obviously been broken many years ago. Perhaps more than once. He just happened to be a genius at developing sensor systems.

In his darkened laboratory, lit only by the faint greenish glow from one of his computer display screens, Vinnie grinned maliciously at us.

"It's simple," he said. "You use the echo-planar MRI to map out the area, tell you which nerve bundles are which, and then you go in with the fiber optics and the laser pulses to get the fine detail."

Jesse straightened up and stretched his back. He had been bent over staring at the detailed map of a small section of a human brain for so long that his spine popped noisily as he stretched.

The darkened little lab was hot and stuffy, as if too many people or too many machines had been crammed into it. The room smelled faintly of something I couldn't identify, something that reminded me of spicy food. Pizza, maybe.

"I know that MRI is magnetic resonance imaging," Jesse said to Vince. "But what is echo . . . whatever it is?"

"Echo-planar," Vinnie replied. "You use much stronger magnetic field gradients than normal MRI and a whole shitful of fast computers to grab the data before the pulse craps out. Call it EPI instead of MRI. It's easier."

"EPI," Jesse repeated.

"Once you have the EPI map," I explained, "you use laser pulses to delineate the individual neurons."

"Right," said Vinnie, making the word sound almost like a gunshot.

"That'll take a long time, won't it?" Jesse asked.

Vinnie said, "Depends on how much computer power you throw in. Anyway, if the guy's a paraplegic he ain't going anywhere, is he?"

Jesse shrugged. "No, I suppose not."

The greenish glow from the display screen made Andriotti's swarthy face look ghastly. He was grinning like a nasty pirate.

I asked him, "You're confident you could map the entire spinal cord on both sides of the cut?"

"Confident as hell," Vinnie snapped. "I could be wrong, but I'm damned confident."

I turned to Jess. "Well? What do you think?"

Jesse rubbed a hand across his chin. Then he looked up. "I think it's worth a try."

"Good!"

I slid an arm around my brother's shoulders and headed for the door.

Vinnie called after us, "Hey, if I'm supposed to work on this, what job number do I charge it to?"

"I'll let you know," I said as I opened the door with my free hand.

Vinnie grunted very much like a wrestler. He had worked for me long enough to understand that "I'll let you know" means that the work should be hidden for the time being. Moonlighted. Charged to some existing project until I could come up with a legitimate account.

I heard Vinnie start humming to himself, "Dah-*dee*-dah, dah-*dee*-dah, dah-*dee*-dah . . ." His version of the "Moonlight Sonata." He'd been down this path before.

* * *

I WALKED Jesse all the way to his car, surprised at how chilly the afternoon had become. Rain clouds were thickening and blotting out the sun.

When I got back to my office, Cassie Ianetta was in the outer room, perched on the edge of the white leather sofa like a nervous little schoolkid waiting for the principal's discipline. Phyllis was at her desk, busily typing away at her keyboard.

Cassie jumped to her feet when I came through the open doorway. I ushered her into my office and gestured to a chair at the little round conference table in a corner of the office, then sat down beside her. That would be better than putting the desk between us, I thought. She looked wound tight, about to snap. Time for the fatherly approach.

"Darrell tells me you've got a problem about the clinical trials."

"Can't someone else handle it?" Cassie blurted. "I can't leave the country. I can't be away for months at a time."

"Problem with Max?"

"He needs me." She was clenching her fingers on the edge of the little table so hard I could see her knuckles going white.

"You mean you don't want to leave him."

"Nobody else understands him!" And she burst into tears.

I let her sink her blubbering face against my shoulder. I put my arms around her, patting her back gently. I really did feel fatherly toward Cassie. I had known her since she'd been a summer intern, working her way through Brown.

I tried to be soothing. "There, there. It's not as bad as all that, is it?"

She sobbed and sniffled for a while, then pulled away and began to apologize. "I'm sorry, it's not your problem, I know."

"But it is my problem, Cass," I said gently. "I care about you, and I care about your work."

Cassie pulled a tissue from the box on the table and dabbed at her eyes.

"You have a brilliant career ahead of you," I told her. "And I don't have to tell you how important your work is."

"But I can't—"

The fatherly approach can take you only so far. What I needed was something more powerful than her damned Max, something that would make her understand where her obligations lay.

"Wait. Maybe I should explain something to you. I ought to be completely up-front with you about this."

"What do you mean?"

I hunched closer to her, until my face was almost touching hers. "I've got a personal stake in your work, Cass. My mother is dying of cancer."

"Oh! I didn't know."

"It's not something that I broadcast around. But she's been in a nursing home for more than a year now. Cancer of the colon. They've operated on her twice, but they didn't get all of it."

"Oh, my god."

"So I want your work to succeed, I want that very much. Maybe more than I should."

"I can understand why."

"Maybe I shouldn't pressure you. Maybe somebody else can get the job done as well as you could. It's just . . ."

I could see Cassie absorbing this new information, her eyes staring off to infinity as she sorted out the data.

"I shouldn't let my personal concerns interfere with your personal concerns. You have to decide what's best for you, for your career, for your future."

"I didn't know about your mother," she whispered.

"I'm sorry I brought it up. Let's face it, nothing you or anybody else can do is going to save her. Even if your clinical trials go without a hitch, she'll be dead long before your tumor suppressant can help her."

I was getting through to her, I could see it. A part of me despised what I was doing, manipulating the kid's emotions. But what the hell, I thought, she's not going to listen to logic. She's all tied up in knots over her stupid Max. She's got her career to think of; she can't hang around his neck and let her own work go to hell.

"I'll do it," Cassie said at last. "I'll go to Mexico or wherever the field tests are set up."

"Don't make the decision right now," I said softly. "It's a big decision. It means a lot to everyone concerned. Think about it. Sleep on it."

"I'll do it," Cassie repeated. She could be very rigid in her decisions. "You're right. It's the right thing to do."

I walked her out of my office, still urging her to think further about her decision, but I was certain that she wouldn't change her mind now that she had made it up. Cassie had that stubborn Sicilian streak in her, I knew from past experience.

Once she left my office I felt almost ashamed of using Momma's illness that way. There was no way Cassie's work would ever be finished in time to help her. God, I thought, it'll take at least another two years. Momma can't hang on that long. Two more years of pain. It made me shudder.

CASSIE IANETTA

Today is Thursday, April twenty-first. I haven't been keeping my diary as faithfully as I promised to, so I'm going to try talking it into this voice recorder every night instead of writing it. Dr. Mandelbaum wants me to keep a diary, she says it'll help me to sort out my thoughts and emotions. Maybe. We'll see.

Arthur Marshak, my boss, wants me to go to Mexico to do the field trials on my tumor suppressant. That means I'd have to leave Max for months. I don't want to do that, but Arthur dumped a whole load of guilt on me and I guess I'll have to go.

When our meeting ended I practically ran from Arthur's office, past my own lab, and out to the pens at the back of the building. The custodial staff is always scrubbing down the tiles, covering up the natural smells of the animals and their excrement with detergents and disinfectants. I don't mind the smell; it's strong and real.

The cage labeled MAXIMILIAN was empty, so I rushed past the two young guys sweeping the floor and pushed through the heavy double doors out to the open-air playground. It was chilly out there, turning gray. I thought it would start raining soon.

I didn't see Max at first. He wasn't in either one of the pruned trees that grow out at the far end of the compound; he wasn't in the jungle gym we had set up for him closer to the doors. I felt a pang of fear in my chest.

And then I spotted him, all the way up the top of the heavy wire fencing that domes in the enclosure. He was hanging up there by one hand and scratching himself on the backside with the other. As soon as he saw me he came scrambling down to the ground and knuckle-walked to me, hooting a great big hello.

He grabbed for me and I let his strong arms enfold me; I knew he would never hurt me. I had worked with Max since he had been a scared, lost little baby, four years ago. Mothered him. Taught him sign language. And I used him as a living biochemical laboratory to generate the antibodies and enzymes that I used in my research. I taught him not to be afraid of my lab, with its strange sterile smells and cold metal tables.

Max trusted me. He performed for me. His body reacted to the injections I gave him and produced the proteins and peptide chains that I needed. It had taken me more than a month of really agonized indecision before I finally injected Max with the carcinoma strain, and I went without sleep for four straight days as my tumor suppressant enzyme destroyed the cancerous cells before they could begin to form tumors. I had watched over Max like a terrified mother, deathly afraid that I had murdered my own child.

But Max lived and thrived. And I swore I'd never use him for experiments again. "You've earned your retirement," I had said aloud to him. And do you know what Max answered? He signed, Banana for me? That's why I loved him. No complications, no conflicts, nothing but trust. And love.

So I sat sprawled on the grass in the animal enclosure with Max huffing and pawing at me like a clumsy child. He made me laugh with his antics.

Play? Max signed.

I nodded.

Max hooted and scampered toward the jungle gym. I scrambled to my feet and ran after him. I didn't have the strength to climb the bars with him, though. The chemo had left me weak and shaky.

But Max climbed right up to the top of the jungle gym and then looked back at me. Play? he signed again.

How could I leave him? He'd be lost without me. Even if Arthur promises not to use him in any more tests, how can I trust any of them once my back is turned?

THE TRIAL:

DAY ONE, MORNING

Before the examiner could frame another question, Arthur said to the judges, "I would like to make it clear that neither I nor any of the other scientists and physicians engaged in this research are attempting to play God."

Rosen started to interrupt but Arthur went on, "Many of the researchers have deep religious feelings. They belong to many different faiths but they all have the conviction that what we are doing is no more playing God than giving medicine to a sick child would be."

A smattering of applause came from the audience behind him.

"Silence," Graves warned the spectators.

"I know that the ability to replace failing organs or regrow lost limbs seems almost magical," Arthur said, warming up to the subject, "but it is simply an extension of knowledge that generations of dedicated men and women have gained through selfless, lifelong effort."

Rosen said, "Dr. Marshak—"

"May I finish?" Arthur looked past the examiner to Graves and the two elderly men flanking him.

"If you can conclude your remarks in under five minutes," Graves said, a little smile playing at the corners of his lips.

Arthur bobbed his head in acknowledgment. "Far from playing God, I think we are doing God's work. If you believe in a supreme deity, why would he—or she—give us the ability to understand these things if we're not intended to use them to make life better? Does God intend for us to wither away and die at three score years and ten? If so, why has he given us the knowledge to extend our life spans? Why allow us to discover medicines? Why have we been able to understand what causes disease and genetic defects? If we failed to use this knowledge we would be spitting in God's face, telling God that we reject the wisdom he has granted us."

The hearing chamber was absolutely silent. Even Rosen, the examiner, stood immobile, his coal-black eyes staring at Arthur.

Graves pushed his bifocals up to the bridge of his nose. "Are you finished, Dr. Marshak?"

"That's all I've got to say," Arthur said. He turned to the examiner. "What's your next question?"

The audience stirred as if coming out of a trance. Rosen made a polite little cough behind the back of his hand, then took a few steps toward the table where Arthur sat.

"You worked with your brother on this idea of regenerating organs?" the examiner asked.

"As I told you, Dr. Rosen," Arthur said with a great show of patience, "at first we were interested only in regenerating spinal cord nerve tissue. We were thinking in terms of helping paraplegics."

"And you worked with your brother."

"I talked out the basic idea with my brother. Until he had to go to South America or Africa or one of those locations."

Rosen walked back to his place at the end of the judges'

table and consulted the notebook computer he had set up there. Arthur glanced sideways at Jesse. He was leaning back in his chair, at his ease, apparently enjoying the show so far.

"Dr. Marshak," Rosen called, "when your brother left the country for Eritrea"—he put a slight emphasis on the country's name, as if he were not so subtly reminding Arthur of something he should have remembered for himself—"had you thought of extending your work on nerve regeneration to the more general purpose of organ regrowth?"

Arthur searched his memory briefly. "We had talked about it, I think. But no, as far as I can recall, we were still thinking strictly in terms of spinal neuron regeneration back then."

"Had you discussed the need for using stem cells in your research?"

"Yes," said Arthur without hesitation. "Adult stem cells. We never even considered using fetal cells."

"Never?"

"As it turned out," Arthur said, smiling, "we found a way to go ahead without using even adult stem cells."

Rosen nodded somberly. "I see. And what about cloning?"

"We considered therapeutic cloning, yes. At that time we thought we could make more of the stem cells we might need by cloning those we obtained from volunteers."

"Murderer!" someone said in a stage whisper, loud enough for everyone to hear. Graves glared at the audience but said nothing.

"If we had needed fetal stem cells, which we didn't," Arthur said, "we would have obtained the fetuses from a reproductive clinic. They were going to be destroyed anyway. They were no longer wanted. We would be able to put them to good use."

Rosen seemed to take a breath. Then he said, "This is not the proper moment to discuss the ethics of fetal tissue research."

"I agree completely," said Arthur.

"So, before your brother went to Eritrea, the two of you were thinking strictly in terms of spinal neuron regeneration."

"Strictly of spinal neuron regeneration, yes."

"You're certain?"

"No, I'm not certain. And I don't see what difference it makes. We're not here to establish precedence, are we?"

The judge on Graves's left said, "That is for the patent office to worry about."

Rosen nodded as if in agreement. He advanced toward Arthur again and asked, "This work that you and your brother did—how was it financed?"

"Out of my discretionary funds. As director of Grenford Laboratory, I had a small fund available for research that's too new to have corporate or other sponsorship."

"Corporate or other?" Rosen snapped. "What other?"

"Now and then we undertook research for an outside customer. As long as it didn't conflict with our corporate products."

"Can you give me an example?"

Arthur thought swiftly. "Several years ago we investigated the possibility of developing a microbe that could concentrate metals dissolved in the ocean."

"Metals?"

"Chromium, manganese, platinum, gold—there are megatons of those metals in the oceans, but they're very dilute and it's not economically feasible to extract them from the water. We looked into the possibility of developing a microbe or a family of microbes that could concentrate such metals in their bodies and then be harvested."

Rosen came close to smiling. "Slave labor on a microscopic scale."

"The microbes are microscopic, but the scale of the operation would have been very large, believe me."

"And what happened?"

Arthur shook his head. "It didn't work. We dropped the program after a year."

"Who was the sponsor?"

"Thornton Mining, if I recall correctly."

Suddenly Rosen was all business again. "And what was the reaction of Omnitech's management when you told them you wanted to regenerate human organs?"

ARTHUR

What was Omnitech's reaction? That depends on who in the corporate management you're talking about. And when.

The first time I mentioned the idea to Johnston, the CEO, was the day I met him at the factory in Yonkers. I visited Momma later that same afternoon.

I drove my own car down to meet Johnston that morning. Usually I enjoyed driving the Infiniti, although the jam-packed morning traffic along the Bronx River Parkway made me wonder why they called it the rush hour. You could hardly move in this snarling, growling jam of automobiles and trucks. The speedometer on the dashboard went up to 160 miles per hour; I remember the salesman at the dealership grinning at me as he pointed out that the government's safety bureaucrats had insisted the car be redlined at 150, but it would actually go much faster. I felt lucky when the traffic inched up to 40. And most of these poor slobs go through this every day. Every morning and every evening. What a life.

There was nothing to do but sit behind the wheel and listen to Chopin on the CD player. It was going to be a tough day. A meeting with Omnitech's chief executive officer over a problem that one of the other corporate divisions had run into. He expected me to solve their problems, as if I didn't have enough of my own. And then a visit with Momma at the nursing home.

And the next day promised to be even tougher. Jess had phoned and invited me to dinner with him and Julia. I accepted, of course. I had to. But I wasn't looking forward to it. It would be the first time I'd seen Julia since their wedding, except for the humanitarian dinner. I wondered how I would get through it.

Omnitech's biomanufacturing plant had originally been an old Yonkers factory building, faded stained brick with row after row of little windows. It still looked old and seedy from

the outside. But it had been completely gutted inside and re-
built to house the people and equipment that produced genetically engineered biotechnology products. This was where
Omnitech still manufactured the oil-eating bugs that Jesse
and I had first developed, back when we were both still students. Still without paying us a penny for them.

When the residents of the neighborhood learned that the
factory would be manufacturing "artificial bugs," they just
about went berserk. NIMBY gone wild. There were demon-
strations and angry city council meetings. People screamed
about "germ warfare" and "mutant monsters." The mayor
made threatening speeches and the TV news shows loved the
whole controversy. Omnitech's public relations staff worked
night and day, showing the news media, the mayor, the city
council, delegations of worried citizens that the "bugs" to be
manufactured could in no way harm human beings. They
showed concerned neighborhood citizens the entire blueprints
of the plant and pointed out the safeguards that ensured no
contamination could get out of the building. None of that
helped. At last they promised to hire as many local residents—
especially ethnic minorities—as possible. That, and some
well-placed emoluments, did the trick.

The city council's vote was close; Omnitech's request for
building permits and zoning variations squeaked through by
one vote. The corporation's CEO, W. Christian Johnston, congratulated himself in front of the board of directors. "We
didn't buy one single vote more than we had to."

The factory opened. Omnitech hired some of the locals.
No mutant monsters haunted the neighborhood. The furor
died away.

Johnston had originally wanted to build the factory in the
Bronx and establish a training center for blacks and other
ethnic minorities next to it. The thought of the Bronx really
shook up the board of directors, though, so they compromised
on this location in Yonkers. The battle to open the factory
had been bad enough, Johnston conceded. He gave up his
idea of helping the Bronx.

Johnston was a big success for Omnitech. He had battled his way out of the black ghetto of West Philadelphia and been hired by one of the corporation's construction subsidiaries. He moved ahead swiftly on a combination of brains and the willingness to work harder than anybody else, and eventually he rose to the top of the corporate construction division in Pittsburgh. Once promoted to the board of directors, he quickly showed that he was much more than affirmative action window dressing. Within five years of his board membership, his election to CEO was virtually unanimous.

He was a big man. Not much taller than I am, but heavy, ponderous, like a football lineman, with huge hands that were still callused from his years of operating front loaders and construction cranes. He looked younger than his years; his rich baritone voice was still strong enough to shout down obstreperous board members when he had to. The only sign that he was nearing retirement age was his short-cropped hair. It was almost pure white. He called it "Omnitech blond."

Now he led me down an aisle of gleaming stainless steel biogenerators, heading for the place on the factory floor where they were having trouble, a massive hulking black man in a three-piece Brooks Brothers suit. I was wearing a sports jacket and slacks.

"You've got that look in your eye, Arthur," Johnston said to me.

"What look?" I said as innocently as I could.

"That look that means you want more money."

"You've been talking to Lowenstein."

"No, Sid's been talking to me."

The factory floor was quiet except for the muted hum of electricity. Off in the distance somebody was playing a country and western radio station, all twanging and wailing. The biogenerators, big ten-foot-tall stainless steel cylinders topped by domes of heat-resistant tempered glass, made hardly any noise at all. The fluorescent lamps high overhead threw curving highlights against the polished steel and glass and made Johnston's deep black skin shine as if he were perspiring.

"So what is it?" he asked me. His tone was bantering, almost. He was smiling but his dark eyes showed no trace of amusement.

"Oh, just something that Jesse and I have started tinkering with. I can handle it with discretionary funding for the time being." I was trying to decide how much to tell him. Corporate support is vital to any research program, but if the corporation refuses its support the program dies. No sense risking a refusal so early in the game. I certainly didn't want to get him worried about stem cell politics.

But Johnston was insistent. "What's it all about?"

"Well . . ." I drew out the word reluctantly. "If this concept pans out, we might be able to do something about paraplegics."

"Do what?"

"Get them up and walking, I hope."

"Like that guy who played Superman?"

It was too late for Christopher Reeve, but at least I had Johnston's attention. I began explaining as we strode along the factory aisle. On either side of us the biogenerators cultivated silent industrious colonies of genetically altered bacteria that were tirelessly producing more of themselves. The microbes had been designed to digest various forms of industrial wastes, crude petroleum, toxic chemicals. They were harvested and shipped to oil spills, chemical factories, paper mills, municipal landfills. There they gobbled up the wastes and converted them to carbon dioxide, methane, water.

Other processors in the factory were producing agricultural products: bacteria that made potatoes resistant to frosts, microbes that fixed nitrogen from the air for wheat and other cereal grains so that they needed far less chemical fertilizers than previously.

Johnston looked intrigued with my idea about paraplegics, but not happy. "Another medical project. A lot of competition there."

"Nobody's doing anything like this," I said.

"Maybe so. But you've got all those goddamned government agencies to deal with. Look what they're doing to your clinical trials. Lowenstein tells me we'll hafta send your team to Mexico, for god's sake. Or maybe Brazil."

"That's part of the cost of doing business," I replied. "You factor that into the price when the product comes on the market."

"Yeah, and then the goddamned government pressures us to lower the price," Johnston grumbled.

I kept a straight face. I'd never heard the CEO use the word "government" without "goddamned" in front of it.

"Medical projects are a big pain in the butt, you know."

"But very profitable," I said.

"Oh, yeah? You heard what the goddamned Department of Agriculture is doing now? They want us to pay royalties for the genetic materials we use. Royalties to some half-assed Third World countries who claim that the raw materials we use come from their territories. Part of the Biodiversity Treaty, they claim. Royalties, by damn! There go any profits we might make."

I let him grumble. There were hardly any other people on the factory floor. The equipment churned along unattended, except for the teams sitting in the monitoring stations up on the iron grillwork balcony above us. They watched their gauges and display screens as intently as any NASA mission controllers.

But there were half a dozen men and women in white smocks standing around the conglomeration of pipes and tubing at the end of the row. They all had radiation gauges clipped to the breast pockets of their smocks.

"This is why I asked you to drop by," Johnston said. "This is where we're having trouble."

There were big red DANGER—RADIATION signs plastered on the tubing and walls all around the equipment. I noticed that Johnston stopped a good twenty feet short of the black and yellow warning lines on the wooden floor.

The corporation had other research operations, in addition to my lab. One of them was under way here at the Yonkers plant, a program to engineer a microbe so that it could take dissolved radioactive uranium and thorium out of contaminated water and convert them into solid pellets. The pellets would be much easier to dispose of safely than tons of radioactive water. They were working with a microbe called *Deinococcus radiodurans,* which could withstand enormous amounts of radioactivity, from what I'd read. The engineers called the bug "Conan the Bacterium." The process was being developed by Omnitech's nuclear power division. It was not a Grenford Lab program, not my problem. Until now.

"Does Habermeir know you've asked me to look into his work?" I asked, keeping my voice low enough so that the technicians attending the apparatus couldn't hear me.

Johnston made a snorting noise that might have been a laugh. "I told him I was doing it. He wasn't happy about it, but what the hell."

I nodded. I didn't like stepping on the toes of other scientists in the Omnitech family. But I needed Johnston's support for my own programs and to keep that support I had to keep the CEO happy. Politics. There was no way around it, you had to be good at politics to get to do the science you wanted to do.

Still, I couldn't help muttering, "How can you expect anything but trouble, dealing with radioactive material?"

Johnston fixed me with a stern gaze. "There's a lot of money to be made in cleaning up nuclear wastes. And it's a *good* thing to do, Arthur. You're always telling me we should be doing *good* things, aren't you?"

"I know, but—"

"Well, cleaning up the environment from radioactive wastes is as good as they come, I think. So does the PR department. We could get a lot of happy mileage out of this, once it works right."

"If it can ever be made to work right."

Johnston smiled with a mouthful of teeth. "You're the scientist, Arthur. I'm just a money-grabbing corporate executive."

"Sure you are."

The black man laughed. "You going to help us out on this one?"

"I'll try," I said, with what I felt was the right amount of reluctance. Let him know I'm doing him a favor and he owes me one in return. "I'll talk to the technicians. And I'll need to see all the reports the project engineers have written."

Johnston beamed at me and clapped me on the back hard enough to stagger a moose.

"Regrow nerve cells so paraplegics can be cured, huh?" he said. "Could put us into a whole new business line. Maybe I could use it to hold off the goddamned Germans and their buyout attempt."

That surprised me. "The Germans are back?"

"They never left, Arthur. And now they've got a whole goddamned consortium of European firms with them. This time it's going to be rough. Really rough."

SO I left Johnston worrying about a hostile takeover and drove up to the nursing home in White Plains with a boxful of reports on the nuclear waste project denting the back seat of my car.

Visiting Momma was never easy. We both knew she was dying and there wasn't a damned thing we could do about it. Me, the big-time scientist, and I had to sit there just as awkward and helpless as some peasant from the Middle Ages.

Momma had always been a fighter. When the auto accident took Dad's life and both her legs, she battled back from her wheelchair, fought the doctors and lawyers and insurance companies and the entire care-giving bureaucracy of New York to stay in her own home and maintain control of her two sons. Gertrude Marshak did not admit defeat, not to anyone.

As the elder son, I became the man of the house, the responsible one who fixed the plumbing and did the grocery shopping and took odd jobs while attending school and studying for scholarships. Jesse could have a more normal life; he was outgoing, gregarious. He kept our apartment in Brooklyn Heights lively with friends and music and his own irrepressible charm.

"Watch out for your brother," Momma told me time and

again. "Jesse has no common sense, you'll have to take care of him."

I did that, without resentment, without stint. When Momma had her first stroke Jesse was spending the weekend at a friend's house and I couldn't find him because he and his friend had decided to take the subway out to Jones Beach and they hadn't come back yet. I was all of fourteen years old. I was frantic, trying to track him down while the ambulance crew wheeled Momma out of the apartment. Even in the hospital, waiting up all night to hear if Momma would live to see the sunrise, I kept telephoning every half hour to see if Jess and his friend had come home yet. It wasn't until the next morning that Jess showed up at the hospital with a single daisy in his fist that he had picked from the hospital's front lawn.

Well, that was Jesse.

Now I climbed the creaking stairs of the Sunny Glade Nursing Home, heading for the corner room on the second floor that had been Momma's home for the past four years. A young attendant in whites smiled at me as she passed me on the bare wooden stairs. I smiled back automatically. I was thinking ahead, beyond this visit with Momma, worrying about tomorrow night's dinner and Julia.

It was hard to think of the pitiful shriveled thing sitting up in the hospital bed as the woman who had been my mother. It looked more like the dried and wrinkled husk of some discarded marionette, its strings long cut, its usefulness long over. An oxygen tube was taped to one nostril. Her once-luxuriant hair was dead white and so sparse her scalp showed through. A faded baby blue nightgown hung limply on her emaciated frame.

The tumors were eating her up, consuming her body and wasting what little strength she had remaining. The strokes had paralyzed her left side and taken away her ability to speak. Yet the fire of life burned in her eyes. Even through her contorted face I could see that Gertrude Marshak was still fighting, still clinging to existence. It was almost as if the pain were the only thing she had left, the only reminder that she was still alive.

I hesitated at the door to her tiny room. It was barely large enough for her bed, a chair, and the bureau on the opposite wall that held a television set. The window was sealed shut and grayed with years of soot and grime from the nearby highway. There was little to see out there anyway except one forlorn maple struggling to survive in a field that had been paved over and turned into a parking lot. The only bright spot in the room was the vase of flowers standing beside the TV.

Momma stirred. Her bed had been cranked up and she could see the doorway. One corner of her mouth twitched in what might have been an attempt to smile.

I stepped into the room, feeling as awkward and helpless as I always did.

"Hi, Momma," I said as brightly as I could manage.

Her eyes shifted to the swivel table beside her bed. The laptop computer I had bought her rested on it, with the oblong black TV remote control unit beside it. I swung the table in front of her and lifted her right hand to the keyboard.

HELLO DARLING, she typed slowly. Momma had been an office manager before the accident, and an excellent touch typist. Now, with only one hand working, it was more difficult.

I pulled the chair to where I could see the blue screen with its white letters and sat down. "How're you feeling?" I asked.

HOW SHOULD I FEEL? It was her feeble attempt at humor.

"You look pretty good," I said, as cheerfully as I could manage. "Better than last week, I think."

FEEL ABOUT SAME

"The flowers look nice."

THEY BRING NEW ONES EVERY OTHER DAY

"They brighten up the room."

THANKS FOR THEM   VERY THOUGHTFUL OF YOU

Her hand looked like a bird's claw. No flesh on it at all. Skin mottled and gray. But her mind was still alert. I couldn't help thinking that Momma's true essence was really in the computer more than the frail dying husk of her body.

I said, "I had lunch with Jesse last week, the day after his award dinner."

I could see her eyes brighten. Quickly she typed, BEST NEWS IN A YEAR!!!

"Has he been to see you?"

LAST MONTH

I made a point of visiting Momma every week or so.

JESS VERY BUSY, she typed. ALWAYS ON CALL

Very busy, I thought. Sure. Like I'm not. Then I said, "I'm having dinner with him and Julia tomorrow night."

WONDERFUL

The wooden chair felt hard and uncomfortable. I confessed, "I'm kind of scared about it, Momma. I don't know how I'll get through the evening."

YOU CANT AVOID THEM ALL YOUR LIFE

"I know," I said. "But still . . ."

YOU STILL LOVE HER

"I don't know, Momma. I don't know if it's love or hate or what. It hurts, whatever it is."

IS SHE COOKING

"No, we're going to a restaurant. Someplace Jesse's picked out."

GOOD

"Still, it's not going to be easy."

BRING A DATE

"Huh?"

BRING A DATE   DONT GO ALONE

"You think I should?"

DEFINITELY

"I don't know if I can find someone on such short notice."

FIND SOMEBODY

I grinned at her. "I suppose I could rent a date if I had to."

DONT BE FUNNY

"I'll see what I can do."

LOVE YR BROTHER

"I do love him, Momma. In spite of everything. It felt great to see him again. We're trying to get past this chasm that's grown between us. But it isn't easy."

COME SEE ME WITH JESS

"The two of us together?"

YES   BEFORE I DIE

I wanted to reply that she wasn't going to die for a long time, but the words wouldn't come out of my mouth. Momma had never hidden behind phony words.

"I'll tell him tomorrow night. It's a good idea, both of us coming to see you together."

GOOD   NOW FIND A DATE

"You're tired? You want me to leave?"

YES

I got up from the chair slowly. "Is there anything you need? Anything I can get for you?"

NEW HEART, she typed. Her hand hesitated a moment, then pecked out, NEW LEGS TOO

"I wish I could, Momma," I said as I bent to kiss her forehead. Her skin felt dry and cold, lifeless, like parchment. "I wish I could."

PATRICIA HAYWARD

In those days I liked to tell myself that I was a novelist who'd been forced to take on public relations assignments to pay the rent on the modest cottage in Old Saybrook, where I lived with my boozy mother and a half dozen cats. Flacking, I called it. Write a flattering piece about some corporate fathead and then watch their PR troops wheedle it into the national magazines.

So I was not in my most jovial mood as I parked my seven-year-old Corolla in the Grenford Lab lot. At least the parking lot had a section for visitors right up front. I locked the car the way I always did, then looked up at the cloudy sky. A good rain would save the price of a car wash. The old red rover was looking pretty sad and grimy. Maybe this Sunday I ought to break down and give her a good wash and a polish, now that the winter was finally over. Been a long time since she sparkled.

I believed in thorough preparation for any job I undertook. But I'd been surprised at how little information was available in Omnitech's files about Arthur Marshak and his Grenford Laboratory. A standard company biography in their PR database, a few clippings that mentioned his name. There wasn't even much in the Columbia University files. A lot more about his brother, but very little on the man I was supposed to interview.

For this meeting I had put on my corporate business suit, a fingertip-length charcoal double-breasted pin-striped blazer with matching slacks. Emphasized my long legs, which were my second-best feature, I thought. Low heels, though; they were much more comfortable and I didn't need any extra height. Thank god I was still almost as slim as I had been when I played basketball in college. My hair had been brick red then, now it had become a reddish brown. Russet, I called it, and I searched in my mirror every morning for that dreaded first sign of gray. My first-best feature was my eyes: green as emeralds and slightly almond-shaped. After that, my face was kind of long and ordinary.

I tucked my shoulder bag under my arm, marched myself up to the laboratory's front door, and entered the lobby.

I had expected to be kept waiting. Corporate bigwigs like to show how busy they are, like to impress a mere interviewer with their importance. But almost as soon as the receptionist put down her phone, a matronly graying black woman came into the lobby and smiled at me.

"Ms. Hayward? I'll take you back to Dr. Marshak's office."

There were no ID badges, no visitors' log to sign. Pretty lax for a high-powered research lab, I thought. Then I noticed the tiny television cameras in all four corners of the reception lobby, up near the ceiling. All four of their red eyes seemed to be watching me. There were more cameras in the corridors as the black woman led me through the building.

"Can I get you some coffee or anything else?" she asked me as she showed me into Arthur Marshak's office.

The office was empty. I saw a broad desk, two upholstered chairs in front of it, a small round table in the corner, bookshelves lined with dog-eared volumes and stacks of reports, one painting of a racing yacht with sails billowing under a bright summer sun, and a lot of smaller frames that held mottoes of one sort or another. No window. A vague scent of something I couldn't identify.

"No, thank you, I'm fine," I answered. Then I asked, "Do I smell vanilla?"

"Heliotrope," the woman replied. "It helps induce harmony."

"Really?"

"He doesn't believe, but it works," she said. "Dr. Marshak will be with you in a minute. Please make yourself comfortable."

I took one of the upholstered chairs, thinking that Marshak was going to make me wait after all. At least his office wasn't very pretentious. Heliotrope, I mused. For harmony.

I scanned the printed mottoes framed on the wall behind his desk. Most of them were about science and scientists. I recognized some of the names: Albert Einstein, Stephen Jay Gould. And, surprisingly, Yogi Berra's *It ain't over till it's over*.

There was one that had no attribution: *Living well is the best revenge*.

"Sorry to keep you waiting."

I turned in the chair and saw Arthur Marshak striding toward me, right hand extended, smiling warmly. Killer smile. Without thinking I got to my feet and took his hand. His grip was firm without being overpowering; he wasn't trying to impress me with macho muscles.

"I've only been here half a minute," I said. He was handsome, in a solid manly way. Not pretty. Silver-gray hair, very distinguished. He was in his shirtsleeves and if he had worn a tie it was gone now. He looked like a busy man.

"Would you like something to drink? Phyllis makes the best coffee in the universe."

"No, thank you. She already asked me."

Dr. Marshak nodded as if satisfied with my answer. Pointing to the round table in the corner, he said, "Let's sit there. We don't need the desk between us."

I followed him to the table. He held a chair out for me, like an old-fashioned gentleman. He wasn't afraid of militant feminism, apparently.

"Do you work at corporate headquarters?" he asked me as he took the chair beside me.

"I'm freelance," I explained. "Your public relations department has hired me to do a backgrounder about you."

"Backgrounder?"

"It's basically a biographical interview that the news media can use for background information. When they send out your next news release your PR people will include the backgrounder with it."

He leaned back in the plastic chair. "I see. Then the newspapers or magazines can blend it into their story about the news release."

"That's right. My work has been in all the major newsmagazines and lots of big newspapers," I said. Then I added, "Although I never get any credit for it."

"They just print your stuff without a byline?"

I made a rueful smile. "I get a check from the client. No byline."

"What about television? Or radio?"

"They use the backgrounders, too. Or so I'm told."

With a shake of his head, Marshak said, "I've been interviewed a few times on TV. They don't seem to know anything except my name. And they get that wrong sometimes, as well."

Thinking of the twinkies I had dealt with at the networks, I laughed and said, "Sometimes they forget to do their homework."

"Well . . ." He inched his chair closer to me. "What do you need to know about me?"

I pulled my little voice recorder from my bag. "Do these things bother you?"

He waved a hand. "No, not at all."

I clicked it on, checked to see that it was running.

Before I could ask a question, though, he said, "Actually, I think it's the lab that you should be writing about. More than two hundred people here, and the work they do is simply fascinating."

"So I've heard."

"How much do you know about genetic engineering?"

I shrugged. "Just the basics. You snip a gene from one organism's DNA and attach it to another organism's DNA."

"Why?" he asked.

Surprised at the interrogation, I replied, "The gene allows the organism to make something—like human insulin, for example. Put a human insulin gene into a microbe and the bug starts producing human insulin for you. You turn it into a little factory."

Arthur smiled again, bigger this time. "That's the basic idea. Good."

"I do my homework," I said.

Soon we were talking about restriction enzymes and endonucleases and oncogenes. Whenever I began to feel out of my depth, Arthur slowed down and explained patiently.

"You must have been a marvelous teacher," I said after nearly an hour's conversation.

"I enjoyed teaching," he said.

"That's obvious. You seem to have an intuitive feel for when I need more explanation."

He threw his head back and laughed. "It's not intuition, not at all. You put on this funny frown; a myopic monkey can tell when you're puzzled."

"Really?"

He made a face: brows knitted, lips pursed. I started to get angry, but then all of a sudden I broke into laughter. "I look like that?"

"Much prettier, of course."

I considered the matter for a moment and decided it was time that I took charge of this interview. After all, I was supposed to be interviewing him, not vice versa.

"Why did you leave teaching?" I asked. "You obviously enjoy it."

Arthur's laughter died. "Well, you might say that teaching left me, in a manner of speaking."

"Oh?"

He looked somber, wary. "Put it this way: Academia is interested in pure research; seeking out knowledge for the sake of knowledge. I'm interested in *impure* research. I want to use knowledge to make the world better. I want to make an impact on people."

"Applied research," I said.

He nodded acknowledgment. "You know the term."

"And that's why you founded the Grenford Lab?"

"And that's why I founded Grenford Lab."

"Tell me about the work that this news release is going to talk about."

For another hour Arthur talked about the new process for inserting antibodies inside cells.

"Normally, certain cells in your body generate antibodies, but they go outside the cell to find and destroy invading viruses."

I nodded as if I understood, mentally dreading the additional homework I was going to have to do.

"With this new process we can make antibodies work inside cells that are infected. Stop viruses from reproducing inside the cell."

I had to hold up a hand to stop him. "Let me get this straight. A virus invades a cell and uses the cell to produce more viruses, right?"

"Right. It's like Toyota taking over a Ford factory and getting it to produce Toyotas instead of Fords."

"So your new technique can get antibodies to work inside the infected cell—"

"And destroy the virus," Arthur said. "Get the factory back to making Fords, the way it should."

"Nobody's done this before?"

"The original research was done at several universities. What we've done is to take their laboratory results and turn them into a practical system that can be used in the clinical world."

"And it can be used against cancer?"

He nodded. "Certain kinds of cancer. The antibodies can attack the viruses that produce the oncoproteins. It might also be useful against AIDS."

"Really?"

"I think so. AIDS is a difficult problem, but I think this technique shows real promise."

"How expensive will this be?"

Arthur shrugged. "You always get into the question of how to pay for the research. The company will want to write off all the research costs against the price of the treatment. Plus a profit, of course."

"Of course," I said. He didn't seem to catch my little touch of sarcasm.

"In the final analysis, though," he said, "our process will help to cure cancer cases. That's what's important. How much is that worth to you?"

I thought about that for a moment. Then I asked, "Is all the work here at Grenford on cancer?"

"Just about all of it."

"Anything else I should know about?"

"Nothing that should be released to the news media."

It seemed obvious that there were things he wanted to talk about.

"Well, I ought to get as much of a feeling for this place as I can, while I'm here. What's going on that might be news-worthy next year? Or the year after that?"

His eyes lit up. "How much do you know about cancer?"

I reached into my memory bank. "It's the number two killer in the United States. There're lots of different kinds. It's got something to do with cells multiplying wildly."

Pointing a finger like a pistol, Arthur said, "Cells multiply-ing wildly. Tumor cells seem to be immortal. That is, ordi-nary cells will multiply for a while and then they differentiate and stop."

"Differentiate?" I asked.

Pointing as he spoke, Arthur told me, "When an ovum is fertilized, that single cell has the power to produce all the different types of cells that will make up the baby's body: the original fertilized ovum is a totipotent cell."

"Totipotent," I said. "It can make any kind of cell."

"Exactly," he said.

"What about stem cells?"

"The first cells the zygote produces are stem cells."

"As it becomes an embryo."

"Right. Embryonic stem cells are totipotent at first; they can make any kind of cells you need. As they multiply and begin to specialize they become pluripotent: they can make some types of cells, but not others. Then, as the cells continue to specialize, they produce eye cells, hair cells, skin cells. That's differentiation."

"I see."

"Tumor cells don't differentiate. And they don't stop multiplying. They don't know when to stop, so they just keep multiplying and multiplying."

I held up a hand to stop him. "Got to switch the recorder's chip," I explained. I did it quickly, then nodded for him to continue.

"So the question is, how do tumor cells keep multiplying? The other side of that question is, how do ordinary cells *stop* multiplying? Find the answer to the second question and maybe you have the answer to the first."

"And you've found it?"

"Not yet. But this antibody treatment I told you about is a step in that direction."

We seemed to have come full circle. I had tried to get him to talk about some of the other projects going on in the lab and he had led me neatly back to the subject he had started with.

Arthur got to his feet. "Come on, I'll introduce you to the woman who's doing the research and she can show you around her lab. You ought to see how the work gets done."

And I'll be out of your hair for a while, I thought. A pretty slick way of getting rid of me. But I followed him out of his office and into the laboratories where "the work gets done."

To my surprise, even after he introduced me to Cassie Ianetta, he didn't leave my side. He seemed as excited about this work as he told me I should be. And as Cassie showed how she had stopped tumors from growing in laboratory rats and macaque monkeys and even chimpanzees, I did indeed become excited.

The three of us walked back through the animal pens to the fenced-over playground behind the laboratory building. A chimp was playing on the jungle gym when we pushed through the double doors. He took one look at me, a stranger, and ran off to the nearer of the two clipped-back trees. He swung up the stunted branches and sat in the highest crotch of the tree, his eyes flicking from Cassie to Arthur to me.

"It's all right, Max." Cassie held her arms out to the chimp. "Come on down and say hello."

Arthur half whispered to me, "Max is Cassie's baby. She taught him sign language when he was just a little toddler."

I watched, fascinated, while Cassie ignored both me and her boss to speak softly, reassuringly, to the chimp. Max clung to his perch, though.

"Max has generated several strains of tumor-killing factors for us," Arthur said while we waited.

"He's a scientist?" I asked, grinning at my own wit.

"He's a factory," Arthur replied. "Cassie has used him to generate various factors. He's now immune to a half dozen different types of cancers."

That made my eyebrows rise. "Could that immunity be given to people?"

With a nod, Arthur said, "Cassie's about to start field trials on human subjects."

"My god," I said. "If she can accomplish that she ought to get the Nobel Prize for medicine! Her and the chimp both."

But Arthur shook his head. "Neither," he muttered.

I was about to ask why not when Max finally decided it was safe to come down and join us. He scampered down from the tree so fast he was almost a blur and went straight to Cassie. He's bigger than she is, I realized with a start, as the chimp wrapped a long hairy arm around Cassie's waist.

Max waggled his free hand and Cassie laughed.

"He's asking you if you've brought him any food," Cassie explained.

I felt suddenly foolish. "I've got a couple of breath mints in my purse," I said.

"No, it's all right. I'll give him his supper in a little while." Cassie was smiling happily, radiantly, like a real mother with a real baby. She really does love this chimp, I realized.

"You and Max seem to get along very well," I said, thinking it was the understatement of the month.

"Max has been a wonderful helper, a real friend," Cassie said. Her eyes shifted toward Marshak. "And now he's retired."

"Retired?" I asked.

"Yes. He's done everything we've asked him to, and now we're not going to use him in any more experiments."

She's talking to me, I realized, but she's still looking at Marshak.

"That's right," Arthur said. "Max has earned a graceful retirement. We're going to put him out to stud."

Cassie frowned at him, almost fiercely.

Max yawned conspicuously and knuckle-walked to the jungle gym.

"I think we're boring him," Arthur said. He and I laughed.

When Arthur finally walked me back to the front entrance, I realized that the receptionist and most of the office staff had already gone for the day. It was past quitting time, although the researchers all seemed to be still in their labs or offices. A uniformed security guard sat behind the reception desk now. I saw through the glass doors that it had indeed showered; the parking lot was puddled.

"I think I'm in sensory overload," I said honestly to Arthur. "I've got a lot of information to sort out."

"Remember that Cassie's work with Max is strictly off the record," he cautioned.

"Why—"

"We don't want to stir up the wackos when the field trials

start," he said. "Can't you just see the headlines: *Scientists Use Chimp Genes on Human Guinea Pigs*?"

I had to admit he was right, although I felt a surge of resentment. Why did you spend half the afternoon showing it to me if you didn't want me to write about it?

As if he could read my thoughts, Arthur said, "I just couldn't resist showing it off to you. Cassie's done a magnificent job and her work could be a major breakthrough in cancer treatment, once we get the clinical results we're hoping for."

I said nothing as Arthur walked me to my rain-spattered car. It still looked dull and dingy. But I was thinking, He showed me Cassie and her chimp because he's proud of the work the kid's done. He's in love with the work; he's excited as hell about it. Like a kid in a toy store.

ARTHUR

I watched Pat Hayward drive away, thinking, She's one very attractive redhead. Sharp mind, too. She appreciates the work we're doing here.

But as I stepped back inside the lab my thoughts turned to that damned question she had asked me. *Why did you leave teaching? You obviously enjoy it.*

It all came surging back, like a black storm-driven tide. Even after eight years I felt nothing but fury toward Professor Wilson K. Potter, the man who had driven me out of the academic world.

The so-called quiet groves of academe are more like a jungle. I had found that out while I was still a graduate student, but I didn't let it bother me. It's just part of the academic world, the backbiting, the personality clashes, the jockeying for position. It was a lot worse in the other departments, I thought. At least in the sciences you had your research and you saw to it that it got published with your name on it. Maybe your professor stuck his name in there first, but everybody knew who really did the work.

When I got an assistant professorship in the department of molecular biology, the competition and gossip and infighting didn't stop, they became more intense. There were a handful of us snotty new assistant professors, each of us full of our own self-importance and determined to reach that one cherished goal: a full professorship. That meant tenure, a safe position for life, an academic home that no one could threaten. I was going to be the one who beat out all the others, I knew that just as surely as I knew that one day I'd get the Nobel Prize for my research.

At first I had almost enjoyed the competition. I saw myself as a sassy young upstart invading the sacred halls of scholarly power. I was intent on making my mark. I was going to get to Stockholm, no matter what.

But I didn't reckon with the quiet, implacable Professor Wilson K. Potter, the department chairman. He was a slight, spare man, almost completely bald, with innocent blue eyes and a constant little half smile playing on his lips. The kind who could knife you in the back without a shred of remorse. Potter had his own ideas about who he would appoint as a full professor and who deserved a Nobel Prize.

I wasn't too worried about Potter. The man was notorious for putting his own name on his graduate students' work and claiming their ideas and sweat as his own. But since everybody knew it, it didn't really matter too much. The anti-Semitic little creep made life as difficult as he could for me, but I held my temper and wrote off Potter as one of the annoyances in life that had to be endured. He wouldn't be department chairman forever. I was young enough to think that I could wait him out. After all, I intended to stay at Columbia for the rest of my life.

It was the cancer patent that tripped me up.

My first warning of trouble came at the annual Christmas cocktail party in the faculty club. A man approached me. He looked several years younger than I, but already soft, round-faced, starting to bloat. Still, he looked prosperous in a way that scientists seldom attained. Most of the other faculty members were in their usual well-worn tweeds or skirts and blouses. This guy was in a dark blue three-piece suit and an actual school tie.

"You're Professor Marshak, aren't you?" he asked me. I had been standing at the bar, getting a refill on my glass of white wine while I squinted through the smoke and laughing conversations and tinkling ice cubes at a certain sultry-looking professor of Romance languages sipping champagne across the crowded lounge. She was wearing a black sheath and looking bored with the older men surrounding her.

"Arthur Marshak," I answered.

"I'm Greg Barrow." He put out his hand. I took it briefly; it felt slightly clammy, but that might have been because he'd been holding his drink in it.

"What department are you in?" I asked. It was a standard question at faculty bashes; an icebreaker, like asking one's astrological sign.

"Actually, I'm not a faculty member. I'm with the university's legal staff."

"A lawyer?" I drew back in mock horror.

Greg Barrow chuckled tolerantly. "I'm afraid you're going to like lawyers even less in a few days."

"How so?"

"It's this patent you've applied for."

"What about it?"

"The rights belong to the university."

I shrugged. "I know that. But the university assigns the rights to me whenever—"

"I'm afraid the rights won't be assigned in this case," Barrow said ruefully.

Puzzled, I asked, "What do you mean?"

"The university will not release the rights to you."

"Why not? They've done it before. It's a special deal that we made a few years back."

"Not anymore."

I felt more surprised than angry. "When you say the university, just *who* in the university made this decision?"

Barrow shook his head slightly. "That's not for me to say."

That aroused my suspicions. I put my wine glass down on the bar. "Just what the hell is going on here?"

"You'll be called to a meeting with the chief legal counsel. He'll explain it all to you. I just thought I'd give you a little warning so you won't be caught completely by surprise."

A Christmas gift from a lawyer. "Well, thank you—I guess."

Barrow put on a regretful smile. "Sorry to spoil the party for you."

"Don't worry about it," I said, for some stupid reason trying to sound nonchalant. "Happy holidays."

"Merry Christmas."

The lawyer melted back into the crowd. For a while I just stood by the bar, my mind in a turmoil of surmises and worried suspicions. Finally I decided that there was nothing I could do until the legal department called me, so I retrieved my glass of wine and made my way through the crowd to the brunette I'd been eying. Maybe a lesson in the Romance languages will make me feel better, I thought.

It did, but only temporarily.

Sure enough, the day before the Christmas break began, I was called to the office of the university's chief legal counsel and was told point-blank that the rights to my patent would not be assigned to me.

"The university will retain the rights," said the counsel. He was a lean scarecrow of a man, cadaverous almost, in a wrinkled dead gray suit. He looked decidedly unhappy.

"The university has assigned the rights to me on my previous applications," I said. "We have an informal agreement—"

"That will no longer be the case," he told me. "The university intends to license the rights to a commercial bidder."

"Who made this decision?" I wanted to know.

The scarecrow spread his long arms. "The, uh, university."

He was trying to stonewall me. "Was it your idea? Did the decision originate with the legal staff?"

"No!" He blurted it like a man proclaiming his innocence.
"Then where did it originate?"

Silence.

"It had to come from somewhere," I insisted. "Someone."

"From your own department," the counsel admitted.

From Potter, I realized.

It was starting to snow when I stormed out of the counsel's office. Blind-angry, bareheaded, wearing nothing heavier than my tweed jacket, I tramped through the falling wet flakes back to my own building and straight to the office of the department chairman.

Potter's office was far from pretentious. Bigger than the cubicles his faculty members were assigned, it was nonetheless a small, stuffy room crammed with bookshelves and a mahogany desk that Potter sat behind like a general looking out at his battlefield from the safety of the walls of his fortress. He was a small man, small in every way; I had often thought that a larger office would merely diminish his stature. There was one window, behind Potter's back. The snow was thickening outside as I took the worn old wooden chair before the desk, my soaked shoes making puddles on his faded thin carpet.

"I'm very busy," Potter said. And he started fluttering papers on his desk, with that venomous little half smile of his ticking at the corners of his mouth.

"You instructed the legal department not to assign the rights to my patent to me."

Potter's lopsided little smile disappeared. "Who told you that?"

"Let's not play games, Professor. You did it and I know you did. The question is, why?"

"Legally, any patent granted for work by the faculty belongs to the university."

"The university has assigned the rights to my previous patents to me. You know that. The arrangement was agreed to more than three years ago."

"Yes, quite true," Potter snapped, his eyes glittering angrily. "And you turn around and license the rights to Omnitech and make a fortune."

"What of it? Other faculty members do the same thing. It's common practice."

"They get rich!" Potter screeched. "They make fortunes for themselves while the rest of us try to live on a professor's salary."

I sagged back on the hard wooden chair. By god, he's jealous. The old bastard is jealous!

"A professor's salary isn't exactly penury," I said, more softly.

Potter's face contorted. "Do you know what Samuels told me last April? His university salary barely covers his income taxes! He invited me out to his big fancy house out on the Island just to show off how well he's doing and then he tells me that his salary is not quite big enough to pay his income tax!"

"But that's no reason to—"

"I won't have any more members of my department using this university as a launching pad for their personal fortunes. Never again!"

"That's unfair," I said. "Dictatorial."

Potter pointed a bony finger at me. "See here, Marshak. You've got to decide whether you're going to be a proper member of this faculty or a money-grubbing businessman. You can't be both. I won't have it."

My insides were trembling. "Are you telling me that you won't allow me to have any of the benefits from the patentable work I do?"

"I'm telling you that you're here to teach and do research, not to build up your private fortune. If you want to get rich, then get out!"

I was fighting to remain calm, reasonable. "I've worked all my life to get where I am. I've seen others take my ideas and make fortunes on them. It's not fair of you to prevent me from getting what I deserve."

"You signed the same disclosure and waiver forms that I did when you accepted your position on the faculty," Potter said. "You're not going to get special treatment anymore. That's final."

I got to my feet. My legs were shaking. "I thought that I had finally found a home, a place where I could work and live for the rest of my life."

"You are using university facilities and students to line your own pockets," Potter snarled at me. "You don't belong in academia, you're just a money-mad Jew."

"I'm not going to allow you to stop me," I said, looking down on the little man.

"Then get out!" Potter snarled. "And don't try to come back!"

Why did you leave teaching? Patricia had asked me. *You obviously enjoy it.*

Yes. I did enjoy the teaching. I did enjoy it. But that gloomy December evening as I stood outside with the thickening snow falling on my bare head, looking up at Potter's window, I felt as if I had been orphaned and thrown out onto the street.

Which was just what Potter had done to me.

PATRICIA HAYWARD

It wasn't until I had driven halfway back to Old Saybrook that I realized that I had gotten precious little information about Arthur Marshak. Hours and hours about the new antibody process and Cassie Ianetta's work on stopping tumor growth. But the background information about the man himself was minuscule.

Is he really that self-effacing? I asked myself. He sure doesn't come across as humble or shy. Then I wondered, Is he hiding something? Is there a bigger story here than the one Omnitech wants me to write?

By the time I got to our weather-beaten old cottage I had made up my mind to phone Marshak first thing the next morning to schedule a follow-up interview.

As I tossed my bag on the kitchen table, I heard Livvie call from the living room, "That you, Patsy?"

Who else? I answered silently.

"Patsy?"

How I hated being called Patsy!

"Patsy, is that you or should I call 911?"

"It's me, Mom. Who else would it be?"

I walked into the tiny front room, suddenly feeling tired and cranky. The picture window had once looked out on a nice lawn and the shore of Long Island Sound. But our landlord had put up another bungalow on that lawn and now all we had to look at was its back windows.

Olivia Hayward—Livvie—was a head shorter than I and forty pounds overweight. She often said ruefully that she got her only child (me) from her second husband (of four) and I got my tall, slim genes from the sneaky, smooth-talking sonofabitch.

"How was your day?" Livvie asked. She sat in her usual recliner, a plastic tumbler in her hand and the vodka bottle at her elbow.

"Pretty interesting," I said. I started to tell her about Grenford Lab and Arthur Marshak while I went back into the kitchen and poured myself a glass from the jug of white wine in the refrigerator.

I sat down beside my mother and told her about my day while the sun went down. Neither one of us made any attempt to begin dinner. I sipped slowly at my wine. Livvie drained her tumbler and poured herself another healthy slug of vodka.

"This scientist guy sounds nice," Livvie said. "He makes a bundle, I bet. Is he cute?"

He's as handsome as they come, I thought. But aloud I answered, "What's that got to do with anything? I interviewed him, Mom. It's work, not romance."

"You never can tell," Livvie said, almost dreamily. "I met your father when he came to the house to fix the bathroom sink."

And divorced him two years later, I added silently.

"Don't you even *think* about marriage anymore?" she asked me.

"Let's not start that again."

"You're not getting any younger."

I gritted my teeth, then leaned forward toward her and said, "Tell you what, Mom. You find somebody who *is* getting younger and I'll write a story about her and win the Pulitzer prize. Okay?"

Livvie gave me a puzzled look. "Just because you made one mistake shouldn't turn you off marriage forever."

No, I said to myself, I should go on like you did and make four mistakes. Or the same mistake four times, really.

To change the subject, I asked, "Did I get any calls?"

My mother frowned with concentration for a moment. "Yeah, the phone did ring. Not too long ago, either."

I got up and went to my bedroom, which doubled as my office. There was only one message on my phone machine:

"This is Arthur Marshak. I hope you don't mind my calling, Pat, after spending a pretty intense afternoon at the lab. I just thought that it might be fun if we had dinner together some evening soon. Maybe tomorrow night, if you can make it. Get to know each other a little better, without the lab around us. Please give me a ring as soon as you can. Thanks."

I plopped down on my bed, grinning foolishly, all my weariness and irritation vanished. The man must really be a mind reader, I thought. Really!

"Anybody important?" Livvie called from the front room.

My grin evaporated at the thought of bringing Arthur Marshak home to meet my mother.

ARTHUR

The next afternoon, the day I was supposed have dinner with Julia and Jess, I drove from the lab to Omnitech's corporate headquarters in lower Manhattan. I stuck to the Bronx River Parkway; I never took the Deegan Expressway if I could avoid it. Superstition, I suppose. Still, I never willingly drove on the highway that had killed my father and maimed my mother.

Find a date, Momma told me. Three o'clock in the afternoon and I've got to find a date for seven-thirty. It had been stupid to call Patricia Hayward. Desperate. Just met her and I phone to invite her to dinner. I must have sounded like an idiot. No wonder she hadn't called back. I began to think seriously of calling a professional escort service.

As a corporate vice president, I had my own office in the headquarters building. It was not as large as my office at the lab but decorated much more richly. The corporate officers know how to spend money on themselves: gleaming walnut paneling and thick luxurious carpeting. Nancy Dubois, one of the more ambitious junior executives, informed me that the carpet's color was pale ecru. At the lab the walls were plain painted plasterboard or cinderblock and the carpeting was industrial heavy-duty gray.

My office had floor-to-ceiling windows, too. Seventy-eight stories up, it was a little scary. The building had been awfully close to the World Trade Center. When the terrorists struck, the police kept us out of the building for weeks until they determined that it was structurally unharmed. Still, it was scary standing there looking out those windows. I imagined an airliner hurtling straight at me.

Ground Zero was on the other side of the building. From my office I could see the harbor far below, and in the distance the small green figure of the Statue of Liberty. My desk was solid walnut. Its gleaming surface was almost always clear of papers or anything that looked like work. I worked at the lab. I came to the corporate office for politics. All the chairs were covered in bottle-green leather, including the big swivel chair behind the desk. I had to insist that they put in a credenza alongside the desk and get me a personal computer. Hardly any of the other corporate vice presidents had computers in their headquarters offices; they requisitioned secretaries to type for them.

Soon as I got in, I phoned Phyllis back at the lab. She assured me that all was well, no emergencies that could not wait until I returned the following morning. Then I phoned Elise Hauser at her UN office. But she was out of the country and would not return for a week.

Through the computer's modem I called up my address book from my database at the lab. I was getting desperate. Maybe Nancy Dubois would be available. We had had a brief fling last year, when I was trying to get over Julia. But she might think I wanted to renew our romance, and that was certainly not what I had in mind.

I was busy scanning the lists for a possible last-minute date when I heard:

"Do you have a couple of minutes, Dr. Marshak?"

I looked up and saw Patricia Hayward standing at the doorway.

"What're you doing here?" I blurted.

"Working."

I waved her into the office as I killed the address list and shut down the computer. "I thought you freelanced out of Old Saybrook."

Pat took the chair at the side of my desk. "I'm spending the day on the company files, doing more research for your backgrounder."

"Oh. I see."

"I know enough now to ask some relevant questions," she said.

She was really good-looking in a coltish, almost aristocratic way. I could picture her in a riding outfit or a form-hugging maillot, outswimming the boys at summer camp. At the moment she was wearing comfortable light gray slacks and a pale blue silk blouse that complemented her reddish hair very nicely.

"Do you have a few minutes?" she asked again. Her voice was a soft purr. Like a cat. I wondered if she liked to be stroked like a cat. But this is no time for that kind of thinking, I told myself. This is business.

"Did you get my phone message last night?"

Her green eyes slid away from mine, slightly. "I was going to call you—but a lot of other things got in the way."

"Well, will you have dinner with me?" As romantic as a dump truck, that's me.

"Dinner? Tonight?"

"Tonight."

"I really can't tonight. I've got to drive back to Connecticut."

"The traffic will be lighter after dinner."

She shook her head. "I don't like to drive in the dark, especially alone."

I thought about that for a moment.

Before I could say anything, Pat added, "I'd love to have dinner with you, but some other night."

"I could get the company to put you up here in Manhattan for the night," I heard myself saying. "We keep a set of condo suites for visiting VIPs."

She smiled. "I'm not a VIP, just a working gal."

"I can bestow VIP status on you."

"For the night."

I saw what was bothering her. "Look," I said, leaning slightly toward her, "I've got to have dinner tonight with my brother and his wife. I need a date. Honestly. I know it's a lot to ask, especially on such short notice, but I really can get the company to let you stay in one of our condos and you can drive home tomorrow in the daylight."

She looked at me, and I could see the wheels working in her head.

I raised both my hands. "My intentions are purely social. Honestly."

"I'm not dressed for anyplace fancy."

"You look fine to me. Jesse said the restaurant's just a neighborhood place down near Gramercy Park."

Pat took in a breath, then answered, "Okay. But I still need the answers to these questions I've come up with."

I relaxed and leaned back in the swivel chair. "Of course. Fire away."

She started asking her questions, but I answered them automatically, like a kid spitting out answers to a school quiz. My mind drifted to Julia and what it would be like to see her again.

IT HAPPENED after a visit to Momma, a little more than a month before Julia and I were to be married.

I had never been in love before. Oh, I had the usual flings when I'd been a student, plenty of them, in fact. Later, there were more adult affairs at the university. And when I became a successful corporate executive it was actually easy to find women. But once I met Julia all that stopped. I fell in love, just like a moonstruck kid. We were going to be married.

Julia was everything I had ever dreamed of: warm, beautiful, loving, intelligent. She was quiet, understated, but always made her point. She never disappeared into the background, whether we were at a corporate cocktail party or attending a Broadway opening. She had opinions, she had ideas, she made me proud to have her standing beside me. And despite that cool facade, she was fiery with passion in bed. She was an executive with British Airways; I met her on a transatlantic flight. Our courtship was a whirlwind: within a month I had taken Julia with me to see Momma at Sunny Glade. Two months after that I proposed.

I had introduced Julia to my brother, of course. Jesse seemed faintly amused by it all.

"You're really going to settle down to married life?" Jesse asked me, a few weeks before the wedding date.

"I certainly am."

Jess was not smiling. "Are you sure she's the right woman for you, Arby? You've only known her a few months."

"She's the one."

"You don't know much about her, do you? I mean—"

"I know enough," I said.

"You think you do."

"I know I do."

Jesse shook his head. "Take it slow, Arby. Don't be in such a rush. Maybe she's not right for you."

I laughed at him. "For god's sake, you'd think you're the one who's getting married instead of me!"

"I don't want you to get hurt," Jesse said, very seriously.

But I ignored him. "You ought to find a woman like Julia and settle down yourself."

"I wish I could," Jesse said.

Momma had been as happy as she could be. She thought Julia was terrific. And she was right, of course. The day it happened, Julia and I had just spent an hour with Momma, me making lists of wedding guests and all the details that had to be taken care of, Momma pecking away at her keyboard with her one good hand. Then they shooed me out of Momma's room; they wanted to be alone for some woman talk, I figured.

When we left, Julia suggested we take a walk around the nursing home grounds before returning to the city. It was a chilly gray afternoon. I remember the wind knifed through my sports coat and it looked like a cold autumn rain was on the way.

"Don't you feel cold?" I asked Julia. She was wearing a light sweater over her short-sleeved dress.

"Arthur, I have to tell you something," she said. I saw that she was somber, grim. The look in her dark eyes was sheer misery.

"What's wrong?"

"It's Jess."

I felt myself go tense with sudden anger. "Has he been bothering you? Saying things he shouldn't?"

"No, not at all."

"He's been telling me to think twice about marrying you," I blurted. I hadn't intended to tell Julia about that. I wanted her to like my brother.

"That's because he's in love with me," said Julia.

I wasn't really sure that I heard her. Or if I did, I didn't understand what she was saying.

"Jesse's in love with me," she repeated.

I just gaped at her. She looked back at me almost as if she were frightened, like a child who's afraid of being beaten. I don't know how long we just stared at each other like that.

Then Julia went on, "And I'm in love with him."

It was as if the world stopped revolving. I took in the entire scene, the gray clouds pressing down on me, the pitiful patchy grass of the lawn, the few trees darkened by grime from the highway, the cars growling past angrily, Julia standing bleakly before me, waiting for my reaction. I imagine she expected anger or tears or questions.

"Neither of us wanted it this way, Arthur," she said, so softly I could barely hear her. "It's just happened and there's nothing any of us can do about it."

I couldn't speak. Ten thousand things I wanted to say, but not a word would leave my throat. I wanted to tell her this was wrong, it was all a mistake, it was a stupid terrible treacherous thing to do to me. But I stood there as mute as a stump.

Julia's eyes were dry, but anguish showed in every line of her face, every tense angle of her body.

"Don't you see, Arthur? He needs me. He really needs me. You're so strong, so capable, so self-reliant. But Jesse needs me to look after him, to stand by his side, to help him in his work."

I wanted to scream, to rage, to find my traitor of a brother and throttle him. Instead I just turned wordlessly away from Julia and walked across the meager lawn to the parking lot, got into my car, and left her standing alone beneath the lowering sky.

I TRIED to drive those memories, that scene, out of my mind as the corporate limo drove Pat and me uptown from the Omnitech offices to Gramercy Park. I'm so strong and self-reliant, am I? Then why are my guts churning as if somebody were twisting a knife in them?

The restaurant was quietly elegant, not glitzy. Small and intimate, with smoked mirrored walls to make it seem bigger than it was without making it look garish.

Jesse was not there when we arrived. Just like Jess, of course. Never on time. The maître d' showed us to the table Jesse had reserved and took our drink orders: Pat wanted white wine, I asked if they had any Tavel.

"Yes, of course," said the maître d' in a smooth near-whisper.

"What's Tavel?" Pat asked.

"A French rosé."

She wrinkled her nose. "Rosés are too sweet for me."

I was glad of the chance to have something that I could talk about. "Tavels are quite dry. I think you'd like it."

"I'll take a sip of yours, okay?"

"Sure."

She liked the wine, though she stuck to her white. For twenty minutes we sipped wine and made small talk while I fidgeted and eyed the front door, wondering when my brother and Julia would show up. And then they came through the door, Jesse chatting laughingly with the headwaiter, Julia searching the room with her eyes.

My heart lurched at the sight of her. More beautiful even than I remembered. Those soulful dark eyes. She still looked fragile, vulnerable, the kind of utterly feminine woman that made me want to wrap my arms around her protectively. Yet her figure was womanly, and beneath that refined veneer she had the heat of animal passion in her blood. I had known that passion, explored every inch of her responsive flesh.

But no more.

She looked depressingly happy. If Julia felt as anxious or reluctant as I did, she gave no sign of it. She was smiling and bright-eyed, her chestnut-brown hair swept back almost carelessly, her Chinese-red dress with its mandarin collar looking modest and sexy at the same time, the way it clung to her. I bounced to my feet as they approached, searching her eyes for some hint of remorse, some sign that she regretted the choice she had made. I found only a kind of hopeful expectancy.

"Arthur," she said, reaching out to touch my cheek.

It was difficult to make my voice work. "It's good to see you again, Julia," I finally managed to croak.

"It's good to see you, Arthur."

I fumbled through introducing Patricia and dreaded having to make conversation. I knew my brain wouldn't work right.

But I needn't have worried. Jesse took over the burden of discourse. He started talking as soon as he sat down and kept right on going through drinks, appetizers, and the main course, his words aimed ostensibly at Pat, although I knew he was showing off for Julia, showing his wife that she had made the right choice.

"So what we're doing, my big brother and I," he was saying to Pat, "is inaugurating the Fourth Era of Medicine." He pronounced it with capital letters.

"The fourth era of medicine?" Pat asked. The expression on her face said that she knew it was just a setup line for Jesse's next quarter hour of lecturing.

"Yep," Jesse said happily. "The first era goes back to prehistoric times. Tribal medicine men found out that if you chewed the bark of a certain tree or drank a tea made from some certain herbs you could stop a headache or settle stomach cramps or induce other simple cures."

"I thought it was the women who did that," said Pat.

Jesse shrugged. "Women, men, what's the difference? Medical practice was a kind of cookbook thing for centuries. They knew certain things worked for certain problems—sometimes. But nobody knew why."

"And they mixed it all up with superstition, didn't they?" Julia said. She looked radiant, glowing. I wondered if she might be pregnant. The thought startled me.

"Yeah, right," Jesse went on, undeterred. "Right up into the twentieth century, just about, medicine was cookbook stuff, hit or miss."

He cocked an eye at me, but I had nothing to say. I was thinking that I'd never seen Jesse looking happier: relaxed, confident, exuding that boyish charm that he used the way other men used money or power to get their way. This is Jesse's night, I thought. The limelight is all his. Again.

Jesse was going on, "Then modern science got into the game. Found out that what cured your headache was acetyl-salicylic acid, so you don't have to chew the whole tree bark, just make a pill out of the effective ingredient."

"Pasteur," Julia murmured.

"Huh?"

"Pasteur was the turning point, was he not?"

Jesse shrugged. "Yeah, sure. He needed the invention of the microscope and a lot of other things, though."

"Yet it was Pasteur who established the germ theory of disease," Julia said firmly.

"Right," said Jesse. "That started the second era of medicine. We began to learn what *causes* diseases. Bacteria, infection. And later on we discovered viruses. Once we started to understand what caused diseases, we could start looking for ways to kill the bugs."

"I see," said Pat.

I was almost amused by Julia's performance. She had always been quiet, self-contained. British reserve, I called it. People thought she was shy, or even upper-class snobbish. But she was a little tigress at heart. She could let Jesse prattle on for a half hour and then bring him up short with a single word. Nobody who knew her could ever take her for granted. Beneath that sedate English exterior she had a first-class mind and an even sharper sense of how to make the most of her intelligence.

"It was Ehrlich who coined the term 'chemotherapy,'" Jesse was explaining, "back around 1910 or so when he came up with his magic bullet for syphilis. We started developing specific chemical compounds to attack specific disease agents. That was the second era of medicine."

"We're still doing that," said Pat.

"Yeah, but there are limits to chemotherapy. For one thing, most of the chemicals we use are poisons. They kill the bacteria that infect you, yes, but they kill healthy cells, too. That's why doses have to be closely regulated and you get side effects from medicines."

"And none of those medicines attack viruses," Julia pointed out. "Not even the most potent antibiotics."

"So now we go into the third era of medicine." Jesse quickly reclaimed the floor. "We start developing antiviral agents through genetic engineering, recombinant DNA, and all that. Antibacterial, too, of course, but it's the antiviral stuff that's the new breakthrough. Monoclonal antibodies to attack cancer cells, for example."

"And AIDS?" Pat asked.

With a vigorous nod, Jesse replied, "There's some work going on at the Cancer Institute on ADA deficiency, trying to restore a damaged immune system. That's a tough one."

"AIDS activists claim that we're not putting enough money into the research."

"More money would help," Jesse said. "But all the money in the world can't buy new ideas, new insights."

Julia chipped in, "It can if it's used to put more researchers to work on the problem."

"Maybe," he conceded. Turning back to Pat, "But I was going to tell you about gene therapy. That's the newest thing. Inserting genes into a patient whose own genes aren't doing the job they're supposed to do. We're starting to cure diabetics, getting them off insulin shots, because we've given them genes that make their pancreases produce insulin naturally, the way normal people do."

"I've written stories about that," Pat said. "They're working on cystic fibrosis, too, aren't they?"

"Yep. And various forms of cancers, especially ovarian cancer, up at the University of Rochester. Malignant melanomas, brain cancer—some group in Shanghai is working on hemophilia, I hear."

"Using gene therapy?"

"Right."

"Then what's the fourth era?" Pat asked.

Jesse gave her a lazy grin. "That's what Arby and I are starting."

"Arby?"

Jesse pointed at me. "The silent dummy that's been sitting

next to you all evening. I think he's had his tongue amputated."

I forced myself to answer, "You're doing so well, Jess, that I didn't have the heart to break in on you."

"First time that's ever happened!" Jesse laughed.

"What are you doing?" Pat asked again. "What about the fourth era?"

"Regeneration," said Jesse, the way a stage magician might say, *Presto!*

The waiter brought our desserts just then and all four of us fell silent, as if we'd been talking about some dark international secret.

I glanced down at my fruit tart, then before Jesse could resume his monologue I said, "Jess and I are tinkering around with some ideas about regenerating nerve cells in the spinal cord."

Jesse laughed. "Arby, you could take the end of the world and make it sound humdrum."

Pat swiveled her head from him to me and back again. Julia quietly spooned up some of her zabaglione.

"What we're doing," Jesse went on, "is going to allow us to reconnect the severed spinal nerves. For paraplegics. We'll make them walk!"

"Really?"

I started to say, "We've just started—"

"That's just the beginning," Jesse said, his enthusiasm growing. "I mean, if we learn how to regenerate spinal neurons, what about other cells, elsewhere in the body?"

Julia put her spoon down and looked at her husband thoughtfully.

"Let's see if we can regenerate a few neurons before we start going off the deep end," I said.

"Yeah, sure," Jesse replied. "But listen, Arby, why *not* other kinds of tissue? It might even be easier."

"Might be," I conceded.

"I mean, think of the possibilities! Grow a new heart, new kidneys, whatever!"

I couldn't help smiling at my brother's excitement. "At least there wouldn't be a rejection problem."

"Wait a minute," Pat said. "You're going too fast for me. Are you saying what I think you're saying?"

Jesse hunched forward so eagerly he nearly dug the elbow of his sports jacket into his dish of spumoni. Julia caught his arm just in time.

"Listen," he said, ignoring his wife's help. "You, me, all of us—each human being was once just a single cell, one teeny little fertilized ovum."

Pat nodded.

"In nine months that one cell grew into trillions of cells, cells that became lungs and hair and brain and muscle and everything else."

"The cells specialized," said Julia.

"Differentiated," I said.

"Okay, okay. Now, you're seventy years old and your heart's crapping out on you. What are your choices?"

"Medicaid," Pat snapped.

"Come on! You need a new heart! What can you do?"

"How much money can I spend?"

"Money is no object."

I said, "This is all theoretical."

Pat grinned at me, then turned back to Jesse. "If money's no problem, then I can get a heart transplant."

"Or an artificial heart," said Julia.

"They don't work."

"Temporarily, until a transplant donor is found."

"Okay."

Jesse was practically bubbling over. "But what if you could grow a new heart? Right there inside your chest? Just like you did originally when you were a fetus."

"Would there be room for two inside?"

I put a hand on my brother's sleeve. "It might be easier to grow the new heart in vitro, from the patient's own somatic cells, and then put it in surgically."

"Well, maybe, yeah." Jesse clearly did not like that approach.

"But the really nifty thing would be to grow it in vivo. No surgery at all."

"Is that possible?" Pat wondered.

"The information is there, in the DNA of your cells," Jesse said. "Same information that built your heart in the first place. All the information is stored in your DNA, everything you need to grow every part of you."

"You mean that if I had an arm or a leg amputated you could grow a new one for me?" Pat asked eagerly.

"Why not?" Jesse answered.

My head was spinning just a little bit. "This goes to show you the effects of Italian wine on Jewish brains," I said.

They all laughed. But then Jesse asked me, "You don't think it's possible?"

"In theory, maybe. Just maybe. In practice—"

"What would the obstacles be?" Julia asked softly.

Watching the expression on Jesse's face as I spoke, I said carefully, "In the fetus the cells grow and differentiate. You start out with one cell, then it multiplies and multiplies until—"

"Yeah, yeah," Jesse interrupted impatiently. "Once the cells differentiate you can't get 'em to regenerate anymore. Right?"

"Not as yet," I said.

Jesse broke into his patented grin. "Ahh! You're not going to be an old fart about this after all."

Julia frowned. "Perhaps you *have* had too much wine, darling."

"I'm just kidding." Turning back to me, Jesse said, "If we can activate the codons for nerve cell regeneration, Arby, we ought to be able to do the same for any kind of cell. Right?"

"In theory," I replied.

"You will need stem cells, won't you?" Julia asked.

Pat said, "Oh-oh."

"We probably will," Jesse admitted. "If the government doesn't get in the way."

"I know there's a lot of controversy about stem cell work," Pat said.

I nodded.

"And the right-to-life lobby is against stem cell research, isn't it?"

"Because the only source for stem cells is from aborted fetuses," Julia said.

"So far," added Jesse. "We'll be able to get stem cells from adult patients. Some lab in Japan or Korea or someplace has produced adult stem cells out of ordinary skin cells."

I put in, "But the fetal stem cells are easier to isolate and we know they're totipotent. Adult stem cells aren't."

Pat started to say, "Totipotent means—"

Jesse couldn't wait. "They can be made to produce any type of cell you need: skin, muscle, neuron . . . anything."

"But it's illegal to use the fetal stem cells?"

"Not illegal," Jesse said. "The government wouldn't fund stem cell research for many years. Now they do, but only under very special circumstances."

"We'll fund the work ourselves," I promised. "We won't use government money, so we won't be hampered by their red tape."

"The rest," Jesse said dramatically, "is details."

Julia asked, "Didn't someone once say that God is in the details?"

Jesse countered, "It was genius, not God."

"The quotation is from Ellice Hopkins," said Patricia. " 'Genius only means an infinite capacity for taking pains.' "

I smiled at Jesse. "I think the proper quotation for this dinner is, 'Genius does what it must, and talent does what it can.' "

ARTHUR

The limousine was waiting for us at the curb when we left the restaurant.

Jesse played at being impressed. "A limo! Rank has its privileges."

"We'll take you home," I said as the chauffeur opened the door for us.

"We could take a taxi," said Julia.

But Jesse went straight to the limo. "Come on, hon. We don't get treated this well very often."

"You don't mind if we drop them off first, do you?" I asked Pat.

She shook her head and then followed Julia into the car's dark interior. Jesse and Julia had taken the rearward-facing seats, separated by a console that held a TV screen. Pat slid across the leather-upholstered bench and I ducked in and sat beside her. The limo was wide enough so that there was considerable room between her and me.

"Give the driver your address," I told Jess.

Jesse twisted around and said to the chauffeur, "Three thirty-four West Eighty-seventh."

As the limo pulled away from the curb, Julia said, "It's getting to be rather a good neighborhood now. You must come up and see us, Arthur."

"Sure," I said.

"I'm learning to cook," she said.

"Is it a safe area?" Pat asked.

Jesse grinned at her. "Safe enough. As long as you don't go out alone in the dark and you walk fast and carry a baseball bat."

"Oh, rubbish!" Julia said. "It's as safe as anywhere else in Manhattan."

"See what I mean?" said Jesse.

I leaned my hands on my knees and hunched forward toward my brother. "We ought to go see Momma together, Jess. She asked me to tell you."

"Sure," Jesse replied easily. "When?"

"My schedule's probably more flexible than yours."

"Yeah. I've got patients to see and rounds to make. All you've got to worry about is board of directors meetings and parties with the rich and famous."

And two hundred people at the lab who depend on me, I added silently. Jesse always did think that he was the only one who had pressures on him.

I asked him, "What's your schedule like for the next few days?"

"We're going to Africa next month," Julia said.

"Africa?" That was a surprise.

"Eritrea," she said.

"But you just got back from Brazil—"

"They need all the medical help they can get," said Jesse, his smile gone. "Malaria, typhus, AIDS; there're even reports of bubonic plague."

"It's because of the famine, you see," Julia explained. "Starvation lowers their resistance to disease."

"But they're still fighting a civil war there, aren't they?" I asked. He's not taking Julia there, I told myself. He can't take her into a pesthole like that.

"The war's over," Jesse said.

"But there's still fighting going on," Pat said. "One tribe raids another. Pillaging, that sort of thing."

And rape, I added mentally.

"We'll be at a UN station," Julia said. "We'll be protected by peacekeeping troops."

"You're not going with him, are you?"

"Of course I am. I wouldn't miss it for the world."

"But . . ." I floundered for an excuse. "But what about your own work? What about—"

"British Airways can get along without me for a month or two," Julia said coolly. "I've arranged for a leave of absence."

"It sounds awfully dangerous to me," I muttered.

"Even airline executives need a little excitement now and then, Arthur," she teased.

"You just got back from Brazil."

"That was last year."

I turned to Jess. "It's one thing for you to go traipsing around the world, but bringing Julia along, exposing her to all those dangers—it's not right."

Before Jesse could reply, Julia said, "I wouldn't let him go without me, Arthur, dear. I'm his wife. I married him for better or for worse. Wither he goest, there go I."

Jesse grinned at me. "I couldn't leave her behind even if I wanted to, Arby."

I sank back in the seat, defeated. But my mind unreeled pictures of Julia dying in some fly-infested tent, sick with a tropical fever while Jesse was out tending to the natives. Or worse, some wild band of marauding bandits breaks into their camp and . . . I squeezed my eyes shut, trying to erase the images from my mind.

We drove in gloomy silence up Riverside Drive, past the piers where the cruise liners dock and the floating museum of the aircraft carrier *Intrepid*. At last the limo cut back into the city streets and pulled up to a gray stone apartment building.

Jesse immediately opened the door on his side, before the chauffeur could get around to it.

"Call me tomorrow and let me know when you can come up to see Momma," I said to him.

"Right," said Jesse as he ducked out the door.

"I'll see that he does," said Julia. She kissed me lightly on the cheek and then she, too, left the limo. I watched them walk up the steps hand in hand. Jesse tapped out their security code on the electronic pad built into the wall next to the front door. The glass door was reinforced with cast-iron scrollwork; meant to look decorative, but actually there to keep thugs from breaking in.

Jess waved nonchalantly as their front door popped open and the limo pulled away from the curb.

"You're really worried about them," Pat said.

"Jesse's a damned fool to take such risks."

"I suppose that's how you get to be Humanitarian of the Year."

I guess I gave her a sour glance. "He can be all the humanitarian he wants to be. But he shouldn't drag her along with him."

"It doesn't look to me as if he's dragging her, exactly," said Pat.

I fumed inwardly, but said nothing. There was nothing I could say. Julia had made that clear.

"She is his wife, after all."

"That doesn't give him the right to risk her life."

"She seems very determined."

I wanted to yell at her, to roar out my fear and anger and hurt, scream to the heavens about my brother's stupid insensitivity. Jesse was taking advantage of her. He knew Julia would go wherever he did. She enjoyed the challenge, she was excited by the idea of living dangerously. It never occurred to her that she could get hurt, get sick, be raped or killed. Those kinds of things did not happen to her. Other people might be blown up by terrorists or murdered in the streets in a senseless drive-by shooting, but that sort of thing never happened to anyone you knew, anyone close to you. How could it happen to you?

But I saw it happening to Julia, and when it did, it would be Jesse's fault. He'd have killed her just as surely as if he'd put a bullet in her brain.

I smoldered in silence while the limo purred softly through the quiet streets, heading for the midtown condo building where the corporation maintained its VIP quarters. Pat said nothing for several blocks. I think she must have sensed how distressed I was.

But after a while she asked softly, "Do you really think you could grow new organs for people?"

It took me a moment or two to mentally shift gears. "Maybe," I said. "It might be possible. In theory, at least."

"Jesse seemed terrifically excited about the idea."

"Sure he is. Why not? He's like a kid with a new toy," I

grumbled. But then I had to admit, "It really is an exciting idea."

She laughed. "You seem to be containing your excitement pretty well, though."

I looked at her. In the shadowy interior of the limo her face was dimly lit by the passing streetlamps, like a speeded-up version of the moon's monthly cycle, waxing, waning, waxing again.

"It's always been that way," I said. "I'm the practical brother; Jesse's the romantic."

And that's when the limousine stopped and the chauffeur hustled around to open the door next to Pat.

"This is it, I guess," she said.

Without thinking, I slid across the seat after her and got out of the limo. We were standing on the sidewalk in front of a modern glass-and-steel high-rise. Through the glass double doors I could see a concierge sitting at an ornate little desk. A uniformed doorman was hurrying across the lobby to open the front door for us.

"The condo ought to have a toothbrush and whatever else you need," I said. "If there are any problems, the concierge will take care of them."

"My car?"

"Tell the concierge when you want it. The garage will have somebody drive it up here for you."

Pat nodded. "You've taken care of everything, I guess."

"I think so," I said. My mind was still on Julia and Jesse. I understood that what really bothered me was not Africa and the danger that they might be heading into. It was the fact that Julia would follow Jesse off the edge of a cliff, that she *wanted* to be with Jesse, go where he went, be a part of his life, merge her being completely with his.

Not with me, I told myself. She doesn't want to be with me.

"Well, thanks for a fascinating evening."

It took an effort to focus my attention on Pat. The expression on her face was strange, part expectation, part puzzlement. With hindsight, I guess she was expecting me to suggest that I come up to her suite with her. But my mind was thousands of miles away.

"No," I said. "I thank you. I couldn't have made it through dinner without you."

And before she could say anything more I turned and went back to the limo, leaving her standing on the sidewalk with the doorman expectantly holding the door open for her and the concierge staring at our little tableau from behind his precious desk.

Jesse's the romantic brother; I'm the practical one. I certainly wasn't romantic that night with Pat Hayward. Not very practical, either.

W. CHRISTIAN JOHNSTON

My workday didn't end at five o'clock. Never does. It didn't even end after I had ushered out the last of my dinner guests from my home in Larchmont. While the caterer's people cleaned up the kitchen and my wife headed upstairs for bed and her latest romance novel, I went to my study, checked the nautical clock on my desk, and phoned Tokyo.

I had to go through several secretaries and underlings, of course. They all seemed shocked that the CEO of Omnitech Corporation was putting through this call himself, with no flunkies doing the up-front work for him. What the hell? I didn't want anybody listening in to this conversation; nobody on my side, leastways. So I sat on the edge of my desk and waited with the cordless phone clamped to my ear. Looking out through the den's windows at the darkened water of Long Island Sound, I wondered when the hell I would *ever* get the chance to sail the ketch before I had to pull the boat out of the water for the winter. Two million bucks for that beauty and she sits at the end of the pier like a goddamned monument.

Finally a man's voice said, "Mr. Nakata will speak to you now, sir." Perfect English, no accent at all.

"Mr. Johnston, what a pleasure to have you call." Ichiro Nakata's voice sounded crisp and friendly.

"It's good of you to take the time to speak with me," I said, feeling relieved that he actually accepted my call. I went around my desk and dropped into my big leather swivel chair.

"It must be close to midnight in New York," said Nakata.

"No rest for the wicked."

Nakata laughed.

"I see that Kyushu Industries is doing very well," I said. "Your stock continues to climb." The compulsory flattery bit.

There was a barely noticeable delay as our words were relayed to a communications satellite and back again. "We have been very fortunate," Nakata said. "Our people work very hard to make us successful."

A dig at American workers. I let it pass. "Success begins with good leadership. You are to be congratulated." There! I can sling the shit with any of these oh-so-polite slopes.

"I understand that Omnitech is also quite successful," Nakata replied.

"We're keeping our heads above the water."

Again the annoying little delay. Then Nakata said, "I remember with great fondness your visit to Japan last year. Perhaps I will visit America this winter."

"Great! I'd like to show you some of our facilities and return the wonderful hospitality you showed me." But I was thinking, Fucking Nip wants to steal whatever he can grab from us.

"That would be most enjoyable."

"You know," I said, easing into the reason why I had made the call, "Omnitech is doing so well that we've become attractive to other corporations."

The delay was longer than normal this time. Finally Nakata said, "I have heard rumors that a European consortium is interested in buying your company."

"Our board is not interested in selling."

"Oh so? Do you expect a hostile takeover attempt?"

This time I hesitated just a little bit before answering. "Could be."

"That could drive up the price of your stock. You could make a considerable fortune."

"A wise investor might buy a block of our stock now," I told him, "and do very well for himself over the next few months."

Nakata said, "That would remove a block of stock from the Europeans' grasp."

"Yes, it would."

"From my slight understanding of your company's position, you seem to be somewhat vulnerable to a takeover."

"Somewhat," I admitted.

Nakata said nothing. I waited as long as I could, but the Jap kept silent.

Finally, I said, "It would help if we were in a better financial position. I'm thinking of getting rid of some of our less profitable divisions, consolidate, tighten the ship all the way up and down the line."

"Always a wise strategy."

"If I can sell off a couple of our divisions it'll improve our cash flow, as well."

"Yes, of course."

The bastard's going to make me ask him, I fumed to myself. "I thought I would give you the first opportunity to consider buying one of our divisions."

The delay, then, "I see. But there is a difficulty. Why would someone wish to buy a division that is not profitable?"

He's interested! I bounced so hard in my chair I made it creak. "Well, some of our divisions are heavily engaged in research, you know. They don't make a profit, but they produce the new product lines that make profits for our other divisions."

"Ahhh. And which divisions might those be?"

"Well, there's our Tulsa Aerospace Division. They've been involved in developing new lightweight materials for airplanes and rockets . . ." I went on and mentioned three other Omni-tech divisions.

Before I could finish, though, Nakata broke in, "And what of your Grenford Laboratory? Are you considering selling it?"

I acted surprised. "Grenford? No. We couldn't sell Grenford Lab. Why, it's the future of our corporation."

"It is very good to see an American executive who thinks about the future. You are not afflicted with the notorious ninety-day syndrome."

"I learned a lot from my visit to Japan," I replied. I knew how to butter up people, too. "We have five-, ten-, and twenty-year plans now, just as you do." But they're not worth the paper they're written on unless we show a profit every god-damned quarter, I thought.

"It might be possible," Nakata said slowly, cautiously, "for us to acquire Grenford Laboratory and then license all the discoveries they make to Omnitech for a nominal fee."

"License their discoveries to us?"

"You could have license to market their products in North America. We would have what remains of the global market."

"I don't think my board would go for that."

"Perhaps not. It was merely a thought."

"Although," I said, leaning back in my chair, "if the price for Grenford was right, it sure would help our cash position."

"And help you to stave off the greedy Europeans."

"Tell you what," I said briskly. "I'll bounce the idea off a few of my board members. Privately, of course. Get their reaction. Then I'll get back to you."

"Very good. In the meantime, I will ask my financial people to make an assessment of Grenford's worth."

"Fine. I'll call you in a few days."

"I will anticipate your call with great pleasure."

I'll bet you will, I thought as I put the phone down. I heaved a big sigh. Well, it's done. Nakata's hot to trot, that comes through clear enough. Hate to sell Grenford to him, but that's better than having those fucking Krauts and Frenchmen take over the whole corporation.

Then I thought of Arthur Marshak. Arthur. He comes up with brilliant ideas, but we can't afford 'em right now. He won't mind working for the Japs. As long as he can do his research he really doesn't mind who the hell is paying his salary.

That's what I told myself.

THE TRIAL:

DAY ONE, MORNING

I didn't tell corporate management that we were aiming at regenerating limbs and organs," said Arthur.

"You didn't? Why not?"

"Because I didn't know it myself. Not at first."

"Are you trying to tell me—"

"The first time I mentioned the regeneration work to the CEO, my brother and I had just had one luncheon conversation about the idea and we were still thinking in terms of paraplegics."

"And you immediately informed Omnitech's corporate management?"

"I mentioned it to the CEO, yes."

"Why did you do that if you could fund this low-level effort out of your own discretionary monies?"

Arthur made a little shrug. "He asked me."

"He knew about it?"

"He did after I told him."

Rosen looked puzzled briefly. But he regrouped and asked, "What effect did this have on the price of Omnitech stock?"

"None whatsoever."

"None? It had no effect at all? No effect on the European bid to take over Omnitech Corporation?"

Arthur looked up at the judges. "Are we going to get into

international business deals now? What's this got to do with the scientific issue?"

Graves knitted his brows and said, "Mr. Rosen, you really are wandering rather far afield."

Rosen stared at the chief judge for a long moment, then turned back toward Arthur. "Did you use any government funding on this work?"

"The paraplegic work?"

"The entire program, including organ regeneration."

"No."

"None whatsoever?"

"Not one penny."

"Any government facilities? Instruments or equipment that your laboratory had purchased on government money?"

Arthur hesitated long enough to let him think he was searching his memory. "No, not to the best of my recollection."

Rosen smiled at him. "That's a lawyer's phrase, Dr. Marshak. Have you been briefed by a lawyer?"

Arthur smiled back at the examiner. "Omnitech's legal department is very interested in this hearing, naturally. But, no, I have not been coached in any way."

Rosen's expression showed clear disbelief.

"Then, to the best of your recollection," said the judge on Arthur's left, "no federal funds were used in your experiments on tissue regeneration."

"That is correct," Arthur said, glancing at the jury. Several of them were scribbling notes. "And we didn't use stem cells, either. Neither fetal cells nor adult."

"Really?" Rosen blurted.

"Really," said Arthur. "Check the reports."

Rosen paced before him a few steps, hands pressed together before his lips as if in prayer, framing his next question. The TV cameras focused on him. The audience waited in silence.

"Dr. Marshak," he said, turning back toward Arthur, "just who actually was the first to hit upon the concept of regenerating organs and limbs? Was it you or your brother, Dr. Jesse Marshak?"

"We did it together."

"Did you?"

Arthur thought a moment, then replied, "If I remember correctly, I first got the idea for regenerating spinal neurons and Jesse amplified it to consider other kinds of tissue."

"Organs?"

"Yes."

"Limbs?"

Feeling nettled by Rosen's seeming obtuseness, Arthur said, "Yes, and toes and fingers, too."

No one laughed.

"Then it was Dr. Jesse Marshak who originated the concept of regenerating limbs and organs, not you."

"What difference does it make?" Arthur shot back. "We're not here to decide who gets a patent on the idea. I thought the purpose of this court was to decide on the scientific validity of the concept. Can we regenerate human organs? Can we regrow a lost arm or leg? I say the answer is yes, we can."

"That is for this court to decide," Rosen snapped.

"Well, then let's get into the scientific evidence on the subject and stop talking about personalities and funding and corporate takeovers."

Rosen looked at the judges. None of them had a word to say. Turning back to Arthur, he smiled tightly. "We will get into the scientific evidence soon enough. First it is necessary for us to establish the background under which the work was done."

"I don't agree," said Arthur.

"I'm sure you don't, but there are other scientists who do. Very prominent scientists, in fact." Rosen went back to his end of the table and riffled through some papers there. "The late Dr. Stephen Jay Gould, of Harvard University, for example. Would you say he was a prominent biologist?"

Arthur answered through clenched teeth, "A paleontologist, I would say."

Rosen gave his wintry smile, then read from the sheet of paper in his hand, "Dr. Stephen Jay Gould of Harvard University had this to say about the human background behind scientific research: 'The myth of a separate mode based on rigorous objectivity and arcane, largely mathematical knowledge, vouchsafed only to the initiated, may provide some immediate benefits in bamboozling a public to regard us as a new priesthood, but must ultimately prove harmful in erecting barriers to truly friendly understanding and in falsely persuading so many students that science lies beyond their capabilities.' "

"That's got nothing to do with the matter at hand!" Arthur protested.

"I'm sure you think so," said Rosen, "but still the fact remains that in your rush to prove your idea a young woman was killed."

Arthur shot to his feet. The audience stirred and all the TV cameras swung to him. "Listen," he said hotly. "I agreed to participate in this hearing because I want the scientific facts laid out clearly and distinctly so that the scientific community—and the general public—can decide on the *scientific* issue of whether or not we can regenerate human organs and limbs. You can debate the social or moral or financial or political sides of the matter somewhere else. This is supposed to be a court of *science* and you're trying to turn it into a political football game. I will not participate in this farce!"

He picked up his leather-bound PowerBook computer from the desktop.

"Dr. Marshak!" called the chief judge, up at the front table. "Arthur—please!"

The hearing chamber was alive with voices now. News reporters whispered hurriedly into their voice recorders. The audience was abuzz. Rosen stood glaring at Arthur while Graves rapped his gavel uselessly.

Over the babel of voices Graves shouted, "Court is recessed for fifteen minutes. Dr. Marshak, Dr. Rosen—I want to see you in the judges' chambers. Now!"

ARTHUR

Actually, the first time I popped the idea of organ regeneration to Omnitech's management was at the board meeting when Johnston tried to sandbag me. It was probably a mistake for me to mention the work so early, but I was trying to fight my way out of a trap.

Omnitech's quarterly meeting of the board of directors took place that summer, as usual, at the corporate headquarters in downtown Manhattan. Over the past two years the meetings had become progressively more tense, as the corporation's sales staggered through a global recession and then slowly recovered. Profits suffered, too, but Johnston and his administrative people managed to keep the net from sinking too far by cutting costs ruthlessly. Which meant laying off workers.

Grenford Lab hadn't been touched by the layoffs. I wouldn't stand for that. Besides, the lab was too small a division for its personnel costs to have any real impact on the corporate financial picture. But more than once I had been forced to fight off moves to cut entire research programs in the name of economy and that most sacred of all cows, the bottom line.

I had a favorite riposte I used on the board whenever they started talking about cutbacks at the lab. "I own a few shares of stock in this corporation, too," I would tell them, "and if you want our stock to be worth anything five years from now, you'd better keep your hands off our research efforts."

At that particular quarterly meeting, though, you could feel a special tension in the air. While the board automatically approved the minutes of our last meeting and then the treasurer's report, I wondered what was making everyone so uptight. Sales had improved; only slightly, but at least the trend was upward. And although Johnston and the other officers were worried about the possibilities of a hostile takeover bid, the European consortium would not be trying to grab the corporation if Omnitech wasn't a valuable asset.

Is it the takeover bid? I asked myself as I sat at the long polished Brazilian cherrywood table. No, I decided, scanning the faces of the other board members. We've been wrestling with the takeover bid for almost a year now. It's something else. Something new in the wind.

No matter how sales and profits went, the board's meeting room remained opulent. Two walls were all glass, from floor to ceiling, glass that darkened automatically when direct sunlight fell on it. Manhattan was spread out on display through those glass walls, from City Hall past the spires of the skyscrapers all the way out to the almost-hidden greenery of Central Park. The emptiness of Ground Zero was off to the left. In the other direction I could see across the East River toward Brooklyn Heights. Not so far away, as the crow flies, from my childhood home. Only a lifetime or two.

The meeting ticked along almost perfunctorily. Johnston kept to the agenda and discouraged speech-making. He sat at the head of the table, with the nominal chairman of the board at his right hand, a doddering old man whose reputation far exceeded his talent, as far as I could see.

Freda Gunnerson was giving a terse report on the Stockholm Division's program to build and operate a modern computer factory in Moscow. The report was pretty glum. Looking around the table, I realized that not all of the board members looked wired tight. Some seemed as unruffled or musingly distracted as they did at every meeting. Fewer than half of the twenty-four-member board ever had anything constructive to say at these meetings, and they were usually the members who also ran operating divisions. The others, mostly white-haired or balding, were on the board because they owned large blocks of stock or had risen to the level of senior statesmen in the corporate world. I often wondered how some of these semi-somnolent old men ever got out of bed, let alone rose to the level of captain of industry. I've got to admit that the few women on the board seemed sharper, more focused than the elder statesmen. Probably they had to be, to rise past the glass ceiling.

The more I studied my fellow board members, the more it seemed to me that only the members of the executive committee were wound up. Something's going on in the executive committee, I realized.

"The Russians say they want capitalism," Gunnerson was complaining in her thin nasally whining voice, "but they are riddled through with corruption and they have no idea of what competition really is or how incentives work."

The executive committee had held its own private little meeting before the regular board meeting, I knew. Something happened that's got them all edgy as hell. Maybe Johnston will get into it when we go to new business on the agenda.

"Thanks for your report, Freda," Johnston said when she turned over the last leaf of the pages before her. "Any comments?"

The board members glanced at one another. Before anyone could speak up, Johnston said, "Okay, we'll go on to new business."

Several of the members looked clearly surprised.

"Before we do that," said Tabatha Young, the only woman among the senior officers of the board, "what's the latest on the takeover bid?"

Johnston squirmed slightly in his chair. I liked white-haired Tabatha Young; she had taken her late husband's seat on the board as a temporary measure nearly five years earlier and had shown that she possessed as much knowledge and drive as anyone sitting at that table; more than most of the men her own age, in fact.

"It looks as if the Europeans are going to go ahead with a hostile takeover bid," Johnston said unhappily.

"That's what you told us last meeting," said Tabatha. "Hasn't anything happened since then?"

Frowning, the CEO said, "I expect them to make a public bid for our stock in a couple of months, three at the most."

That sent a shudder of sighs and whispers down the table.

"And what are we doing to prepare for that?" Tabatha could be relentless when she wanted to be.

"The one thing we've got to do is improve our cash position," said Johnston. "That should up the market price of our stock, make the takeover attempt too expensive for them."

"And what steps are you taking toward that end?"

Johnston hesitated, then replied, "I'm not prepared to discuss that yet. The executive committee is working out a plan, but it's not finalized. It may be necessary to call a special meeting of the board in a few weeks specifically on that subject."

"I see," said Tabatha.

"Any new business?" Johnston asked eagerly from the head of the table.

Sid Lowenstein said, "I hear Art's started down another new trail. Maybe he can tell us something about it."

My annoyance at Lowenstein's calling me Art was swallowed by my surprise at being asked to report on the new work I had started at the lab. I had only had that one brief discussion with Johnston about the paraplegic work and now Lowenstein wanted me to talk about it in front of the entire board. Why?

"It's very early," I said cautiously, trying to think it out while I talked. "And very small. I can handle it out of the division's internal funds for the time being."

"What's it all about?" asked Tabatha.

"Don't be coy, Arthur," Johnston said. "Tell the board what you told me two weeks ago."

Have they rehearsed this? I wondered. I felt as if I were stepping into a quicksand bog. "It's much too early to let this information go beyond these four walls." I knew that corporate board members kept secrets about as well as congressmen or White House aides.

They all leaned forward in their plush chairs and looked expectantly down the table at me.

There was nothing for me to do except plunge ahead. Gingerly. "We've started very preliminary work on experiments that may lead to a way to cure paraplegics."

"Cure them?"

"If this idea works, we may eventually be able to reconnect the severed spinal tissue and allow paraplegics to regain control of their legs."

Surprisingly, one of the oldest men there asked, "What about their bladder functions? It's kidney and bladder infections that kill most paraplegics, isn't it?"

He must have one in the family, I thought. "Yes, it should allow them to regain control over their bladders, as well. Reconnect the spine, and the brain regains control over all the parts of the body that were lost when the spinal cord was severed. If they haven't degenerated too far."

"Can you really do that?" the woman next to me asked.

"Not yet. We've just started some preliminary work on the concept. That's why it shouldn't be repeated outside this room."

Johnston was smiling happily down the table. But Lowenstein asked, "How many paraplegics are there in the United States, Art?"

That surprised me. "I don't really know. But there must be hundreds of thousands, at least. Maybe a million or more."

"I looked it up," Lowenstein said with a thin smile. "About ten thousand cases per year in the U.S. Most of them are the result of trauma—injuries. Automobile accidents, motorcycles, things like that."

"How many altogether?" someone asked.

"Can't be more than three, four hundred thousand altogether," said Lowenstein.

"How many of them would you be able to cure?" Gunnerson asked.

I waved a hand in the air. "I don't know. A fair percentage of the accident victims, I should think. If we get to them early enough so that their legs haven't atrophied."

"That's not a very big market," one of the older men muttered. He pulled a pocket calculator from his vest and tapped on the keys. "Let's say fifty percent of ten thousand. Not much of a market at all, really."

That nettled me. "There's the rest of the world," I pointed out. "And quadriplegics, too."

"There's about two hundred thousand quadriplegics," Lowenstein said. "In the U.S., that is."

"Even so." The old man shook his head as if in disappointment.

Feeling as if I had to defend myself, I said, "Well, there are some things that we do because they're the right thing to do. If we can make paraplegics and quadriplegics get out of their wheelchairs and walk, lead normal lives again—"

"How much would it cost?" someone asked.

Another board member said, "If the market's this small, there won't be any profit in it."

"I don't see why we should invest money in a program that's not going to be profitable. Your burn rate is already too high, Arthur."

"The money my lab burns," I shot back, "produces this corporation's profits five years downstream. And I'm not asking for more funding."

"Not yet," someone muttered.

"But you will," the old man said with a knowing smile. "Sooner or later you'll come to us for money, won't you?"

I had to admit, "Sooner or later."

"I think you ought to drop this project right here and now, before you pour too much money into it."

Johnston pursed his lips as if he wanted to say something, then decided against it.

"Now, wait a minute," I said. "Do you mean that if we could save the lives of ten thousand people, we wouldn't do it unless we could make a profit at it?"

"We can't engage in programs that lose money," Lowenstein replied. "For god's sake, Art, we're not the government! We can't print money, we've got to *earn* it."

Most of the board members chuckled.

I tried to hold on to my temper. "But what if this technique would have wider applications than *merely* a few tens of thousands of paraplegics?"

"What do you mean?" Johnston asked.

"Suppose we could find out how to regenerate other types of tissue, in addition to spinal neurons?"

"Like what?"

"Hearts. Livers. Kidneys. Amputated limbs."

That stunned them. They all sagged back in their chairs as if I had slapped their faces, all at the same time.

"Are you serious?" asked the oldest member of the board. I knew he had undergone quadruple bypass surgery and several other cardiac procedures.

"I am serious," I told him.

"Regenerate a heart?"

"Regenerate any organ in the human body," I said firmly. Then I added, "Eventually."

The woman next to me asked, "Do you mean you could grow a new heart for a person? Inside her own body?"

"Without surgery," I answered. "That's the goal of our work."

"New breasts for mastectomy cases?"

I nodded.

Johnston gave Lowenstein an intense stare, then said to me, "I had no idea you had come so far . . ."

Waving my hand again, I confessed, "We haven't done anything so far except talk. And think."

"But you think you might be able to regenerate organs?"

"Maybe."

"Wait a minute," said Tabatha. "This is going to need stem cells, isn't it?"

She was even sharper than I had thought. "It might. At the outset, at least."

"Can we do that?"

"If we fund it ourselves, without government money," Johnston answered for me.

"Regenerate any kind of organ? Like lungs?" one of the older men asked again, in a wheezing voice.

"Eventually we'll be able to regenerate any kind of tissue," I said, knowing that *eventually* would probably be too late for him and most of the others around the table.

"That's a different kettle of fish," said the man with the calculator. "That—it's kind of staggering, isn't it?"

I had them hooked. There was no way they were going to order me to drop the work now. But I didn't want to build their expectations prematurely.

"Look," I said, "I don't want to give you the idea that we'll be able to do this by Christmas. All we've got right now is a few basic ideas—and the talented people who might be able to turn those ideas into reality. But it will take time. I have no idea of how long."

"It would be very nice," said one of the old men, "if you could have it done before my next physical."

Everyone laughed. There was no question of stopping the research now. No one asked about how much money it would take, not even Lowenstein.

And I almost forgot that the executive committee was keeping secrets from the rest of the board.

But as the meeting broke up, I noticed once again that all six of the executive committee members drifted up to the head of the table and huddled with Johnston briefly, whispering. One of them even glanced back my way, like a guilty little kid plotting against me.

Something was definitely cooking, that was certain. I picked my PowerBook from the table and headed slowly for the door. Sure enough, I was barely out in the corridor when Johnston clapped me on the shoulder, like a policeman grabbing a suspect.

"That's a nice fast one you pulled on me in there," the CEO grumbled.

"Fast one?" I feigned innocence.

Johnston started toward his office, one massive paw still gripping me by the shoulder, almost hard enough to hurt, dragging me along the corridor with him.

"That business about regenerating hearts. You never told me about that before."

You didn't tell me you were going to sabotage the paraplegic work, either, I retorted silently.

Aloud, I replied, "It's new. We've just had a couple of conversations about it, nothing more."

"But you made it sound to the board like it's almost a done deal."

Johnston was clearly angry, I could see that. Why? What's going on?

"I told them it's just in the talking stage, didn't I?"

Frowning as he strode into the anteroom of his own office, Johnston said, "The board members aren't scientists, Arthur. You know that. You tell them something might be possible, they assume you've got it in the bag."

"Well, it's not, and I'll be happy to explain that to them at the next meeting."

"Yeah, you do that." Johnston finally let go of my shoulder and headed for his broad, curved, ultramodern desk.

"What's going on?" I asked.

Johnston looked up at me as he sat behind his desk. "What do you mean?"

"Why are you so upset about what I said? Why's the executive committee so wired?"

"I don't like being surprised at board meetings."

"I told you about the paraplegic work."

"But not about growing new hearts."

I put on a grin, trying to lighten the mood. "Well, you don't think I'm going to let Sid shoot me down without fighting back, do you?"

Johnston did not grin back. "Sid's fighting to save this corporation from being bought out by a bunch of European bastards who'll gut the company, milk it for all it's worth, and then throw us all on the garbage heap."

"Is that what the executive committee's so tense about?"

"Yeah," said Johnston. "What else?" But his gaze did not meet mine.

The desk phone buzzed and Johnston's secretary's voice announced, "Your call to Tokyo is coming through, Mr. J."

"All right," he said to the phone speaker. As he picked up the handpiece he shooed me toward the door with his free hand.

STILL WONDERING what was really burning Johnston's guts, I drove back to the lab and got there by late afternoon. I made a brief stop at my own office, then wandered out to the laboratories where the research work was being done. The real world. I loved the sights and sounds and smells of the working labs. I knew each one of the researchers and their technicians by name. I chatted with them about their work, their families; I exchanged jokes with them. I knew every inch of the elaborate glassware apparatuses they were using, every humming, beeping, blinking instrument on their benchtops. Like a good general, I wanted to know exactly what my troops were doing, and I let them do their jobs without sticking my fingers into their experiments.

The real world. The board of directors can play their games and talk their talk, but out here is where the real work gets done. You can't bullshit with science. It either works or it doesn't. Like Omar Khayyám's moving finger: it writes and neither piety nor wit can change any of the words.

I ended up in Darrell Walters's office, a ramshackle corner room stuffed to the ceiling with gadgets and shelves full of reports and pictures tacked to the walls and a well-scarred wooden drawing table and a big flip-chart easel covered with scribbled lists in half a dozen different-colored felt-tip marking pens in Walters's scrawling hand lettering.

Darrell had no desk. He preferred a broken-down stuffed sofa and an eclectic scattering of chairs, some wood, some plastic, one a high swiveling barstool.

I sat on the barstool. Darrell had stretched out on the sagging sofa. Vince Andriotti had joined us, scowling darkly, his natural expression.

We were brainstorming the idea of regenerating organs.

"Whatever made you tell the board of directors about it?" Darrell asked from his supine position.

I shook my head ruefully. "It was either get them excited about growing new hearts or have them direct me to stop the nerve regeneration experiment."

"I guess most of the board members could use new hearts," Darrell said.

"Some of them have never had a heart," I joked.

"What about growing brains for 'em?" Andriotti suggested.

Swiveling the barstool back and forth, I said, "You know, one of the women on the board asked me if we'd be able to regenerate skin and muscle tissue. Instead of plastic surgery for face-lifts and breast replacements."

"Now, *that's* a moneymaking idea!" Darrell said.

Vince was sitting backward astride one of the wooden chairs with his heavy forearms draped on its back and his chin buried in his hairy arms. He asked, "Does this mean I can stop moonlighting and get a legitimate charge number for the job?"

"Haven't you got one?" I was surprised.

"Not yet."

"Tell Accounting to open a charge for you first thing tomorrow morning. I'll okay it."

"Great."

Darrell's mind was on more esoteric matters. "Arthur, how in hell can you grow a new heart in a patient's chest without squeezing the heart and lungs that're already in there? There won't be enough room for the new heart to grow."

"I don't know how elastic those organs are, do you? Maybe they can be squeezed to a certain extent, or pushed aside a little."

"They put artificial hearts in peoples' chests," Andriotti pointed out.

"After they've removed the natural heart," said Darrell.

"Not always. Sometimes they leave the natural ticker in there and use the artificial heart as a booster pump, to help the natural one 'cause it's gotten too weak to pump blood all the way through the body."

"It's a point we'll have to check out with Jesse," I said.

"Is your brother going to be working with us on this?"

"Yes," I said automatically. Then, remembering, I added, "Until he goes to Africa."

"We'd better get a team of tame physicians, then," said Darrell, "and bring them on board the program."

"Surgeons?" Vince asked.

"No!" I snapped. "This work should not involve surgery. Never."

"What about if we have to grow the organs in vitro and then implant them in the patient?"

"Well—maybe then, I suppose."

Andriotti's swarthy face went crafty. "So maybe we oughta have at least one little surgeon on the team? As a consultant, not regular staff."

I conceded the point with a reluctant nod.

"What kind of experimental animals should we be thinking about?" Darrell mused.

"Pigs, minihogs," said Andriotti. "Their cardiovascular systems are damned close to ours. Same blood clotting times, too, I think."

"Macaques," Darrell said. Most of our animal experiments were done on lab rats first and then the monkeys.

"Chimps, eventually," I said.

Darrell pretended to be shocked. "Lord, don't let Cassie hear you say that!"

"Where is she?" I asked. "She ought to be here; we could use her brains on this."

"She's prob'ly having dinner with Max," Vince cracked.

I looked at my watch. It was well past the nominal quitting time. I got down from the stool and went to the phone on the wall by Darrell's sofa.

"Page Cassie Ianetta for me, please," I told the security guard at the switchboard.

"And Barry Logan," Darrell suggested. "He's good at this kind of brainstorming."

Andriotti gave a grunt. "Zack O'Neill, too."

That surprised me. O'Neill was a fairly recent addition to the research staff. "Why him?" I asked.

Vince's face eased into a big smile full of white teeth. It made him look like a pirate or a Mafia hit man.

"Because," he said with a great show of patience, "Zack is the kid who did his doctoral work on cell division suppression factors, remember? He gave us a talk on the subject when we interviewed him last year. That's why we hired him, right?"

"Oh, yes. Right," I said. I should have remembered that. The truth is, Zack O'Neill wore an earring and kept his brick-red hair chopped so short it looked like a patch of rusty spikes. And he dressed like a punk rocker, almost: leather jackets and T-shirts with outrageous pictures and slogans. But despite his appearance he was one of the brightest youngsters we had found in several years. I realized, to my surprise, that the inspiration for my idea about paraplegics probably came from my half memory of Zack's presentation, more than a year ago.

So I had O'Neill paged, along with the rest of them. Within a quarter hour Darrell's cluttered office was ringing with opinions and arguments as the six of us batted around ideas, suggestions, plans about experiments that would lead to the ability to regenerate organs. I kept my eyes on Cassie. Was she in remission or had she really licked the cancer? She seemed strong enough, completely at home in this kind of atmosphere, no longer the sad-eyed little waif but an energetic, animated thinker who could hold her own in the fast-moving free-for-all debate.

"I don't care what kind of experimental results you get," Andriotti was saying stubbornly, "sooner or later you're gonna hafta use chimps. That's all there is to it."

Cassie gave him a hard stare.

"That's not necessary at all," said Zack O'Neill. He still wore the earring but at least he had bought some decent shirts instead of the sloppy tees he used to wear. He was one of those types who would look youthful even in his seventies. Strong jaw, clear light eyes, bright personality. Either he was going to a better barber or I was getting accustomed to his haircut.

"Scientifically it may not be necessary," I explained to him. "But before we can go to human trials we're going to need to do some chimp experiments."

"To impress the politicians," Darrell added.

O'Neill frowned at us.

"But I thought that pigs have the cardiovascular system closest to our own," Barry Logan countered.

"They do," answered Darrell, "but we're talking about a lot more than hearts here. Chimps have a similar body size to humans, same organs."

Cassie asked, "When we do animal experiments, we'll have to induce trauma or debilitation, won't we?"

"Not at first," I said.

"We'll want the animals to be as healthy as possible, in fact," Darrell said.

"Yes, but eventually we'll need to cause cardiac insufficiency or kidney failure, stuff like that," Cassie insisted. "To make certain that the regeneration brings the animal back to full normal function."

"Amputate limbs?" O'Neill asked.

Andriotti grunted. "Gonna have a lot of pissed-off chimps on our hands."

"Is it legal?" Cassie asked. "Won't the animal rights people go through the ceiling?"

I sighed. "I'll get our legal department to look into it. Either way, it's certainly not something we'll want to tell the news media about."

"Oh, boy, I can see the stories on TV," Darrell moaned. "Evil scientists chopping up cute little chimps."

"Anybody who thinks chimps are cute has never worked with them," Logan grumbled.

Cassie said, "The public always thinks of baby chimps. They seldom see adults."

"They never have to dodge the shit they throw when they're pissed with you."

"We're drifting into scatology," said Darrell, still stretched out on his sofa. "Let's get back to the problem at hand. Where do we start this program? What do we do first?"

I smiled inwardly. Darrell Walters looked and often behaved like the least practical person on the staff. Yet he was the rock on which the rest of the scientific staff depended. The kids looked up to him, and he guided them with firm patience.

Which leaves me free to do the things that need to be done in order to keep the staff's freedom to conduct their research.

I got down from the barstool. "I've got to make a few phone

calls," I told them. "I'd like the five of you to get together in my office tomorrow morning, first thing. Come for breakfast—eight o'clock a hardship for any of you?"

"Long as you don't mind my sweats," Andriotti said. "I jog in to work, y'know."

"If you smell too bad we'll throw you into the shower," I said as I headed for the door.

By the time I reached my own office, though, my grin had faded away. Brainstorming was fun, but I had other things to do and if I didn't do them right, my staff wouldn't get to do the science they were brainstorming about.

Phyllis was working away at her computer.

"You still here?" I realized the inanity of the question as soon as I said it.

"Helping to type up this report that's due Monday," she said.

"Can you set up coffee and buns for tomorrow at eight?"

Without looking up from her screen, Phyllis asked, "How many people?"

"Six, including me."

She nodded.

"Maybe a couple extra," I added as I headed into my inner office. "Just in case."

"Will anybody want tea?"

"Cassie might, come to think of it."

I closed the office door. No sense disturbing Phyllis with my phone calls. I booted up my desktop computer and put the address file on-screen. Scrolling down to the name I wanted, I highlighted the phone number and tapped the ENTER key. The computer automatically dialed the number.

A recorded male voice told me that I had reached the number and, if I left a message, my call would be returned as soon as possible.

"Nancy, it's Arthur Marshak," I said. "I was wondering if you'd be free for dinner some evening this week."

I heard a click, then Nancy Dubois' slightly suspicious voice said, "Arthur, is it really you?"

"Yes, of course. Why not?"

"It's been such a long time since you last called. I thought you had forgotten all about me."

Nancy was one of Sid Lowenstein's assistants. She was young, attractive in a stylish trendy way. She had not yet made up her mind between career or marriage or both. I had turned to her on the rebound from Julia, and during the brief time that we were going together she had made it clear that she thought I was much too old for a potential husband, but as long as she was shopping around she didn't mind the difference in our ages. I had stopped calling her after a few weeks. I dated other women, but none seriously.

My thoughts had returned to Nancy, though, because she was in Sid's office and she was also clever enough to know what was going on inside the executive committee. At least, I hoped so. It was time to renew my acquaintance with her.

I bantered lightly with her, then returned to my invitation to dinner.

"Not this week," she said. "I'm busy. How about Monday?"

"Can you come up to Connecticut?" I asked. "Meet me at my fencing class and we'll go out to dinner afterward."

"Fencing? You mean, with swords and all?"

"Yes. I go two or three times a week. It's great exercise and a great sport."

"*That's* how you stay so slim!"

"It helps."

"Sounds very sexy."

"If you'd like to try it, I'm sure the maestro can work in a beginner's lesson for you." I made a mental note to phone the coach and make certain he would give a newcomer a half hour of his time. Not give, I reminded myself. Sell.

"Will I need any special clothes or equipment?"

"Just a regular gym outfit will do. One of the other women will lend you a jacket, I'm certain."

"It sounds like fun."

"Whatever turns you on," I said. A corny lie, but it was all I could think of at the moment.

We set the time and place. I hung up, then called one of the quiet little restaurants in the area to set up dinner for Monday. Nancy was smart enough to know I'd be probing for information about the executive committee, I felt certain of that. The question was, did she still like me enough to let me know what was going on?

My next call was to Jesse. I had seen my brother exactly once since our dinner in Manhattan. The planned visit to Momma had never come off. I had visited her alone; Jesse couldn't get free from the hospital. Or so he said.

Julia's voice said, "Hello?"

I realized that I had dialed their home number, even though I knew that Jesse was hardly ever at home this early in the evening.

"It's me, Julia," I said.

"Hello, Arthur. Jesse's not back from the hospital yet."

"I need to talk to him as soon as he gets a minute free. We're going to be starting work on this regeneration business—"

Julia laughed gently. "Arthur, darling, if you wait for Jess to have a free moment you'll have a long gray beard down your shirt."

"That bad?"

"Even worse than usual. We're preparing for this African jaunt. I'm in the midst of packing and setting up inoculations. Dreadful things, needles."

"You don't have to go," I blurted.

"Ah, but I do."

"Julia, it isn't right for Jess to drag you off to these places. They're dangerous!"

Very patiently, Julia replied, "As I've told you before, Arthur, dear, he's not dragging me anywhere. I want to go. I want to be able to help him, to help those poor miserable people. I couldn't remain here while he's off in the bush somewhere risking his life."

"So you've got to risk yours?"

"Oh, I was only being dramatic. There's very little risk, actually."

"Stay here where it's safe," I said, meaning, *Stay with me*.

"No," Julia said, as if she knew precisely what I meant. "No, I really can't, Arthur. My place is beside Jess, wherever he goes, whatever he does."

Trying to keep the anger out of my voice, I said, "Well, I hope you're both very happy."

And I slammed the phone back into its cradle.

THE TRIAL:

DAY ONE, MORNING

The "judges' chambers" was actually a stuffy little anteroom off the main hearing room. It held a single small desk, a few wooden chairs, and a heavy plush maroon sofa that looked ludicrously out of place.

Milton Graves sat wearily in the desk chair. The other two judges—the Caltech professor of biochemistry and the Yale professor of jurisprudence—took the wooden chairs that flanked the desk. That left Arthur and Rosen to sit side by side on the sofa.

Graves was a slight, slim man, almost frail-looking. Arthur saw beads of perspiration on his balding dome as he nervously polished his bifocals with a tissue.

"Now, look," he said, putting the glasses on again, "I will not have any grandstand plays out there. Is that understood?"

"There won't be any grandstand plays as long as we stick to the science of this issue," Arthur said.

"Why are you dragging in all these extraneous matters?" Graves asked Rosen.

"I wouldn't call wrongful death an extraneous matter," Rosen replied.

"Well, I do," Graves snapped. "At least for now. This is a

court of science, not a homicide investigation. We're not the criminal justice system."

Arthur's guts clutched inside him. Homicide. Criminal justice. He realized that if this science trial went the wrong way he might face criminal charges.

The examiner seemed completely calm, totally at ease in the tension of the room. "It is important to establish the background in which the scientific work was done."

"Bullshit!" Arthur snapped.

"Now, wait—" said the law professor.

"We're going to have half a dozen scientific witnesses," Rosen said, his strong baritone voice cutting the Yale professor to silence. "That's in addition to the tons of written reports and papers that the jury has already reviewed. The scientific evidence will be laid out very clearly before we're finished."

"So why all these questions about funding and priority? Why keep harping on that unfortunate woman's death?" Graves demanded. His voice was scratchy, testy, a voice that had frightened an entire generation of biology students.

"I need to show the background of the work. This research wasn't done in a vacuum. Dr. Marshak had a purpose in mind when he started the work. He directed the program toward certain goals. That had a powerful influence on how the work was done, how quickly it advanced, and what kind of results they got. It had a very powerful effect on the woman who died."

"Those are not scientific questions," Arthur insisted.

"Yes, they are," Rosen shot back. "You want to limit this trial strictly to the results that came out of your lab. We could read your research reports for that."

"That's what this court is all about," Arthur said. "Examine the research results and make a public declaration of whether or not it's possible to regenerate human organs and limbs."

"And forget about the human consequences?" Rosen asked stubbornly.

Graves said, "The human consequences will be examined elsewhere."

Slowly, with great dignity, Rosen got to his feet. "The purpose of this court"—he began to pace the tiny room as he spoke—"is to make a public recommendation on the efficacy of human organ regeneration."

"A *scientific* recommendation," Arthur reminded.

"A recommendation on which public policy will hinge," Rosen said. "No matter how you look at it, once this court says yes or no about organ regeneration, the political debate is a foregone conclusion."

The Yale professor said, "I'm not so certain that's valid. There are ethical issues here. Stem cells. Cloning."

"That's not our problem," Graves snapped. "We are supposed to be debating the scientific possibilities, not ethics or politics."

Rosen gave them the ghost of a smile. "Think of the debate in Congress over whether or not to fund organ regeneration. If this court says it is scientifically possible, what congressman could vote against it? His constituents would tear him apart!"

"Then he'd need regeneration," quipped the Caltech biochemist. Graves glared at him.

"And consider the opposite situation," Rosen went on. "If this court says regeneration is scientifically impossible, no politician in his right mind would ever put up a penny for further research."

Arthur shook his head vehemently. "No, it's not supposed to work that way. This court decides only the scientific validity of the concept. Others debate the political, financial, social aspects."

Rosen gave him a pitying look. "Dr. Marshak, you just don't understand the way things work. Once this court makes a decision, all the other debates will be foregone. What we decide here will decide *everything*. Including whether or not you are responsible for your researcher's death."

The little room fell absolutely silent.

"The morality question," said the law professor in a whisper.

"Oh, I suppose there will be the usual debates about the

morality of it in the media and among the ethicists," Rosen conceded. "But the political steamroller will already be running. If and when this court recommends proceeding to human trials, nothing will be able to stop the program from moving forward."

"Not even the people who oppose fetal tissue research?"

"Not even the right-to-lifers," Rosen insisted.

"Good!" Arthur snapped.

Rosen gave him a hard stare, then turned back to Graves. "That's why I've got to have the latitude to determine all the background influences on this work. We're not just looking at the cold technical data. We're making a decision for the entire nation here. Maybe the entire world. A life-and-death decision."

Graves puffed out a little sigh. "My god, Arthur, I think he's right."

Arthur started to object, but he saw the look on Graves's face and the faces of the other two professors. He knew he had lost the argument.

And maybe the entire case.

WASHINGTON:
THE CAPITOL

Reverend Roy Averill Simmonds transferred from his Mercedes to the rented school bus at the preselected rendezvous point on Maryland Avenue, twenty blocks from the Capitol. His chauffeur stayed with the car, looking rather nervous to be left alone in the run-down neighborhood. Simmonds heard the door locks click behind him. The two aides who had been riding with him accompanied Reverend Simmonds as he climbed aboard the shabby, rickety bus. They were both big men, their faces expressionless as statues.

The people aboard the crowded, sweaty bus were over-joyed to have him among them. They were mostly youngish, in their twenties and thirties, new parents from a suburban church outside Baltimore. Reverend Simmonds worked his way along the aisle, shaking hands with each man and woman in the seats as the bus lurched and swayed through the hot summer sunshine.

"God bless you!" they called to him. "Thank the Lord for your strength!"

He smiled at each and every individual one of them, a bright beaming smile full of confidence and goodwill. He was a tiny man, even in his elevator shoes, almost delicate. Compactly built, a feisty bantam who stood out in a crowd because of that glowing smile and the palpable radiance of his personality. Sandy hair cropped short, light hazel eyes that could peer into the depths of your soul, he looked youthful and energetic, except for the shaggy eyebrows that showed a few strands of gray. And the faint scars behind his ears. But only an expert would notice such traces of cosmetic surgery. He wore plain tan slacks and a summer-weight sports jacket of slightly darker brown. No tie. He was no better dressed than the people with whom he rode.

One of his aides held a tiny oblong black cell phone in one beefy hand, with its receiver plugged into his ear. He whispered to Reverend Simmonds as they made their way down the length of the bus, hand over hand along the grips set into the seat backs.

When they got to the rear of the bus and all the passengers had turned in their seats to watch him, Reverend Simmonds raised both hands above his head and announced:

"We have more than a thousand people already at the Capitol, and more on the way!" His voice was strong and surprisingly deep.

Everyone cheered.

"Are you ready to show the world what God wants of us?" he demanded. The strength of that voice never failed to move people.

"Yes!" they shouted back, as one voice.

"Are you ready to force those godless scientists to obey the Lord's will?"

"Yes!" they screamed louder.

The bus was braking to a stop, still some two blocks from the Capitol.

"Then let's get out there and win the day for Jesus!"

They boiled out of the bus, impatiently yanking their printed placards from the bus's luggage compartment and joining the growing crowd that was marching along the avenue toward the Capitol building, waving their signs like battle standards.

Simmonds descended from the bus, but did not join the march. He watched while another aide in a dark suit and string tie came running up to him, sweating and breathless.

"CNN van just arrived," he gulped out.

"What about the other networks?" Simmonds asked, squinting into the bright sunlight.

The young man bobbed his head. "They're all there, including Fox."

Simmonds smiled. Turning to the aide with the cell phone, he said, "Get them ready."

The sweaty young man said, "There's others here, though."

"Others?"

"People who're *for* Marshak."

Simmonds blinked with surprise. "Who brought them here?"

The young man shrugged inside his loose-fitting dark jacket.

"They're not organized," said the aide with the radio. "According to our front men, they're just a bunch of old folks and cripples."

"A spontaneous demonstration?" Reverend Simmonds smiled ironically. "How quaint."

"They could cause trouble," the other aide said.

Simmonds's smile widened slightly. "Good," he said. Then, motioning to his little group of assistants, he started walking toward the Capitol. "Let's get cracking. If there's going to be trouble, it'll be on the news this evening. And if it's on TV, I've got to be on the screen, right in the middle of it all."

THE TRIAL:

DAY ONE, AFTERNOON

At least we're talking about the science, finally, Arthur said to himself.

The morning's nonsense about funding and priorities and corporate business was finished at last. They had taken a break for lunch, and Arthur had been surprised to see the crowds of demonstrators milling around across Independence Avenue and all the way to the barricades around the Capitol steps, marching past a grim line of blue-uniformed Capitol Police and helmeted soldiers carrying assault rifles. He saw his own name on many of their printed placards. Even from this distance he could hear their chanted slogans. My god, he thought, if they see me they'll come after me like lions chasing down Christians.

Arthur canceled his idea of going to one of the nearby restaurants and ducked back inside the Rayburn Building to grab a quick bite at the cafeteria. He ate alone; neither Jesse nor anyone else associated with the trial was in sight. Arthur relished the brief respite of solitude.

Once the trial reconvened they finally started to get down to the scientific evidence behind his work. The hearing chamber had been darkened so that Arthur could show the PowerPoint slides he had set up in his notebook computer.

Standing at the witness table, Arthur tapped the tiny computer with his forefinger, which slightly shook the image on the screen set up on the side wall of the room.

"And as you can see, the new kidney has already started to assume the shape and size of the original. You can compare it to the left kidney, which was left intact in the animal."

Someone coughed in the darkness. Otherwise the hearing chamber was still.

He tapped the computer's keyboard, and the image on the

screen changed. "This is the final X-ray in the series. The new kidney has reached juvenile size and is functioning nominally. The animal was returned to its normal life at this stage, and is still living quite normally."

"The animal in question was a chimpanzee?" Rosen's voice came out of the shadows.

"A macaque monkey," said Arthur. "We didn't do any chimp work at this stage of the program."

"Thank you."

"Can we have the lights, please?" said Graves.

Arthur felt a twinge of surprise. He had dozens more slides to show. But the overhead fluorescents blinked on and the people in the crowded room stirred and muttered as if coming out of a dream.

"I have no further questions for Dr. Marshak at this time," said Rosen. "Although I may need to recall him later."

Graves nodded. "You are excused, Dr. Marshak."

Feeling slightly off balance at the abrupt termination of his testimony, Arthur pleaded, "But there's a lot more evidence to show."

"The jury has your written reports," Graves said. "And you will be allowed to respond to the jury's questions later in the proceedings."

Nettled, Arthur said, "Well, then, I have a prepared statement that I want to read into the record." He pecked at the keyboard, shutting down the PowerPoint program.

"Later," said Graves. "We will accept prepared statements at a later stage of the proceedings."

Feeling frustrated, Arthur slapped the notebook closed. He had deliberately chosen not to allow an assistant to help him operate the computer. He wanted to show the slides by himself. Now, as he toted the computer back to the front bench where all the witnesses had been seated, he heard Graves announce:

"Court will adjourn until ten o'clock tomorrow morning." But before anyone could move he asked, "Mr. Rosen, who do you plan to call next?"

"I'll start tomorrow morning with Dr. Jesse Marshak."

WASHINGTON:
THE CAPITOL

Larry Corrigan had taken a haircut and shaved and even worn a tie and jacket for the rally. He didn't want people to think of him or his friends as a pack of motorcycle bums. Some of the other guys wore their leathers in the hot summer sun, sweating and cursing as they wheeled themselves across the special parking lot set aside for the handicapped right up to the line of cops and soldiers at the base of the Capitol barricade.

They had come from some pretty distant places, many of them. Their black jackets proclaimed club affiliations from New Jersey, Minnesota, Texas, even California. Paraplegics and quadriplegics, most of them injured in cycle accidents. Larry felt kind of proud of them.

His own bunch, from the VA hospital in Bethesda, had been tooling around the parking lot since morning, watching busload after busload of religious nuts arriving and forming ranks like a bunch of toy soldiers. Kids, most of them, although there were plenty of older folks carrying banners and placards, too; mostly women, gray-haired and grim-faced.

"What a bunch of pissants," grumbled Spider Zee, sidling his wheelchair hub to hub next to Larry's. Spider had cleaned up for the day, too. Even washed his hair and pulled it back in a long ponytail.

"Watch the language," Larry warned. "We don't want the reporters to think we're Hell's Angels."

Spider laughed. "More like Purgatory's Spooks."

When the wheelchairs had first arrived in front of the Capitol that morning they had had their few moments of fame. The TV cameras had focused on them while Larry, suddenly a spokesman for the whole, smiled and squinted up at a bottle-blond reporter who held a microphone under his nose.

"If anybody can get us on our feet again," he had said for the TV news, "we're for it."

"Even if it means experiments on animals?" the reporter had asked.

"Hell, they can experiment on me if they want to," Larry had snapped, instantly regretting the expletive. "I'm not goin' anywhere."

The reporter had smiled professionally. "Critics of Dr. Marshak claim he's using fetal stem cells in his experiments. Are you in favor of abortions?"

Larry sucked in a breath before answering. Are you still beating your wife? It was a no-win question. Finally he said, "I put in my time in the Middle East and Afghanistan, when I was in the Army. I've seen lots of kids die. I'm against killing."

"Even if fetal stem cells are necessary to cure you?"

"Those scientists are pretty smart, I think. They'll figure out a better way, you wait and see."

The reporter looked disappointed that she could not get him to say anything controversial. She tried a few more questions, then turned to her camera operator and said tartly, "Wrap it up. Let's get somebody else."

As he sat in the hot afternoon sunshine that baked the parking lot and Capitol grounds, Larry watched the organized platoons of protesters and the signs they carried:

MARSHAK KILLS BABIES
NO ABORTIONS FOR PROFIT
USING STEM CELLS IS MURDER

Most of his guys were off in a corner of the asphalt parking lot, grabbing sandwiches and beers from the truck that had accompanied them. Some of the club were drinking from bottles or flasks they had brought along with them. Then Larry saw Spider and a couple other of the guys wheeling themselves over toward the orderly lines of protesters marching by the barricade. Ed Frank was with them, leading the charge in his electric-powered chair. They're going to get themselves into trouble, Larry thought. He called to two of his most reliable club members to follow him as he started wheeling after Spider and Ed.

Sure enough, by the time Larry got within earshot, Spider was shouting at a squad of earnest-looking young men and women in dark suits and modest dresses.

"Hey, why d'you people want to keep me crippled, huh?"

They tried to ignore him and continue their carefully paced march along the barricade that blocked off the Capitol steps. On the other side of the picketers the Capitol Police stood grimly waiting for trouble.

"Hey, I'm talkin' to you!" Spider yelled.

"Pay no attention," said the marchers' leader, up at the head of the line.

That was the worst thing she could have said. Spider angled his chair sharply and cut into the middle of their line, forcing a placard carrier to stop or fall over him.

"Spider, leave them alone!" Larry called.

But Spider's face was red with more than the afternoon's heat. The placard the young man was carrying proclaimed ABORTION IS MURDER. Spider glared up at the kid.

"You want me to sit in this fuckin' wheelchair the rest of my life?"

"I don't want to interfere with God's plan," said the young man. A little smugly, Larry thought.

"You think God wants me to stay crippled?" Spider demanded.

"You brought it on yourself, didn't you? Nobody forced you to ride a motorcycle."

"You stupid little shit!" Spider screamed. "I was drivin' a fuckin' school bus!" And he reached up with his powerful arms to wrestle the kid's placard away from him.

The young man tried to hold on to the placard. A couple of his friends jumped in to help him.

"Stop it!" Larry yelled at the top of his voice. "For god's sake, stop it!"

But Spider had wrestled the sign away from them and was swinging it like a two-handed broadsword. He knocked down one protester and several others grabbed at him, at the placard, at his chair. The cops just stood there doing nothing. Larry saw it all dissolve into a wild, fist-swinging, screaming melee within an instant. Then the cops moved in. Ed's chair toppled over and he spilled out, totally helpless, people stepping on him as he screeched with pain. Larry tried to ram his own chair into the growing riot, to protect Ed as much as he could, but somebody clipped him behind the ear and everything went gray and blurry.

The TV camera teams came running to the growing scuffle as police and protesters and wheelchairs and reporters all converged on the fight. An Army-green helicopter hovered overhead, its engine roar and downwash smothering everyone.

From more than a block away, Reverend Simmonds broke into a sprint, his two beefy security men galumphing along behind him. Get there before the camera crews leave, Simmonds gasped to himself as he ran. Got to get there before the camera crews leave.

WASHINGTON:

EVENING

When the hearing adjourned late that afternoon and the room began to empty out, Arthur realized that he was facing the prospect of dining by himself.

He hated to eat alone, especially away from home, in a hotel. He needed people to talk to, to review the day's events and prepare for tomorrow's. But none of his own researchers had come down to Washington for the trial; Arthur had thought that their written reports would be sufficient and both the Omnitech legal staff and his public relations consultant thought it would be best if Arthur made his presentation by himself. Now he was starting to think that he might get Darrell Walters, at least, to come down and bolster his own testimony. Rosen was going to use Cassie's DVDs, he was certain. And Graves would let him do it. Talk about murder, Arthur said to himself.

Patricia Hayward had been at the hearing, she was serving as Arthur's PR consultant, but she must have ducked out as soon as the session was adjourned.

Arthur stood uncertainly in the emptying hearing chamber. Everyone else was rushing out. Jesse was nowhere in sight and Arthur could not share a meal with his brother now, anyway. Then he saw Milton Graves come out of the door behind the judges' desks.

"Milton," Arthur called to him. "How about dinner?"

The chief judge actually blanched. "Arthur, I simply can't! I shouldn't even be speaking to one of the witnesses outside the court chamber."

He hurried away, leaving Arthur standing alone. But not for long. As soon as Arthur stepped out into the corridor the news reporters raced up to him.

"Dr. Marshak! One minute, please!"

Arthur was quickly surrounded with microphones thrust in his face and video cameras staring at him. Good thing Graves ran away, he told himself. What would they make out of a harmless conversation between the two of us?

"Dr. Marshak, you seemed very upset at the hearing today."

"Dr. Marshak, what did Judge Graves say to you and Mr. Rosen when he called you into his chambers?"

"Dr. Marshak, how do you think today's testimony went?"

"What do you think of this afternoon's riot?"

"Riot?" Arthur felt his stomach clench. "There was a riot?"

"A big fight between some paraplegics and the religious demonstrators."

"Was anyone hurt?"

"A few bruises, nothing more serious. About a dozen or so were arrested."

Arthur shook his head. "That's awful."

He saw Pat Hayward rushing down the corridor toward

him. She must have gone to the toilet, Arthur realized. Now she stopped at the fringe of the crowding reporters and made gentling motions with her hands. Arthur got her message: stay cool, don't give the sharks any blood.

"What was the prepared statement that you wanted to read into the record?" asked one of the reporters. "Do you have it on you?"

"Why wouldn't Graves allow you to read it?"

"Do you think you're getting a fair trial?"

Spreading his hands to quiet them down, Arthur said, "Wait! Wait! One at a time."

"Do you think you're getting a fair trial?" repeated a determined-looking woman holding a miniature voice recorder in one hand as she pushed a microphone under Arthur's chin with the other.

He made a photogenic smile for her while he thought swiftly. Pat tried to look encouraging from behind the reporters' backs.

"I'm not on trial here," Arthur said at last. A dozen microphones inched closer to him. "Science is on trial. A particular new capability is on trial."

"Do you really think you can grow new organs in people?"

"Yes. And I have the scientific evidence to back up that belief."

"What about the people who say that you'd be tampering with things that should be left alone? Playing God?"

Arthur stretched his smile a bit. "Their great-great-grandparents said that vaccinating children against smallpox was playing God. Their earlier ancestors burned people at the stake for espousing new ideas."

One of the bright-looking young men grinned as he asked, "Do you think you're going to be burned at the stake in there?"

"I think a good idea might be thrown away," Arthur replied. "I think that if that happens, people whom we could cure are going to die."

"Is your idea getting a fair hearing?"

Careful! Pat's expression suddenly told him. They're just waiting for you to say something they can use against you.

He cocked his head slightly to one side, thinking before he spoke. Then, "I was surprised, obviously, that the examiner was allowed to bring in questions about priority and funding sponsorship. I had expected the court to deal strictly with the scientific questions, nothing else."

"Are you worried about being accused of homicide?"

"No," Arthur lied. "It was a suicide, not a murder. That's obvious."

"Do you feel any responsibility about her suicide?"

"No," Arthur snapped. Another lie.

"So who did get the idea first, you or your brother?"

With only a fraction of a second's reflection, Arthur answered firmly, "Jesse thought of regenerating organs first. I was still thinking in terms of regenerating spinal neurons when he broadened the scope of our concept."

"Hey! There he is!"

"Thanks, Dr. Marshak!"

Like a school of fish the reporters flashed away, surging through the corridor toward a new bit of bait. Arthur saw who they were chasing. Jesse.

"Dr. Marshak!" they were yelling as they scampered down the corridor. "Dr. Marshak!"

Suddenly there was no one between Arthur and Pat Hayward, looking coolly attractive in a crisp beige miniskirted suit that showed off her long legs to advantage.

"How'd I do?" he asked her.

"Fine," she replied. "I liked that line about science being on trial instead of you."

"Well, that's what's happening in there."

They walked together down the corridor and out into the soggy summer afternoon. The heat hit them like a load of steamed towels dropped onto their shoulders. Not a breath of air was stirring. Independence Avenue was clogged with slow-moving traffic: a sluggish artery of cars and buses and taxis, motors grumbling and growling while they inched along.

As they waited for the light to cross the avenue, Arthur was tempted to invite Pat to dinner. He knew plenty of people in

Washington, but none of them were the kind of acquaintances that he could phone at the last minute for a dinner engagement. Of course, he could get some of the local Omnitech people to go out with him. The corporation had a big office in downtown Washington. But they were virtually strangers who would do it out of duty, and he did not feel like keeping them from their own families and evenings.

Probably better to just order dinner in my hotel room, he said to himself as he walked with Pat across Independence Avenue to the taxi stand where the corporate limo was supposed to be waiting for him. It was not there. A sea of cars, but the limo was nowhere in sight. Arthur could see the tired, exasperated drivers sitting behind their steering wheels with their windows rolled up, the air-conditioning on full blast and their radios blaring. At nearly four dollars a gallon, Arthur thought. The heat from their engines and the sullen glowering sun made the street broil. Arthur felt himself sweating, his shirt sticking to his back and ribs.

As he peeled off his suit jacket he thought, I'll meet with the corporate lawyers over breakfast tomorrow morning, go over today's testimony, and get set for Jesse's day at the witness desk.

"They said there was a riot out here?" Pat asked. Somehow she still looked cool and crisp.

Jolted out of his thoughts, Arthur saw that the Capitol grounds and parking lot were almost empty. No lines of buses, no marching files of protesters.

He shrugged. "It'll probably be on the six o'clock news."

"If it really was a riot," Pat said. "The reporters can turn a little scuffle into World War III."

He almost laughed.

Then he saw the limousine inching through traffic toward them. Should I ask Pat to dinner? Arthur had a rule against socializing with his female employees, a rule that he had bent considerably but never truly broken. At least, that was his view of it. Pat was a consultant, not really an employee, yet he felt doubly uncertain about her. She was very attractive, and

Arthur had the feeling that she felt attracted to him. Yet they had both kept their relationship pretty much centered on business, despite the obvious temptation to do otherwise.

The limo pulled up to the curb and the liveried driver hopped out, all apologies and excuses about the traffic and the police, who wouldn't let him stay parked in the taxi stand. As Arthur helped Pat into the blessedly cool interior of the car he heard himself ask, "Do you have any plans for dinner?"

"No."

He sat beside her and shut the car door. "Where would you like to go?"

She hesitated a moment, then seemed to come to a decision. "Someplace quiet, where we can go over the day's testimony and prepare for tomorrow's."

An hour later they were sipping wine at a small table in an intimate French restaurant in Georgetown. The place was crowded, tables crammed in with barely enough room between them for the waiters to push through. But a generous tip to the maître d' had gotten Arthur one of the few quiet booths at the back of the room.

"It's not going the way you thought it would, is it?" Pat was asking.

He nodded gloomily. "I thought we could separate all the emotional and political factors and show the world that the science really works. But it doesn't look as if I'll be able to do that."

"Do you think they're going to use Cassie's videos?"

"I'm certain of it."

"But it's so unfair!" Pat said heatedly. "You're not responsible for what Cassie did."

With a wry smile, Arthur said, "Tell it to the judge."

"It's got nothing to do with the scientific facts."

His gloom deepening, Arthur said, "You know that and I know that and even Graves knows it. But this trial has been bent out of shape already, on the very first day. God knows what's going to happen tomorrow."

Pat looked angry, sad, and worried all at the same time. "Why is Jesse so opposed to you?" she asked. "Back when you two first talked about this, he seemed more enthusiastic about it than you were."

"I wish I knew," Arthur said. "He's my brother, but he's become a stranger to me. And an enemy."

PAT WAS staying at a motel near the airport. Arthur drove her there in the limo after dinner, said a polite good night, and returned to his suite in the Four Seasons. All the way there he wondered what would have happened if he had tried to make a move on Pat. Would she have rebuffed him? Or gone along because he was her employer? Or was she disappointed that he had done nothing but say good night?

Restless, unable to sleep, he put his clothes back on and walked for almost an hour along Wisconsin Avenue, unnoticed by the people who crowded the cafés and movie theater.

They were young, mostly. The singles crowd, roving the bars and fast-food joints, laughing and searching for romance, for excitement, for sex, maybe even for love. How many of you will die of heart disease? Arthur asked them silently. Plenty of the youngsters were smoking, he noticed with some disgust. How many will need new lungs? Or come down with cancer? How many of you realize that we'll be able to help you, if only they'll allow us to?

None of them, Arthur thought. None of them know. None of them give a damn.

But I care, he knew. I care. They're not going to stop me. I'm going to give you all the gift of life, maybe the gift of immortality.

Then he saw a pair of teenage boys in grimy T-shirts and jeans, spiked hair, dangling earrings. Puffing cigarettes. Christ, he said to himself, do you really want everybody to live forever?

THE TRIAL:

DAY TWO, BREAKFAST

There was a miniature television set in the bathroom of Arthur's hotel suite, and he watched *CNN Headline News* as he shaved. It startled him when the screen showed the riot that had erupted in front of the Capitol. As Pat had guessed, it was little more than a scuffle. But he had never seen his name on placards before yesterday, never realized the emotions that his work was stirring.

"My god," he said to himself, "what do they want of me?"

On the front page of the *Washington Post* there was a picture of demonstrators punching each other. The story about the trial itself was on page three.

Arthur was knotting his tie when the concierge called to tell him that his three visitors were on their way up to him. His doorbell chimed a moment later, and he went in his shirtsleeves to admit three lawyers: an old man, a young man, and a middle-aged woman, all in funereal dark business suits. They reviewed his testimony from the previous day over breakfast in his sitting room.

They accomplished nothing, Arthur thought. The young lawyer felt that Arthur had conducted himself brilliantly, especially when he tried to insist that the court stick to nothing but the scientific evidence. The woman worried that Rosen was maneuvering to establish Jesse as the rightful originator of the regeneration idea and thereby strip Omnitech of any patents or other proprietary rights. The third, older and grimmer, said very little but looked as if the world were going to come to an end within minutes.

Finally, just when Arthur thought they were finished, the older man cleared his throat and said in a rasping voice, "About this business of wrongful death . . ."

Arthur fixed him with a hard stare. "That's got nothing to do with this trial, no matter what Rosen says."

"It's not *this* trial that worries me," said the lawyer. His two colleagues, sitting on either side of him, nodded their heads in unison.

"What do you mean?" asked Arthur.

"It seems clear to me that Rosen is trying to establish a connection between your research project and the unfortunate woman's suicide."

"That's nonsense."

"Perhaps so. Perhaps not. But the testimony in this trial can and undoubtedly will be used in whatever civil or criminal suits are instituted back in Connecticut in regard to her suicide. You are going to have to defend yourself against charges of responsibility for her death."

"She killed herself," Arthur snapped. "She was emotionally unbalanced. Is that my fault?"

"You have a high visibility in this matter," said the old lawyer, his voice like a creaking hinge. "That makes you highly vulnerable. And Omnitech, of course, has the deep pockets that personal injury attorneys look for."

"Personal injury?"

"She had a family," said the younger man. "If they can prove wrongful death and fix the blame on you—"

"Nonsense!"

The old lawyer grimaced. "That is for a court of law to decide. A jury of your peers."

Christ, Arthur told himself, I thought I had picked a jury of my peers here in Washington. If I have to stand trial over Cassie's suicide—

"You must not respond to any questions about the suicide," the lawyer said in a tone that sounded already like impending doom. "You must not give them any material they can use against you and the corporation later on."

"I understand," Arthur said, realizing that the corporate lawyer was worried about the corporation, not his own life or reputation. "Thanks for the warning."

Arthur ushered them out of his suite, glad to be rid of them, then went to the bedroom to put on his jacket. *A civil or criminal trial in Connecticut. Great. Wonderful. Just what I need. Maybe they will burn me at the stake, after all.*

CNN Headline News was still on in the bathroom; they were showing yesterday's riot again.

The damned limo was nowhere in sight. Feeling angry and depressed, Arthur took a taxi to the Rayburn Building. *The limo's probably taking the lawyers back to their office,* he told himself. *I'll have to get Pat to call the service and straighten them out.*

The taxi driver was an elderly black man who seemed just as somber as Arthur felt.

"You goin' to that trial 'bout the doctors?" he asked as they inched through the morning traffic on Pennsylvania Avenue.

"I'm one of the doctors," Arthur replied.

The driver glanced up at his rearview mirror. "Yeah, yeah—they had a picture of you in the paper Sunday."

Arthur saw the dark, red-rimmed eyes study him as they waited for a stoplight to change.

"You really can grow a man a new heart?"

"That's what we're trying to do," Arthur said.

"You ain't really done it yet?"

"Not in humans."

"Well, hurry it up, Doc. Some of us cain't wait all that long, you know."

Arthur smiled at him. "We're doing our best."

When the cab pulled up at the entrance to the Rayburn Building, Arthur gave the man a ten-dollar tip.

THE TRIAL:
DAY TWO, MORNING

"Dr. Jesse Marshak, please."

Jesse looked fine, completely relaxed. He was wearing a light brown Western-cut suit with a bolo string tie. He took the oath with utter seriousness, but that boyish careless smile of his broke out as he sat in the witness chair. He carried no papers, no computer, no notes at all. He just sat down and smiled at Rosen and the judges. Arthur thought for an instant that Jess might throw one arm across the back of the chair and put his feet up on the desk.

"Dr. Marshak," said Rosen, from his seat at the end of the judges' row of desks.

"Dr. Rosen," said Jesse.

"You are the brother of Dr. Arthur Marshak?"

"That's right."

"And what is your professional affiliation, sir?"

"I am chief of internal medicine at Mendelssohn Hospital in New York City, and director of research at the La Guardia Medical Center in Manhattan."

Rosen glanced down at the list of questions he had prepared. "Are you now, or have you ever been, an employee of Omnitech Corporation?"

"No. Never."

"Have you ever been a consultant to Omnitech?"

"Not in a formal sense."

"What do you mean by that?" Rosen asked.

Jesse glanced at Arthur, then, "I batted some ideas around with my brother, but I never had a formal, legal agreement of any kind with Omnitech."

"Did you work in any way with your brother on this program to regenerate human organs?"

"I did not." Firmly.

"And why not? If the idea was originally yours, why didn't you work on the program to bring it to fruition?"

Jesse smiled again. "I was busy."

JESSE

Eritrea. I could smell the poverty the instant the plane's hatch opened.

The acrid tang of dung. Human sweat. Dust. Above all, overpowering heat. The blast of sun-scorched hot air coming in through the hatch was like standing in front of an enormous oven. And I had to step into it.

Julia was right behind me as I clambered down the cargo plane's flimsy ladder and to the dusty airstrip runway. The rusted hulk of a burned-out truck stood baking in the sun with a mangy starving cow tied to its battered front bumper. Talk about the contradictions of the Third World! I could count the cow's ribs. I wondered what the hell a cow was doing in the middle of the airstrip. Beetles crawled in the dust. Flies droned in the air. Off in the distance the brown hills shimmered in the heat haze. I wanted to turn around and climb back into the plane and fly home to New York.

Julia's voice sounded bright and certain. "Well, here we are! It feels good to be out of that awful plane, doesn't it?"

Even Cairo, filthy and crowded and plagued with every disease known to medical science, was starting to look good to me.

A team of dark-skinned men in shabby clothes helped the plane's crew to unload the medical supplies that had been our main cargo. Even the pilot helped to unload, while Julia and I stood in the hammering sun, feeling lost and uncertain, looking totally out of place in our clean new khaki shirts and slacks and white baseball caps.

Within minutes all the crates and cartons were piled up on the dusty runway. My soft-sided glitzy black Samsonite luggage sat there in the bug-crawling dust, with Julia's handsome blue matched set beside them.

The pilot mopped his face with a dirty handkerchief as he came toward us. His shirt was dark with sweat, sticking to him.

"UN blokes should be here soon enough," he said.

"You're not leaving us here alone!" I said.

The pilot stretched his arm and pointed. "That'd be your reception committee, I expect."

A cloud of brown dust was scurrying along the road toward the airstrip. I squinted and made out a truck. But it seemed to be a grayish brown color, not the glaring white of the UN.

"Well, good luck," said the pilot. He stuck his hand out.

I didn't take it. "What if that's not the UN?"

"Who else could it be?"

Julia smiled and said, "I'm sure the captain has a schedule to maintain. We shouldn't keep him, dear."

The pilot laughed. "Well, yes, sort of. Got to taxi over to the fuel dump and fill up the tanks and all that."

"Carry on," said Julia. "We'll be fine."

I wanted to say otherwise but I didn't want to look like an asshole in front of them. So I strained my eyes watching the approaching truck, then looked at the gaggle of laborers who had unloaded the plane, then at Julia. She seemed completely in charge of herself, totally unperturbed. What if that's *not* the UN? I asked myself. What if it's bandits or one of those warlords come down here to steal the medical supplies?

But I just stood there like a dumb jackass while the pilot climbed back into his rattletrap cargo plane and started the far-side engine with an explosive roar that made me hop almost out of my skin. Julia sat on one of the wooden crates. I stared at that approaching truck with my stomach churning inside me, and the plane trundled off noisily toward the fuel dump at the far end of the flyblown, almost deserted, sunblasted airstrip.

"It is the UN, darling," Julia said. I saw that she held a small pair of field glasses to her eyes. Where did she get those? I had never seen them before.

But I sure felt relieved at her announcement. And even more relieved when she passed the binoculars to me and I could see the blue United Nations symbol on the side of the white truck. It was all covered over with a film of gray-brown dust, of course.

The truck bore four Pakistani soldiers and a Canadian captain in desert camouflage uniforms and blue UN helmets, plus the doctor who was leaving Eritrea. He was an Indonesian, small, dark, and very happy to be on his way home.

"It is hopeless here," he told me somberly, while the plane taxied back from the fuel dump. "Absolutely hopeless."

Great news.

"Surely it can't be all that bad," Julia said with a smile.

The Indonesian merely shook his head. As soon as the crew popped open the hatch in the plane's side he scampered for it, without another word. While the local laborers sweated to load the truck, the plane took off, engines howling, blowing gritty dust in our faces. Then it dwindled into the burning sky and disappeared. All of a sudden I felt very alone in a strange and barren landscape of brown hills and unbearable heat.

Julia snapped me out of it. "Well, then," she said cheerfully, "shall we put our bags on the truck?"

The Pakistani soldiers did nothing to help us. They stood around—uneasily, I thought—and squinted toward the distant bare hills, heavy automatic rifles slung over their shoulders. Their fingers were never far from the triggers.

The Canadian captain introduced himself as Ralph Eberly, from Vancouver. He supervised the loading, even helped Julia with her luggage.

"It's not far to the field hospital," he told us. "Then we can get out of this awful heat."

"It's air-conditioned?" Julia asked hopefully.

"It has a roof and some shade," answered Captain Eberly. He was very young, tall and gangling. His uniform was cov-

ered with dust but his square-jawed face was freshly shaved
and his blue northern eyes looked alert and undefeated.

We rode the rattling, jouncing truck over the rutted un-
paved road away from the airstrip, with me, Julia, and Captain Eberly squeezed onto the bench behind the driver, Julia
in the middle. The young Canadian explained the local situation as he kept his eyes straight ahead, watching the road
over the driver's shoulder.

"Most of the fighting's down toward Massawa and As-
mara. And along the border with Sudan, of course. Things
have been fairly quiet here for a while. Occasional band of
thugs, but they're driven by the famine more than anything
else. Steal food when all else fails."

"The hospital?" I asked.

The captain glanced at me, looking glum, then returned to
watching the road. "Not much, I'm afraid. Converted from
an old church. We've patched up the roof and put up as many
tents as we could. Was hoping there'd be more tents in the
supplies you brought in with you."

"We had nothing to do with the supplies," I said.

"Understood. But still . . ." Eberly shifted unhappily on
the bench, turned to eye me directly, with Julia between us.
"You see, the countryside's been devastated by the fighting.
People are starving. And sick. Everything from typhus to
cholera. Schistosomiasis, dengue fever, you name it and
they've got it."

"Is that smoke?" Julia asked, pointing past the driver's ear.

"Dust," said Captain Eberly, shaking his head. "That's the
settlement. Your destination."

It had been a town once, I saw as we approached the field
hospital. Or at least a village. There were burned-out remains of circular huts and cinder-block houses on both sides
of the stony, rutted road. The only building that looked occupied had obviously once been a church, with a pitched roof
and the charred stump of a steeple.

Beyond the church-turned-hospital was the tent city. There
must have been a thousand tents there, at least. Big khaki-
colored army tents close to the hospital's dried mud walls,

neatly laid out with military precision. But farther on the tents were smaller, scattered haphazardly as if they had been set up quickly, desperately, to keep pace with the growing influx of the sick and dying.

And they were dying, you could tell just by looking. It was like a scene out of Auschwitz, gaunt hollow-eyed men and women and children, too weak to do more than stare blankly at their own doom, arms and legs like sticks, flies crawling on their faces, into the corners of their eyes, clothes in dirty rags. Babies too weak to cry, their bellies bloated, lying naked on the filthy ground.

"They keep trickling in," said the Canadian grimly as the truck squealed to a stop by the hospital. "Emptying out the countryside. They know there's some food here. Not enough, though. Not nearly enough."

It took a real effort to pull my eyes away from the haunted black faces and glance across at Julia. She looked stricken.

"My dear lord," she murmured. "My dear lord."

ARTHUR

The trouble with spying is that it's so damned difficult to get disentangled once you're involved in it.

Nancy Dubois had fallen in love with fencing. Once I had arranged her first lesson, and dinner afterward, she had promptly gone out and bought herself a full outfit—padded jacket, trousers, mask, glove, and several foils—and shown up the following Monday evening ready to pay for a season's worth of lessons.

Now she showed up each Monday evening. She had become one of the gang. We usually went out for a bite to eat after each session, eight to twelve men and women ranging from a couple of teenagers to my age pushing tables together at the local HoJo or McDonald's.

The hell of it was that I had learned virtually nothing about what the executive committee was up to. Six weeks of fencing lessons, six evenings out with Nancy, and nothing to show for it except some veiled hints about deals with Japan aimed at stopping the European takeover bid. Nancy seemed pleasant enough, sociable with the other fencers and friendly with me. No hint of romantic inclinations, though, and I was afraid to push in that direction for fear of driving her away. And, to tell the truth, I really wasn't that interested in her. I wanted information from her, not sexual gratification.

Yet she didn't look as if she would drive away easily. I thought that perhaps she was waiting for me to make a move.

To call our run-down little gym a fencing academy was overly grandiose, but there was something about fencing that encouraged such formalities. Our teacher—a Latvian immigrant who worked daytime as a Federal Express driver—was by nights our maestro. He was almost a midget, slim as a saber blade, with a wild shock of strawberry-blond hair. On the fencing strip he could move faster than the eye could follow. He was excitable, and that unruly shock of hair sprang up when he took off his fencing mask. He often lapsed into his native tongue when a student particularly annoyed him.

I whipped off my mesh mask after my lesson and saluted formally with my saber. The maestro returned my salute.

"Thank you for the lesson, maestro," I said perfunctorily. I was sweating hard; physically tired and emotionally weary.

On the other side of the gym a pair of fencers danced up and down the long narrow mat of their fencing strip, blades clicking as they grunted or shouted, "Eh-lah!" when they lunged. Others were working out in the corners of the bare room, practicing the elaborate steps and hand movements. The gym smelled of perspiration, rang with shouts and fervent discussions that often rose to arguments.

"Your mind is not on the lesson," said the maestro. A stranger would have had difficulty understanding the Latvian accent.

"I'm sorry—"

"Since you brought that little brunette here, you think more about her than about your lessons. No?"

It was so. With a sheepish grin I replied, "I imagine you're right."

"So"—the maestro was peeling off his cracked, stiff old leather glove as the two of us walked off the strip, his voice low and confidential—"put her in bed, make love to her, and get her out of your thoughts. The first tournament comes in two weeks and I need all your attention on it."

I had to laugh. The maestro didn't know or care about what his students did while he himself was driving his Fed-Ex truck. Fencing was all that mattered.

"Good advice, maestro," I said. And I had to admit that it probably was damned good advice.

Instead of going out with the gang after the session, I invited Nancy to dinner. She easily accepted and we each drove our own cars—my Infiniti and her Taurus—to the quiet little seafood restaurant by the Sound where we had gone the first time, six weeks earlier.

Nancy was in the frilly blouse and knee-length skirt she had worn at the office. As we chatted over our meal and I kept pouring the wine, I tried to maneuver the conversation to the inner workings of the executive committee. Nancy skillfully stayed away from the subject.

Finally, in exasperation, I came out with it. "Nancy, I've got to know what the executive committee's up to."

"Up to?" She managed to look innocent, almost.

"Something's going on."

Nancy gave me a coy smile. She had a heart-shaped face and she could dimple very prettily. "Oh, Arthur, something's *always* going on. You know that."

"I think it involves the lab."

She made no reply.

"If it does," I said, "I've got a right to know what it is."

"Have you talked with Johnston?"

"He was evasive."

Nancy made a shrug that said, *So what do you expect me to do about it?*

"There are more than two hundred people at the lab," I said. "Very dedicated, very talented people. If the executive committee is doing something that's going to affect them, I ought to know about it."

She sighed. "Sid would go spastic if anybody gets a whiff of this."

"A whiff of what?"

"I really can't tell you, Arthur," she said, looking genuinely troubled. "You wouldn't be able to keep it to yourself and Sid will know I'm the one who told you about it."

"About what?" I insisted.

"I can't." She shook her head.

I reached across the table and took both her hands in mine. "Nancy, you've got to. You can't tell me that something's so important that Sid Lowenstein is about to go ballistic over it and then not tell me what it is!"

"He'd fire me."

"He won't know you told me. I'd never tell him—"

"He'd know it was me. Nobody else would let you in on it."

She's playing with me, I realized. She's leading me on, reeling me in like a fish. She wants something from me and she's not going to spill the beans until she gets it.

"Nancy, is there some way I can protect you from Sid? Would you like to transfer to another position at headquarters?"

Her eyes widened just for a flash of a second. Then she regained control of herself. "I work for Sid. If he finds out I'm even suggesting that the executive committee's thinking about your division, he'd boot me out on my butt."

"So how can I help you?" I asked. "What can I do to protect you?"

She hesitated a moment, the tip of her tongue peeking out between her teeth like a little girl waiting to unwrap a big birthday present.

"There's going to be an opening next month in the marketing department. The chief assistant to the VP of marketing is quitting."

"And you want the job."

"I'd be good at corporate marketing, Arthur. I could make vice president in a few years."

"Who else is in line for the position?"

"Nobody even knows it's going to open up! Not yet. The guy who has the job now hasn't told anyone he's quitting."

"Except you."

She smiled knowingly. "Except me."

"You really want to work for Uhlenbeck?" I asked. "The man's something of a dimwit, isn't he?"

"That's the whole point! I can take over the department, do his work, take his job. I'd do a better job than he can, really I would."

I could feel myself starting to grin. "So moving you to marketing would be a good thing for the corporation."

"Of course it would. I wouldn't think of doing it if it weren't. We're all loyal Omnitech people, aren't we?"

I laughed. But then I got back to the point. "So what's going on inside the executive committee? What are Sid and Johnston up to?"

She took a deep breath, as if she were about to tackle some monumental undertaking. I have to admit that I enjoyed the way the frilled neckline of her blouse moved when she breathed.

"So?" I asked again.

She leaned across the table, lowered her voice. "They're talking with Kyushu Industries about selling the lab."

"Selling?" I felt as if I'd been punched. "To Japan?"

"Omnitech would keep a license to develop any new product lines the lab produces and sell them in the U.S. Japan gets the rest of the world market."

"Jesus H. Christ on a motorcycle."

"It's merely in the talking stage, from what I hear," Nancy said swiftly. "Nothing may come of it."

"But they're willing to sell the laboratory?" I could barely believe it. "*Sell* it? Sell *us*? Like a bunch of baseball players?"

"They're desperate to fight off this takeover bid."

I sat there, stunned, wondering what I could do now that I knew what was going on. Would being owned by the Japanese make any real difference? Yes, of course it would. I'd had a virtually free hand with Omnitech; Johnston and I understood each other. With the Japanese it might be very different. Very different. They'd want to control their investment. Maybe I could quit and start a new lab somewhere else. Most of the staff would come with me. But the lawyers would try to stop me. It'd be a mess, a god-awful mess.

With a start, I realized that the waiter was standing beside our booth.

"Coffee, sir?" the waiter asked for the second time.

Neither I nor Nancy wanted anything more. I handed the waiter my platinum American Express card and signed the bill with hardly a glance at it. We left the little restaurant and stepped out into the sighing breeze of a late September night.

"It's chilly," Nancy said.

I looked down at her. In the light from the parking lot she smiled up at me. Invitingly, I thought.

"Do you live far from here?" she asked.

"About fifteen, twenty minutes," I replied.

"I've got to drive all the way back to the Bronx."

Without really thinking about it, I suggested, "Why don't you come up to my house?"

She said, "I'll follow your car."

She had expected the invitation, obviously.

Nancy seemed quite sure of herself; not at all hesitant or nervous. She parked on the driveway behind my car and we entered the house through the garage. She gave the kitchen an approving once-over as I led her toward the living room.

"I don't do much cooking in here," I admitted. "That's why it looks so sterile."

She smiled and murmured, "That's a shame."

The living room, with its cathedral windows and sunken fireplace area, really impressed her.

"A fireplace!" Nancy went straight to it and ran her hand along the white-painted bricks.

I turned on the gas flame, low, and she sighed and sat on the curving sofa facing the fire. As I went to the bar to pour a couple of snifters of cognac, I knew where we would make love. But you've got to be careful, I warned myself. Don't rush things. Don't scare her off.

I needn't have worried. I had forgotten that Nancy liked to play games; before the snifters were half finished she was playfully auctioning off her clothes.

"Now the bra," she was saying as she sat on the thickly carpeted floor at my feet, the firelight warming her bared shoulders, a sly smile on her lips. "The bra costs twenty-nine ninety-nine, retail. But under the circumstances I think I should get a lot more for it. A lot more."

Grinning down at her, I said, "It's used."

"That's what makes it worth so much."

"I'll give you . . . thirty dollars."

She shook her head.

"Thirty-five."

"Nope. Fifty dollars or bust." She giggled at her pun.

"How about forty-five?"

She tilted her head slightly, thinking it over. "Okay. Forty-five dollars. But for that price you're going to have to take it off yourself."

I pretended resignation. "Well, if I have to, I have to." I slipped down off the sofa and sat on the floor next to her.

I was a little afraid that the cognac was hitting her so hard she would pass out, but her drunkenness was only an act, I found once we started truly exploring each other's bodies. We made love eagerly, almost fiercely, there in front of the fireplace, Nancy yelling like a cheerleader while I gasped and snorted and gripped her so tightly I could see my finger marks on her flesh afterward. Then we padded to the bedroom and did it all over again.

Finally, as we drifted to sleep with her body warm and cuddled next to mine, I thought, Well, she said she wanted to make vice president. At least she's made *a* vice president. Twice.

But my dreams were haunted by Japanese samurai who were trying to slice me open with their bloodstained swords.

ZACK O'NEILL

Arthur didn't like me. He didn't like the way I dressed, he didn't like the way I did my work, and he especially didn't like the fact that I was younger than him and probably a helluva lot smarter.

For an old guy, though, the boss wasn't too bad. He was no feeb, far from it; Arthur was sharp and he was probably a helluva good scientist in his day. But you know what happens once you pass thirty-five or so: you stop doing any original work and get yourself bogged down in administration. Or worse, you go through the motions of doing research and just get in the way of the morfs who're trying to get some real work done.

So I was surprised when he called me into Darrell Walters's office that afternoon and told us to start thinking about organ regrowth. Like it was his idea. Shit, I did the basic work on differentiation factors when I was still at Berkeley. Got my PhD on it.

It wasn't that I didn't try to fit in with Arthur's idea of how his staff scientists should behave. Once I started getting a salary I bought myself the first new clothes I could afford since my graduate fellowship had run out. And I knew he got freaked about my 'do, so I found a barber who could tone it down a bit, make it look more like a military buzz cut. I figured the boss would like a haircut that reminded him of West Point or Annapolis. I kept the earring, though. Well, a smaller one. I was willing to go so far in pleasing the boss, but no farther.

Of course, I didn't endear myself to him at the office Christmas party.

It's a very informal bash. Everybody just sort of stops work around four o'clock on the last working day before Christmas and we all get together in the cafeteria. BYOB. No drugs, which kind of surprised me a little. Arthur ran a clean operation that way. There were plenty of bright people who knew enough about chemistry to blow the roof off the place, but I never even sniffed any pot at the lab.

So I brought a bottle of Jamaican rum that my roommate at Berkeley had left behind when he cracked up and ran off to the woods to get away from the grind.

Arthur saw to it that the lab provided plenty of ice, chasers, soft drinks, and munchies. His chief of the administrative departments sent everybody a memo the Monday before the party, reminding us of the evils of liquor and telling us to pick designated drivers and all that shit. Got the company off the hook, I guess, in case anybody racked up his car driving home.

We had canned music and people were dancing where they'd cleared away the cafeteria tables. No spouses allowed at the office party. From what I heard about earlier parties, some pretty hot romances got started under the mistletoe.

But as I looked across the crowded cafeteria floor, I could see that there were about six guys to every woman, and a lot of the women were older, like Arthur's secretary, Phyllis. Nice lady, but nobody's going to screw around with her.

I had sort of hoped to get a chance to dance with Vince Andriotti's daughter, Tina. She's an exotic-looking knockout, but you couldn't get close to her with her father snorting right down your neck. At least at the party I figured I could dance with her and get to know her a little better. Maybe something good would come of it.

But there was Arthur, clutching Tina's hand and not letting go. The two of them were standing by the makeshift bar that Darrell and some of the technicians had put together. Arthur was smiling out at his people on the dance floor like the head of the family at a big Polish wedding. Tina looked to me as if she wanted to get out of his grip, but Arthur wasn't letting go of her hand. Vince, her father, was all the way over on the other side of the room, running the CD player that they had plugged into the cafeteria's sound system. Maybe he figured his daughter was okay as long as she was with Arthur; the boss would scare off any of us young, virile types.

Well, the hell with that. Tina was the best thing going at this party and I wasn't going to let Arthur monopolize her, boss or no boss.

The sound system was playing some ancient Beatles tunes, old enough so that even creaky geeks like Darrell could go out on the dance floor and hop around. So I walk up to Tina and say, "May I have this dance?"

She looked surprised and turned to Arthur. He looked surprised, too, and let go of her hand. I gave him a grin and took Tina out onto the floor. She's really a knockout, with almond eyes and high cheekbones. Great bod, too. She sort of looked embarrassed, wouldn't let her eyes meet mine.

As we danced I maneuvered her the best I could away from the bar, where Arthur was standing, and toward the other side of the room. Her father was on that side, but hey, my intentions were strictly honorable. Well, more or less.

By the time the CD had played out we were both puffing a little. I had let myself get out of shape, I guess.

"Well, thanks for the dance," I said. It was the first chance I had to say anything since we started dancing.

"Thank you," she said, her eyes finally looking straight at me.

"For what?"

"For rescuing me," Tina said.

So she *did* want to get away from the boss. We drifted apart; Tina stayed near her dad and I danced with a few of the other younger women. Once I figured a decent interval had passed, I tracked her down again and we had another dance together, a slow one, so I could hold her and talk to her a little. It was really nice, almost romantic, except I could feel two pairs of laser beams staring at me from opposite sides of the dance floor.

Tina and I dated now and then afterward, nothing serious. She was a good kid, great to be with, great sense of humor, but she wasn't going to get serious with any guy and I didn't want any commitments, either. We just had some fun together, that's all. But I was certain that Arthur had it in for me after that. I didn't see him at my lab all that winter, and when I had to give presentations on the work I was doing he seemed to frown at me all the time I was on my feet talking.

So it was sort of a shock when I was brought into Darrell's office that afternoon to brainstorm Arthur's new idea about curing paraplegics. His new idea! My first impulse was to remind him that half of what he was talking about came straight out of my doctoral work. But I stayed cool, because I quickly saw that only half of it was from my work. Arthur had strung together some other ideas; I didn't know where he had gotten them, but he had put them together brilliantly, I had to admit. Maybe he wasn't generating the original ideas anymore, not at his age, but he sure could put things together. He was super sharp, all right, and before long we were shooting the shit like equals.

That's when it came to me. This work he wanted to do, curing paraplegics and regrowing organs and limbs—this was my big chance! It was right down my alley, and I could really sink my teeth into this program. I was going to become Arthur's fair-haired boy, by Jesus. I was going to become the lead man in this research effort. Phat city. I'd make them all proud of me, especially the boss.

And maybe even Tina. I realized that I wanted to be a shining star in her eyes.

It wasn't until a lot later that I finally realized that this was the way Arthur got his people motivated. He could get you excited about a new program, so excited you'd bust your balls trying to succeed. You wanted to please him, he had that power to make you want to make him smile at you. Because the best way to please him was to break new ground, make a success of yourself. Push ahead and get the job done, no matter how tough it was. Make a success of yourself and you made him happy.

I guess that's what they call leadership.

JESSE

Within two days we got down to a routine at the tent city surrounding the field hospital. And within three days Julia came down with a high fever.

I was frantic, even though Captain Eberly assured me that most Westerners are hit by fever or dysentery when they first arrive.

"Goes with the territory, I imagine," he said calmly. "We're aliens here; even the local bugs don't like us."

Yeah, sure. But I could see Arby's face frowning at me and hear him saying how he warned me not to take her with me. I didn't have anywhere near the diagnostic equipment or facilities that I needed. I took blood samples from Julia's arms, checked her temperature hourly, dosed her with antibiotics and aspirin.

"Don't neglect your real patients," Julia said from her cot, sweating and shivering.

"I just hope it isn't malaria," I muttered as I sat on an empty wooden crate beside the cot. I mean, they didn't even have decent chairs for us.

"Eberly told me it's the wrong season for malaria," Julia said weakly. "The mosquitoes don't come 'round until the rainy season."

Then it might be dengue fever, I thought, trying to remember how long the incubation period for dengue was. She couldn't have come down with it so soon. I radioed back to the UN medical center in Cairo for as much information as I could get, and faxed the results of Julia's blood tests to them over the radiophone. It took days before they sent back the results, and at that all they said was that it was negative on dengue fever.

"It's just the heat," Julia assured me. "I'll get acclimated in another day or so."

I stared down at her, trying to make her fever disappear by sheer willpower.

"There are all those other people who need you," she urged. "Don't waste your time on me."

"They can go fuck themselves," I snapped. "You're the only one I care about."

Julia pushed herself up on one elbow. The sheet covering her dropped away slightly and I could see that her shirt was soaked through with perspiration.

"Jesse, darling," she said in the tone she reserved for out-stubborning me, "we are here to help those poor starving people out there. I'll be fine in a day or so. Go out and do the work you came here to do."

So I went, reluctantly, and spent the day among the hopeless, examining, tapping, testing, inoculating, looking at babies with famine-bloated bellies and mothers too weak to move. I gave injections, bound up wounds, handed out pills, prescribed ointments for open sores. A half dozen Ethiopian nurses assisted me, three grave men and three silent women, with dark unsmiling eyes in their darker faces. The line coming into my examination tent seemed to go all the way out to the horizon and then some. When I took a break to dash back to Julia, the line was just as long as it had been when I'd started.

"What they need is food," Captain Eberly told me while he and I grabbed a quick bite of the prepackaged stuff the plane had brought in.

It didn't take a medical genius to figure that out. "Most of what I'm seeing is hunger-related," I agreed. "Parasites, infections; they haven't got the somatic vigor to fight them off."

"How's Mrs. Marshak?"

"Holding her own," I said. "I've put enough antibiotics into her to make a herd of elephants get up and fly."

"She should be better in a day or two. Almost everyone comes down with a fever when they first arrive here."

I guess he was trying to cheer me up, but every time he repeated that dumb line it irritated me more. I got up and headed back toward the examination tent.

"I'll look in on her, if you don't mind," Eberly called after me.

By the end of the first week Julia was strong enough to leave our tent for short, wobbly walks. Eberly went with her when I was too busy with his endless stream of starving, dying people. Mothers came in, scarecrow-thin, carrying babies that had been dead for days. Children burned and blasted by artillery shells up in the hills. Men without legs, women with tapeworms in their intestines twenty feet long and festered sores all over their bodies. AIDS was spreading through the camp and we didn't have enough prophylactics to do a damned thing about it. The Ethiopian nurses gave lectures about it, but it didn't do a bit of good. I started wearing surgical gloves all the time. And a mask and goggles, when I had to work on their mouths.

When does it end? I asked myself as I sat bone-tired on my cot at sundown one day. The line was still standing silently by the examination tent, all those big dark eyes staring at me accusingly. I didn't do this to you, I wanted to tell them. You did it to yourselves. But of course I knew that they hadn't. They were victims, just ordinary people who'd been kicked in the guts by the civil war and the famine and their own endemic poverty. They needed all the help I could give them. They need a lot more.

Eberly had been in the tent with Julia when I had come in. I felt so exhausted, so emotionally drained, that I couldn't eat. I just went to the cot and plopped down on it, still fully dressed.

"I think I'll catch a few winks," I said.

"Don't you want dinner?" Julia asked.

The thought of eating while all those hungry hopeless people waited in the endless line made me feel almost ill.

"Not now," I said, turning over on my side, away from her, away from them. "You go eat. Keep up your strength."

"I'll take care of her," Eberly said.

"Yeah," I said, staring at the olive-drab fabric of the tent.

It wasn't until the two of them had left that I began to think about stories I had read about American women and white hunters in Africa. Julia was English and Eberly wasn't a white hunter, of course, but he was young and good-looking. A soldier. Just as good as a white hunter. And he's spending more time with Julia than I am, I thought.

I tossed on the cot for what seemed like a few minutes, but when I got up and pushed through the tent flap it was fully dark outside. Stars hung up in the black sky, glittering, almost close enough to touch. I expected to hear a lion roar or wolves howling or something, but there was no sound out in this barren desert except the eternal buzz of the damned insects.

The line had dispersed. Thank god, I thought. They've gone away, or at least they've scattered back to their tents and lean-tos on the other side of the church.

I went into the abandoned church, where the UN soldiers had set up a rough mess hall. Julia and Eberly were sitting together at one of the folding tables, across a corner, close enough to touch hands. Nothing between them but the plastic mess kits we used. We only ate the prepackaged rations that the plane had brought. Boiled our water to hell and back. No local foods for us, although the Pakistani soldiers seemed to be getting along well enough. But they boiled their water, too, and cooked everything to death.

I felt as if I were staggering as I walked up to the table. Eberly shot to his feet, looking almost flustered, if you ask me. Red-faced. Julia smiled warmly at me.

"Feeling better, darling?" she asked.

"I'm okay," I said, sitting down across the little table from her. "Just tired, that's all."

But I was thinking, Another seven weeks of this. Seven more weeks. Forty-nine more days of all those people in line and forty-nine more nights of wondering what this Canadian soldier boy is fantasizing about my wife.

CASSIE IANETTA

I was walking with Max today around lunchtime in the fenced-off area behind the lab. It's starting to get too chilly for Max to stay outdoors for long, even at noontime; chimpanzees can be very susceptible to colds and lung infections.

"So I'll be away for six months or so," I was saying to Max.

Max knuckle-walked alongside me, then swung up onto his favorite tree. I smiled at him. He needs the exercise. The kids that take care of the animals never give Max enough exercise time.

"I've got to go away for a while," I said out loud as I signed, Cassie go away.

Max waggled one hand from up in the tree branch: No. No.

"You will miss me, won't you?" I said to him. "I'll miss you, too."

You stay, Max signed. You good.

My eyes filled with tears. I wanted to clamber up there next to him and give Max a good hug. But one of the caretakers might see; they made enough crude jokes about the two of us already. And sometimes Max forgot how much stronger he was than me; he had bruised my ribs more than once.

They just don't understand. None of them do. I know that Max isn't human. I'm not crazy or weird or anything like that. But Max is trusting and loving in his own way. He's loyal. He doesn't run out on you because you've got cancer. He doesn't go off with some other woman the day you enter the hospital for radiation and chemotherapy.

"There you are!"

I turned and saw Darrell Walters striding busily up the concrete walk that meandered along the grassy enclosed yard; old "Uncle Darrell," lean, lanky arms and legs pumping away, a stern expression on his long-jawed face.

"I've been looking all over for you," Darrell said.

I felt a surge of annoyance. I have a right to spend my lunch hour wherever I want to, I grumbled to myself.

"I need your help on this analysis that O'Neill and his technicians are trying to do. They're getting bogged down. They need somebody with your fine touch for these things."

I looked up at Darrell. He wasn't teasing, not being sarcastic. He meant exactly what he said.

"What's their problem?" I asked.

Darrell glanced up at Max, who was watching us from his tree with sad brown eyes. "It's this nerve-regeneration experiment they're running for Arthur. They're trying to do an analysis of the chemical pathways between neurons and they're swamped with all kinds of spurious signals."

With a resigned sigh, I signed good-bye to Max. He shook his head, a very human gesture.

Darrell was so much taller than I that I had to crane my neck to look up at him as we started back toward the lab. I asked him, "What equipment are they using?"

"Come on back to Zack's lab. He can show you the whole setup."

As we came up to the building's rear door I stopped and said, "Darrell, I want you to look out for Max while I'm gone."

"Me?" He looked startled.

"Please."

"But the caretakers—"

"They don't exercise him enough. They don't give him any special attention. Max needs companionship. He's not a lab rat or a minihog. He's practically human!"

Darrell just stood there, looking upset.

"And it's starting to get colder. It's going to be winter soon. Max catches cold easily, you know. You've got to look out for him."

Finally Uncle Darrell broke into a gentle smile. "I'll look out for him. Don't worry about it, Cassie. I'll see that Max gets all the attention he needs."

"I'll make out a list of what he needs. And the foods he likes best. Treats, you know, like gumdrops; he's crazy about gumdrops."

"Any special flavor?"

"Spearmint's his favorite. But he likes lemon, too. And raspberry. But don't let him have too many."

Darrell shook his head, and I could tell exactly what he was thinking. Maybe she'll find some nice guy down there in Mexico and start to feel just as much for a man as she does for the damned dumb chimp. I knew that's what he thought. Just like Arthur and all the rest of them. That shows how much they know about anything.

As we stepped through the door and into the laboratory building, I told Darrell what was really important to me. "Max is not to be used for any experiments while I'm away."

"Now, wait a minute, Cass. We can't—"

"That's the deal I made with Arthur. Nobody touches Max until I get back. Arthur promised."

"He did?"

"Yes, he did." It wasn't a lie, exactly. Arthur had said he had no plans to use Max for anything while I was away.

Darrell shrugged. He knew Arthur even better than I did, so I was certain he never believed for a moment that Arthur would flatly promise to put Max on the retired list while I was away. I was sure Darrell figured that maybe Arthur said he'd try to leave Max alone, or waved his hand and smiled when I asked him not to let anybody use Max until I came back.

"Well," Darrell said, "you know that we're going to mate him with the female chimps."

"Yes," I said. "That's all right."

A slow smile broke out across his horsey face. "Not such a bad life, at that."

I didn't dignify his smirk with an answer. But I hoped that Darrell realized I would cause a bundle of trouble if anybody tried to use Max for any experiments while my back was turned. And maybe that was as good as a promise from the boss.

JESSE

I kept telling myself that it's crazy. I'm not a jealous man. And there was nothing to be jealous of.

I turned on that damned stiff, uncomfortable cot and looked at Julia, sleeping soundly on the cot next to me. We were practically touching, we had put our cots so close together. In the darkness of the tent I could barely make out the profile of her form against the slightly lighter side of the tent. I thought of how god-awful awkward it was going to be to try making love on these damned contraptions. Once she felt strong enough again.

Her breathing was deep and regular. That was reassuring. The fever seemed to have disappeared as suddenly and mysteriously as it had come. Some doctor. Can't even diagnose your own wife.

And what about yourself? Are you jealous of some Canadian kid in a soldier suit? He does spend a lot of time around Julia; a helluva lot of time. Shouldn't he be out there chasing down the bandits in the hills or inspecting the troops who're protecting this hospital or something?

I turned over cautiously on the creaking cot, worried that it might tip over. I listened for a minute or two longer to Julia's breathing—and for the terrifying sound of a mosquito inside the tent. Nothing, thank god. I bug-bombed the tent every evening, while Julia was outside having dinner.

With Captain Eberly.

I couldn't sleep. Every time I closed my eyes I saw that long line of people out there, needing, hurting, waiting for me to do something for them, ease their pain, make their lives better. I could feel their pain, their misery. Every time I started to fall asleep all their stares and moans coalesced into one lone person: Ma, lying haggard and shriveled in her nursing home bed.

It had been almost impossible to get to see her, with so

much else to do at the last minute before leaving for the airport. Patients at the hospital. The custodial staff at the medical center was threatening a job action. Inoculations and a ton of paperwork for the UN and the African officials and the damned snotty State Department bureaucrats.

And Arby chewing on my ass every day about driving up to see Ma.

"I'll send a limo for you," Arthur promised. Threatened, really. "The driver will wait for you and then take you wherever you have to go."

What good would it do to see Ma? She's dying and there's nothing I can do about it. Not a damned thing. But Arby's pushing and I guess I really should see her before I go. What if she dies while I'm overseas?

Ma looked no different than the last time I had seen her. Emaciated, withered down to wrinkled skin and bones. Somebody had smeared some lipstick on her and brushed what was left of her hair. But that's not Ma, not that dying little bag of bones that can't even smile at me. It's not her. There's nothing left of her. She'd already died, only she wasn't ready to admit it yet.

That was just like Ma. Strong and gutsy. The mother who fought the whole goddamned New York City school board to get me into the Bronx High School of Science. The mother who sat by my bed every minute when I was sick with hepatitis and the doctors thought I was going to die only she wouldn't let me die because she loved me so much she kept me alive and made me strong again. The mother who told Arby that if Julia wanted me instead of him it wasn't my fault and there was nothing he could do about it.

But this half-paralyzed old lady in this lousy little room—I had to force myself through the doorway and into her room.

Someone had put an extra chair beside her bed. Probably Arthur had phoned ahead to tell them that we'd both be coming.

Ma's eyes fastened on me. I made myself smile and go to her and bend over and kiss her forehead. It felt like kissing a corpse.

"How are you, Ma?" I asked, feeling totally stupid as soon as the words left my lips.

Arby bustled around and pulled the tray with the computer on it over to the bed. I had to scrape my chair across the floor to get it to a position where I could see the display screen.

Painfully, Ma typed, GLAD TO SEE BOTH

"How are you feeling?" Arby asked, his voice strangely low, tight.

OKAY. HOW YOU JESS

"I'm fine," I said with a heartiness I sure didn't feel. "Going to Africa for a couple of months, working at a UN hospital."

VERY PROUD OF YOU

That made me smile.

HOW JULIA

"She's fine, Ma. She's going with me."

WHEN WILL I BE GRANMA

Christ, I should have known she'd bring that up. Nothing but pressure, every time.

But I kept the smile on my face and answered, "Not yet, Ma. We're not ready yet."

I DONT HAVE LONG

"Oh, you'll be okay," I said. "You'll be at his bar mitzvah."

SURE

I looked up at Arby, hovering over Ma. They didn't need an extra chair for him, he wouldn't sit down anyway. Say something, for chrissakes, I begged him silently. Take me off the hook.

But Arby just stood there in his handsome suit and tie, looking as pained and helpless as I felt. If only there was something we could do for her, I thought. Some way to help her. They're standing in line all over the place, waiting for me to help them somehow, all their eyes on me, at the clinic, at the field hospital. Humanitarian of the Year and I can't even help my own mother, for chrissakes, can't help all those frightened, sick, beaten people. AIDS victims, rape victims, addicts and drunks and people starving in Africa and kids dying of dysentery within sight of the big high-rise apartment blocks on the beaches of Rio. And they all want me to cure them, save them, feed them, and make them happy again.

And Julia's spending more time with that damned Canadian than with me. In my mind's eye I saw her with the UN captain sitting in the shade of a plane tree in the late afternoon while I worked my ass off with these damned hopeless cases. Only it wasn't Captain Eberly that she was sitting with, chatting with, laughing with. It was Arby who was sitting with her. Julia had gone back to Arby and left me alone with the endless needy and my dying mother.

I sat bolt upright on the cot, drenched in sweat.

Julia stirred, woke up. "What is it, darling? Are you all right?"

"Go back to sleep," I said. "It's nothing. Just a bad dream."

THE TRIAL:

· DAY TWO, MORNING

So, after originating the idea for organ regeneration," said Rosen, still seated at the end of the judges' desks, "you went to Africa to work with a UN mercy mission."

"That's correct," Jesse replied.

"And you did not work on the organ regeneration program at Omnitech's Grenford Laboratory?"

"I did not."

"Not at all?"

"Oh, I talked with my brother about the progress of his program when it first got under way, but by the time I got back from Africa he had already put together a team of Omnitech employees and medical consultants from several hospitals and research centers."

Rosen seemed to think that over for a few moments, hands pressed together prayerfully before his face. Then he asked, "Did you receive any financial remuneration from Omnitech Corporation?"

Jesse grinned at him. "Not one penny."

"Did you ask for compensation?"

"No. Why should I?"

"Again I ask," Arthur called from his seat on the front bench, "what does this have to do with the scientific facts?"

Jesse turned in his chair to see his brother. Arthur was clearly angry, his face a storm cloud. "Does it really change the scientific data if someone was paid by Omnitech or not? Are you implying that the scientists who worked on this program biased their results according to who signed their paychecks? That's monstrous!"

Graves reached for his gavel, a pained look on his face. Rosen gave Arthur a wintry smile.

"Dr. Marshak," said the examiner, "you are the one who has used the word 'biased,' not I."

"If you're implying that my staff people deliberately altered their research results to suit some corporate objective, I'll sue you for libel!"

Jesse had never seen Arthur so boiled. He almost laughed out loud; Arby never let his emotions show like this. Rosen must really be getting to him.

The chief judge was pointing his gavel at Arthur, saying, "This is not the proper forum for such an outburst!"

Arthur got his feet. "This isn't the proper forum for smearing honest, dedicated scientists!"

"Dr. Marshak, sit down and be quiet!" Graves screeched.

"I will when you instruct that inquisitor to stop maligning my staff scientists!"

Rosen, still in his chair, raised both his hands, palms outward. "I assure you, Dr. Marshak, that I have no desire to malign anyone."

"Then retract your insinuation," Arthur snapped.

"I made no insinuation. I merely asked if your brother received any compensation from Omnitech. If you like, we can have the clerk read it back from the transcript."

"The implication was clear," Arthur said. But he sat down.

Jesse turned back toward the judges and the examiner. Wow! he thought. Arby's going to pop his cork before this is over.

ARTHUR

I stood at the big picture window of my living room with my morning mug of coffee warming my hands and watched Nancy back her red Taurus out of the driveway. Heading toward the corporate headquarters in Manhattan, I surmised. Probably she'll stop at her apartment first and change into fresh clothes. I didn't know and didn't care.

Nancy had awakened early, all smiles, and pranced off to the shower with barely a good morning. I had gotten out of bed, pulled on my robe, pissed in the guest bedroom's toilet, and gone to the kitchen to grind some coffee beans.

"I'll get breakfast in town," Nancy told me, declining even a cup of fresh-brewed coffee. She swept out of the house with nothing more than a peck on my cheek.

But she whispered into my ear, "It was wonderful. See you next Monday night."

And I felt my heart sink.

As I stood by the window and watched her Taurus disappear behind the hedges of the front lawn, I wondered if the price of Nancy's information wasn't going to be too high. I didn't mind helping her to get the advancement she wanted. But I shuddered at the thought of having a regular Monday night date with her. Or anyone. Like paying the rent on the first of the month. Too cold-blooded. It becomes an obligation. A business deal.

Well, I asked myself, that's what you set up, isn't it? A business deal. She tells you what you need to know and you help her move up the corporate ladder. The fucking is just there to clinch the transaction, like the signatures on a contract.

In blood, I thought. She's going to be more trouble than she's worth. I could feel it in my bones.

As I showered and shaved and dressed, I wondered what I should do about this Japanese deal now that I knew about it. Confront Johnston? Find out who Johnston was talking to and go to Japan to see them personally? Find my own buyer for the lab?

Maybe I should just barge into Johnston's office and ask him what the hell he was doing. It might bounce back to Nancy, but why should I care about that? Could be the best way to get her off my neck.

I wanted to be angry with Johnston, sore at him for even thinking of selling off the lab. But I couldn't work up the emotion. Johnston had saved my life, back when Potter had driven me out of Columbia, out of academia. I owed Johnston a lot.

I started thinking back to the first time I had met W. Christian Johnston, nearly fifteen years earlier, at a fund-raising party at Columbia one snowy January evening.

It had been a tepid affair, at best. Weak punch and thin finger sandwiches. Not much to offer the university's big money people, I thought as I looked around the darkly paneled old room. Nobody under sixty except me. All gray heads. I should talk. My hair was already silver.

There was only one black man in the room, a big man, physically. And he must have been big in the wallet, too, I saw from the way the president and other university officers were clustered around him.

Wilson K. Potter, my department chairman, came out of the crowd around the black man and made his way through the gathering directly toward me. Even back then Potter was nothing more than a pinch-faced bald little gnome who hadn't changed his teaching plan since he had achieved tenure ages ago.

"There's someone that the president wants you to meet," Potter told me. The expression on his face was even more rancid than usual, as if this was a distasteful duty. "He's the new CEO of Omnitech Corporation."

Johnston behaved like a salesman at first, all toothy smiles and his voice too loud. He insisted on being called "just Johnston. That's all. No Mister or anything. Just Johnston. With the tee."

He doesn't want to be called Chris, I figured. And whatever his first name is, he must hate it.

The crowd slowly melted away, until Johnston and I found ourselves alone in a corner of the room. Through the narrow mullioned window we could see the snow floating softly through the lights of the streetlamps outside.

"I hear you have some very practical ideas about genetic engineering," Johnston said, his voice much lower than before.

"My brother and I have played around with a few things," I replied.

"Bugs that eat oil spills?"

He knew all about that, I was certain. "I think your company is already using some of our ideas."

"Yes, we are."

I made a rueful smile. "So we get the credit in academia for the work and companies like yours make the money out of it."

"What are you working on now?"

"Toxic wastes."

That made his eyes widen. "A bug that eats toxic wastes?"

"Several different strains, yes."

"In landfills?"

"In landfills. Or wherever."

Johnston made a soft whistle between his teeth. "That could be worth a lot of money, Dr. Marshak. A *lot* of money."

"To Omnitech."

"To whoever owns the patent on the bug."

Now my eyes widened. Of course! I told myself. If I could get the university to grant me the rights to the patent . . .

"Omnitech will pay very handsomely for a license to produce and sell your bug," said Johnston, his voice even lower. Then he grinned and added, "Providing it works, of course."

But my excitement ebbed as quickly as it had peaked. "I imagine the university will want the patent."

Johnston gave me a sly smile. "We can work out a deal. They're after me to make a big contribution. I'll get them to assign the patent rights to you. Then you license the rights to Omnitech and Omnitech puts up the money for the new gym or library or whatever they're after me for. Everybody gets happy."

My relationship with Johnston has truly been happy ever since that snowy evening, I realized. If it hadn't been for Potter, I could have stayed at Columbia and licensed Omnitech to develop whatever I invented and I never would have had to get involved in corporate politics. But Potter put an end to that. Potter and his academic politics.

I should have stayed and fought. I should have demanded that Potter resign. Or retire. But that would have caused more damage to the university than I could deal with. And inevitably I would have been blamed for breaking the collegial code of brotherhood. Funny how they only threw that collegial crap at you when they knew they were in the wrong and had no other defense. No, there were plenty of older men and women on the faculty who would have sided with Potter. They considered me a young upstart. They were furious that some of us were getting rich while they still toiled along at academic salaries. Even some of the other Jews on the faculty were sore at me.

I let Potter win. I was so shocked and shattered by his hatred that I just walked out of his office and spent the whole Christmas break that year wondering what I could do, where I could go.

It was Phyllis who set me straight. She was a departmental secretary in those days, mother-henning all of us young snot-nosed assistant professors. By the time I showed up in my cubbyhole of an office in January she had heard the whole story. I was on the way out.

"You and that nice Mr. Johnston from Omnitech seem to get along so well," she said as she poured coffee for me. "Why don't you see if he'll take you in?"

"I don't want a job," I told her, "I want a laboratory. With a staff of my own."

"So?" And Phyllis left me at my cluttered desk, wondering if she knew more about this than I did.

So I bit the bullet and called Johnston and asked him if Omnitech would set up a laboratory for me.

"Not just any lab," I told him. "I want it to be the best research center in the world. I want to bring in the best and the brightest young scientists we can recruit."

Even over the phone he sounded intrigued. "To do what, Arthur?"

"I've got some ideas about cancer," I said.

"Patentable ideas?"

I didn't hesitate even a fraction of a second. "Yes," I said, even though I knew the university would claim the patents for the work I had done so far. The hell with them. Let them have everything I'd done to date. I'd do more. Better.

"We've never gone into the medical field," Johnston said.

"Pharmaceuticals are a multibillion-dollar business," I said.

"Yeah, I know. But it's a crowded field, Arthur. And the goddamned government's got its big boots all over it."

Wishing he were in the office with me so I could calibrate the expression on his face, I answered, "Cancer is a major killer. That makes it a major market."

He didn't reply for several moments. Then, "Both my parents died of cancer."

"And it'll come calling on both of us, one of these days."

"Let me see what I can do," Johnston said.

It took him a couple of weeks to get the idea past his board of directors, a couple of weeks while I cleaned out my office at Columbia and wondered where my next meals would be coming from. I knew that Potter would do his best to black-ball me throughout the academic community. I began to think about going to Europe or maybe Israel.

Then Johnston phoned me, in my apartment in Washington Heights.

"Would you mind working in Connecticut?"

He not only let me set up Grenford Laboratory and hire the staff I wanted, he even made me a corporate vice president in the bargain.

"Be good to let the board of directors see you," Johnston told me. "Get yourself some clout with them."

I owed him my life.

But how could he sell me off? I asked myself for the ninetieth time that morning. Like some has-been baseball player.

I went down to the garage and slid behind the steering wheel of my Infiniti, ready to start out for the day's work. But I still had no idea of how to handle the problem, how to deal with the information that Nancy had fed me. How to face W. Christian Johnston with the knowledge that this man I owed so much to was ready to stab me in the back.

JESSE

I woke with a start. Somebody was in the tent, touching my shoulder.

"Wha—"

"Sshh." Somebody was bending over me. I couldn't make out the man's face in the darkness. "No need to wake up your wife," he whispered. It was Eberly. "Come outside."

I scrambled out of my cot and followed the Canadian out through the mosquito netting and the tent flap, wondering what the hell he wanted with me this early in the morning. A duel at sunrise, maybe?

Eberly was fully dressed. It was almost dawn, gray and chilly, no stars left in the pale sky.

"There may be some trouble," he said. His youthful face was very serious. I saw that he had a pistol strapped to his hip.

"Shooting trouble?"

"I hope it doesn't come to that. A group of bandits has come down from the hills. They want our food supplies, I imagine. Poor devils must be desperate."

"What are you going to do?"

"I've radioed to Massawa for support. They'll send helicopters."

"How soon?"

Eberly looked off toward the hills, eyes narrowed. "A few hours, at best."

"What do you do till then?"

"Talk to their chief, I suppose. Or fight. It's really up to them."

"How many of them are there?"

"Hard to say. I suppose they've got RPGs. That's what worries me."

"RPGs?"

"Rocket-propelled grenades. Antitank weapons, actually, but they make pretty effective short-range artillery."

"Jesus!"

"I doubt that they'll do any shelling, though. If it's the food they're after they wouldn't want to blow it up."

"What's going on?"

We both turned to see Julia stepping through the tent flap, still in the khaki fatigues she slept in, her face pale, her hair pulled back and tied into a ponytail, her eyes blinking sleep away.

"Trouble," I said. I realized I was wearing striped boxer shorts and an undershirt. It made me feel slightly ridiculous.

"There may be some shooting," Eberly said. "The two of you had better get into the church. It's the safest place."

"What about the others?"

"We'll get the women and children into the church. As many as we can."

"Perhaps we should set up a dressing station," Julia said.

Eberly nodded. I was thinking that I didn't come here to be in the middle of a firefight.

The church was already jammed by the time we got to it.

Women and children, and a good many men, too, I could see. Crippled, mutilated by earlier fighting. Huddled and silent, staring at their own fear with wide, frightened eyes. The smell of them was enough to turn my stomach, almost. I had never been bothered by their smell before, out in the open air. But packed inside the four thick walls of the church it was overpowering. Like being pushed inside an overripe garbage bag.

Human garbage, that's what they were. The unwanted leftovers of humanity. Black, poor, starved, maimed, sick, and now some band of thugs was going to start shooting up the place.

Not much of a shelter, I thought as I looked around the crumbling church. The walls were thick, true enough, but already cracked from earlier shellings. Half the roof was gone and the front wall, where the altar was, had a wide-open hole in it where a big window used to be. Sunlight streamed through, onto the altar that we were turning into a surgical table.

Julia and I and the six nurses set up a dressing station at the altar. The silence in the church was eerie. More than a hundred people packed in here and nobody's saying a word. Like they're children; they think if they can be quiet nobody will know they're here. Pull the covers over your head and the night monsters won't know you're in the bed.

Some of them were moaning, of course. Couldn't help themselves. The UN soldiers had dragged the bedridden cases into the church. But even their groans and whimpering cries were muffled down to a soft background hum.

"Nothing to do but wait," Julia said as we stood by the white-sheeted altar table. She spoke in a near-whisper.

"Maybe it'll all blow over," I said. "Even starving bandits ought to know better than to mess around with the UN troops."

A rattling sound, like the distant popping of firecrackers.

"Is that gunfire?"

An explosion off in the distance.

Julia ran to one of the empty windows. I raced after her and pulled her back. "Don't! Stay down."

"It's too far away to be dangerous," Julia said. But she didn't try to get out of my arms.

"Who made you an expert on battlefield matters?"

Then silence. Feeling kind of sheepish, I edged to the long narrow window and looked out. One of the white UN armored cars was moving across the barren landscape about a mile away, its diesel engine growling and sending up spurts of black sooty smoke. Another was moving, too, farther away, barely discernible except for the spray of dust it kicked up.

Julia pressed against my back and peeped over my shoulder. "Is it all over?"

"I hope—"

The nearer armored car exploded in a red fireball. I felt as if I'd been punched in the gut. All kinds of firing broke loose, guns popping everywhere, smoke and dust rising like a pall. Another explosion, smaller, farther away. And then a third, even more distant. The armored car was burning. I could see men staggering out of its rear hatch, stumbling and collapsing onto the ground. Even at this distance I could see that they were black with burns.

"My lord in heaven," Julia murmured.

As abruptly as it had started the firing stopped. The other armored car chugged over a bare little rise and I could no longer see it.

Christ, what do we do if they kill Eberly and the other troops? Where the hell can we hide? What if those bastards come into the camp and they see Julia? What the hell can I do? There's no place to run to.

The people in the church were whispering now. I turned and saw that they were clutching fearfully at each other, whispering in hissing sibilances. Prayers, maybe. Or curses. Most of them had their eyes squeezed shut. They were just as scared as I was.

"Those men out there . . ." Julia was still staring out the window.

"Not yet. It's not safe out there."

"But they're hurt."

"It won't do them any good if we get our asses shot off."

Julia started to reply, thought better of it.

The other armored car came back into view, thank god. It stopped at the wreck of its mate. Men hopped out and began to tenderly pick up their wounded comrades.

"Looks like it's over," I said. "They're bringing the wounded in."

The tension inside the church broke visibly. The crowd swayed, sat up straighter, released their death holds on one another. People began to talk. A baby squalled. I felt my own breath come back to me; I sucked in a big lungful of the fetid air. Nearly gagged on it. Julia smiled worriedly at me.

Within a few minutes the armored car clattered to the church door and the Pakistani soldiers gently carried their blackened, burned comrades through the crowd up to the altar. The Eritreans made a path for them like the Red Sea parting for Moses.

Then I fell into my work, the one thing I knew how to do, treating burns and shrapnel wounds, cutting away blackened flesh and digging out sharp-edged chunks of metal, sewing up jagged torn meat, stapling arteries together, bandaging bloody arms and legs and chests and heads. I'm not much of a surgeon but I was all they had. I had to amputate one leg. Had to tell one of the soldiers, through his sergeant who spoke English, that he had lost one of his eyes permanently.

By the time I was finished, the sun was high overhead, blazing through the shattered roof of the church. My T-shirt and slacks were stiff with drying blood. My hands ached and the back of my neck throbbed painfully. Julia was also blood-spattered, somber.

Then we heard helicopters thrumming overhead, coming in low and fast, heading for the distant hills.

Stretching tiredly as the last of the wounded was carried off, I slid one arm around Julia's shoulders and we made our way out of the now-empty church. It was hard to tell who was propping up who.

Eberly was standing out there, binoculars to his eyes. I saw the helicopters off in the distance, angry white hornets buzzing through the blazing afternoon sky.

The Canadian put his field glasses down and said, "The choppers will pound them. They'll pay for what they did."

The captain was quivering as if he had drunk six pots of coffee. "Bloody-minded bastards didn't want to talk, all they wanted was to fight. Well, we showed them some fighting. We showed them, all right. They got one of our cars but we shot the bloody hell out of them. And now the choppers will blast them but good."

"Was anyone killed?" Julia asked quietly.

Eberly sobered a bit. "Two. The driver of the armored car that got hit and one of the riflemen."

"What about their side?" I suddenly realized that we had treated no wounded Eritreans.

"We killed sixteen of them."

"No wounded?"

Eberly looked away from us. "The Pakis don't take wounded, not once some of their own have been killed. Can't say I blame them."

I just stared at the captain. This was the kind, courteous, charming young swain who had been so attentive to Julia. Fire a few shots and he's a homicidal maniac!

But Julia said, "I'm glad it wasn't your armored car that got hit."

Eberly suddenly looked embarrassed. "I am, too," he said softly.

JULIA

Eritrea was a mistake. I had miscalculated terribly in my plans to raise Jesse's reputation. It changed Jesse. I doubt that anyone could see that except me, but I realized it within a few days of our landing at the UN station.

He seemed almost dazed by the poverty and hunger we found there. I wasn't very much help to him, at first, because

I came down with a tropical fever almost the minute we landed there. He was so solicitous, so worried about me, it would have been touching if I hadn't felt guilty that he was spending more time with me than with his real patients.

He became very moody, tired all the time. He even seemed to lose interest in sex, which worried me terribly. Not that I was such a ravishing desirable love goddess; I lost more than ten pounds to the fever and must have looked rather bedraggled most of the time. But Jesse was simply too weary to be interested, and I became convinced that his weariness was in the soul, more than physical.

I realized that I had pushed him too far. He worked night and day with the poor in New York, and then I had urged him to go to Brazil as part of a UNESCO team to teach the latest medical practices to young Indian men and women from the villages in the Mato Grosso. At least we had been quartered in Brasília then, a reasonable city, the national capital. The politicians and lawyers made certain that they lived in comfort.

But in that dusty flyblown UN camp in Eritrea my husband was driving himself to physical and emotional exhaustion with overwork and some strange illness of the soul that I couldn't fathom at first.

I thought it might be a more subtle form of the fever that had knocked me down, or perhaps some kind of parasite eating away inside him. But it was neither, as it turned out. Thank heavens.

I was actually almost glad when he began casting suspicious scowls at Captain Eberly. It showed that he still cared about me, but more importantly it showed that he still cared about himself. There was nothing going on between the captain and me, of course. Eberly was a solicitous young man, well behaved in every respect. He had an incredibly difficult job on his hands, protecting this field hospital with its wretched accumulation of human detritus from marauding bands of murderous thieves. I admired his courage and his coolness under fire.

But by the time I was feeling almost normal again, Jesse was virtually growling at Eberly whenever the captain came near me. We usually ate together at the end of the day, although Jesse was barely picking at his food and losing weight alarmingly.

"You're overworking yourself, darling," I said to him one evening as we sat down to dinner. I must admit, the prepackaged rations the UN provided did not give much stimulation to one's appetite.

"Tell them," Jesse mumbled, pointing with a plastic fork toward the tent village on the other side of the falling-down church.

Captain Eberly said earnestly, "It won't do them any good if you collapse from exhaustion, you know."

Jesse glared at him. "I'm here to help those people. You do your job and let me do mine."

Eberly looked rather shocked. We lapsed into an uncomfortable silence.

I decided to bring the matter to a more reasonable resolution. "Perhaps, darling, you could set regular hours for examining patients. Then you could have a little time to rest, get your strength back—"

"My office hours are from sunup to sundown," he snapped at me. "As long as there's enough light to see by, I'll do what I can for them. If we had some decent electric lights I'd work nights, too."

"But you can't work all the time," I said.

"And what about them?" He pointed again, his voice shaking. "Do you expect me to take walks with you or sit down and listen to a BBC concert while they're standing there bleeding and dying?"

"Of course not," I said. Eberly remained silent, watching us, his eyes shifting back and forth.

"So what am I supposed to do?" Jesse asked. "Just let them die?"

"You can't help all of them," I said, as reasonably as I could. "It simply isn't possible, dear. I know you want to, but it's not physically possible to take care of them all."

"Then I'll take care of as many of them as I can. As long

as there's enough light to see by and I can stand on my two feet, I'll take care of as many of them as I can."

I had been an utter fool, pushing Jesse into this horrible situation. It had sounded so noble and right, back in New York. Help the poor starving Africans. Volunteer to work for the UN. It was the right thing for the Humanitarian of the Year to do. It would look good in media interviews; it would help bring in donations to the hospital and medical center. But I realized that I didn't care about the Africans or the UN or anything else. What did they matter to me, compared to my husband? I had pushed Jesse too far; he was close to cracking.

I had created the problem; I would have to help solve it. "You're right, of course," I said. "I should have seen that from the outset. Very well, then, I'll help you."

Eberly's brows shot up.

"I've had some training in first aid," I said, rather haughtily, actually. "I'll stand beside you, darling, and do as much as I can."

"I didn't mean that you—"

"No, no, you're quite right. The problem is overwhelming and we must all do whatever we can to help. I shouldn't be sitting around like a pampered princess. The captain has his work to do and you have yours. I'll help you in whatever way I can."

Jesse smiled at me weakly. "You really are something, aren't you?"

"I'm your wife, darling, and I've been terribly stupid about this entire mission. There's more than enough work for the two of us, and from now on I intend to do my share."

It was very hard work. The worst part of it was the endless hopelessness of it all. Of course, it was physically punishing to be attending to patient after patient, hour after hour, all day long in that exhausting, smothering heat. But the emotional drain was even worse. No matter how long we worked, the line was always there, always longer, it seemed. I began to pray for sunset by the middle of the day, pleading with a god I didn't believe in to hurry the darkness so we could drag ourselves back to our tents.

Day after day we worked in the blazing heat. At night we barely ate a thing, then crawled into our cots for a few pitiful hours of sleep.

I began to hate those sick, starving people who needed so much from us. It wasn't their fault, I knew, but still I felt as if they were sucking the life out of us, draining us, bleeding us dry. No matter how much we did for them there was always more to be done.

But after several weeks of this, one night Jesse pushed his cot next to mine and then, in the darkness, began fumbling with the buttons of my shirt.

Surprised, I whispered, "Are you going to examine me, Doctor?"

"Thoroughly," he said.

We giggled like a pair of teenagers and I felt a tremendous surge of relief gust through me. I knew Jesse was going to be all right. Despite it all, he would be all right.

WASHINGTON:

DIRKSON SENATE OFFICE BUILDING

Franklin J. W. Kindelberger had been a senator long enough to stop wincing at the fact that his office was in one of the buildings known as an S.O.B.

He sat relaxed in the small conference room that was part of his suite of offices, long legs stretched out across the carpeting and a heavy cut-crystal glass of bourbon on the rocks in one massive hand. He had the lanky build of a cowboy, big bones and long limbs, but his eyes were slitted, evasive, with the slightly crafty look of a banker or insurance salesman. He combed his thinning hair forward over his receding hairline. For years he had wanted to grow a beard, but thought it would lose votes, especially among the women. By now it would probably come in all gray, he told himself wistfully.

Kindelberger was relaxing with his three key aides after a tedious morning of meeting constituents and making promises. Most of the others on his staff had gone downstairs for lunch. Kindelberger was skipping lunch, except for his usual bourbon. He sat with his three aides on the comfortable leather chairs in the conference room, watching C-SPAN as a fellow senator made a long and boring speech to the empty senate chamber. Only Kindelberger was drinking.

"This is a waste of time," he muttered. "She's making an idiot of herself."

"Plays well back home," said Laureen Jarvis, the senator's chief of staff. She was in her early thirties, round-faced and slightly plump.

Kerry Tate shook his bald head. "They show the empty chamber. Anybody can see she's talking to herself."

"It still goes into the record," Jarvis insisted.

"Let's get something else on," Kindelberger insisted.

Ed Bloomfield held the remote control. The most brilliant manipulator of demographic data on Capitol Hill, he was grossly overweight, asthmatic, pasty-looking from spending every possible moment indoors, preferably in front of a computer screen. He clicked away until *Headline News* came on the screen.

"Aw, hell," groaned Tate, "we've seen the financial report three times this morning. It's not going to change." Tate was the senator's chief political advisor, the most trusted person in the room, the one who had been with Kindelberger from his beginnings as a hungry lawyer in Pocatello. Tate had been bald and nervous even back then.

"I wanna see the latest stock market numbers," Bloomfield mumbled, his eyes on the screen.

"They might have more on the riot," Jarvis said.

"Riot?" Kindelberger asked. "Where?"

"Right here," said Tate. "In front of the Capitol."

"When?"

"Yesterday afternoon."

Looking a little guilty, Kindelberger said, "I must've missed it. Didn't see the news last night."

"Picture on page one of the *Post* this morning," Tate said.

"Didn't get a chance to see the paper, either," the senator muttered defensively.

They had to wait until the end of the half hour, after the sports report. The Colorado Rockies had lost to the Cincinnati Reds after beating them two straight. "Broke their winning streak," Bloomfield quipped.

Then came the footage of the scuffle between the wheelchair-bound paraplegics and the sign-bearing religious picketers. Kindelberger muttered, "Bunch of nuts," but it was not clear which side he meant. Reverend Simmonds appeared on the screen briefly, his eyes piercing beneath their shaggy brows.

"These godless scientists must be stopped before they destroy us all," he intoned. "We must draw the line here and now."

Kindelberger nodded.

The coverage went on to show Arthur Marshak's stormy testimony and his threat to walk out of the hearing.

"What hearing is that?" the senator asked. "I don't recognize anybody there."

Jarvis said, "It's not a regular hearing. It's that science court thing."

The news report ended and commercials came on. Bloomfield muted the sound.

"It's getting a lot of people worked up," said the senator.

"A few religious zealots," Tate scoffed. "And some motorcycle thugs."

"It's more than that," said Bloomfield. He always sounded breathless, as if each word were an effort.

"What do you mean?"

"This could be bigger than abortion rights." He sucked in air noisily. "They're talking about growing a new heart inside you . . . when your old one starts to fail." Bloomfield sank back into his leather chair, mouth hanging open from the exertion of talking.

Laureen Jarvis took over. "The scientists think they can grow new organs inside your body when you need them. Regenerate amputated limbs, stuff like that."

Kindelberger grunted thoughtfully. "Can they grow new hair?"

Everyone laughed, except Tate.

"Is there something in here for me?" the senator asked.

Bloomfield raised a hand and ticked off his fat fingers. "Religious vote. Senior citizens. Stem cells. Abortion rights. Insurance industry. Birth defects. Health care."

"Which adds up to the women's vote," Jarvis added.

"And no two of them on the same side," grumbled Tate.

"What's AARP say about this?"

Jarvis shrugged. "They haven't come out with a position yet."

"Nobody has," said Bloomfield. "Too early."

"I've never seen people so worked up about scientific research," Kindelberger said.

"Stay out of it," Tate snapped.

The senator gave him a quizzical look. "You always say stay out of it, Kerry. Hell, you wanted me to stay out of the health insurance fight."

"You were lucky then."

"Maybe I could get lucky again," Kindelberger said. "After all, I am on the Human Resources Committee."

Tate shook his head vehemently. "This is a no-win situation, Franklin. If you go with the scientists the religious right will attack you as pro-abortion. If you go against the scientists the AARP will crucify you. And who the hell knows which way the insurance and medical lobbies will jump? They don't know themselves, yet."

"Stem cells are a trigger issue," Bloomfield said. "Gets everybody hot, one way or the other."

Kindelberger slumped back in his seat and took another

sip of his bourbon. The room fell silent. The news was back on the television, but it was still muted.

"I've got to face that sonofabitch Maklin next November," Kindelberger muttered. "And he's got the governor behind him."

"All the more reason to avoid slitting your throat over this issue," warned Tate.

"Good TV coverage," Bloomfield suggested. "Better than speeches on C-SPAN."

Tate scowled at him.

"Suppose he just sits in on the hearings?" Jarvis suggested, pushing back a stray lock of hair that had fallen over her face. "As an interested member of the Senate. A concerned senator."

"Yeah!" Kindelberger brightened. "I wouldn't have to take a stand, just say I'm there to see for myself what this is all about. I'll look smart and be on TV."

"If they continue to cover the hearings," Tate pointed out. "The TV crews were there yesterday only because it was the first day. Nobody expected the demonstrators."

"This Dr. Marshak," said Jarvis, "the guy who threatened to walk out of the hearing. He looks like good TV material to me."

Kindelberger shrugged. "We could check and see if the demonstrators intend to keep it up. Get in touch with that reverend."

"We could make certain the networks know that the senator will sit in on the hearing," Jarvis said. "That will guarantee news coverage, at least for the first day you show up."

"Right. And if they stop covering the hearings I'll stop attending."

Tate still glowered, unconvinced.

"It'll give us some time on the tube that we wouldn't get otherwise," Jarvis urged.

"Make him look like he's on top of a coming issue," Bloomfield agreed.

Very reluctantly, Tate said, "Maybe you're right. Maybe it could be a plus."

"So set it up for me, Laureen," said the senator eagerly.

"But don't say anything at the hearing," Tate insisted. "Don't you open your mouth."

Kindelberger grinned at him. "I'll be quiet as a li'l ol' mouse." Then he added, "In the meantime, get ahold of that guy Simmonds for me."

ARTHUR

In the months after I first learned that Johnston was negotiating to sell off Grenford Laboratory to the Japanese, I couldn't seem to decide what to do about it. I toyed with the idea of visiting Japan and meeting the people who were attempting to buy the lab, but I hadn't been able to work up enough enthusiasm for the idea to actually put it into motion. Neither had I braced Johnston with the fact that I knew what was in the wind.

I procrastinated. I put off any decisive action because I truly couldn't decide which course of action might be best. I saw Johnston regularly, but the CEO gave me no hint that the lab was on the block. I saw Nancy Dubois almost every Monday evening, and—despite everything—we spent most of those Monday nights in bed. She was acting as if she expected it; she wasn't going to let loose of me until she got the promotion she was after. If then.

Indecision ruled my life for months, and I hated it. I felt testy, tense all the time. I've got to find a way through all this, I told myself constantly. Yet the weeks drifted past, one after another. Even my fencing fell off; I wasn't good enough to make the tournaments and for the first time since I had taken up the sport I really didn't care.

All that time, the scientific work went extremely well. Darrell Walters acted like a gangling paterfamilias over an enthusiastic research team that included Vince Andriotti, Zack O'Neill, and several of the younger staffers.

O'Neill was doing especially spectacular work then. If he had been at a university he would be heading for a Nobel Prize. He took the existing work on stem cells and carried it further, engineering a family of peptides that he playfully dubbed "regentides." Properly inserted into a somatic cell, the regentides could lock onto the cell's DNA and alter gene expression by binding both to key repressor genes and to the enzymes that control the regulatory genes. The cells actually reproduced almost the way they did in the womb. In effect, he was able to regress normal body cells so that they became pluripotent, like adult stem cells.

We were on the right track. Zack was already starting to plan experiments to use his regentides to regenerate specific organs instead of merely making cells multiply in a culture dish.

While all this was going on, I received a phone call from Jesse. Phyllis came to the door of my office with a big grin on her face and told me to pick up the phone.

"Hi, Arby!" he said brightly. "How's it going?"

"Jesse!" I almost jumped out of my chair. "Where are you?"

"London. We're on our way home."

I felt a huge surge of relief that Jess and Julia had made it safely through that pesthole. "How are you? How's Julia?"

"Julia's pregnant!" The joy in my brother's voice came bubbling through the phone connection.

It felt like a shock in the pit of my stomach. "That's wonderful," I managed to say. "Congratulations."

"You have no idea what an achievement it was," Jesse prattled on, "doing it on Army cots and all that."

"What's it going to be," I forced myself to ask, "a boy or a girl?"

"Too early to tell. We just arrived in London last night and confirmed it this morning. We'll wait until we get back to the States for a sonogram."

"Julia's all right?"

"She's terrific!"

"And you're in good health? You didn't catch anything while you were in the bush?"

"Naw, I'm fine, Arby. Couldn't be better. Lost a few pounds, that's all. A couple of English trifles and I'll be right back where I was."

"When will you be back home?"

"Don't know yet. We're going to hang out here in London a couple days, relax, get used to civilization again. I'll give you a call."

"Have you called Momma?"

"Not yet. Can you give her a ring for me?"

Telephone calls to Momma were difficult, of course. She needed a nurse there to hold the phone and speak the words she tapped out on her keyboard.

"I'll run up and see her," I said tightly.

"How is she?"

"About the same. She'll be happy to hear about Julia."

"Yep. She's going to be a grandma after all."

It almost made me smile. "Yes, that's right, isn't it?"

"Gotta run now, Arby. See you soon."

"Wait!" I almost shouted. "When will you be back here? When can you come up to the lab and see the progress we've made?"

"Progress?"

"On the regeneration work."

"Oh, that."

"We've developed a set of peptides that can regress cells to their pluripotent state," I told him. "Differentiated cells like bone or muscle start to reproduce just like they did when they were in the zygote stage."

"You can make somatic cells reproduce?"

"Like they do in the womb," I said.

"In vivo?"

"No, in a culture dish. But we're starting to plan experiments to reproduce specific organs in vitro. Then we'll go on to actual animal experiments."

"Not bad," was all that Jesse would say.

"I want you to be part of this, Jesse," I said. "It's your idea as much as mine. We could use your expertise on this."

He laughed carelessly. "Like I don't have enough to do."

"Well, if you're going to be a father, it wouldn't hurt to have a consulting fee coming to you, would it?"

That made him think, at least for a moment or so. "No, I suppose it wouldn't hurt, at that. But where would I get the time to come up there and work with your people?"

I waved a hand in the air. "We'll figure that out once you get back. But I want you working with me on this, Jesse. I really do."

"Okay," he said. "We'll talk about it when I get back."

"Fine," I said.

For a long while after Jesse hung up I sat at my desk, thinking. Not about Jesse's coming to work with us at the lab. About Julia's pregnancy. With his baby. And I had to go down to Sunny Glade and tell Momma about it.

I don't know how long I sat there, staring at nothing, my thoughts spinning. Julia had conceived a baby with Jess. He sounded so goddamned happy about it. She let him do it to her. She wanted him. She'd been doing with him all the things we had done together. All the—

Phyllis buzzed on the intercom. I shook my head, trying to clear it of the images that I was seeing.

I pressed the intercom switch. "What?"

"Cassie wanted to see you before she left."

I pulled in a deep breath. "Okay. Now's as good a time as any."

Within minutes Cassie showed up at my office door, her face sallow, her eyes sad, as if she were going to a funeral. She looked like I felt. She was wearing a long-skirted maroon dress instead of her usual jeans.

"Cassie, come on in." Putting on a smiling front, I waved her into the office. "You look wonderful." In truth she looked on the verge of tears.

She perched on the edge of the cushioned chair in front of my desk. "I'm going to the airport this afternoon. The field trials."

"You'll love Mexico," I said as heartily as I could manage. "Especially once you're outside Mexico City. The pollution there is pretty bad, but the countryside is beautiful."

"I'm worried about Max," she said.

"Max will get along fine. It's only a few months."

Cassie sniffled. "He doesn't want me to go."

I sighed inwardly. "Cassie, we'll take good care of him. We've got all your instructions about his diet and his exercise and everything, right?"

"I don't want him used in any experiments."

"We have no plans for that. I've told you a dozen times."

"Zack is already talking about animal experiments for the regeneration work."

"That's on lab rats, Cassie. You know that. You'll be back long before we're ready for monkey work, let alone the chimps."

"I don't want anybody touching Max."

I forced a smile. "What do you want from me, Cassie? A written promise? In blood? Will that do?"

She hesitated, obviously struggling within herself. "I trust you," she said at last. But it didn't sound convincing.

"Good." I got up from my chair and came around the desk. "Good. I'll personally look in on Max every day, if that'll make you happy."

She got to her feet. "I'd appreciate it."

"Then that's what I'll do." I put my arm around her skinny shoulders and walked her to the door. "Now you go to Mexico and do the field trials and don't worry about a thing here."

She looked up at me with those big solemn waif's eyes.

"And watch out for those Mexican caballeros," I joked, smiling. "They're very romantic, I hear."

She almost smiled back.

After Cassie left the outer office, I turned to Phyllis, who was watching the empty doorway with a thoughtful look on her face.

"Remind me to look in on Max once a day," I said.

Phyllis cocked a brow at me. "You gonna learn sign language, too?"

I shook my head wearily and went back into my office. I got a barely discernible whiff of peppermint. Phyllis's aromatherapy again: peppermint for pep. Sitting at my computer, I pulled up the latest written reports on the regeneration work. When in doubt, dive into the science. Do some useful work instead of letting your emotions drive you crazy. The computer file showed nothing but lab notes and fragments of commentary that would one day be incorporated in publishable papers. I'll have to get Darrell and Zack and the rest of them together and have them give me a complete rundown on where we stand, I told myself.

Long after darkness had fallen, I had the small group sitting in my office. Darrell Walters had commandeered the couch; Vince Andriotti was astride one of the conference table's chairs, sitting on it backwards, as usual, his chin on his hairy forearms.

Zack O'Neill was saying, "I don't see why we shouldn't go right into animal tests."

"Do in vitro first," said Darrell. "It's easier and we can avoid the complications of in vivo work."

O'Neill frowned. "Hell, what good is growing a rat's heart in a flask going to do us? We want to grow it inside the experimental subject, don't we?"

"Once we know we can grow it in a flask," Darrell countered. "Never add an experiment to an experiment, Zack. Pare down the unknowns and the risks."

Zack shook his head, obviously disappointed with such a conservative approach. He was all fired up, full of youthful piss and vinegar, certain that he was on the right track and ready to push the throttle all the way.

I said nothing, but I was thinking that we couldn't be the only research team working along these lines. I knew that several university labs were moving in the same general direction, to say nothing of other outfits overseas.

Andriotti piped up. "The computer simulation of the spinal neuron growth pattern is just about ready. Do we publish or not?"

"Not," I said. "Not yet."

"When?"

"After the patent application is filed."

"Then I better start talking to the lawyers," Andriotti said, in a tone that showed clear distaste.

"I'll handle that end of it," I said. "You prepare the documentation."

"Another six hundred pounds of paperwork," he grumbled.

O'Neill asked, "Once the computer simulation is finished, what do we do about it?"

"You mean, do we go to animal tests?"

"Right."

I looked around at my researchers. They all seemed agreed. "Animal tests, then," I said.

"What about funding?" Andriotti asked. "We start doing multiple animal tests—"

"On the spinal cord neurons?" Darrell asked, looking puzzled. "Or the organ regeneration?"

"Spinal neurons," said Zack.

"We can't keep using the IR&D number," Andriotti said. "The accounting people are already turning purple whenever I charge to it."

I knew that the internal research and development account was almost completely drained. I'll have to get a special appropriation from Johnston, I told myself. The prospect did not cheer me.

But then an idea struck me.

"Zack," I asked, "do you really think you could grow a new heart in a lab rat, based on what we know now?"

He didn't hesitate a microsecond. "Yes."

"How soon?"

Darrell started to protest, but I waved him down.

O'Neill turned thoughtful, then said, "Two, three weeks, maybe. Give me a month."

Swiveling my chair to face Darrell, I said, "I want to push ahead on this as hard and fast as we can."

"But—"

I told them, "I want to do a demonstration for Johnston. And Lowenstein."

Darrell's long face broke into a canny grin. "Oh-ho! Want to impress the money boys, do we?"

"You're damned right," I said.

But it was more than that. When I finally left the lab that night, I decided it was time to stop fumbling around and start a determined offensive. Sell my lab off to the Japanese, will they? Not if we make them think we're on the verge of the biggest breakthrough of the century. I grimaced in the darkness as I drove along the winding Fairfield County roads. I'll make the lab so goddamned important to them that they'll sell off their mothers before they touch my lab!

The problem was that I wasn't supposed to know about Johnston's dickering with the Japanese. It's impossible to fight a battle when you're not supposed to be aware that the battle is going on. To reveal what I knew would be to betray Nancy's confidence, which would poison a damned good source of information into the inner workings of the corporate office. I had to fight fire with fire; I had to use Nancy to smoke out Johnston and his offer to Japan.

I worried about that. Not that using Nancy troubled me; she was using me to get ahead on the corporate ladder, so what the hell? But exactly because our affair was based on our individual ambitions rather than passion, it was dangerous. She could be playing a double game: telling everything she finds out about me to Johnston. Or Lowenstein, more likely. I distrusted the corporate comptroller. Probably Sid was the one who was pushing Johnston to get rid of the lab, in the name of the almighty bottom line.

Perhaps because I was so guarded with her, making love with Nancy had become less exciting, almost a chore instead of a joy. Let's put it this way: I didn't get any great ideas during sex with her. But she seemed to expect a tumble in bed, as if it bound me to her. If she noticed that my performance had become routine, mechanical, she never mentioned it.

I've got to find a way to break off with her, I told myself as I pulled up on my driveway and reached for the garage door control on the panel over my head. I've got to end it with her. The garage door swung open smoothly and the light inside came on. But not yet, I figured. I've got to carry it on a little while longer.

The following Monday night I met Nancy at the fencing academy as usual and took her home with me. We shared a precooked dinner in front of the fireplace, then went to bed. I felt especially interested in her and we had a rousing good time.

"You've never visited the lab, have you?" I asked her as we lay side by side, warm and wet after sex.

"No," said Nancy drowsily.

"You really ought to. It's a fascinating place. Especially if you're going to move over to marketing. The lab is the key to the corporation's future."

"Then why is Johnston ready to sell it?" she asked, almost like a challenge.

I hesitated. Peering into the shadows of the darkened bedroom, I could barely make out Nancy's face on the pillows next to me.

"Johnston is making a mistake. A big one. What we're doing now at the lab will be worth billions, eventually. That's why the Japanese are interested in us, I'll bet."

That stirred her. She turned toward me and propped herself up on one elbow. "What are you talking about?"

"In a month or so we'll be regenerating hearts inside of living animals."

"Really?"

"Imagine what that could mean to the corporation."

"You're actually ready to do experiments on animals? So soon?"

"Yes. The work has been going extremely well."

"Does Johnston know about this?"

"Not yet," I said. "I'm going to tell him about it the next time I'm in the office. This is too hot to talk about over the phone. I want to get him in complete privacy."

"If news about this leaked out . . ." Nancy's voice drifted away into silence.

I knew what she was thinking. The effect on the price of Omnitech stock. If the stock goes up it makes it harder for the Europeans to mount their hostile takeover. We won't have to sell off the laboratory. The lab will be too important, too precious, to even consider selling it.

"I'm telling you about this," I said softly, almost whispering, "because I have a terrible fear that the Japanese might have a pipeline into the lab."

"A pipeline?"

"Or more likely into corporate headquarters. They know what we're doing, I think. And I think that's why they're prepared to buy the lab from Johnston."

Even in the darkness I could see her eyes widen. "Do you think that Johnston has been telling the Japs what you're doing?"

"I don't know," I replied honestly. Then I added, "But I'm afraid that somebody has been. I think there's a leak in corporate headquarters and the Japanese are benefiting from it."

Once I said it, I realized that it might even be true. I smiled in the darkness of the bedroom. Let's see how that goes over downtown.

JESSE

There've been times when I've had to wonder whether Arby has a heart inside him. Here I phone him, practically the instant we get to London, to tell him that I'm going to be a father and all he wants to talk about is his goddamned organ regeneration work.

I put the phone down and turned to Julia, standing on the other side of the bed, unpacking. We had come in late the previous night and spent the morning in an obstetrician's office getting Julia checked out.

We had splurged and taken a suite, very nice in a kind of stuffy, old-fashioned way. Cost an arm and a leg, but Julia got a pretty good discount through British Airways, so we could afford it, just about. What the hell, I thought, we were back in civilization after all those weeks in purgatory and London was Julia's town, after all, and she was going to have a baby and why shouldn't we celebrate a little? The hell with the cost!

It's true that most of my income was from the royalties on the patents that Arthur filed while he was at Columbia. He put my name on them alongside his because we worked on the ideas together. I deserved to be there; we were partners back in those days. My salary from the medical center was nominal, of course, and my income from the hospital was negative, when you figured out all the hours I put in. I wasn't hurting, financially, but then I didn't have all the corporate perks that Arthur did, like limousines and private jets and swanky condos in midtown. Of course, once he went to work for Omnitech, they got the patents, not us.

Anyway, I hung up the phone and said to Julia, "Arby says congratulations."

She looked up from her unpacking. "Is that all? You were on the phone for quite a while."

"He said I should phone Ma and tell her about the baby."

"Of course you should."

I tugged the biggest of my own suitcases up on the bed and opened it up. "Naw, telephoning Ma is sheer torture. We can go see her when we get back."

"But—"

"Arby can tell her about the baby."

Julia looked as if she wanted to say something, then thought better of it.

"He's offered me a consulting position with his lab," I told her. "Says we could use the money."

"Ah, that's what you were talking about when you said you wouldn't have the time."

"Yep." I started taking the slacks and jackets out of the suitcase. They all looked frayed, dusty, caked with the dirt and sweat of Eritrea. All of a sudden I had an urge to throw them all away and go out and buy a whole new wardrobe. In London, yet. That'd be terrific.

"Could you actually find the time to work with Arthur?" Julia was asking, very seriously.

"I don't see how."

"Perhaps instead of the time you put in at the medical center," she suggested.

"They couldn't get along without me," I said. It sounded arrogant, I guess, but it was true.

Julia pursed her lips for a moment, thinking. Then, "Why not arrange a consulting agreement between the medical center itself and Arthur's laboratory?"

"Between La Guardia and Grenford?"

"Yes, that way you could use the facilities at the center for whatever work you'll be doing for Arthur. It would save you going up to Connecticut every week, wouldn't it?"

I had to admit that she had something there. "If I could get Arthur to take on the center as a kind of subcontractor, have all the medical work concentrated there—it'd pump a lot of bucks into the center, that's for sure."

"It would help La Guardia and it would give Arthur a firm medical team to work with his researchers."

I dropped the clothes on the floor and went around the bed to grab Julia. "Forget about unpacking," I said. "Let's go out and see this town of yours."

She wrapped her arms around my neck and kissed me. "Yes, let me show you London." Then she added, "After we've finished the unpacking."

That was Julia. Always fun, but always practical. Me, I was wondering if we had enough left on our credit cards to buy a new wardrobe on Savile Row.

ARTHUR

Johnston arrived at the lab two days later. Just happened to be driving through, on his way to Boston, he claimed. As if he drove to Boston instead of flying in the corporate jet.

I kept a straight face and walked him straight down to Zack O'Neill's lab. I watched Johnston closely as I introduced him to Zack. The earring and semi-wild haircut didn't bother the CEO at all; he didn't even blink. Good.

Zack's lab was neat as a pin. He ran a pretty tidy operation, normally, but I had given orders to make certain his lab was especially gleaming on this day. Visitors seldom realize that a clean, shipshape lab is one in which little creative work is being done. A *working* lab looks frantic, haphazard, busy. So Zack's lab was sparkling. It was crammed with equipment, of course, so much so that there was barely room to walk between the benches. But everything was in its place, all the equipment shining as if it had never been used. One entire wall of the room was covered with cages for several dozen purebred laboratory rats.

Johnston's face twitched unhappily at the rats, who twitched their whiskers back at the CEO and stared at him with beady eyes through the wire doors of their cages.

"Don't like rats," Johnston said. "Saw plenty of 'em when I was a kid."

"These are purebred laboratory strains, made to order, genetically," I told him. "They won't hurt you."

"I still don't like 'em."

"Then you should have gone into biology," I said jovially. "You get to slaughter them by the thousands."

Zack O'Neill did not laugh at my little joke. He was smart enough to sense that something was going on between the CEO and me, though. I could see a cagey look in his eyes. He showed Johnston through his laboratory setup like a square-shouldered lieutenant briefing a visiting general. Zack seemed to enjoy the CEO's obvious aversion to the lab rats.

"This little fella here," O'Neill said, opening a cage labeled 3C278 and taking a trembling white ball of fur into his hands, "is going to have the honor of growing a second heart pretty soon."

"How soon?" Johnston asked, staying an arm's length away from O'Neill and the rat.

"About a month from now," I said. "Isn't that right, Zack?"

O'Neill nodded. "If things keep going as well as they have been."

Johnston made a toothy smile. "That's great. Just great." Then he headed for the door.

I patted O'Neill on the shoulder before following the CEO out of the lab. Zack grinned at me and returned 3C278 to its cage.

"I just don't like rats," Johnston mumbled as I caught up with him in the corridor. "Not even those tame ones." The man was almost shuddering.

"If everything goes right with the rats, we'll be able to move into minihogs and then monkeys," I told him.

"How soon?"

I waggled a hand. "That depends on a lot of factors."

The CEO stayed silent until we returned to my office. I could hear the gears whirring in his head. Once the door to my inner office was firmly shut, I opened the miniature bar behind my desk.

"You look as if you could use a medicinal drink," I said.

Johnston sat slumped in the leather chair in front of my desk. "Yeah. Bourbon, if you got it. Neat."

I poured two fingers of bourbon into a heavy shot glass, then a bit of sherry into a similar glass for myself. I never drink during the working day, but this was a special occasion.

The CEO took his down in one gulp.

"This could be big, Arthur," said Johnston, putting the empty glass on the edge of the desk. "It's almost scary."

"Will it help you fight the takeover?"

"Hell, yes! If you can really regrow organs in people, we'll be untouchable."

"I think we'll really be able to do it. The coming year should tell us whether it'll work or not."

Johnston seemed to relax slightly. "A year, huh?"

"I think so." I hesitated, then said, "I don't think we ought to be making any announcements until we're sure we're on the right track."

"Yeah, yeah. It's too soon to make any public announcements." Then he grinned a little. "But maybe we can juice up the rumor mill some."

I raised my brows.

"Wouldn't hurt to have a few rumors circulate around. Raise the stock a few points. Make people wonder."

"You know," I said, "even when we succeed with the various animal trials, we'll have to deal with the FDA and god knows how many other government agencies."

But Johnston's grin only widened. "You'll probably get flack from the right-to-lifers and the animal rights people, too, once they find out what you're doing."

"That's not really funny," I said. "They can be dangerous. They've dynamited laboratories, you know."

"Pushes up the stock, publicity like that. Maybe we ought to try a little dynamite here and there."

"The SEC would love to hear talk like that."

Johnston laughed. "Wait'll the SEC hears the rumors about this work of yours. I know just the guy they'll send to visit me; little mousy mother who thinks he's Dick Tracy."

"Why would the SEC get into the act?"

"Because once we start the rumors running and the stock goes up, they'll want to see if we're manipulating the stock price illegally."

"Is it illegal to spread rumors?"

Johnston raised his hands, pink palms out. "Hey, we're not gonna spread any rumors. We're just gonna plant the seeds in the right places and watch 'em grow."

"But will that cause trouble with the SEC?"

"Long as we can show that the rumors are based on fact, there's not a damned thing they can do about it."

I thought about that for a moment. "Then we'd better make very certain that we've got the goods before we start any rumors circulating."

Johnston nodded soberly. "Right on. That's what I'm depending on you for, Arthur. You've got to be absolutely straight with me on this. No hype. Just the straight poop, nothing else."

Before I realized I was saying it, I replied, "Okay, but I want you to be absolutely straight with me, too."

"About what?"

"About rumors I've heard that you're talking to the Japanese about selling the lab."

His eyes went wide. "Where the hell you hear that?"

"Rumors," I said. "Some friends of mine on Wall Street."

"It's bullshit," Johnston snapped.

"Is it?"

Johnston snorted angrily. "Look, even if somebody in the corporation did talk to the Japs, it was only very preliminary talk. Very preliminary. And nothing but talk. Just to keep all the bases covered, protect ourselves against this takeover bid as much as we can."

"That's all it is?"

"That's all it is now. I guarantee you."

I studied Johnston's face. He'd always kept his word with me. Our relationship had started with a handshake, a long time ago, that snowy night at Columbia. We'd had our ups and downs, but he'd always kept his word.

I felt tremendously relieved. I reached across the desk and extended my hand to Johnston. The CEO took it in his big paw, gripped it firmly.

"You can trust me, Arthur," he said.

"Then tell me the truth. Were you negotiating to sell the lab?"

"No. I had mentioned the possibility to the Japs, but it was only one possibility among several. They said they'd consider it, but they haven't made a solid offer and I haven't pressed them on it."

"All right," I said.

"If your organ regeneration program goes as well as you say, the lab'll be much too valuable to sell off."

"And the corporation will be much too strong for the Europeans to take over," I added.

Johnston nodded. But then he said, "Unless . . ."

"Unless?"

His face went somber again. "You've got me thinking, Arthur. The goddamned government's gonna want to get their sticky fingers into this, one way or another."

"You mean the FDA? I don't see—"

"If this gets as big as we both think it will, there'll be more than the FDA coming at you. You'll have congressional committees crawling all over you. They'll demand studies and evaluations and all kinds of crap, won't they?"

I realized he was right. "The National Academy of Sciences ought to be brought into the picture, I guess. Once we're ready for human trials."

"Every politician in the country will get involved."

"Maybe you're right." I felt a sinking sensation in the pit of my stomach.

"If we get strung up on red tape by the goddamned government," Johnston said, "it could open the door for all kinds of takeover maneuvers from overseas."

"I see."

Strangely, Johnston did not seem at all depressed. "If that happens, maybe the best road to take is a merger with one of the big European pharmaceutical companies."

"Merger?"

"Might make sense, in the right circumstances."

"But I thought—"

Johnston got to his feet. He loomed over me like a smiling thundercloud. "Let me worry about the business end of it, Arthur. You stick to the science."

PART OF sticking to the science was attending scientific conferences. I encouraged my researchers to go to the more important conferences and present papers reporting on the scientific work they were doing. It was always a delicate matter, balancing the lab's need to maintain corporate secrecy against the individual researcher's need to maintain his or her scientific credentials. I always pushed for more openness; I wanted my researchers to be recognized by the scientific community for the top-flight scientists that they were. Too often men and women working at industrial laboratories are slighted or forgotten altogether because their corporate employers won't allow them to publish in the scientific literature or present papers at conferences.

And I had another reason to push for openness, too. By getting my people to tell the world what they were doing, I pushed them to keep moving forward with their work. No resting on your laurels once everybody else in the field knows what you've accomplished and can duplicate it. You've got to move on, go farther, break new ground. That was my contribution to the management of research. I believed in it when I was in academia and I thought it was absolutely essential at an industrial lab, where corporate secrecy can be a cloak for laziness or timidity.

The annual genetic engineering conference was taking place in Las Vegas. Cassie Ianetta was due to fly up from Mexico, Vince Andriotti was going to deliver a paper on his latest work in high-resolution imaging, and several of my younger researchers were giving papers also. Zack O'Neill and his development of regentides were definitely *not* going to show up at the conference.

I was set to go, though. I had been invited to make one of the luncheon speeches; not a scientific report but a "senior statesman" type of speech on the state of the field of genetic engineering. It would be hard to keep from talking about our organ regeneration work, but we weren't ready to reveal it to the world yet. Not yet.

The day before I was to fly to Las Vegas, Jesse called.

"We're back home," he announced, "and Julia wants you to come over for dinner."

"You should have let me know sooner. I'll be in Las Vegas for the next three days," I said.

"You've taken up gambling?"

Frowning as I held the phone against my ear, I replied, "It's the annual genetic engineering meeting."

"In Las Vegas? Where're they going to hold next year's, Atlantic City? Or maybe some Indian reservation where they've put up a casino?"

I didn't laugh. "I'll be back Sunday night."

"Can't wait that long, Arby. Come over tonight."

"But you just got back. Julia won't want to cook dinner before you've unpacked."

"So we'll send out for pizza or Chinese," Jesse answered carelessly. "Don't worry about it."

I thought swiftly: If I pack this afternoon I can drive into town, have dinner with Jess and Julia, and then stay at the corporation's condo overnight. That'll be easier than driving to Kennedy from Connecticut in the morning rush traffic, even in a limo.

"What time?" I asked.

"Doesn't matter. We'll be here when you show up."

"I'll be there at seven-thirty."

"Great," said Jesse.

But Jesse was not there at seven-thirty, of course.

I left my car and travel bags in the corporation's midtown condo and took a cab to Jesse's apartment. It was dark by seven-thirty, the end of an unseasonably warm late winter day. After weeks of gray overcast and icy wind blowing in from the river, this day had been bright with sunshine and the promise of springtime. The streets in Jesse's neighborhood seemed reasonably clean, and I didn't see any homeless people shuffling about or huddled in doorways. The only pedestrians appeared to be well-dressed local residents. Down the street cars hummed by on Riverside Drive; lights were twinkling in the condos on the Jersey side of the Hudson, outlining the high-rises that overlooked the river.

Tucking the bottle of wine I had brought from home beneath my arm, I found the Marshak nameplate in the doorway and pressed the button under it.

"Yes?" It sounded like Julia's voice, barely recognizable in the ancient speaker.

"It's me, Arthur."

"Lovely." The door buzzed. I pushed it open; heavy glass with ornamental iron scrollwork. The lobby felt overheated and stuffy. One elevator; it, too, was very old, the door squeaked, and the cables groaned as I rode up to the fifth floor, hoping it would make it all the way there.

Julia was standing in their open doorway when I got off the elevator. She looked pale and thin, but she smiled broadly as I stepped toward her.

"Arthur, dear," she said.

It felt strange not to take her in my arms, and Julia showed no inclination toward even a sisterly kiss on the cheek, so I awkwardly thrust the bottle of wine at her.

"Put it in the freezer," I said, "so it chills down for dinner."

"Yes, of course," she said as she ushered me into the apartment. She was wearing a fuzzy sweater and dark slacks. It was too early for her pregnancy to show.

"How are you?" I asked, as I looked around the apartment. High ceilings with real moldings, the kind nobody bothers with anymore. Eclectic furniture, no two pieces seemed to match, yet it all came together in a pleasing, comfortable whole. Everything painted off-white, walls, ceilings, woodwork, everything. "How do you feel?"

"I'm fine, really," Julia said. "A few problems, but that's to be expected, I suppose, in my delicate condition."

"Where's Jess? Isn't he here?"

"Oh, he popped in at the hospital to see how they've managed without him. He'll be back soon."

It was after ten o'clock when Jesse finally showed up, cool as a breeze, relaxed and happy. I was steaming. Julia and I had drunk about a quart of fruit juice each, waiting.

Julia kissed her husband warmly. Jesse grinned when he turned to me and stuck his hand out.

"So how's things with you, Arby? Made another million while we were gone?"

"Would you have stayed away this late if Julia had been here alone?" I asked him.

"Aw, don't start growling at me, Arby."

Julia stepped between us. "Arthur, dear, he came home early to see you. If you hadn't been here, Jess would still be at the hospital." Turning to her husband, "Wouldn't you, darling?"

Jesse made the same sheepish grin that had gotten him out of a thousand scrapes. "I don't know. Maybe."

Julia phoned the neighborhood Chinese restaurant and half an hour later we were hunched over the coffee table in their living room, picking from cardboard cartons with wooden chopsticks.

"In Eritrea they eat with their fingers," Jesse was saying. "Three major eating styles in the world: the fork, chopsticks, and fingers."

"We've tried all three," said Julia, "and I must say I prefer the fork."

"Cultural bias," Jesse said.

"Perhaps."

"How was it in Africa?" I asked. I had already heard Julia's version of their time in Eritrea: the hunger, the disease, her own bout with fever, the skirmishes with starving bandits. Now I wanted to hear Jesse's.

"Looks pretty hopeless," Jess replied. "If it weren't for the UN they'd all starve to death or kill one another."

"Then why—"

"Interesting medical problems, though. All kinds of parasitic diseases. I'll bet they've got parasites there that haven't even been catalogued by Western scientists."

"Sounds charming."

"It's a terrible tragedy," Julia said. "Especially for the children."

"So we feed them and help them medically," I heard myself say, "but we don't improve their basic situation."

"No, not at all," Julia agreed. "All we're doing is putting a Band-Aid on their problems."

"And feeding them enough so they can go out and make

another generation of starving, sick people who can't take care of themselves."

Jesse looked up from his rummaging through the cartons. "What do you want us to do, Arby, leave them to die?"

"I don't think we're helping them," I said. "I think we're just making their situation worse."

"You want to send in the Marines?" Jesse asked. "Take over the country and straighten it out?"

I shook my head. "I wouldn't risk killing one American soldier over a problem that's none of our business."

"But Arthur, the children!" Julia said. "We can't leave them to die."

I looked into her dark eyes; they were steady, unwavering, no tears or unreasoning sentiment. She had made an unemotional ethical decision.

"Julia," I said, "you can't keep bringing children into the world if you can't take care of them properly, can't even feed them. It's not right, and they shouldn't expect us to take care of them."

"They don't expect anything," Julia said calmly. "I don't think they have any hope left in them at all."

"Then why are we prolonging their agony?"

Jesse made a wry grin. "Arby, suppose they could pay us for the food we give them. Suppose Omnitech could get a contract to feed them and make a profit at it. Would it be okay with you then?"

"That would mean they have enough money to feed themselves, wouldn't it?"

"Okay, so the U.S. taxpayer is footing the bill. Is that what bothers you, that you have to fork over a fraction of a penny to feed starving black people?"

"What bothers me," I said, holding on to my temper, "is that what we're doing is not solving the problem. In fact, it's making things worse."

"So you'd let them starve?"

I looked at my brother. Jesse was smiling that lazy, careless smile of his, but underneath it he was just as adamant as I was.

"Jess, do you support a woman's right to have an abortion?"

"Certainly."

"This is the same thing. Why bring children into the world when you can't take care of them?"

"There's one rather large difference," Julia pointed out. "The choice of abortion is up to the mother, at least in most cases. The women in Eritrea—"

"And elsewhere," Jesse butted in.

"And elsewhere," Julia added with a nod toward him, "those women *want* to have their babies. They don't want abortions, and they certainly don't want to watch their babies starve to death."

We argued around and around, getting nowhere, of course. Finally I decided it was useless and changed the subject.

"Have you thought about the consulting agreement?" I asked.

Jesse seemed surprise by the abrupt shift of gears. He blinked a few times, then said, "Yeah, I have."

"It's very generous of you to offer it, Arthur," said Julia.

I contradicted, "The basic ideas here are as much Jesse's as they are mine. And we're going to need the best medical advice we can get on this."

"I've been thinking," Jesse said, with a long glance at Julia, "that maybe you ought to work out an agreement with the medical center to work with your people."

That surprised me a little. "La Guardia?"

Jesse nodded. "We've got a top-notch medical team there, Arby. Just what you need."

I had to admit that he was right. "But what about you, Jess? I want you to be part of this."

He flashed his boyish grin. "I'll be part of it—through La Guardia."

"Don't you want a consulting contract of your own?"

He flicked another glance at Julia, who remained absolutely silent.

"Well?" I asked.

"I don't know, Arby. We could sure use the money, but if I

sign a consulting agreement, then I'd be committed to spending a certain number of hours on the program and I don't think I want to be tied down like that."

"The agreement could leave the amount of time entirely up to your discretion," I said, starting to feel impatient with his reluctance. I thought I knew what was bothering him, but he wasn't going to come out and admit it.

"Yeah, yeah," Jesse said. "The amount of time I spend on the project would be up to my discretion. Sure. And you'd be breathing down my neck every minute of the day."

He just did not want to work for me. Not even as an independent consultant. That was the trouble.

Julia said softly, "If you make a contract with La Guardia, Arthur, you get the entire medical team, including Jesse. I'm sure he'll become fully involved in your program once the medical center is a part of it."

I looked into those steady brown eyes of hers. "I thought that a consulting arrangement with Jess would be good for you two financially."

"We're all right financially," Jesse said.

"We're fine," Julia added.

My stubborn idiot of a brother didn't want to feel beholden to me, especially in front of his wife. I heard Momma's voice telling me, *Watch out for your brother, Arthur. You're the practical one; Jesse's a dreamer.*

But how can I watch out for him if he won't let me? I wondered.

"All right," I said, admitting defeat. "We can work out a contract for La Guardia Medical Center to work in partnership with Grenford Laboratory."

Jesse smiled as if he'd won some kind of a victory.

"Lovely," said Julia.

THE TRIAL:
DAY TWO, MORNING

Graves banged his gavel and called for order. Slowly the hearing room quieted down. Jesse watched his brother sit back down in his front-row seat, his face still flushed with anger.

Rosen seemed totally unperturbed by Arthur's outburst. He sat immobile, hands pressed together before his face, waiting for the buzz of conversations to subside.

At last the chamber was still. Without getting up from his chair at the end of the judges' desks, Rosen asked Jesse:

"Dr. Marshak, you say that you did not actively engage in the research going on at Grenford Labs on organ regeneration."

"That's right," Jesse replied. "There was some talk about my consulting with the Grenford Lab, but nothing came of it."

"Why not?"

Jesse flicked a glance back at his brother, then took a deep breath. "A lot of reasons," he said. "I was extremely busy at the hospital and the medical center. Grenford had its own research team working; they had started up while I was in Africa and they seemed to be barreling right along. They didn't really need me, and—frankly—I got the strong impression that they considered me an outsider. You know, the boss's brother."

A few titters from the audience. Graves looked up and frowned.

"Did you have any misgivings about the direction the research was taking?" Rosen asked.

Jesse hesitated a moment, then answered, "No. In all honesty, I didn't think much about that until some time later. No, I was just busy in my own sphere. I figured if my brother needed my help or my opinions, he'd ask me."

"You and your brother—Dr. Arthur Marshak—were still on good relations then?"

"Oh, sure. I didn't see much of him, but there was no falling-out between us. Not until later."

ARTHUR

I had never been to Las Vegas before. The city is tawdry, a triumph of greed over common sense. The casino hotels, each more garish than the last, look impermanent, as if they're actually movie sets, painted fronts with nothing behind them. I'm not religious, but I thought of how the old Hebrew prophets must have felt about Sodom and Gomorrah.

Yet the conference organizers had set the annual genetic engineering conference here. Cutting-edge science among the slot machines. Some two thousand scientists in with all the gamblers. I shook my head as I stood in line to register at the hotel. Last year the conference had been in San Francisco. A reasonable choice. Next year it would be San Antonio.

It was all so damned inconvenient! The hotel was miles away from the conference center. To attend the conference sessions, you had to ride on a chartered bus that trundled along the tasteless flamboyance of the Strip, stopping at each of those monuments to cupidity before finally arriving at the vast and crowded conference center, baking in the desert sun. Beyond the center were tract after tract of cookie-cutter housing developments, far out into the brown dusty waste of the desert.

Once inside the conference center, though, things started looking better, even though the place was air-conditioned cold enough to freeze glycol. I met men and women I hadn't seen since the last annual conference. Luncheon dates were made. I scouted out the bar; many of the attending scientists spent more time there than in the sessions listening to the presentations. There's more science going on in the bars and hotel suites than in the sessions at conferences like this. The papers presented at the official presentations addressed what had been accomplished in the past, even if it was the very recent past. The excited, intense conversations going on at the bars, in the suites, in the hotel corridors—they dealt with what was going on *now*: what's new, what ideas were percolating, which directions research was taking.

Of course, there was a lot of job-hopping going on, too. And some industrial espionage, I suppose. Lots of information flying around. I had instructed my people to stay strictly silent about the regeneration work. Too early to say anything; too important to tip off any possible competition.

Within a few minutes of stepping off the confounded bus, I had forgotten the inconveniences of the conference arrangements and was deep in conversation with my peers. I try to be a good listener, and this year my objective was to find out if anyone else was working on organ regeneration. I resolved to do what Polonius advised: give every man my ear, but few my voice.

The only session I attended the first day was the one in which one of my young researchers was giving a paper on cancer inhibitors. I sat in the front row, beaming encouragement at my offspring as the youngster delivered his first paper before a national conference.

I was climbing aboard the bus at the end of that opening day when I recognized Patricia Hayward's red hair and long legs on the top step ahead of me. I followed her to one of the last rows in the bus, glad that she picked a seat that had no other occupant.

"Mind if I sit with you?"

She did not seem surprised as she looked up at me and smiled. "Dr. Marshak. Hello."

I sat beside her. "How've you been?"

"Pretty busy. And you?"

"Pretty busy."

The bus huffed and lurched and we were on our way back

to the center of town. I realized that I hadn't seen Pat for months, not since that dinner with Jess and Julia before the two of them went off to Africa.

"I didn't know you were attending the conference," I said.

Patricia tapped a fingernail against the plastic badge pinned to her blouse. "I'm on assignment for *Discover* magazine."

"Something specific? Or just covering the conference as a whole?" Suddenly I realized that she knew about our regeneration work. As a consultant to Omnitech she must have signed a nondisclosure agreement, of course, but still I felt uneasy about her being here among so many potential competitors.

I tried to keep the worry off my face as we chatted until the bus stopped at Pat's hotel: one of the more modest emporiums along the Strip. On impulse, I got up and followed her out onto the hot, sun-baked street.

"Are you staying here, too?" Pat asked.

"No. I'm farther up the street, at the Bellagio."

"Wow," Pat kidded. "The big time."

"Do you have any plans for dinner?" I asked her.

"Actually, I do. I'm interviewing three women: a staff researcher at La Roche Laboratories, a professor of molecular genetics from the University of Texas, and a graduate student from Caltech."

I felt disappointed. "Sounds like a full evening."

"I'm free tomorrow night."

That old familiar thrill of excitement surged through me. I had to remind myself that this was business and nothing more. "All right. Fine. Tomorrow at . . ."

"Seven? Eight?"

"Make it eight."

"Eight o'clock, then," she said.

"I'll meet you here. In the lobby."

"Fine."

I watched her disappear into the hotel's smoked-glass lobby. Then I turned and decided to walk through the late desert afternoon back to my hotel instead of waiting for the next bus. For some reason I found myself whistling an old Beatles tune as I walked along the avenue: "Let It Be."

The next day I was really busy, going to meetings and attending sessions and pumping colleagues for information all afternoon. But despite spending hours at the conference center's bar (drinking fruit juice, mostly), that evening I arrived precisely on time at Pat's hotel. The lobby was crowded, bustling. Slot machines lined every wall, and through a wide archway I could see the casino, filled with intense men and women grimly having the fun of gambling their money away. It made me shake my head. It was mathematically certain that the longer you gambled, the more you lost. If the house didn't have the odds stacked in its favor, gambling casinos would have gone extinct sometime in the fifth dynasty of ancient Egypt.

Yet the lure was undeniable. Even some of the scientists attending the conference hit the gaming tables, each of them convinced that he had finally figured out a mathematical way to beat the odds.

Turning, I spotted Patricia making her way through the crowd toward me, looking both elegant and casual in a cool white silk long-sleeved blouse and burgundy tapestry vest that accentuated her lean, trim figure. Dark slacks hid her legs, which was a shame, but still she looked great. I felt overdressed in a business suit and tie; this was the Wild West, after all.

We went by taxi to a tiny restaurant in a crumbling old adobe house out in the desert, highly recommended by the concierge at my hotel. Probably owned by a relative of hers, I thought. The house looked as if it had been built in Kit Carson's day and left to bake in the sun since then. To my pleasant surprise, though, the place was more than decent. Quiet, small, almost intimate, almost empty. The restaurant was set up in what must have originally been the house's dining room. A small round fireplace in one corner; cracked smoke-darkened beams supported the ceiling. There was only one other couple in the tile-floored dining room: a rather stout woman working on a slice of chocolate cake and coffee while her gray-haired husband scrutinized the bill.

The specialty of the house was barbecued ribs. The host

was the only waiter, and the restaurant's owner: a rangy, leather-faced old-timer who personally tied huge napkins around our necks, but only after I had stuffed my tie in my jacket pocket and then taken off the jacket and draped it on the back of my wobbly wooden chair.

The ribs came, steaming, with corn on the cob, french fries, and a family bowl of coleslaw. And a pitcher of foaming beer.

"My cholesterol fix for the year," I muttered as we dug into the ribs.

"Cholesterol doesn't count when you're having fun," Pat said. "I did an interview with a Nobel Prize winner who told me that."

"Did he?"

"Something close to it," she admitted with a laugh.

We had the place to ourselves after the older couple left. Our host busied himself feeding sticks into the fireplace. Pat and I chatted about the conference.

"You know," I said as casually as I could, "we're not mentioning a word about our regeneration work. Not a peep."

She looked up from the ribs. "Is that why you asked me out? For a security check?"

"Why, no, not at all."

The fine line of her jaw was set stubbornly. "You told me back in your laboratory that the work was confidential. I don't blab proprietary information to strangers, Arthur. I don't sell information, either, if that's what's bothering you."

She was angry with me. I tried to apologize, and as I did so I started to think that my concerns over her reliability had been only a part of my reason for asking her to dinner. A minor part. She was really an elegant-looking young woman. Even angry as she was, with those green eyes snapping at me, she was gorgeous.

When forced into a corner, try telling the truth. So I said, "Pat, the security business was just an excuse to myself so I could work up the courage to ask you to dinner."

"Work up the courage?" That seemed to surprise her. "Come on, now."

"You're very lovely, and much younger than I. You must have had a dozen invitations to dinner. And then some."

A smile was trying to work through her anger. "And you're a very powerful, very successful man. You could have your pick of the women at this conference."

"I did," I said. "I picked you."

"Because you were worried about my keeping your secrets."

"If that had been the only reason I would've talked to you on the street in front of your hotel yesterday when we got off the bus."

She thought that over for a few moments. "All right," she said at last. "I'll take you at your word. The business part of this dinner is over. Let's forget it and be sociable."

Just like that? I wondered. Can she just drop it and change her mood so easily? Or is it all an act?

I decided to follow her lead. Truce. I asked politely, "How are your ribs?"

"Fine," she said. Then she grinned. "I assume you mean these here on my plate."

I had to laugh. It felt as if a dark storm cloud had passed and the sun was shining again.

"Do you know that for thousands of years the most learned men in Europe actually thought that men had one less rib than women because the Bible said God took a rib from Adam's side to create Eve?"

Soon we were talking and bantering as if the storm cloud had never been there. Our host brought a second pitcher of beer and once we had finished with the ribs he brought us bowls of water and a dish of lemons for us to wash our hands.

"Don't hold with them wet paper things they got all wrapped up in tinfoil," he told us in a gravelly voice. "Got all kindsa chemicals in 'em, I bet."

We used the finger bowls and dried our hands on the cloth towels he provided. I was talking to Pat about molecular genetics when our host came to our table with a trio of shot glasses in one hand and a bottle of mescal in the other.

"Can't sell this stuff to you, my license is only for beer and wine," he explained. "So I'll have to give it to you free."

And he pulled out a chair and joined us, uninvited. Pat wrinkled her nose as he lit up a cigarette, but said nothing. I went back to talking about molecular genetics. The fire burned low, the mescal warmed the three of us. I realized I was talking nonstop, but Pat looked intrigued, our host spellbound.

After a while, though, the grizzled old man said, "Yeah, but what you're doin' is kinda like tryin' to play God, isn't it?"

I had heard that line a thousand times before. From professors of philosophy. From news reporters. From doctors of divinity. From worried, frightened parents.

I leaned back on my creaking chair, the mescal making me feel expansive. "God's a lazy engineer," I said. "We can do better."

"What do you mean?" Pat asked.

Waving at the cigarette smoke, I explained, "The human body is a slipshod design. It's the result of an accumulation of accidents and adaptations. That's why it doesn't work as well as it should."

"Works pretty well for me," the host said, stubbing out his cigarette in one of the dishes as he gave Pat a sly wink.

"It's falling apart," I said. "Your body is, mine is, even this lovely woman's is. Little by little, but sooner or later something major breaks down and you die."

"Well, that's natural, ain't it?"

Gesturing to the ceiling, I asked, "Is this house natural? Are the clothes we wear natural? The whole history of the human race is to improve on nature, to do better for ourselves."

"Have we really improved things for ourselves?" Pat asked quietly.

"Do you want to drop dead of exhaustion and malnutrition at thirty? Or be clawed down by a leopard because you can't outrun it and don't have any tools to protect yourself?"

"But we still die," said the host. "We live our three score and ten and then return to the dust from which we were made."

"Three score and ten," I muttered. "Despite all the advances we've made in medicine and sanitation and nutrition, the human body still seems to wear out around then. On the average."

I caught the look in Pat's eye, then added, "Until now."

"Until now?" the old man echoed.

Maybe the mescal was making me too relaxed. But what the hell, I thought, this old guy isn't an industrial spy. And besides, I felt like showing off a little for Pat.

"What would you say if I told you we'll be able to replace the parts of your body that wear out with new ones?"

"Like puttin' a new carburetor in a truck's engine?"

"Better than that," I said, waggling one finger in front of his face. "It will be like *growing* a new carburetor in the truck's engine, and letting the old one fade away."

Our host shook a fresh cigarette from his pack. "That— that'd be somethin'."

"You're damned right," I said.

Pat leaned closer to me and asked, "What you said earlier, about the human body being a slipshod design. I've always thought it's a marvel of intricate workings. At least, that's what I've always been told."

I grinned at her. "You've been talking to old fogies in the medical profession too much. The real marvel of the human body is that it holds up for seventy years. Just about everything in your body is an accident of history. A very lovely set of accidents, in your case."

"What do you mean?"

I shrugged. "Take this regeneration work. Turns out there's a protein that induces neurons to grow. It's called noggin. Silly name, but that's what its discoverers called it."

"So?"

"So how does it work? If you or I or our genial host here had designed the system, we'd design a protein that makes the neurons grow. Right?"

"That's what you said noggin does, didn't you?"

I waggled my finger again. A habit I can't seem to break. "Noggin doesn't do the job directly. It suppresses the activity of another protein that prevents neurons from growing. Instead of a chemical that says, 'Grow!' we've got a chemical that stops another chemical from saying, 'Don't grow.' "

"I see . . . I think."

"The whole human body is like that. More redundant systems than a NASA spacecraft. Nothing works directly. Enzymes telling other enzymes to stop repressing still other enzymes. Hell, when you stop to think that we're the results of an amoeba trying to reproduce itself, you realize what a haphazard set of mutations we really are."

"And you're goin' to do better than that?" our host asked.

"Damned right," I snapped. "We're going to improve the model—eventually. Right now we're just trying to figure out how to rebuild it, piece by piece."

He shook his head. "I don't know. Sounds kinda scary to me."

"It won't sound so scary when you need a new set of lungs."

He looked startled. Then he took another long drag on his cigarette. "Hell, if you can grow me a new set of lungs I can stop feelin' guilty 'bout these coffin nails."

We all laughed. Pat glanced at her wristwatch and suggested that we get back to town. Our host insisted on driving us, claiming there was little chance of getting a taxi at this time of night.

"Morning," Pat corrected. "It's past midnight."

"Even worse," he said. "You folks don't mind ridin' in a pickup, do you?"

"Can you drive all the way into town without smoking?" Pat asked.

"For you, pretty lady, I'd drive all the way to Yuma without smokin'."

The cold night air braced me, drove away the pleasant cobwebs that the mescal had spun in my brain. It was a gorgeous desert night, stars glittering like jewels in the sky, moonlight making the dry dusty landscape look silvery and romantic. I helped Pat into the cab of the battered pickup, then climbed in myself.

Even through the truck's smeared windshield the stars hung out there like friendly beacons.

"That's Deneb, in the tail of the Swan," I said, pointing. "And there's Altair, in the Eagle."

Sitting next to me, her shoulder pressing against mine, Pat asked, "And the bright red one, down near the horizon?"

I hesitated a moment, thinking. "Must be Mars."

"Nope," said our host. "That there's Antares, in the Scorpion."

"By god, I think you're right," I said.

"It must be fun to know all the stars," Pat said.

"It's fun to know anything," I told her. "That's why people do science, because it's the greatest thrill in the world to find something that no one has found before."

I could sense Pat nodding in the darkness.

"We're hunters, basically," I went on. "For millions of years our ancestors lived by hunting. Our bodies, our minds, even our societies are based on that heritage of hunting. That's why scientists are happy at their work. They're hunters. Out on the frontier, always moving into the unknown, always hunting."

"And what are you hunting for?" Pat asked.

I heard myself chuckle. "Me? I don't hunt anymore. Too old. I'm a big chief now. I send out younger men and women to hunt."

"Can you get the same kind of satisfaction out of that? The same thrill?"

I had to think awhile before answering. "No. That's gone. Now what I want to do is make an impact. I want to have an effect on our society. I want to change the world, Pat, change it for the better. That's my kick."

"And recognition? Do you want that, too?"

"I don't want to be buried in an unmarked grave, if that's what you mean. But I'll never get a Nobel Prize," I said, surprised at how much of the bitterness showed up in my voice. "I'll never even get recognition from the National Academy of Sciences. I'll just have to settle for money."

"And power?" she asked.

I laughed. "No power. That's for the politicians and the captains of industry. All I'm looking for is the chance to change the world. I don't want to run it."

"But you have to run a little piece of the world, don't you, to make the impact you want to make? You have to have the power to run your lab."

"Yes, that's true. That's the one piece of the world that I have to run. It's a tiny piece, but I'll fight to keep control of it."

Soon the lights of Las Vegas blotted out the stars. The Strip was just as crowded with traffic as it had been at noon, even more so. Pat directed our host to her hotel. I got out of the pickup with her.

"Thanks for the lift," I said.

The grizzled old man grinned at us. "Hell, thank you for the most int'resting evening I've had since the hookers' convention two years ago."

He drove off, laughing and lighting up a fresh cigarette.

The sidewalk was bustling with people. Standing there in front of the hotel, I asked Pat, "Can I buy you a nightcap?"

She seemed to think it over. Then, "I don't think so, Arthur. It's already pretty late."

"There's nothing much happening tomorrow until my luncheon speech," I said.

A faint smile touched the corners of her lips. "I think it's best that I go straight to bed. Sleep, I mean."

I smiled back at her. "All I'm suggesting is a drink, Pat."

"One thing leads to another, and if I have another drink I'm not sure where we'll go from there."

"Where would you like to go?" A part of my mind realized how ridiculous it was to be attempting to seduce this attractive young woman on the crowded sidewalk in front of a garish hotel. But what the hell? You fight your battles where they happen to fall. That's how Napoleon got to Waterloo.

Pat's smile faded. "Arthur, you have quite a reputation, you know."

"Me?"

"You. And Nancy Dubois, at the moment."

That staggered me. "Well, that's not . . ." There was nothing I could say that wouldn't make me sound like an unfeeling bastard.

"Good night, Arthur," said Pat, almost solemnly. "Thanks for a lovely evening."

"Good night," I replied lamely.

Pat turned abruptly and strode into the hotel. I watched her enter the lobby and head straight for the elevators. Then I started walking up the Strip to my own hotel, thinking, She knows about Nancy and me. Of course she knows. Pat's been around the corporate office long enough to hear the gossip. Nancy must be shooting off her mouth to the other women. I wonder if Lowenstein knows as much as she does.

THE TRIAL:
DAY TWO, MORNING

You say there was a falling-out between you and your brother?" Rosen asked. Jesse kept his eyes on the examiner, still sitting at the end of the desks facing him. "Yes," he answered.

"What was the reason for this . . . falling-out?"

"A difference of opinion."

"About the work on organ regeneration?"

"Yes."

Rosen asked, "Could you be more specific about the cause of this difference of opinion?"

Jesse felt annoyed. He had gone over this with Rosen and the others a dozen times in the weeks leading up to the trial. Now the lawyer was acting as if he'd never heard it before. But that's the way they do things in a court of law, Jesse told himself. They've got this antiquated way of getting at the information they want you to say.

"Well, among other things, Arthur wanted to go into human trials right away," he said patiently.

"And you did not?"

"I didn't think they had enough knowledge from the animal experiments to rush into human trials."

"Butchers!" a man yelled from the back of the chamber. "Animals have feelings!"

Whipping around in his chair, Jesse saw a rake-thin elderly man shaking his fist in the air. "You've no right to hurt poor, defenseless animals!" he bellowed.

Graves banged his gavel and shouted, "Remove that man from this chamber!"

Two of the uniformed guards standing at the rear of the room moved in on the man, who glared at Graves but allowed himself to be hustled out into the corridor.

"I will not tolerate any more interruptions like this." Graves almost snarled the words. "One more outburst and I'll clear this chamber entirely!"

The audience went very silent, just as Graves's lecture students used to hush when he fixed that baleful gaze of his upon them.

"Go ahead, Dr. Rosen," Graves said.

Rosen nodded to the chief judge, then returned his somber gaze to Jesse.

"Your brother wanted to go ahead with human trials, but you felt the work was not yet sufficiently advanced for them?"

"That's right," Jesse said.

"And just when did this difference of opinion first arise?"

Suddenly Jesse felt tongue-tied. There were so many ways to answer the question he couldn't decide which one to say. The winter of the big blizzard. The day our mother died. The day Julia lost the baby.

JESSE

It had been snowing for more than six hours, with no end in sight. The city was already buried in drifts driven by the gale-force winds. Even the ambulances were having trouble getting through the foot-deep snow that covered most of the streets. The cold was numbing, killing.

We'll be getting frostbite cases down in the emergency room, I knew. Exposure and hypothermia. A lot of homeless people aren't going to make it through this night.

I was up in the women's ward, facing row upon row of beds occupied by the poor, the sick, the battered wives, the drug-addicted kids, the rape victims, the tuberculosis cases, the pneumonia and bronchitis and influenza cases, the pitiful helpless dregs who were prey to every predator, microbe or human, that stalked the deadly streets out there. The ward was jammed to overflowing; they had already started putting beds out in the corridors, and more were coming in as the ambulances and police cars struggled back through the howling blizzard. As I made my rounds through the ward, a flash of déjà vu hit me with almost overpowering force.

I saw myself back in Eritrea, facing that endless line of hopeless, helpless blacks staring at me out of eyes already dead, waiting for me to do something, accusing me. It's the same thing here, I realized, and the truth of it almost made my knees buckle.

It's endless! Day after day, night after night. The more we do for them, the more there is to do.

Yet they were there, waiting for me, moaning in their pain or staring with blank-eyed desperation at a future as bleak and pointless as the storm raging outside. What can I do? I asked myself. Over and over, as I made my way from bed to bed, I silently asked myself, What can I do? What can I do?

I was halfway through the ward when a nurse came hurrying after me, grim-faced, a cordless telephone in one hand.

Wordlessly, I took the phone. "Yes?"

"Jess, it's Momma," I heard Arthur's voice. "I just got the call. Another stroke. Bad one. They said she won't live through the night."

"Jesus."

"I'm going to try to get down there," Arthur said.

"Where are you?"

"At the lab. The state police say that the major highways are being plowed constantly; they're trying to keep at least one lane open."

"I'll drive up."

"Don't take any risks you don't have to."

"What about you?"

"The state police have offered to drive me to the nursing home."

"Maybe I can get an ambulance to take me."

"Okay. See what you can do."

I handed the phone back to the nurse. "Who else is on the ward tonight?"

There were half a dozen residents hanging around, trapped by the blizzard. I swiftly made arrangements for a couple of them to take the rest of my rounds. I actually felt relieved to be out of the ward. And I felt ashamed at my sense of relief. Like a kid playing hooky from school; it's great to be out but you know you ought to be in.

I went to my cubbyhole of an office and phoned Julia to tell her what was happening.

"I can drive you," she said.

I nixed that idea right away. "No. You stay home. There's nothing on the streets except emergency vehicles and crazy people. Not even the buses are running, I hear."

"Then how will you get to Sunny Glade?"

"I'll get one of the ambulance guys to drive me."

Julia was silent for a moment. Then, "That isn't terribly fair, is it? Someone in difficulty might need that ambulance."

"Julia—"

"I can drive. I'm not totally helpless."

"No," I said firmly. "You stay in the apartment and don't

budge. I'll phone you from Sunny Glade." Or from the car, I thought, if I get into trouble.

I didn't bother with an ambulance. I went down to the underground garage, pulling on my overcoat and gloves as I rode the oversized elevator, wrapping a scarf of heavy English wool around my neck.

The streets were treacherous. It was still snowing hard, with the wind driving the flakes almost horizontally through the weak cones of light from the swaying streetlamps. Snowplows had obviously been at work: the middle of most of the main avenues were covered with only a few inches of snow while huge banks of white were piled up along each side. God help anybody parked under those piles, I thought as I inched my Firebird along the plowed lane. Plenty of cubes under her hood, but there was ice just beneath the new-fallen snow; I could feel the wheels slipping and sliding.

At least the streets were empty, almost. Half a block ahead a minivan slid through a red light, spinning a full three-sixty as it sailed through the intersection. Good thing nobody else was in the way. I slowed down even more and inched my way through. Two bashed-in cars were off to one corner of the intersection, the hood of one rammed against the side door of the other. Nobody in sight. From the depth of snow on them, the collision must have happened an hour ago or more.

Even the bars looked dark and closed. I drove carefully past a snow-shrouded Yankee Stadium and up onto the Deegan Expressway, slipping and sliding on the ramp. The Bronx was silent and cold as an Arctic wasteland, except for a siren I could hear wailing in the distance. Ambulance, it sounded like. Then I got lucky. There was a nice big public works truck plowing the new-fallen snow and spreading sand behind it at the same time. I followed it for miles, feeling like I had a battleship escorting me through enemy territory. I had to turn off at the Cross County Parkway, though, and head for the Hutchinson.

The snow began to ease off, and I even thought I saw a few breaks in the clouds. Not too bad now. The worst is behind me, I thought. Then I hit a patch of glare ice. The Firebird spun wildly and thunked sideways into a huge snowbank. The seat belt cut into my shoulder but the air bag didn't go off, thank god.

For long minutes I just sat behind the wheel, grateful that both the car and I were still in one piece. It took a while for my hands to stop shaking. It was damned cold, despite the car's heater. Gas gauge read about half, so that was okay. Hell of a time to think about that now.

I gingerly downshifted to the lowest gear and gently put a little pressure on the accelerator. The engine purred, the wheels spun, but the car didn't move. I tried shifting to reverse and back again, thinking maybe I could rock her loose. The car rocked, all right, but it didn't go anywhere. The wheels just whined on the ice. I couldn't get free of the snowbank.

I sat hunched over the wheel, wondering what to do. The cold was seeping into me, getting past my coat and muffler and gloves, leaching the warmth from my body. I could run out of gas, stuck here, and freeze to death. So I picked up the cell phone and punched star 911.

It took about ten, fifteen minutes of waiting out in the cold and dark. I was never so glad to see the red and blue flashing lights of a police car. The cop pulled up behind me and came out into the cold and snow, bundled in a thick hip-length pile coat and heavy boots.

I rolled my window down a crack. Wind-whipped snow stung my face.

The police officer bent low and said, "Kinda lousy night for a drive, ain't it?"

"I'm a doctor," I told him. "I'm trying to get to an emergency case up in White Plains."

The policeman did not ask for identification. He told me to stay in the car, then went back and hooked a chain to the rear of the Firebird. Backing slowly, the police car pulled me free of the snowbank.

The cop came crunching through the snow again.

"Thanks," I said.

"I'll lead you. Gimme the address where you've got to go and follow me."

Feeling unutterably grateful, I followed the blinking red and blue lights all the way to Sunny Glade.

Arthur was sitting in the lobby wrapped in a cashmere overcoat when I came in. I had to stamp snow off my shoes. Just the few yards from the parking lot to the front door and my shoes were soaked through. Then I saw the look on Arby's face and I knew I was too late.

"She died?"

Arthur looked up at me. "Half an hour ago."

I sank down onto the sagging old sofa beside my brother. "She's dead?" It was like that feeling you get after Christmas, after all the presents have been unwrapped and opened up. It's over.

"There's nothing you could have done, Jess. She was so far gone."

"Was she in much pain at the end?" I asked him.

Arby shrugged inside the overcoat. "I only arrived here a few minutes before the end. She was unconscious, completely out of it."

"That's something, at least."

"It's good that it's finally over. She suffered enough."

My eyes were misting over. "I want to see her."

Arthur looked bleak, too. "Yeah. I think they've moved her back to her own room by now."

We got to our feet.

"Julia's called three or four times," Arthur said. "She sounded pretty worried about you."

"It wasn't easy sledding out there," I said.

"You came by ambulance?"

"Naw. I drove my own car. Slid into a snowbank at one point."

"That was brilliant."

Ignoring Arby's sarcasm, I realized I had left my cell phone in the car, so I looked around the lobby for a telephone.

"There's a phone in Momma's room," Arthur said. "You can call Julia from there."

Ma was back in her bed when we entered the little corner room. In the dim light from the bedside lamp, she looked as if she were asleep, but I realized that I had never seen Ma sleeping with her arms lying straight at her sides like that. She'll never open her eyes again, I knew.

"Phone your wife," Arthur whispered.

It took a real effort to tear my eyes away from Ma's body. I went to the telephone on the bedside table and tapped out my number. Julia picked up before the first ring was finished.

"Jess?" Her voice sounded frightened, almost frantic.

"Yes, hon. I'm here with Arby."

"Oh, god, I was so *worried* about you! I was afraid to phone and distract you from your driving. The TV news is showing nothing but smashups on the roads. I was afraid I'd see you."

I smiled into the phone. "I'm okay, nothing to it. Nothing to worry about."

"You'll stay there overnight, won't you?"

"Hadn't even thought about it. Yeah, I suppose that's the best thing to do."

"How's your mother?"

The question brought me back to the reality of the moment. I had to swallow hard before I could speak again. "She died, Julia," I said, struggling not to cry. "Half an hour before I got here, from what Arby says."

"Oh, dear, I'm so sorry."

"Yeah. Well, it's a blessing, really. She'd been in a lot of pain for a long time."

"Yes."

"Are you okay?"

"I'm fine. The usual twinges, that's all."

"Stay warm and don't go outside. If you need anything, phone for delivery."

"Of course," she said. "The streets are positively swarming with delivery boys."

"I mean—"

"I'll be fine, Jess. Don't worry about me."

I glanced at Arthur, who was staring out the window at the snow, his back to the bed, making a big show of not listening to our conversation. "I love you, Julia," I whispered.

"I'm mad about you," Julia answered.

"Is she all right?" Arthur asked as soon as I hung up the phone.

"I guess so. It hasn't been an easy pregnancy."

Arthur turned to face me. "Oh?" The room was dimly lit, shadowy, but I could see the concern on his face.

I waved a hand at my brother. "It's nothing, really. Everything's under control."

"Well, is it nothing, or is it something that's under control?"

"A bit of both," I said, starting to feel a little pissed off at his big-brother act. "Julia just has to be a little careful, that's all. There's been some bleeding. She's going in for tests—that is, she was going for tests tomorrow. I don't think she'll get there, with this storm and all."

"You shouldn't have left her," Arthur said.

I stared at him, not certain I had really heard Arby correctly. "I shouldn't have left her?"

"There's nothing either one of us could do here," Arthur said. "You should have stayed with your wife on a night like this."

"Arby, this isn't the Victorian Age. Julia's fine."

"You shouldn't have left her."

He was standing on the other side of the bed, our dead mother between us, and giving me his usual *I know better than you do* routine. "I suppose that's what you would have done: let Ma die and stay with your wife."

"On a night like this that's exactly what I would have done," Arthur said. "I wouldn't have left my pregnant wife all alone."

"What's the matter, you pissed off that you didn't have Ma all to yourself at the end?"

"Don't be an idiot. There was no reason for you to risk your neck driving out through this storm. There was nothing you could've done for Momma."

"Oh, but it's okay for you to drive out here, isn't it?"

"I came in a police cruiser."

"Big deal. So you're an important man."

Arthur looked like he was going to say something, but then he bit it back. Looking down at Ma's body, "We shouldn't be arguing like this, Jess," he said, dropping his voice low.

That was another one of his tricks. Stick you with the point he wants to make and then say we shouldn't argue.

"It won't bother her now," I said.

"It's just—if I were Julia's husband I would've stayed with her on a night like this. I wouldn't have left her side."

"Well, you're not her husband. And you don't know much about Julia, really, if you think she'd want me to be holding her hand when my mother was dying."

Arthur seemed to retreat into the shadows. He backed away from the bed, then turned to the window again. I heard him mumble, "You're right. I don't know much about Julia."

LOOK, THE last thing in the world that I had wanted was to break up Arby's romance.

It had struck me funny, at first, to see Arby so crazy about this Englishwoman. He was usually so damned serious about everything he did. Like the last thing in the world he wanted was to look even the slightest bit foolish. He'd think about something for a year before moving an inch. What did that guy on television say about doing carpenter work? Measure twice, cut once. All his life Arby would measure until the damned sun went down and then start in all over again the next day.

But there he was, all of a sudden gone totally bonkers. In love, yet. Like he had watched a video on how to have a torrid romance and now he was acting out his part. Flowers and moonlight and the whole nine yards.

I was almost always too busy at the hospital or the medical center to even think about romance. Almost. Sure, there were plenty of women available. Trouble was, sooner or later they wanted to get married. Usually sooner. I used to think that hell was a cruise ship filled with Jewish women and their mothers, and they all know that I'm a doctor.

The idea was to have fun. Don't get emotionally tangled up. There'd be plenty of time for marriage and kids and all that. Later. After I was more settled.

Arby insisted on our going out on double dates.

"You can't work all the time, Jess," Arthur would repeat over and again. "You've got to have some relaxation or you'll drive yourself into an early grave."

Truth was, Arby just wanted to show off his girlfriend. Oops, make that his fiancée. He had asked Julia to marry him and she had said yes. Imagine Arby married!

But Arby could do strange things sometimes. I never thought he'd leave Columbia, but all of a sudden he up and quit and started this research laboratory of his. Moved out to Connecticut, for chrissakes. Maybe he really was getting old enough to want to settle down.

So there we were, the four of us: Arby and his fiancée and me and my date—a buxom Latino X-ray technician from the hospital named Gloria who claimed she was into channeling and reincarnation. And oral sex, if the rumors were right.

Julia was the quiet type, but those dark eyes of hers could look right through you. I felt almost uncomfortable when she studied me from across the dinner table.

Arby was bragging about how many Nobel Prize winners he had hired as consultants for his lab. Gloria was fascinated with him, maybe because he looked so well off and sure of himself. The silver hair gets them, I think; gives Arby a fatherly look. But although Julia was smiling in all the right places of Arthur's stories, every now and then she looked at me as if she were X-raying my mind.

My beeper went off, and it turned out to be an emergency back at the hospital. I had to leave Gloria with Arby and Julia and grab a taxi outside the restaurant. It was past dawn by the time I got back to my apartment. I pulled my clothes off and flopped on the unmade bed. I dreamed of Julia; nothing erotic, I was just talking to her in some kind of an office. Arby's office, I recognized it, at his lab up in Connecticut.

I didn't see Julia again for more than two weeks. Then Arthur insisted that I come up to his house for the weekend.

"Bring a date with you, if you like," Arthur said. "Julia's going to be here. We can make it a foursome."

I didn't bother with a date. I couldn't get away for the entire weekend, anyway, only Saturday night.

It was midafternoon when I got there. Autumn, at last. Football weather, crisp and clear after months of heat and humidity. We always had more violent crime injuries in the emergency room during the hottest part of the summer. But now leaves were falling on Arthur's vast lawn and tempers were cooling in the ghettos. We could play football out on Arby's lawn, I thought as I looked out the window at the green expanse and the drifting leaves. Hell, the National Football League would have room enough to play a game on that lawn.

Arby looked happy and perfectly relaxed in a green velour pullover and chocolate brown slacks. The country squire at his leisure, I thought, smiling to myself. Julia wore a pale yellow turtleneck sweater and light blue skirt. Very pretty. I had come in my Saturday jeans and the shirt that had been at the top of my bureau drawer.

Arby was showing off again. He had bought new furniture, redecorated the house, and he was like a real estate agent showing the damned house off, room by tedious room. I thought maybe Julia had picked out the furniture. Maybe Arby's just trying to make her happy. Who the hell knew?

A phone call from the lab took Arthur to the den he had built next to the living room. He closed the door, leaving Julia and me standing next to the picture window, drinks in our hands, looking like a couple from the pages of the *New Yorker*: rich, sophisticated, slightly hostile.

"You see," Julia said, "you're not the only one who gets called away for emergencies."

I made a smile for her. "On a Saturday afternoon, yet. I guess Arby doesn't have everything under control, after all."

"What makes you say that?"

I shrugged. "He's always in charge of everything. Always calculates all the angles before he moves ahead. Arby's always been the organized one."

"And you?"

What is this, I wondered, an interrogation? So I answered, "I'm the baby brother. I don't have to be organized."

"Arthur thinks the world of you, you know," said Julia.

"I know."

An uncomfortable silence fell between us. She was waiting for me to tell her how much I adore my big brother.

Before I could make up my mind to speak, Julia took a step closer to me. "You have this peculiar little smile on your lips, you know."

"I do?"

"It's almost a smirk."

"I wasn't aware of it," I said.

"I've noticed it before. Perhaps it's your natural expression."

"A smirk?"

"As if you know something that no one else knows. It gives you this slightly superior, slightly bored look."

She was smiling. Not a big smile, just enough to show that she wasn't trying to pick a fight.

"Well, I certainly don't feel superior," I said.

"No, of course not. You're rather in awe of Arthur, aren't you? You don't have to live up to him, you know. You're quite a marvelous human being yourself, actually."

That's how it started. With that conversation. We doubledated a few more times and the more I saw Julia the more I felt like I was being drawn into some kind of a whirlpool. I mean, I couldn't stop thinking about her. I never wanted to hurt Arby or get between him and Julia, but I couldn't help it. It was overwhelming. Like there was some force pulling at me, dragging me in a direction that I knew I shouldn't go.

Not that I did anything about it. I never said a word to her, never even saw her without Arby being present. Oh, okay, so we were alone for a few minutes at a time once in a while, when Arby had to answer the phone or whatever. I tried very hard not to let anything show, but the smile that Julia always gave me—that smile. It seemed to know what was going on inside me, the turmoil, the wanting, the pain that was better than any pleasure I had known before.

So help me, I never took a step toward her. But I made time to go out with her and Arby as often as I dared. Sometimes I brought a date along, but usually the poor kid just sat there, ignored, while I talked with Julia. Arby never seemed to notice anything. Not a thing. You could have whacked him on the head with a frying pan and he wouldn't have noticed it. Not when he was with Julia.

And then, at dinner one night Julia said, "Your work at the hospital must be fascinating."

I sort of shrugged. "It's drudgery, most of it. Poor people don't have exotic diseases. They've got parasites or infections or complications from do-it-yourself abortions. AIDS. Women beaten up by their boyfriends. Kids, too; more and more child abuse. Oh, yeah, there's a fair amount of stabbings and shootings, especially on the weekends."

"And that's your practice?" she asked.

Arby said, "Jesse's a doctor of internal medicine. He's director of research at the La Guardia Medical Center. But he spends most of his time in the hospital in the ghetto."

I didn't like the way he said that. "Hey, Arby, you know at one time it was our people in the ghetto."

He looked a little surprised. Then he said, "Our people got themselves out."

"Some of them did."

"And those who did helped the others to break out. We didn't get welfare."

Julia ended the incipient argument. "Would it be possible for me to visit your hospital?"

I felt stunned.

"I'd like to see what it's like."

"It's not pretty," I said. "It doesn't even smell good."

"I think it's time I saw where you work," she insisted. My heart was thudding in my chest so loud I was sure that Arby could hear it. But he seemed not to notice a thing.

Julia went on, "We see enough of good restaurants and people who are well off. The poor are rather hidden from us, don't you think?"

I couldn't answer because I had the wonderful fantasy that what Julia was really saying was that she wanted to see where I work, what I do. She wanted to be with me!

Arthur shrugged. "If you want to. I'm sure one look will last you a long time."

"Perhaps," Julia murmured.

"Frankly," Arby said, "I don't see how you put up with it, Jess. Doesn't it ever get you down, all those needy people, day after day, year after year?"

I made the best speech of my life. I said, "They need help."

So two days later Julia showed up at the hospital. Without Arby, who was busy running his lab. She stuck right beside me all through my rounds. We grabbed a couple of soggy sandwiches in the cafeteria and then I took her through a typical afternoon of seeing patients and conferences with hospital staff and administrators. The guys on the resident staff all gave me leering grins, that's how great-looking Julia is. The administrators looked flustered that an outsider was listening to them whine about shortfalls of funding and new insurance regulations.

We skipped dinner. There was too much to do, too many sick and bleeding people to deal with. She stayed with me every step of the way until it was past ten o'clock. Finally I signed out and we went out onto the street, surprised that it was dark. I was pretty tired.

And damned depressed. It had been a wonderful day with Julia beside me. But now she was going home. And in a few weeks she'd be married to Arby.

JULIA

If there's any blame to it, it's mine. I could sense that Jesse cared about me, perhaps he even loved me, but he wasn't going to do anything about it. I was Arthur's and he wouldn't interfere, no matter how much he wanted me.

It was tremendously flattering, of course. Very romantic. Even dangerous. Here I was, making arrangements with Arthur for a big wedding bash and fantasizing about his brother. I told myself a thousand times that I was being a foolish little girl. Arthur offered the kind of world that a woman could only dream about: a posh lifestyle and social position and considerable wealth. It was all right to fantasize about the romantic, forbidden brother, but I had no intention of allowing those fantasies to rule me.

And yet . . .

No matter how I tried to avoid it, I was drawn to Jesse. I found myself asking to see his hospital. I wanted to see where he worked, I told myself. Truth to tell, I wanted to be with him. Alone. Without Arthur.

Most of Mendelssohn Hospital was grubby. The buildings were old and dingy, the staff harried, the patients poor and dark-skinned and desperate. It was huge, of course, taking in several city blocks. Inside, it was quite confusing, a haphazard conglomeration of wards and offices and waiting rooms, the painted walls faded and worn-looking. Pitiful families wandering through the labyrinthine corridors, trudging along the scuffed floor tiles, looking confused or worried or frightened. Patients moaning in their beds or calling for a nurse or just lying there resigned and helpless. In some wards they had filled all the beds and had patients on gurneys out in the corridors.

There was one modern section, however: a surgery that looked quite futuristic, with big electronic display screens all around the operating table, surgeons wearing strange goggles as they manipulated tiny lasers instead of scalpels. I watched, fascinated, from the observation room behind a big window, as they cut away at the patient's abdomen.

"Cancer of the pancreas," Jesse muttered as he stood beside me.

"It looks like an absolutely up-to-date facility," I whispered. Silly, whispering like that when we were safely behind that thick window.

"Took four years of my life to raise the money for this facility," Jesse said. "We needed it, but it was tough as hell to find people willing to put up the money for it."

"Do you operate there often?" I asked.

He looked shocked. "Me? I couldn't be a surgeon. Cut up people day in and day out? Not me!"

"But they're curing that cancer patient, aren't they?"

"They're cutting out the tumor. That's not a cure."

Jesse turned away from the window and I followed him out toward the corridor.

He put that knowing smirk of his back in its place and said, "Surgery's an admission that you don't know enough about medicine."

"You don't approve of surgery?"

"Only when nothing else can be done."

"You never do it yourself?"

He shrugged. "I can sew up a slashing if I have to. I've done my share of stitching in the emergency room."

He walked me to the cardiac intensive care ward, where patients were waiting for angioplasty and bypass operations. Most of the patients were elderly, confined to their beds, although a few were shuffling along the corridor in their baggy green hospital gowns, pushing their rickety IV holders along with them, plastic tubes leading from the dangling bags to their bandaged arms. They looked weary, frightened.

"A heart attack is scary," Jesse said. "Makes you realize how close to death you can be."

"They're all going to have surgery?" I asked.

"Wish we knew enough to cure them without surgery," Jesse told me. "I wish we could give them new hearts."

Gradually, several other doctors started to walk along with us. Younger men and women. Even some nurses began following us. Jesse knew them all, bantered back and forth with them. He stopped here and there, chatted up some of the patients, looked at their charts, squinted at the monitor screens that showed their vital signs, leaned across their beds to examine them, held brief discussions with the younger staff people who clustered around him.

It was an entourage, I realized. These young men and women gathered about Jesse; they were drawn to him. He was their leader. They followed him and watched him and hung on his every word. They idolized him.

He could be a great man, I thought. With the proper backing, the proper drive, he could make this hospital into the finest medical center in the city.

"It must be a heavy responsibility," I said as he led me out of the ward.

He stopped and looked back at the patients, the staffers, the patients and doctors and nurses and orderlies who were all looking at him. Depending on him. With a boyish grin and a wave, he pushed open the big door and we headed for the elevators.

But I saw tears in his eyes. "There's not a damned thing I can do for most of them. Postpone the inevitable, that's about it. Give them another few years of life. Another few years of pain. It gets pretty hopeless."

He *was* a great man, I knew. But he didn't know it, and neither did the rest of the world. I could change that.

It was fully dark outside.

"I'll have to get a taxi," I said as we walked slowly down the hospital steps. An ambulance was coming in, we could hear its siren echoing off the buildings down the street.

"Tough to find a cab up here after dark," Jesse said. "I'll drive you to your place."

"Oh, no, it's much too far. Practically at JFK."

"I don't mind," he said.

"You're much too tired for that long a drive." He did look tired, but I wondered if I was trying to convince him of it or myself.

We were walking under the bright anticrime lamps back to the guarded parking lot for hospital staff. The uniformed security guard in the shack nodded to Jesse, who gave him a sloppy salute and a grin.

"He was a Marine in Kuwait," Jesse told me once we were out of earshot. "Now he's a sedentary overweight middle-aged rent-a-cop with a beer belly, waiting for his first heart attack."

He sounded strangely bitter. Or perhaps frustrated, as if he should be able to do something about the guard.

"Okay," he said, "I'll drive you downtown and you can pick up a taxi there."

"Why don't you drive me to your flat?"

The words just popped out of my mouth. I felt just as stunned as Jesse looked.

He said, "Huh?"

"Your apartment," I said. "It's not far from here, is it?" I felt rather like a ventriloquist's dummy, with someone putting the words in my mouth. But the ventriloquist was me, myself, my deepest desires.

"No, it's not far," Jesse said slowly, hesitantly. "Just ten minutes or so."

"You have a sofa, don't you? I could sleep there."

But I didn't sleep on the sofa, of course. Once Jesse closed his apartment door behind us it was as if the world speeded up and went into overdrive. One instant he was reaching for my hand and a blink later we were tossing around in his bed like a pair of tigers mating and I didn't think about Arthur at all. Not until morning.

WASHINGTON:

THE RAYBURN HOUSE OFFICE BUILDING

There were fewer news reporters out in the corridor when the hearing recessed for lunch than there had been the first day, Arthur saw. Most of them clustered around Jesse, who had been giving testimony all morning.

A couple of them approached Arthur but he brushed them off, saying, "I won't have anything more to give you until I start cross-examining the opposing witnesses."

They seemed to accept that, grudgingly, and went back to the group poking their microphones at Jesse. I'll have to cross-examine him, Arthur told himself. That's going to be sweet.

He saw Pat Hayward waiting for an elevator.

"Going to lunch?" Arthur asked.

"Yes. There are several very nice places within a couple minutes' walk."

"The congressmen and senators have all the conveniences, don't they?" Arthur said as the elevator doors slid open.

They rode down to the ground floor and left the building by a side door. As they crossed Independence Avenue they saw a gaggle of demonstrators slowly trudging their picket lines out by the Capitol steps. Their placards seemed to be drooping in the hot sun.

"Not as many as yesterday," Arthur said.

"I don't see any of the wheelchair contingent," said Pat.

Arthur sighed. "We're yesterday's news. No riots today."

With a laugh, Pat said, "We could start one, if you like. Just walk over to those religious zanies and let them see who you are."

Laughing back ruefully, Arthur said, "I'd much rather have a nice, quiet lunch with you."

"Me, too," said Pat.

When the hearing reconvened Arthur saw that an extra man was sitting at the desks in the front of the room. He looked like an aging cowboy, a face made of rawhide. Arthur took his seat on the front bench, wondering who this stranger was. He wanted to ask Pat, but she was back at her seat in the rear of the chamber.

Graves cleared his throat and the crowd quieted down.

"We would like to welcome Senator Kindelberger to this hearing," said the chief judge. "I would like to express my personal gratification that the senator recognizes the importance of these proceedings."

Kindelberger smiled toothily and hunched over the microphone in front of him. "I just want to say that I am here as an interested observer. The results of this trial will undoubtedly have a very deep and long-lasting effect on the American people and I firmly believe that it is important for the Senate to understand what is at stake here."

"It certainly is," said Graves. "Thank you, Senator."

"You're entirely welcome, sir."

Jesse was back in the witness chair, Rosen was at his seat, riffling through pages of notes. The TV cameras were still watching, although Arthur thought they were aimed now at Senator Kindelberger rather than the examiner or the judges.

"If I may recapitulate this morning's testimony," Rosen began, "Dr. Marshak, you told this court that although you helped to invent the concept of regenerating organs, you did not take part in any of the work done at Omnitech Laboratory."

"That's Grenford Laboratory," Jesse said. "It's a division of Omnitech Corporation."

Rosen bobbed his head up and down. "Yes, yes, Grenford Lab. Excuse me."

Jesse leaned back in his chair. Arthur looked past him, at the jury of their peers, a dozen of the nation's top scientists. So far they've heard precious little about science, Arthur said to himself.

"Now, then, Dr. Marshak," said the examiner, "we have heard Dr. Arthur Marshak, your brother, testify that, in his opinion, this work in organ regeneration is ready for human trials. Yesterday he showed us the results of work done at Grenford Laboratory on various animal test subjects, including monkeys. Yet you say you are opposed to human trials. On what grounds?"

Arthur felt himself tensing, waiting for Jesse's answer.

"On the grounds that I do not believe that organ regeneration will work in human beings," Jesse said, carefully enunciating each individual syllable.

Damn! Arthur said to himself. He's lying through his teeth.

JESSE

When Julia finally told Arby that she had fallen in love with me, Arby did what he always did: He turned cold as an iceberg and walked away from both of us. Didn't say a goddamned word. Just absolute frigid silence. Like he didn't know that we existed or didn't care.

He showed up at the wedding. Ma insisted on that. I wanted to bring Ma to the ceremony; I could have had an ambulance and a complete mobile life-support system for her, but Arby just pulled his big-brother act and flatly refused to allow her to be moved from the nursing home. Instead he arranged for a closed-circuit TV link to be fed into her bedroom; Ma watched Julia and me getting married on her TV set, live and in full color.

Arby sat in the front row, looking like a statue of ice. He didn't say a word to either one of us, didn't kiss the bride at the reception. When we returned from our three-day honeymoon at Niagara Falls (Julia had insisted on it) there was a Federal Express envelope waiting for us. Arby had started a trust for our children's education, the legal papers said, and funded it with a hundred thousand dollars.

Christ! What could I do? I phoned him a couple of times but I could never get past his secretary. So I wrote him a thank-you letter. Then we had to go off to Brazil for a few months and when we got back I found out that I had been named Humanitarian of the Year. So I invited Arby to the dinner at the Waldorf and Ma insisted that he had to attend, it would look terrible if he didn't. He came, but he wouldn't sit with us. Moved his place card to the other end of the head table.

Then that night—actually early the next morning—he phones me all hotted up over this idea of regenerating spinal neurons. He invites me to his lab for lunch. It goes fine and we're starting to heal the wound. Julia and I went to Eritrea for a couple of months and I phoned Arby from London the first day we got there. Everything seemed to be going along well. He even seemed genuinely pleased when I told him that Julia was pregnant. When we got back to New York we had him to dinner at our apartment.

Then Ma died and Julia lost the baby.

I had fought my way through a blizzard to get to Ma, damned near wrecked my car in the snow, but she had died before I could get there. Arby gave me that fish-eye look of his, like I should have been at her bedside at her last moments. As if I hadn't tried. I guess he was upset about her dying, but he took it out on me, like he usually does.

I had to stay over at the nursing home that night. Next morning I phoned Julia. She sounded a little strange to me; her voice was kind of shaky.

"You okay?" I asked her.

"Yes, I think so." Before I could ask her what she meant by that she added, "I seem to be bleeding."

Julia's anything but the panicky type. "A lot?" I asked.

"More than before." She had been bleeding a bit ever since the pregnancy had begun.

"Hemorrhaging?" I asked.

"I don't think it's that bad," she said. But there was that frightened little quaver in her voice.

"Stay in the apartment. Lie down and take it easy. I'll be there in an hour."

"But the roads are still treacherous." I heard real alarm in her voice now.

"I'll take it easy. Don't worry. I got here all right, I'll get back to you. Now go lie down."

Arby had already left for his laboratory. I was glad that he hadn't been standing over my shoulder while I talked with Julia. He'd start pestering me with questions and blaming everything on me.

The sky was bright blue when I went outside. It must've stopped snowing soon after I had arrived, because the one plowed lane in the lot was covered with less than an inch of snow. So was my car. I didn't bother sweeping the snow off my Firebird or chipping the ice off the windshield. I just revved up the engine and turned on the defroster and rear-window defogger. The engine heated up slowly, but in a few minutes I could push most of the crap off with the windshield wipers. Still couldn't see out the back too well, but another five minutes or so would take care of that.

The wheels spun on the ice underneath the snow. I hate that whirring sound they make. But I jockeyed the car back and forth until the tires found something to grab on to and then I shot out of the parking lot like a torpedo. Banged the god-damned fender against one of the posts at the covered front entrance to the nursing home; there was another patch of ice on their curving driveway. I didn't stop. The car wasn't badly dented, I figured, and I was in a hurry to get home.

Julia lay unconscious in a pool of blood on the bed when I got there.

It was a nightmare. Took forty fucking minutes to get an ambulance. I couldn't stop the hemorrhaging and I knew I was too rattled to drive. Besides, the damned Firebird probably didn't have enough gas to make it to the hospital. It had been reading empty the last ten minutes before I found a parking spot among the snowbanks along our street where somebody had shoveled his car out and gone to work.

The paramedics came pounding at the door at last and we bundled Julia off to the hospital. I put her in a private room and got the chief of obstetrics/gynecology by the scruff of the neck, just about, to come in and examine her.

It was a miscarriage. Nothing anybody could do about it. I didn't give a shit. Julia was the one I was worried about.

"She'll be all right," the ob-gyn told me. "She's lost a lot of blood, though. She'll need—"

"Not from the bank," I told him flatly. "I'll give her blood. I'm the same type as she is."

I wasn't going to run any risk whatsoever of Julia getting tainted blood. I know they do all kinds of screening and there's practically no chance of an HIV carrier donating to the blood bank anymore. But that was my wife we were talk-ing about and I wasn't going to take any chances.

"We're supposed to screen blood from donors, even family members," she told me. Like I didn't already know.

"Consider it already screened," I said. It'd take more than a week to schlepp the goddamned blood up to Syracuse and back for the screening procedure.

The ob/gyn hesitated, then caught the look in my eye. "It's on your responsibility," she said.

"Damned right."

"She'll need more than one donor can provide," the ob/gyn said. "Is there anyone else in the family with the same blood type?"

That's how Arby found out about the miscarriage. I phoned him at his lab and begged him to come down right away. For once in his life he didn't pester me with a million questions. Soon as he heard Julia needed blood he was on his way.

We both spent a pretty miserable day at the hospital, giving blood, drinking orange juice, hovering in the corridor outside Julia's room. Despite it all, I had to laugh at Arby. He was scared green of needles. I don't think he'd have given blood for me or Ma or anybody else in the world except Julia.

He hardly said a word to me all through those long hours of worrying. The doctors kept telling us that Julia would be fine; even the nurses said there was nothing to worry about except the stray chance of an infection. One of the staff psychologists looked in on her, then gave me her card and told me Julia and I both might want some counseling about the loss of the baby.

Arthur's face clouded up like a thunderhead while the psychologist talked to me. I think up until then the realization that Julia had lost the baby hadn't really sunk in on him.

I looked in on Julia constantly, of course. She was very pale, but her pulse was good. They had given her sedatives, naturally, and she was either out completely or in a dreamy, drowsy half stupor. By late afternoon, though, the sedatives were wearing off and her eyes began to focus again.

"I'm sorry," were the first words she said to me.

I leaned over the bed and kissed her on the lips, lightly. "It's not your fault."

"I know," she said in a tired whisper. "But I'm still sorry that we lost the baby."

"Don't worry about it. We'll make another one."

"Yes."

I tried to grin down at her. "We'll start trying as soon as we get home."

She made a smile for me. "Do we have to wait that long?"

I felt tremendously relieved. I know that miscarriages happen all the time and even though it can be a life-threatening situation, I had reached Julia in time and gotten her the best medical attention New York City can provide and she was never really in danger. Not really. But still I felt as if a block of cement had lifted off my shoulders. She was going to be okay. She could smile and make a joke with me. She had come through it all right. We wouldn't even need the damned psychologist.

But outside in the corridor Arthur was waiting for me, his shirtsleeve still rolled up and a Band-Aid on the puncture in his vein.

"She's going to be all right," I said to him. I guess I was smiling pretty broadly.

Arby wasn't smiling. Far from it. "How did it happen?" he asked. Like a police investigator.

"A miscarriage. It happens."

"But why?" he demanded. "What caused it?"

I shook my head. All of a sudden I felt enormously weary. Ma's death, the harrowing ride up to the nursing home, then Julia and the wild drive back. I hadn't slept much last night and all this stress and tension was wearing me down. And now Arby acting like the Grand Inquisitor.

"Infection can cause a miscarriage, can't it?" he snapped.

"In some cases."

"Julia came down with a fever in Africa, didn't you tell me so?"

"Oh, Christ, Arby, that was months ago."

"But the infection might have lingered in her system. A slow virus or a parasitical bacterial strain."

He knew just enough about medicine to be a pain in the ass.

"Okay," I said. "Soon as she's strong enough I'll do a complete blood workup. If there's anything hiding in her system, I'll find it. Okay?"

"This wouldn't have happened if you hadn't dragged her off to Africa with you."

"So you're blaming me for this?" My weariness disappeared. I was blazing mad.

And so was Arby. "I *told* you not to take her with you! I *warned* you that you were putting her in danger!"

I pushed my face so close to his we were practically butting our noses together. "I don't give a shit what you said or what you think. This is our business, my wife's and mine, and you stay the fuck out of it!"

There must have been other people in the corridor, but I paid them no attention. Didn't see anybody except Arby and that goddamned crack-of-doom expression on his face that he always used whenever he wanted to lord it over me.

"You might have killed her," he said.

"So what? She's my wife, big brother, not yours. Why don't you just roll down your sleeve, put on your coat, and get the fuck out of our lives!"

Arby's face went from red to ashy gray. His chest was heaving and I'll bet his blood pressure was popping two hundred diastolic. He clamped his mouth shut so hard I could hear his teeth click. Then he did just what I told him to. He rolled down his sleeve and, without bothering to button the cuff, grabbed his coat from the chair against the wall and strode off down the corridor like a rhinoceros charging. People scattered out of his way and I realized that half the hospital staff must have heard us screaming at one another.

ARTHUR

I couldn't deal with Jesse after the miscarriage. I simply could not stand even the idea of being in the same room with my brother. He had exposed Julia to disease and danger without even thinking about the risks to her. And now she had paid the price for his self-centered indifference.

It was the end between us. Momma was no longer there to hold us together. Jesse had taken Julia from me and then nearly killed her and she apparently didn't blame him at all.

I went into mourning. Ostensibly, it was for my mother, but actually it was for the loss of Julia, the loss of my brother. I suppose it really was for me, myself.

We held a small funeral service for Momma. Very small: only the three of us and a few distant cousins from Florida who flew up to Connecticut and spent most of their time complaining about the weather. The winter had turned gentle, I thought: temperatures in the forties and clean blue skies. Spring was on the way. The only reminder of the blizzard was the big banks of graying snow piled along the streets and highways. But the Florida contingent shivered and moaned and made it clear they couldn't wait to get back to the warmth and their golf courses.

Jesse and Julia sat on one side of the chapel's central aisle; I sat alone on the other. I did not speak a word to Jess, nor he to me. The ceremony was brief and impersonal. The rabbi had never met my mother; he just went through the motions of a memorial and inserted Momma's name in a prepackaged little speech. I took the vase with her ashes from his hands and walked straight out to the parking lot, where the snowplows had left mini-mountains that were slowly melting under the pale sun. The lot was dotted with big puddles and streams of meltwater pooling around clogged drains.

Julia came to me as I pressed the remote control key that unlocked my car. I held the little vase with Momma's ashes in my other hand. I thought that perhaps Jesse had sent his wife over to negotiate his getting some time with Momma's remains.

But Julia never mentioned the ashes.

"How are you, Arthur?" she asked. She was wearing black, of course. It made her look pale, I thought. Or perhaps she hadn't regained her complete strength yet.

"I'm all right," I answered. "And you? Have you recovered from . . ." For some reason I suddenly felt embarrassed.

"Oh, yes, I'm fine," she said. "But you look as if you haven't been sleeping well. Are you certain you're all right?"

I didn't know what to say.

While I was trying to find some words, Julia said, "It's really wrong of you to blame Jesse for my miscarriage, Arthur."

I felt the heat rising in my face.

"I made up my own mind to go to Eritrea with him," she went on. "I knew the risks. If I hadn't wanted to go, I wouldn't have gone."

I heard myself mutter through clenched teeth, "If Jess wanted to drive a motorcycle over a cliff you'd ride with him on the back seat."

Julia actually laughed. "I don't think so, Arthur, dear. I really don't."

"Well, I do." And I opened the door to my car.

"I feel as though this separation between you is my fault," Julia blurted.

"Isn't it?" I snapped. I ducked into the car, put the vase on the seat beside me, and slammed the door shut.

I suppose I should have taken the day off, taken the week off, perhaps, and gone sailing or taken a trip to someplace where I could be by myself and get my equilibrium back. Instead I drove straight to the lab and spent the afternoon pestering my researchers at their work. They didn't seem to mind too much having the boss look over their shoulders. But it reminded me that for years now I'd been an administrator, not a performer; an observer, not a scientist.

"Can I say something?" asked Tina Andriotti. I was standing behind her in her little cubicle of a lab while she bent over her worktable, dissecting a rat. The smell of formaldehyde almost completely overpowered the softer fragrance of her perfume.

"Of course. What is it?" I asked her.

Tina was Vince Andriotti's daughter, barely twenty-six years old. She had come to the lab the previous summer as a student intern and quickly proven to be a first-rate biologist. I had approved her request to work with us full-time for a year; she wanted to take a break from schooling before starting her postgraduate studies.

"You're making me nervous," she said.

"I am?" She surprised me. I had poked around her lab before and she had never complained.

She put down the scalpel she'd been using and turned around to face me. Tina bore the exotic genes of her Armenian mother very well. Almost as tall as I, she was dark of hair and eye, her complexion smooth and smoky, her figure lush. She tended to wear tight jeans and sweaters that hugged her form. Several of the younger men in the lab had tried to date her; they complained that it was unfair of her to look so tempting while her father was in the building, watching over her.

She seemed very serious. "It's not you, really. It's—Oh, never mind." And she turned back to the dissecting table.

I watched her for several minutes in silence. She was working for Zack O'Neill, pushing hard toward the experiment where we would try to grow a new heart in one of the lab rats.

"There's a couple of women in the lab," Tina muttered, still bent over the remains of the rat, "who're dying to nail you on charges of sexual harassment."

I could feel my jaw drop open. "Sexual harassment? Me?"

"They've asked all of us to let them know if you do anything actionable."

"Of all the—" I was going to say *ungrateful bitches*, but I held my temper back. "Who are they?"

Tina shook her head, her back still to me. "It's enough that I warned you, Dr. Marshak. I'm not going to squeal on them."

"But what makes them target me? I've never harassed any-one. I've always treated women fairly, haven't I?"

"You've always treated me fairly," she admitted.

My mind was going over the recent past. I hadn't come on to any of the women at the lab. Never. I don't believe in mixing work and sex, it causes too much trouble. Well, there was Nancy Dubois, of course, but that was different, and besides, Nancy didn't work at the lab.

Tina straightened up again and went to the sink, peeling off her surgical gloves as she said, "Women are very sensitive about harassment, you know. It's something we've got to watch out for."

"But I've never . . ." A new thought struck me. Was Tina merely trying to keep me off balance? Was she worried that I was about to hit on her and she used this sexual harassment ploy to stop me before I started?

"Well," I said, "thanks for the warning. Can I look at the animal now?"

"Sure, go right ahead." She smiled and it looked to me as if she thought she'd pulled one over on the boss. On the other hand, there was no way that a smile on a young woman as beautiful as Tina could not be inviting.

I stuck strictly to business. I went over to the table and peered at the rat's insides. Tina obligingly swiveled a magnifying lens over the cadaver. I saw the rat's regular heart and a little pink node next to it, where a new heart had started to grow. And dozens of ugly gray tumors clustering all through the thorax, crowding the lungs and blocking off the aorta.

"Zack can get a new heart started," Tina said, all business now, "but the tumors start to spring up and choke off the natural organs."

"The regentide isn't specific enough," I said. "We've got to determine how to concentrate it specifically on the heart cells."

"And then there's the problem of getting rid of the old heart once the new one kicks in."

I said, "Let's worry about that problem after we've gotten a new heart to work without killing the animal with tumors."

Tina shrugged. Deliciously. "Okay, you're the boss."

I had to admire her. Tina had a really sharp mind and the special kind of dexterous hands that would allow her to be either a first-class surgeon or a first-class experimental biologist—whichever she eventually chose. But she also had this ravishing physical beauty, and she was bright enough to realize that it could be a handicap to her career. Men saw her face and figure before anything else; she had to make them see her brains and dedication, just as they would in another man or a less-beautiful woman. Maybe this sexual harassment ploy was the right way for her to go. I just hoped she wasn't really telling the truth about a cabal of women in the lab looking to make trouble.

I made a mental note to ask Phyllis about this sexual harassment business.

ABOUT A week later we had a review meeting in my office. Zack, Darrell, Vince Andriotti, and I went through all the data we had accumulated. I was impatient with their results so far.

"What you're telling me," I said, "is that the attempts to grow a new heart cause cancer."

Zack nodded somberly. We were sitting at the round conference table in my office, the four of us. I had received a phone call from Johnston that morning. He wanted to know how the work was coming along.

"We'll beat the problem," Darrell said, almost casually. Then he added, "But it's going to take time."

"The CEO wants to see a rat with a new heart in it," I said.

"He will," Darrell said.

"By the end of the month?" I asked.

"Hell, no."

Should I tell them about Johnston's approaching the Japanese? No, I told myself firmly. That's my worry, not theirs. Don't pressure them more than you have to.

Zack's boyish face had a sly look to it. "You said the CEO wants to see a rat that's grown a new heart?"

"That's what we promised him. Remember?"

"Sure, sure." Zack's eyes shifted away from mine slightly and he asked, "What's wrong with showing him a rat with two hearts?"

"And a shitload of tumors," Vince said.

"So what?"

Darrell shifted uneasily in his chair. "What are you proposing, Zack?"

Gesturing with one hand, Zack said, "I can produce a rat that's grown a new heart. It might not be fully functional, but we can show the CEO fluoroscope imagery in real time and he'll see two little hearts going pitty-pat."

"And a shitload of tumors," Andriotti repeated.

"Not if we use the right dye," Zack countered.

"Now, wait a minute—" said Darrell.

But Zack didn't wait. "We can inject the dye into the bloodstream and stick the rat in the fluoroscope for a couple of minutes. The CEO will see two hearts and we turn off the scope before the dye gets to the tumors. Simple."

"That's cheating," Darrell said.

"It would be cheating if we tried to tell the scientific world that we had successfully generated a new heart in the animal with no harmful side effects," Zack said.

"But it's not cheating if we let the CEO think that's what we've done?" Vince looked disgusted.

"We can tell him it's the first time we've done it and there's still a long way to go before we've got the procedure perfected."

Darrell ran a finger across his long jawline. "In other words, we'd just be putting on a show to satisfy the management."

"Right."

All three of them turned to me. Vince was clearly unhappy with the idea; Darrell seemed almost amused at the thought of pulling one over on the top brass. Zack had already convinced himself that this was the way to go.

I let them sit there, waiting for my decision.

"All right," I said at last. "We'll do it your way, Zack. But I'll tell Johnston clearly that this is merely a demonstration, that there are still plenty of problems to be solved before we can even move to minihog experiments."

"Clearly," Vince emphasized.

"Clearly," I affirmed.

Darrell chuckled. "You can be as clear as you want to, Arthur. All that Johnston's going to see is a rat that's grown an extra heart. All that he's going to think about is that we're on the right track to the biggest medical breakthrough in history."

"Well, we are," Zack said. "Aren't we?"

I had to admit that we were.

ZACK WAS bold and ambitious, but he was no fool. He worked out the procedure and tried it on three rats in a row. They grew new hearts, and the new hearts even started to pump blood. But the tumors grew uncontrollably and each rat died within two days of the new heart's growing to full size.

Good enough.

I invited Johnston to the lab. He brought Sid Lowenstein and Tabatha Young with him.

We had set up Zack's lab for the demonstration. He had, as planned, reserved 3C278 for the starring role. The little ball of white fur nestled trustingly in the palm of Zack's hand as he showed it off. As usual, Johnston shied away from it. Sid looked as if we were asking him to eat broccoli. Tabatha cooed over the rat and stroked its back with one bony finger.

"This little fellow was injected with the peptide sequence that we've developed specifically to initiate the growth of new heart cells," Zack said as he placed the rat in a glass box and started walking back toward the fluoroscope apparatus.

We formed a little parade behind him: Johnston, Sid, Tabatha, Darrell, and me.

Talking to them all the time, Zack put the glass cage beside the fluoroscope screen and powered up the equipment. Then he took a hypodermic syringe from the table at his elbow.

"I have to inject our subject with a dye that will make his bloodstream visible in the fluoroscope," he said. "It's a painless injection."

"Painless to you, maybe," Sid Lowenstein muttered. No one laughed.

"The injection includes a sedative," Zach continued, "so the subject will be unconscious."

I looked the other way while Zack injected the rat. Once the fur ball slipped into sleep he closed the glass lid and placed the cage behind the fluoroscope screen. Darrell turned off the room's lights.

"It will be easier to see the screen if the room's darkened," I explained.

"I can see its bones!" Tabatha said.

"Look for the blood flow," Zack said, pointing. "See, here's where I injected the dye. It'll be reaching his original heart in a few seconds."

"Yeah, there's the heart," Lowenstein said. "See it beating?"

"And here," said Zack, "is the new heart."

"It's beating, too!"

"Both of them!"

I was watching Johnston's face. In the greenish glow of the screen his skin looked eerie. But slowly a smile spread across his features.

"Look at that," he said, in a near whisper that had more than a little awe in it.

"The test subject has grown a functional second heart," Zack said crisply. "Just as we intended it to do."

Darrell clicked on the ceiling lights. We all blinked like kids at the end of a movie.

"By god, you've done it," Lowenstein said, genuinely impressed.

"We've started on it," I said. "We're a long way from anything useful in the clinical sense. There are a lot of problems still to be solved."

"I think it's wonderful," Tabatha said. "How soon can I get a new heart?"

I thought of the masses of tumors already clogging 3C278's thorax and gave Tabatha a patient smile. "It's going to take a while longer, I'm afraid. Maybe quite a while longer."

JULIA

There was a side to Arthur that I didn't like at all. He was strong, self-reliant, and utterly capable—most of the time. In American parlance, he was a "take charge" kind of person. But when he couldn't have his way he dashed off and sulked like a little boy.

He ran away from me when I broke the news to him that I had fallen in love with Jesse. And he ran away again after their mother's funeral service, when I tried to heal the breach that I had caused between them. I suppose I can't really blame him. In his own way, Arthur was just as vulnerable as Jesse. It's just that usually he didn't show any chinks in his armor at all. Completely unlike Jesse, who was always wearing his heart on his sleeve. Jesse was impulsive, and you could always see what he was thinking just by looking at his face. Arthur was much stronger, self-contained. But when he hit an obstacle he couldn't climb over, he ran away from it.

For weeks I agonized over Arthur. I had hurt him terribly, I knew, and just when that wound seemed to be healing my miscarriage drove him even further away from Jesse and me.

"Don't worry about Arby," Jesse told me. "He's like a cat. He always lands on his feet."

"I've seen cats mashed flat by lorries, you know," I said.

Jesse gave me a slightly hurt look. "You're thinking more about him these days than you are about me, you know that?"

We happened to be in bed at that moment. "Really, darling," I said, "you *are* a spoiled little boy, aren't you? Both of you, actually."

Jesse smiled at me, took my hand in his, and slid it down the length of his torso. "Does that feel like a spoiled little boy?" he asked.

"Well, it's not little."

"And it's not spoiled."

"But it's definitely male."

After more than a year of marriage and all we had been through, I still had to reassure Jesse that he was the center of my universe. The reassurance was great fun, actually.

Jesse insisted that I take a full physical examination shortly after I came home from hospital. He was concerned that perhaps some exotic infection was lingering in my system and this had caused the miscarriage. I spent several days at the medical center, allowing Jesse's best people to stick me with needles, probe, tap, palpate, and otherwise investigate every pore of my body. I came out of it with flying colors.

"My god," said Jesse, reading through their reports over dinner at our flat, "you're as healthy as a horse."

"Then why did I have the miscarriage?" I wondered aloud.

He shrugged. "It happens. Even to healthy women. For no apparent reason."

"But would it happen again?"

"There's no reason to expect it to."

"There was no reason to expect it the first time," I said.

He leaned across our tiny dinner table and kissed me gently. "First pregnancies are always the toughest. You'll see, the next one will go fine."

I certainly hoped he was right. It was clear from the expression on his face that he was as worried about it as I was, but he didn't want to alarm me.

Still, as the weeks wore into months I found myself worrying not about having a baby, but about Arthur. Should I try to call him? Or perhaps drive up to his laboratory and drop in unannounced? Neither, I decided. I would write instead. His birthday was coming up, and instead of a silly commercial card I would write a long and heartfelt letter.

Which I did. I told him how terrible I felt and how wrong it was for him and Jesse to remain separated. I told him how much we both missed him, and how unhappy Jesse was over their falling-out. That was a bit of a stretch, I'm afraid; actually Jesse seemed to have dropped Arthur out of his mind altogether. At the very end of my letter I invited Arthur to have dinner with us on his birthday.

Before mailing the letter, though, I showed it to Jesse. He

came home close to midnight that night, bone-tired. Perhaps I should have waited until morning, but I was too excited by the prospect of setting everything right between them to think of that.

Jesse sat down wearily in the easy chair in the living room and I handed him my letter.

"What do you think of this?" I asked.

He frowned when he saw it was addressed to Arthur, and muttered something about my terrible handwriting as he started scanning the letter. I sat on the sofa and watched his face: it went from unease to displeasure to outright anger. He crumpled up the sheet of paper in his fist and threw it across the room.

I was shocked.

"You're not going to beg my brother's forgiveness, goddammit! He's the one who ought to be asking you to forgive him, for god's sake."

"I wasn't begging—"

"The hell you weren't!" He shot up to his feet, strode across the living room, and picked up the crumpled letter. "This goes straight into the trash."

I followed him into the kitchen. "Don't you want to be reconciled with Arthur?"

"Sure. When he's ready to admit he's been a pigheaded jerk. Not before. I won't have you crawling to him. Never!"

His anger stunned me. Until that moment I had never realized that Jesse was just as furious with his brother as Arthur was with us.

THE TRIAL:
DAY TWO, AFTERNOON

Jesse could hear, behind him, the stirring of the people who packed the hearing chamber. All the TV cameras were focused squarely on him now.

Rosen asked again, "You don't think that organ regeneration will work on human subjects?"

"No, I do not," said Jesse. He expected Arthur to object, but nothing happened. He shot a swift glance at his brother. Arby's face looked ominously dark, furious; he was obviously struggling to hold himself in check.

"What leads you to that conclusion?" Rosen asked.

"The fact that there are undesirable side effects from the procedure."

"Undesirable side effects?"

"Yes."

"Such as?"

Jesse took a longer look at Arthur. Strangely, Arby's expression seemed slightly more at ease. He looked more as if he were genuinely intrigued by what Jesse was saying, rather than angry about it. The same old Arby, Jesse thought; he covers up his emotions right away, never lets his feelings show. Not for long, anyway.

"Such as?" Rosen prompted again.

Turning his full attention back to the examiner, Jesse said, "The growth inducers used to initiate the regeneration tend to also cause unwanted growth of other cells."

"Other cells?"

"Yes. In the reports that Grenford Laboratory has offered as evidence there's clear indication that regeneration attempts have led to tumor growths in the test animals."

"Tumors?" Rosen asked, as if this were all new to him. "Malignant tumors?"

He wants me to say "cancer," Jesse knew. I wonder how long I can go along this line without using the word. "Some of them become malignant," he said. "Apparently the peptides used to initiate regeneration can trigger the proto-oncogenes in the nearby cells, as well."

"And that leads to cancer?"

The crowd gave a little collective gasp. There! Jesse thought. The C-word is out in the open.

"It certainly does lead to cancer," he said.

"And for that reason you are against any attempt to conduct human trials of organ regeneration?" Rosen asked.

"Yes, that's right." Jesse shifted uneasily in his chair, then went on, "Now, understand that the tumors aren't always cancerous. Most of them are benign."

"But all of the regeneration trials have led to the growth of unwanted tumors, have they not?"

"Yes, I believe so."

"Objection!"

Jesse turned in his chair and saw that Arthur was on his feet again. He looked calm and in control of himself, but Jesse knew what ferment must be seething below his brother's facade.

"Dr. Marshak," said Graves, the chief judge.

Almost smiling, Arthur took a few steps from his place in the front row toward the witness chair where his brother sat.

"Have you read all the reports we offered in testimony?" he asked Jesse.

Rosen got to his feet and came around the table. "This is not the proper time for cross-examining the witness."

Arthur ignored the examiner. "Well, have you?" he asked.

Jesse looked from Arthur to Rosen to the judges. Graves's face was twisted into a worried scowl.

"Dr. Marshak," he said to Arthur, pointing with his gavel, "you said you have an objection and I am willing to listen to it. But you may not cross-examine the witness at this time."

A grimace of anger flashed across Arthur's face but he quickly suppressed it. "I do have an objection," he said to Graves.

"Well, what is it?"

Looking down at his brother for a moment, Arthur said, "The witness is basing his testimony only on the earliest reports of our animal trials. The later reports show quite clearly that we've been able to control the tumor growth to a considerable extent."

He's calling me a liar, Jesse realized. Or an incompetent boob.

"I read all the reports," he snapped, staring straight at his brother.

"Then why don't you admit that we've solved the tumor problem?"

"Because you haven't!"

"That's just not true," Arthur insisted.

Graves banged his gavel on the desktop. "Quiet! Both of you!"

Arthur stood facing his brother, fists on his hips. Jesse could feel his insides boiling. It took an effort to keep himself from yelling back at his brother.

"Dr. Marshak," said Graves to Arthur, "you have made your objection and it will be duly noted in the record of these proceedings. Now kindly sit down and let us go on. You'll get your chance at cross-examination later."

Arthur went back to the front bench and sat. Rosen returned to his seat. Jesse thought of two prizefighters going back to their corners at the end of a round. He turned back to face the judges and saw that Senator Kindelberger was grinning at him.

JESSE

There was no way that I was going to work with Arby or any of his people, not after the way he blew up over Julia's miscarriage. He had even snapped at Julia at Ma's funeral service, for god's sake. So the hell with him. No sense even thinking about La Guardia and Grenford working together. That was finished before it ever started. Arthur's the big-shot executive with his own laboratory and a whole staff of sycophants kowtowing to him all the time. Let him go tinker with nerve regrowth or organ regeneration. See how far he gets.

I had more important things to attend to.

Like every hospital in the world, Mendelssohn always needed more money. We were even more in the red than most because the hospital is right on the border of the worst ghetto in the city and we had this constant tidal wave of welfare and charity cases. Poverty is ugly. Poverty is kids with sores on their skin and lice in their hair. Crack babies. AIDS babies. And violence. When I worked the emergency room I bet I saw more gunshot wounds than the medics with the First Cavalry.

That's why it seemed to be a perverse sort of godsend when Reverend Roy Averill Simmonds, one of those television evangelists, was rolled off an ambulance into the emergency room that Friday night.

It'd been months since I'd seen Arby. Julia was completely recovered from the miscarriage and back at work at British Airways. In fact, she was off in London the night Reverend Simmonds was brought in.

He was only a small-time evangelist in those days; you could see him on cable TV late at night. He had come to New York as part of a summertime revival bash at Yankee Stadium, where he had to share the pulpit—or whatever they used—with half a dozen other Bible-thumpers. Even at that they only half-filled the stadium. But it was still the most excitement the Bronx had seen all summer, what with the Yanks doing so miserably.

I was down in the cafeteria, grabbing a quick cup of coffee after being on duty for several hours. I made it a point of honor to do my share of the ER duty. Nobody on the hospital staff got special privileges, starting with me.

One of the Hispanic orderlies came barreling through the empty cafeteria, breathless.

"Quick, they need you!"

"What is it?" I asked, gulping down the last of the coffee.

"A very important man. He's been wounded."

"Who?"

"Some priest. Not a priest, a minister. He's on TV all the time."

At that point, I had no idea who Reverend Simmonds was or that he'd been working the crowd at the stadium. I tossed my Styrofoam cup into the waste bin and hurried toward the elevators, thinking that we had an assassination attempt on our hands. Urban violence had found another victim. Or maybe terrorism.

But when I started examining Reverend Simmonds, in a curtained-off corner of the emergency room, I saw that he had been neither shot nor stabbed. He was suffering from a concussion, a pretty bad scalp wound, and contusions along the side of his head and face.

Two deathly pale young men had come in with the evangelist. They were standing at the foot of the gurney while I examined him, both of them sweating in dark suits with narrow ties.

"What happened?" I asked as I watched the patient's pupils. He was semiconscious, unfocused; a concussion, all right.

"One of the light standards collapsed and fell onto the stage," said the young man nearer me, in a hushed voice.

"Right in the middle of his sermon," said the other, also whispering.

"Must've been pretty heavy," I said, starting to clean the scalp wound. The patient winced and groaned.

"It's a miracle that it didn't kill him."

I wisecracked, "Thank god he's got a thick skull."

Neither of them so much as smiled.

"Will he be all right?"

"I think so." I called out to the volunteer on station at the desk outside, "Schedule this one for X-ray. Skull, left cheek-bone, and jaw."

"I think it was an assassination attempt," one of the young men whispered.

I looked up at him. He was entirely serious.

"Who'd want to kill him?"

"The forces of evil."

"Like who?" I asked.

His eyes shifted around as if he were searching for de-mons in the air.

"A man of God has many enemies," the other one said.

"Like who?" I asked again.

"Those who serve the devil," he whispered so low I could barely hear him.

I almost laughed in his face. The forces of evil were most likely a couple of sloppy electricians who didn't set up their stage lights properly. Instead of worrying about the devil, these guys ought to be more careful about who they hire, I thought. Probably nonunion workers.

I bundled him off for X-ray, warning the orderly that this was a concussion case and he'd probably upchuck sooner or later. Then I quickly forgot about Reverend Simmonds. It was a busy Friday night. Early summer, not the muggy dog days yet, but the bars and street corners were producing a heavy stream of fights and slicings. Then an apartment block caught fire and we started getting burns and smoke-inhalation cases. Reverend Simmonds had it easy.

It was Sunday before I saw him again. I was at my desk, wading through the eternal ocean of paperwork, when two other aides—fresh-scrubbed young girls this time—pushed his wheelchair into the doorway of my office. The bandaging on his head made it look like he was wearing a white turban, almost. The swelling on his cheek had gone down, but that side of his face was still purple. He was dressed casually: light slacks, crisp white short-sleeved shirt, no tie.

"You work on the Lord's day," said the reverend. I was surprised at the depth and power of his voice, especially since he was just a little guy. A bantamweight, really.

"People get sick and injured on the Lord's day," I said. "Somebody's got to take care of them." I didn't tell him that as far as I was concerned, the Sabbath had already passed.

He gave me a penetrating look from under those graying shaggy eyebrows. "You're the chief of internal medicine here, I understand."

"That's right," I said.

"Yet you were working in the emergency room Friday night."

"It was my turn. Every doctor on the staff takes his turn, that's the way we do it here."

"That's very unusual."

"So is getting bonked on the head by a light stand."

He threw his head back and laughed, which told me that he wasn't in any real pain. "You see?" he said to the two silent girls behind him. "It's just as I told you. It all has a meaning, a significance."

"What does?"

Reverend Simmonds motioned for them to push his chair closer to my desk. There really wasn't much room for him; my office is barely big enough for the desk and file cabinets.

"There's no such thing as a coincidence," he said to me in that deep basso voice. "Everything happens according to God's plan."

"Everything?"

"Everything. My accident and the fact that you were in the emergency room—both part of God's plan."

"So what's God planning next?"

He took my question as if I had really meant it. "I think the Lord is telling me that I should help your hospital. I think the Lord wants me to help the poor, downtrodden, hopeless people of the ghetto."

"They can use all the help they can get," I said.

"Helping this hospital would help them, wouldn't it?"

"Ninety percent of our patients are from the immediate neighborhood," I told him. "Most of them are on welfare or Medicaid or Medicare."

He nodded as if he had just made up his mind. "I'll help you to raise funds for this hospital. Together we will do God's blessed work."

So help me, those were the words he used. God's blessed work. He took off to complete his tour of revival meetings that he was scheduled to do. Went all across the country, mostly to small and medium-sized cities in the Midwest, although I heard he made stops in Seattle and Salem, Oregon, and then swung back East to Portland, Maine, and Hartford. His TV ministry resorted to tapes of old shows while he was on the road.

All through those weeks several of his people were in constant touch with me by phone, making arrangements for a fund-raising rally in Central Park. At first I just went through the motions, figuring that's what they were doing and the whole wacky idea would fall of its own dead weight sooner or later. But these guys were serious. I mean, *serious*. I was tempted to call them the reverend's disciples. Utterly intent on producing a mammoth rally in the park; not a smile on any of them, ever.

The reverend's business manager seemed more human, though. He was a chubby, jovial-looking older guy named Elwood Faber. Always wore a tweed suit, no matter how hot it was. And he never perspired, despite his chunky build. I wondered what kind of metabolism he had. He was from somewhere out in Kansas or Nebraska, someplace like that. He could crack a smile, at least, and knew a joke when he heard one. Mentally sharp, too, despite his fat farm-boy looks and his seedy clothes.

Little by little, I began to see that Elwood was the real brains behind Reverend Simmonds's operation. And he was dead-set on making this Central Park gig a mammoth success.

"You can really get people to fork out thirty bucks a head

for these revival meetings?" I asked Elwood once, when he had come to my office at the hospital.

"Surely do," he answered cheerfully. "We give them a lot for their money: entertainment, rock music, gospel singing— and salvation."

I looked at him. He was grinning at me.

"Salvation," I said.

"People need to feel that there's something bigger'n them, something in control of the world. It's pretty scary out there all by yourself. Folks feel better when they can believe that God loves 'em and is lookin' out for them."

"Do you believe any of that?" I asked.

Still grinning, he said, "That's not important. The customers do. We make them feel good."

"Does Simmonds believe any of it?"

Faber's smile clicked off like an electric light. "He surely does. Don't doubt it for a second. He believes, all right. If he didn't he wouldn't be able to do what he does. You can't sway thousands of people with something you don't feel in your heart of hearts. He's convinced of the truth, don't doubt that for a second, son."

"But you don't swallow it," I said.

The grin came back. "Like I said, that's not important. The reverend has important work to do, powerful work. And I help him."

Faber helped a lot. He was the one guy in Simmonds's operation who seemed to know what he was doing. I started to get calls from the mayor's office, from the Parks Department, from Broadway show people, for god's sake. The hospital's board of directors was overjoyed; they would have made me a saint, at least the Catholics on the board would have.

Simmonds flew into town specifically to nail down the final plans for the rally. He invited me to dinner at his hotel and I took Julia.

"Where is he staying?" Julia asked when I told her about dinner.

I grinned at her. "At the Pierre."

She looked impressed. "The Lord's work must pay pretty well."

"I guess it does."

It was over dinner—served in his suite, no less—that I started talking about the research we were doing at the La Guardia Center. Simmonds didn't seem interested at all. He looked bored, in fact.

And then, somehow, I mentioned Arby's work on organ regeneration. I don't know why I did that, it had nothing to do with me or the hospital or the medical center. But I did, and it perked him up immediately.

"Grow new organs right inside your body?"

We were halfway through dessert and coffee. Julia and me, Simmonds, and Elwood Faber, the business manager. The hotel had sent up two waiters to set things up and serve the various courses. They were out in the hall now, waiting for him to call them when we were finished. No wine with the meal. No after-dinner drinks, either. Simmonds ran a dry ship.

I took a sip of coffee from the delicate china cup. "That's what he's after. When you wear out the organs you were born with, you can grow a new set as you need them."

He gave me a fishy stare. "Then you wouldn't die when your time came."

"How would one know when one's time has come?" Julia asked sweetly.

Simmonds was a little guy, like I've said. He was sitting in one of the hotel's fake Louis XIV chairs, across the white-clothed table from us. The chair was big and ornate; it made him look even smaller. He frowned like a petulant kid.

"That's interfering with the Lord's plan," he rumbled.

"So's taking antibiotics," I said.

"No, no, this is serious." He seemed really troubled. "This would allow people to prolong their lives indefinitely, wouldn't it?"

"If it works," Faber said, as he reached for a second helping of dessert.

"Oh, it'll work," Simmonds growled. "Sooner or later the scientists will make it work. They always do."

He had more faith in Arthur than I did.

Julia said, "But if it can be made to work, wouldn't that mean it's part of God's plan?"

The reverend shook his head doggedly, lips pursed, brows pinched together. "It would be the devil's work," he said. "So it must be stopped."

Well, we argued *that* point long into the night. All very politely, mind you. None of us raised our voices. I was amused by it, more than anything else. Here was this little guy who thought he was plugged into God's personal Web site worrying that what Arby and other scientists were doing was the work of the devil. It was ludicrous.

But Julia took it all much more seriously. In the taxi going back to our apartment she said to me, "I wish you'd never mentioned Arthur's work to that man."

"He did get clanked up about it, didn't he?"

"He's dangerous, Jess. I'm afraid of him," she said.

"Him? Dangerous?" I laughed. "He's just a showman who uses religion instead of performing dogs. One step up from a con man."

Sitting beside her on the back seat of the cab, I could feel the tension in her. She had been more relaxed in Eritrea.

"You're wrong," she said. "He believes what he's saying. That's what makes him dangerous."

That was just what Elwood had told me: the reverend really believes.

"He's going to raise a great deal of money for the hospital, isn't he?" Julia asked me.

"If Elwood and his people can pull off this rally in the park, yeah."

"That means he'll be attracting a huge crowd to the park, doesn't it?"

"Sure, but—"

"That's his power, Jess. He can draw crowds."

"So do the Rolling Stones," I said. "And bigger crowds, too."

"That kind of power can be used for more than just raising money," Julia said. "He can turn it into political clout. Or worse."

All of a sudden I got a picture of the mob from the last scene of every Frankenstein movie I had ever seen when I was a kid. Always brandishing their torches and marching up to the castle and burning the place to the ground.

"Aw, don't be silly," I said to Julia. "This is just a little guy who can sweet-talk people out of a few bucks by spouting that old-time religion. It's show business, not politics."

But Julia shook her head and said, "You're wrong, Jess. He's dangerous."

ARTHUR

The demonstration for the CEO had gone extremely well. By the time Johnston, Lowenstein, and Tabatha Young had left the lab, they were assuring me that the regeneration work was going to be the salvation of Omnitech Corporation.

"Send me a budget plan for the coming year," Johnston told me as I walked them to their waiting limo.

"I'd like to see a copy of that myself," said Tabatha.

I smiled and nodded.

"No gold-plating, Art," Lowenstein warned. But he was smiling.

"When have I ever gold-plated a budget?" I replied, with as much innocence as I could muster.

We all laughed together. The best of friends, the four of us. As long as I could hold up before their eyes the prospect of a golden future. Tabatha even kissed me on the cheek, for god's sake!

By the time I got back inside the building, Zack O'Neill had already sent poor little 3C278 down to Tina's dissection lab.

"Seems a shame to sacrifice him," I said to Zack.

He shrugged. "I'm building up a timeline study to see how fast the tumors grow. Old 3C's part of the study. And she's a her, not a him."

"Couldn't you let her hang in there for a while longer?" I asked.

Zack grinned at me. "You're not getting sentimental over a lab rat, are you?"

"That rat has earned us a year's operating budget, maybe more."

"I could have her stuffed and mounted for you," he joked. "She'll look great on your desk."

I thought about hurrying down to Tina's lab and making a dramatic rescue of our brave little rat.

Zack was saying, "Besides, the tumors'll kill her anyway in a few days. Why put her through all that pain?"

"Yes," I said. And to myself I added, Stay away from Tina, you fool. Life's complicated enough without chasing an employee—who's the daughter of an employee, yet.

I left Zack's lab and went to my own office. Phyllis was at her desk, as usual, pecking away at her keyboard.

"Phyllis," I asked, "have you heard any complaints about sexual harassment?"

She looked up at me warily. "I wouldn't call them complaints, exactly. But there's some talk, here and there."

"About me?"

"Not to my face, no."

Of course, I realized. They wouldn't talk about me in front of Phyllis. She'd fry them.

"Well, if you hear anything, would you let me know?"

She gave me her schoolteacher look. "I told you, they won't talk in front of me."

"Oh. I see," I said. "Well, if you do hear anything about anybody, please let me know."

"Sure," Phyllis answered, but there wasn't much conviction in it.

I went into my office, wondering what else I could do about it. Then I remembered that I should call Nancy. Tomorrow, I decided. Or maybe the next day. Spend the weekend with her, maybe. After she's had a chance to observe what Sid and Johnston really think about the demonstration they saw here today.

* * *

FOR SOME reason I didn't call Nancy at all. I spent the weekend by myself, the first really hot weekend of the summer. Families streamed to the beaches or the mountains. I took off by myself in my Infiniti, with the air-conditioning turned up nice and high, and drove all the way up to Rockport, Maine. Ate a lobster dinner in a crowded ramshackle tourist joint built on a pier that swayed with every incoming wave. Then drove back home to Connecticut, listening to Ravel and Debussy on the CD player. And Schubert's Unfinished Symphony; perfect for that dark, breezy summer night. Slept late Sunday, read the *Times,* poked around the house until early afternoon, then finally went down to the lab to work on the budget that Johnston had asked for.

Anyone who thinks you can make a schedule for research is a fool. I don't care what the corporate management wants or needs, no one on earth can write a schedule for work that is essentially a trek into the unknown. That's what research is, a safari across the frontiers of knowledge. Trying to make a neat little budget with a schedule of goals to be accomplished, well, it's as if Jefferson had insisted on a schedule from Lewis and Clark before they set out on their exploratory trip across the Louisiana Territory: you will arrive at the River Platte by such-and-such a date. They didn't even know the River Platte existed when they started out!

So creating a research budget is a work of art. The management types think it's simple: you determine how many researchers and technicians you need for the program, tote up their hours, throw in estimates of the equipment and supplies they'll require, and then add a generous figure for overhead and administrative costs.

Yes, but how many researchers do you need to get the work done? To some extent, manpower buys time, true enough. The more people you can put on a job, the sooner it gets done. Up to a point. More important, in research, is the quality of the people working on the task. And not just their qualities as individuals, either, but the mix of their personalities. You can't have an entire team made of chiefs, you need some Indians. And even among the Indians there are prima donnas, personalities that will clash with certain other personalities.

That's what I wrestled with all that long sunny Sunday afternoon: building the right team and providing them with the equipment, supplies, and—above all—the flexibility they'd need to get the job done.

I wasn't alone in the building, of course. I could hear the distant yowls of Max and some of the other chimps around feeding time. Their handlers took turns working the weekends. Vince Andriotti stuck his swarthy face in my doorway, but I waved him off.

"Budget," was all I needed to say. He grinned and vanished like a genie, minus the puff of smoke.

I realized, as I crunched through the numbers with my desktop computer, that we could use Cassie's tumor-killer to help us. If we couldn't make regentide specific enough to avoid sprouting tumors, we could at least use the tumor-killing antigen that Cassie was testing to knock the tumors out. I felt better about that. We had a backup, a way to solve the biggest problem that had come up so far.

The next evening was Nancy night. The fencing season had ended weeks ago, but we still met almost every Monday evening. I was feeling good enough about the way things were going to start thinking about how I might disencumber myself from her. But I had to be graceful about it. Hell hath no fury and all that. If she thought I was dumping her, she might turn very nasty. I still wanted her friendly; she was a valuable ally in the corporate office.

She had obtained her promotion to the marketing department and was busily getting herself acclimated to the new position. And already beginning to undermine the vice president of marketing. Uhlenbeck seemed an easygoing character, quite pleased to have Nancy taking over his chores for him. He reminded me of a character out of Dickens: tall and gawky, bald except for a fringe of white hair, slightly out of focus with the world around him. He must have been a good man once, but now he seemed to be resting on his laurels, waiting for retirement age or his golden parachute. Nancy was already right there behind him, ready to push him out of the plane.

I called her that Monday afternoon to cancel our date. She had her answering machine on, and I felt grateful to give the message to the machine instead of Nancy herself. I actually felt relieved. Then I started to ask myself why I wanted to get Nancy out of my bed. Time for a reality check. Well, I told myself, for one thing, she'd been bragging about our relationship to the other women in the corporate office. That's bad news. It could cause trouble, sooner or later. For another, it was tough to think about dating other women when I knew Nancy was hanging around my neck. I didn't want a scene with her accusing me of two-timing her.

If there had been some real emotional commitment from either one of us it would have been different. But Nancy didn't really care about me and I certainly didn't care about her. She had wanted that promotion and I had wanted information. The sex was a by-product, not a reason for our affair. We had both gotten what we had bargained for, so what was the point of keeping the relationship going?

The truth was, I was getting bored with her. And she probably felt exactly the same way about me. One of us had to put an end to this affair, and I told myself it was my responsibility. Just do it nicely, I thought. With tact and kindness.

That's what I was thinking about when I visited corporate headquarters in the middle of the week after our demonstration for Johnston et al.

Nancy sauntered into my office unannounced and sat herself primly on the chair in front of my desk. She was dressed in a power suit: no-nonsense beige slacks and jacket, hair done up slickly, just the right amount of makeup to show that she was a hard-driving executive who happened to be an attractive female.

"So what are you doing with your Monday nights?" she asked.

One Monday night I had begged off and she was acting like the wronged woman already. I looked up from a computer screen filled with cost estimates. "The same thing I do almost every night," I said. "Working at the lab. This regeneration program is moving ahead now, accelerating. It's taking almost all my time."

"Weekends, too?"

"Weekends, too," I said.

She seemed to think that over for a moment. Then, "I know that Sid and Johnston were tremendously impressed with their visit to the lab."

I nodded. Nancy had never come to the lab, despite my invitations.

"But you can't be working *all* the time," she said.

I had to bite the bullet. "Nancy, I think it's best if we let things cool down a bit, don't you?"

"Cool down? What do you mean?"

She wasn't going to make it easy for me. "We should stop seeing each other." There. I said it.

Her face crumpled. One moment she was a self-assured executive, cool and in command of herself, then all of a sudden she looked like a child who'd just been told there is no Santa Claus. Her eyes filled with tears.

"But I thought you cared about me!"

I looked past her to the door to my office. She had left it open and people were walking by in the corridor outside.

"I like you a lot, Nancy," I improvised, keeping my voice low, "but I don't think we should—well, I'm just not ready for any kind of a commitment. It's best if we break it off, right here and now."

"But I love you!" she blurted.

My jaw must have dropped six inches.

"Do you think I'd go to bed with you just because I wanted a promotion? Do you think I'm some kind of company whore?"

I jumped up and went for the door. I wanted to close it.

Nancy turned in her chair. "You can't run out on me! I won't let you!"

I shut the door and leaned against it. "I'm not running out on you, Nancy. I just want to keep our conversation private."

"Private?" she fairly shrieked. "I'll tell everybody! I'll tell them all what a coldhearted bastard you are!"

I pulled up the only other chair in the office beside her and, leaning close, keeping my voice low and controlled, I said, "You'll do nothing of the kind. You have your own career and your own dignity to think of. This isn't some soap opera, and don't think you can turn it into one."

The tears were streaming down her face but her eyes were blazing with anger. "What are you going to do, get me fired? You try that and I'll have you in court on harassment charges so fast your head will spin."

"Nobody's going to fire you," I said, trying to keep calm and sympathetic. "But you really ought to behave like an adult."

"What do you think we were doing in bed? Wasn't that adult enough for you?"

"Nancy, please. I'm sorry that I didn't realize how deeply you felt for me. I had no idea, honestly."

"And you don't give a damn about me, do you?"

"I think you're a wonderful person, but—"

"You're a piece of shit, Arthur Marshak. You know that? A cold-blooded goddamned piece of shit. A turd, that's what you are."

I didn't feel cold-blooded. I could have happily strangled her at that particular moment.

I got up and went back behind my desk and took a box of facial tissues from a drawer and handed it to her. Nancy dabbed at her eyes, took a deep breath, and rose to her feet.

"I should have known better," she said, her voice shaky. "I've been dumped before, but I never thought you'd be so damned shitty to me."

"I'm really sorry . . ."

"Go to hell, Arthur." She turned and stamped out of my office.

I sagged back in my desk chair, thinking, Well, at least that's over. I hope.

CASSIE IANETTA

I know it's been months since I've put anything into this diary. I've been very remiss. I've even been dragging out my work here in Mexico; the human trials could be going much faster, if I put more effort into them.

But none of that seems terribly important right now. I've fallen in love!

It isn't the first time for either of us, of course, but it's like I was a kid again. I'm trying to forget everything else, forget all the times I've been hurt, forget how treacherous men can be, even forget my work—just about—so I can spend every waking minute with Bill.

Bill Ventriss. He's a filmmaker, from Los Angeles. "A serious filmmaker," he told me the first day we met. "Not one of those commercial hacks."

Which is why he's here in the provincial city of Querétaro, a few hours' drive out of Mexico City. He's living here while he gathers material for his film on the Mexican Revolution.

"None of this Pancho Villa stuff," he says. "I'm going to do a film about the real people, the people of this land."

Querétaro is where I'm doing the human trials on my tumor suppressant, working with the city hospital and a small staff of doctors, nurses, and administrative assistants in a set of offices that Omnitech has rented for me. The offices are just across the street from the hospital, really very decent although not fancy at all. I'm not spending Omnitech's money foolishly.

We're doing a double-blind series, of course, inoculating cancer patients and other patients who don't have a single tumor. Some of the cancer patients get my enzyme, some get a placebo. Then we keep track of them to see how—or if—their tumors develop and what the side effects of the treatment might be. Most of our volunteers are mestizo women, stolid and silent until they see the needles. They never complain, though; they want the miserable few pesos I'm paying. But their black, black eyes always go wide the first time they see me coming at them with a hypodermic syringe.

The first moment I saw Bill it was like an electric shock. I was taking a break from inoculating volunteers, taking the afternoon off, strolling through the street market in the center of Querétaro. The Mexicans do beautiful work: cabinetry, sculptures in wood, fancy mirrors—if I had a house I could have furnished it completely for practically nothing. And opals! Querétaro is a center for those incredible Mexican fire opals: *opales de fuego,* they call them. I've been buying them by the palmful, as many as I can afford.

I first saw Bill from across the central lane of the market. He was wearing real tight jeans and cowboy boots, with a black leather vest hanging unbuttoned. He was holding one of those ritual masks in both hands and talking about it very seriously with the shop's proprietor. He happened to look up and our eyes locked. Like I said, I felt an electric shock.

. He must have felt something, too. He put the mask down, very gently, and left the shopkeeper standing there and came across the crowded lane to me. The shopkeeper scowled after him with disappointment, but then he must have noticed me standing with my mouth hanging open like somebody who's been hit by a lightning bolt and he smiled at me.

By that time Bill had stopped no more than a yard or so in front of me. He didn't say anything, just stared at me with the most incredible sky-blue eyes I've ever seen. And a two-day growth of beard on his rugged jaw. He was just a little taller than I, wiry, very intense. I never really knew how old he was. I supposed he was somewhere around my own age, but his face had that craggy, weathered look to it. Tanned really dark, like he had spent most of his life outdoors.

"Christ, what a face." Those were the first words he spoke to me. "It was made to be photographed."

No one ever thought of me as a photographer's model before. I had always thought my face was real plain, kind of mousy.

"Look at those cheekbones," he went on, slowly circling

around me. "And the planes of your cheeks and jawline. And your profile!"

I didn't know what to say. He looked serious, sounded serious.

"Can I buy you a beer?" he asked. "I want to know all about you, where you're from, what you're doing here, why you dropped out of the blue to this exact spot at this exact time."

So we went to the nearest cantina and spent the afternoon talking. I forgot about my work, forgot about all the other times men had betrayed me, even forgot that cancer ran through my family like the Grim Reaper swinging his scythe. All I could see was Bill smiling at me, telling me about the films he wanted to make, the stories he wanted to tell.

To say I was swept off my feet would be an understatement. I was mad for him! Bill brought me out of myself. I realized that for years I had been just going through the motions of living, terrified of the cancer that always came back, afraid to get myself involved with a guy who'd run away once he found out about me, like the others had. I had built a shell around myself so I wouldn't get hurt again. Over the past few years I'd spent most of my social time with Max; at least he would never turn his back on me.

Bill was different. He was caring, he was sensitive, a gentle and patient lover who could turn me on with just a touch or a kiss. Two days after we met I checked out of the hotel where I'd been staying and moved in with him. He had a tiny little row house in one of those winding streets off the market area. And an old MG convertible, the square kind, forest green.

We drove everywhere, top down, engine roaring so loud we couldn't hear each other even if we yelled. Over the mountains into Mexico City to spend whole days at a time in the anthropology museum staring at the massive stone monuments of ancient civilizations.

"Layer on top of layer," Bill told me. "The Aztecs were newcomers, you know. Just the latest tribe to claw its way to the top around these parts. There's been other civilizations, much older, before them. What stories they could tell, if these stones could speak."

We became pyramid hunters. We drove out into the countryside to see the pyramids and temples built by those ancient peoples. I was letting the work slide, but it didn't matter. It was going along more slowly, that's all. I was getting good solid results. Okay, I didn't write my reports as fast as I should have. I sent excuses back to Darrell and Arthur. They didn't complain.

Once we went all the way out to Lake Chapala, above Guadalajara, and found a lovely hotel nestled in the flowering hills. But there were lots and lots of retired American military officers living in the area, stretching their pensions in Mexico, and they were almost always in the dining room at mealtimes, ordering hamburgers and bourbon in loud, abrasive voices.

"They've been here twenty, thirty years, some of them," Bill said, frowning across the dining room at them. "Never learned a word of Spanish. Never even tried real Mexican food."

I smiled at him over the candle on our table. He was wonderful.

One weekend we drove out to Parícutin, the volcano that rose out of a cornfield in the 1940s. It's a big cinder cone now, more than seven thousand feet high; still active, of course. We rented horses and rode up to the ruins of the town that the volcano's lava had destroyed. Nothing left standing except the two ends of a big church. The lava ran right through the middle of it. There were lots of other visitors climbing around the ruins, most of them Mexican, although I heard plenty of midwestern voices yakking back and forth.

Bill took one look at the teenagers who had climbed to the top of the ruined church's old bell tower and decided he had to go up there, too. It looked dangerous to me, but I thought that Bill could do whatever he set his mind to. Fly up there, if he wanted to.

I went up with him, scrabbling across the glassy black stone that had once been a red-hot river of lava, climbing up the crumbling wall of the church. We made it to the top, where a pack of Mexican kids gave us a round of applause. I guess we looked pretty elderly to them. The view was incredible: the gray cinder cone of the volcano, the colorful town down the road, the lush green of the valley, the purple mountains making a sawtoothed horizon all around us. And the sky: That bright, bright blue Mexican sky with its hot sun pouring down on you. No wonder the ancients worshipped the sun. It was almost overpowering.

On the way back down I slipped on the smooth black lava and twisted my ankle. Bill and one of the Mexican boys had to carry me back to the horses. I felt like an idiot, but the pain from my ankle scared me. I thought maybe I had broken a bone.

Bill drove me back to the hospital at Querétaro, where they X-rayed my ankle and found nothing broken. Just a bad sprain. For the next few weeks I hobbled around on a crutch while Bill did all the housework. He never grumbled once. He almost always did the cooking; he was a much better cook than I was. He drove me to the office every morning and took me back home again in the evening. He would lift me up out of the MG and carry me in his arms into the house, up the stairs, and straight to the bed. I hoped my ankle would never heal.

I was still on the crutch when it came time for my monthly Pap smear. It was just a precaution; the last series of chemotherapy had cleaned me up good. At least that's what I told myself. I skipped the test. I didn't need it. I'll go next month, when I'm on my two feet again, I thought.

Besides, if they found something I didn't know how it would affect Bill and our relationship.

JESSE

I'll say this much for Elwood Faber: he knew what he was doing. He put the Reverend Roy Averill Simmonds on the map. Before the rally in Central Park Simmonds had been just another evangelist on late-night TV wheedling his audience for money and playing to mediocre crowds in minor cities.

The Central Park rally was a smash success. Must have been half a million people showed up, the crowd just blackened the grass and swarmed up trees and lampposts. Like another Woodstock. Using the hospital as a focal point, Faber got *everybody* to show up and pitch for contributions, from the mayor on down to a bunch of ragtag kids sobbing into the microphones that they had ruined their lives with drugs and crime.

"We was doin' the devil's work," they cried, and their cracked voices boomed out over the loudspeakers.

By the time Reverend Simmonds himself trotted out to the bank of mikes, that whole giant crowd was absolutely silent, as if they were expecting him to pull off some kind of miracle right there before their eyes. I noticed that he swung wide of the metal poles holding the lights. Made me laugh, and the people sitting in the makeshift bleachers all around me hissed—actually hissed—to shut me up.

I squeezed Julia's hand. We were packed into those bleachers like sardines, shoulder to shoulder, the guests of honor seated right behind the wooden temporary stage with the podium in its center, bathed by the spotlights.

Julia was watching Simmonds as intently as any of the would-be saints sitting with us.

"Bless you, one and all," Simmonds began, his bass voice low and rumbling like distant thunder.

"And blessings on you!" shouted a voice from the crowd. A shill, I figured. The crowd was deep in darkness now, the sun had gone down sometime while the second or third rock group had been playing.

"We are here tonight to do the Lord's work," Simmonds intoned, and he slowly, smoothly went into his speech. He spoke about the hospital and asked me to come down and stand beside him. Faber had told me he'd do that, so I wasn't surprised.

"Here is the man who saved my life," he said to the crowd. A major exaggeration, but what the hell? The mob cheered and applauded as Simmonds laid his hand on my shoulder. He was standing on a little platform behind the podium, so he was almost as tall as I was, as far as the crowd could see.

I stood there with a sappy smile on my face while Simmonds spoke about how the hospital was "doing the Lord's work, toiling in the vineyard among the poor and dispossessed, a beacon of blessed light in the midst of the darkness of violence, crime, and poverty."

He worked himself up, little by little, and I could feel the crowd getting excited. Couldn't see them, with all those spotlights blazing in my eyes, but I could *feel* them, like a big panting animal out there in the darkness, breathing and stirring, its pulse beating faster and faster as Simmonds stirred them up. He stirred himself up, too. I could see perspiration trickling down his face. Pretty soon he was worming off his jacket and throwing it to the floor of the stage; he loosened his tie, got red in the face.

He went from the good work that the hospital was doing to the evil that surrounded us all. "Every one of us is in the midst of mortal danger. Every minute of the day Satan and his legions are trying to pull us down to everlasting hellfire."

On and on. I had to stand there at his side while he ladled out fear to the crowd the way a man pours dog food into his pet's dish. Not fear of God; he was scaring them with fear of the devil. To hear him tell it, the devil was after each and every one of us, every minute of the day. Not even our dreams were safe. His words blurred into a long, rhythmic string of cadences that became hypnotic. His voice boomed and I could feel the crowd swaying and sighing to his words.

Me, I never believed in any of that stuff. Our parents weren't religious; the only time they made us go to temple was during the high holy days. I hadn't seen the inside of a synagogue since Ma had her first stroke. Arthur was the same, although—come to think of it—he felt about his research the way some men feel about God. No, not really. What Arby worshipped was success. He didn't want heaven, he just wanted the Nobel Prize.

"The legions of evil are everywhere," Simmonds ranted on, "even in the laboratories of science where men attempt to tamper with the will of God."

That woke me up.

"Only a short hour's drive from this very spot, secular scientists are striving to interfere with God's plan of life. They seek to make men immortal, in defiance of God's will. I say to you, they will fail! They will fail just as the heathens of Babylon failed when they tried to build a tower that reached unto heaven. They will fail because these things are not meant for man to know. They will fail because God will strike them down."

The crowd roared like an angry beast.

"In their blasphemous quest for immortality, these godless men of science are killing babies! They take human fetuses, living human beings, and destroy them so they can harvest their stem cells. And then they clone the cells!"

"Monsters!" roared a voice out of the darkness. Whether he meant the scientists or what they were cloning wasn't clear to me.

"Monsters indeed," Simmonds agreed. "Who knows what kind of soulless devil's spawn they're creating in their laboratories?"

I was so stunned I didn't know what to do. I guess I should have interrupted, said something, but instead I just stood there like a dummy.

Reverend Simmonds moved on to other matters, but his reference to Arthur's lab rang in my mind like a fire bell. Why the hell did he do that? Did he mean what he said, or was he just using whatever came to his mind to stir up the crowd? Was Julia right; was this little man dangerous?

Sweat was pouring from his face, soaking his shirt.

"Now it is time for you to make your choice," he bellowed into the mikes. "Are you for good or for evil? Are you ready to make a sacrifice to help further the work of the Lord?"

"Yes! Yes!" they screamed out of the darkness. I began to realize how Hitler could get kids to march their neighbors off to concentration camps.

"Let me see my people!" Simmonds exhorted. "Light your candles of faith."

Thousands and thousands of candles lit up the darkness like the world's biggest birthday cake. I found out later that Simmonds's people had sold a candle to every person who came to the rally for a buck apiece. We could've run the hospital for a month on the candle money. Now they all lit up, a sea of lights flickering and dancing out there like an ocean of fireflies.

They surged toward the stage, where a solid wall of New York City police stood between them and Simmonds.

"Now is the time to show that you are prepared to sacrifice for the Lord," Simmonds told them, lowering his voice slightly. The crowd hushed and stilled.

"Now is the time to give generously to this fine hospital, so that this fine doctor can continue the Lord's work here among you."

The inevitable pitch for money.

"I want to see a sea of green," Simmonds told them. "As my helpers go among you, fill your hands with cash and raise your hands to the Lord."

God almighty, I thought, if I were a pickpocket I'd follow this guy wherever he went. I peered into the candlelit crowd and, sure enough, they were digging into their pockets and purses and waving bills over their heads. I couldn't tell if they were ones or bigger, but whatever they were, it must have totaled up to plenty.

When it was all over, it took a full squad of police to get us from the bleachers, through the milling crowd, and out to the buses that waited to drive us to Simmonds's hotel. He was staying at the Marriott this time, down near Grand Central. His people had set up a small reception, small in comparison to the rally, that is. Must have been close to a hundred people in one of the hotel's function rooms. Nonalcoholic drinks, cheese, and fruit. A lot of tuxedos. This was the big-money crowd and Simmonds worked them as expertly as he had the mob in the park. I saw a lot of checkbooks opening up.

I had to stand there with him and chat with just about everyone who was there. Simmonds acted as if we were old friends, almost brothers. Julia stayed by my side, the expression on her face somewhere between worried curiosity and reluctant amusement.

"Tell me more about this scientific work you mentioned," said one of the men as he shook Simmonds's hand. He was elderly, overweight, his shirt collar at least a size and half too tight for his throat. His wife was rake-thin, and had a pained look on her gaunt face. Bleeding ulcers, she looked like to me.

"Dr. Marshak can explain it better than I can," Simmonds said, patting the man's hand and moving him and his wife on to me while he turned to smile at the next couple.

The man gave me an expectant look.

"It's research into organ regeneration," I said, almost mumbled, in fact. "Instead of transplanting organs from a donor, they want to learn how we can grow new organs within our bodies."

Before the man could reply, his wife snapped, "They're not using animals for experiments, are they?"

"Of course they are," I answered without thinking. "You wouldn't want to use humans."

"What kinds of animals?" she asked.

I must have shrugged. "Lab rats, to begin with."

"Dogs?" she demanded.

"I don't think so," I said.

But she wasn't satisfied with that. "They always use dogs. Scientists always use poor defenseless little doggies. They *enjoy* torturing the poor things."

I should have told her she was wrong. I should've told her she was crazy. But instead I just said, "As far as I know, they're not using any dogs."

Clearly unsatisfied, she dragged her husband away to the fruit punch.

By the time we crawled into a taxi to go home, I was exhausted. I'd put in a regular day at the hospital, then been on my feet all through Simmonds's sermon and the reception afterward. My feet hurt. For the first time in my life, my legs ached from standing all those hours.

Julia seemed tired, too. At least she was quiet all the way back to our apartment.

But as we undressed for bed, she asked me, "Don't you think you should warn Arthur?"

"Warn him? About what?"

"That Simmonds has targeted his lab."

"Targeted?"

"He practically identified Arthur's laboratory as being the center of all the evil in the universe, didn't he?"

She slipped off her bra, then padded barefoot into the bathroom. I sat on the bed and called out to her, "Don't you think you're exaggerating things?"

"No, I don't."

I was so tired it was an effort to take off my loafers. I could hear Julia brushing her teeth. I slumped back on the bed and closed my eyes. Falling asleep instantly is an important survival tactic for practicing doctors.

But Julia wasn't ready for sleep yet. "I told you he was dangerous and now he's attacking your brother."

My eyes popped open. "He was just working up the crowd, for Pete's sake. Just saying whatever came into his mind."

"I don't think so," Julia said as she pulled the sheet back and climbed into bed. "I think he'll use Arthur as a target to whip up his followers into a frenzy."

"And do what? Burn down the lab? Don't be silly."

"Jesse, dearest, he's dealing with very disturbed people. Don't you realize that? Look at that elderly woman at the reception. She'd rather see experiments on human beings than on dogs. Really!"

"You're getting worked up over nothing," I said, even though I worried that she might be right.

"Perhaps. I certainly hope you're right. All the same, shouldn't you call Arthur and warn him?"

She was still trying to get Arby and me together. I didn't go for it. "Arby can take care of himself."

"I wonder," Julia said, sounding totally unconvinced.

I turned toward her in the bed and stroked her thigh.

"I thought you were tired," she said.

"Not that tired." I went to kiss her.

But Julia put a finger against my mouth. "Lips that have not touched toothpaste shall never touch mine," she said.

So I brushed my teeth and brought the whole tube of toothpaste back to bed and squirted it all over her naked body.

THE TRIAL:

DAY THREE, MORNING

Your name, please?"

"Professor Doctor Xenophon Zapapas."

A hint of suppressed tittering rippled through the hearing room. Graves silenced the audience with a stern look.

"Your affiliation?" asked Rosen.

"I am head of the department of molecular biology at the University of Athens and a visiting professor at the University of South Florida in Tampa."

Zapapas looked like the Hollywood version of a European scientist: he was small, dark, and intense. Dressed almost formally in a striped gray suit with matching vest and precisely knotted cravat, he appeared to be something of a dandy. His face was lean, with large expressive dark eyes and a pencil-slim black mustache, pointed little goatee, and thinning slicked-back hair that glistened in the overhead lights.

Arthur Marshak sat in the front row of the hearing room, watching Zapapas intently. He knew the man by reputation only: Zapapas put out a steady stream of research papers that were all variations of the same basic work he had done more than ten years earlier. He kept on publishing, and journals kept on accepting his papers, even though he had apparently not had a new idea in a decade.

When the National Academy of Sciences had agreed to convene this science court, Arthur had provided Graves and his staff with the names of more than a dozen knowledgeable researchers who could be called on to testify to the court about their evaluations of the scientific evidence he had prepared. Zapapas had not been among them. Rosen, as chief examiner, had gone out and dragooned his own experts.

Sitting at his place alongside the three judges, Rosen asked, "Professor Zapapas, can you give us your estimation of the research done so far on organ regeneration at Grenford Laboratory?"

"Yes, of course."

As the professor launched into his scientific testimony, Arthur noticed that Senator Kindelberger's eyes soon began to glaze over. The senator had shown up on time for this morning's session and taken his place at the front row of desks, on the opposite side of the judges from Rosen.

Zapapas wanted to show slides to illustrate the points he was going to make. Clerks duly lowered the window drapes and set up a slide projector on the table where Zapapas sat. The judges, Rosen, and Senator Kindelberger all came down from their seats at the front desks and took chairs in front of the jury, facing the projection screen that now covered the chamber's side wall.

Except, Arthur noticed, that Kindelberger walked quietly through the darkened room and out the door at the rear. He's had enough, Arthur said to himself. The reporters have noted he's here; now he can duck out without being bored by the science.

But then, as Zapapas droned on about his own work in fetal tissue transplants, Arthur saw Jesse quietly get up from his seat on the front bench and tiptoe out of the chamber, too.

WASHINGTON:

DIRKSON SENATE OFFICE BUILDING

Jesse felt nervous, apprehensive as he walked into the air-conditioned lobby of the Dirkson Building. Like a little boy sneaking into an X-rated movie.

I shouldn't even have bothered going to the hearing this morning, he said to himself. Zapapas and a couple of other so-called experts were scheduled to give their testimony all day. Instead of putting in an appearance at the hearing, I could have slept late for a change.

After going through the metal detector in the lobby, he asked for Senator Kindelberger at the information desk. The security guard phoned, then told him that someone would be down shortly to escort him. Jesse clipped the plastic badge the guard handed him onto his jacket's breast pocket.

Why does Simmonds want me to see Kindelberger? Jesse asked himself. It's obvious that the reverend and the senator have joined forces. That must be Faber's doing. But why do they want to drag me into it?

Looking around the spacious lobby, Jesse saw that the senators had no objections to making themselves comfortable. This building's a goddamned marble palace, he thought. It must have cost a fortune and a half. A young black woman came to the information desk, shoes clicking on the marble floor, and introduced herself as one of Senator Kindelberger's aides. She led him to the elevators, then down a handsome wide corridor to the senator's suite of offices. Bigger than most of the wards back at Mendelssohn, Jesse thought as he gaped at the rich wood paneling and the young staffers who didn't seem to be straining themselves too hard with work. A lot of talking going on; a lot of telephoning.

Jesse wondered what Julia would think of it. She had applied for U.S. citizenship before getting pregnant again. He wondered how the Congress would stack up against the House of Commons in her eyes.

Elwood Faber had set the meeting for ten o'clock. But although Jesse had made certain to be precisely on time, when his guide ushered him into the senator's office he saw that Faber and Reverend Simmonds were both already there, seated in front of the senator's desk. And another man.

He looked familiar: a round, puffy-looking face with baggy eyes. Twenty pounds overweight. Unhealthy grayish pallor; Jesse guessed that he suffered from a circulatory disorder. Forty-five, maybe fifty years old. The guy wasn't much bigger than Simmonds, except in his bulging middle. Jesse knew he had seen him somewhere before. Those sleepy, hooded eyes. When you looked into them they were cold gray, calculating, cynical.

"Dr. Marshak." Kindelberger got up and came around his massive desk, smiling warmly, hand outstretched in greeting. He towered over Jesse, a big rawboned man with a tanned, craggy, weatherbeaten face. He's had a couple of melanomas removed, Jesse saw. At his age, he's vulnerable.

"You know Reverend Simmonds, of course, and Mr. Faber," said the senator, not letting go of Jesse's hand. "I'd like you to meet Joshua Ransom."

That's who it is! The face clicked into Jesse's memory as soon as he heard the name. Joshua Ransom. The self-styled activist. The man who had stopped or delayed a dozen new biotechnology programs with legal maneuverings. Neither a scientist nor a lawyer, Ransom had still managed to carry his objections against new scientific breakthroughs all the way up to the Supreme Court.

"King of the Luddites," Jesse said to Ransom with a smile.

Ransom did not smile back. "I've been called that," he said in a reedy tenor voice. "It's a title I accept as an honor."

Kindelberger looked uneasy.

"It's all right, Senator," said Simmonds. Turning to Jesse, "We're all on the same side here, aren't we, Dr. Marshak?"

Jesse realized the reverend was right. "I suppose we are," he said reluctantly.

Kindelberger sat Jesse between Ransom and Simmonds, then went back behind his desk to the big swivel chair. Faber sat off to one side of the office, fading into the background like a professional servant.

"Have you had your breakfast, Doctor? Would you like some coffee, tea, whatever?"

"A cup of coffee will be fine," Jesse said.

Kindelberger jabbed a finger at the woman who had ushered Jesse into the office. "I'll have a cup, too. What about you fellas?"

Simmonds and Faber both asked for decaffeinated coffee.

Ransom said, "Pure fruit juice for me. No concentrates, no preservatives."

Jesse wanted to ask Ransom if he ever took aspirin, but decided not to. Ransom represented a powerful political force, and the senator had invited him to this meeting for a purpose. No sense starting an argument right off the bat. With Simmonds's religious zealots and Ransom's antiscience activists, Kindelberger was putting together a serious coalition.

Kindelberger leaned so far back in his chair that Jesse thought he was going to put his feet up on the desk. But instead, he grinned and said, "I bet you're wondering why we asked you here this morning."

"It's obviously got to do with the trial," said Jesse.

"Damn right," said the senator. Immediately he looked at Simmonds and apologized, almost sheepishly, "Sorry, Reverend. No offense."

Simmonds said, "The senator needs to know why you oppose your brother's work."

Jesse felt alarmed. *Why do they want to know? Isn't it enough that I'm ready to stick my neck out and testify in the trial? What are they digging for?*

The same black woman who had escorted Jesse to the office came in again, carrying a Lucite tray with four heavy mugs and two silver coffeepots, plus a tall glass of juice, giving Jesse a few moments to frame his answer while she put the tray on the senator's desk and poured the coffee and then left the office, closing the door softly behind her.

Simmonds has been damned good to the hospital, Jesse was thinking as he reached for his mug and sipped at the steaming brew. I don't want to lose him. But what's this senator after?

Ransom's eyes seemed to be boring into Jesse. "We all know why *we're* here. But what about you? What's your angle?"

"I see this as a moral issue," Simmonds said, "and I assume that Dr. Marshak does, too."

"In a way," Jesse temporized.

Kindelberger's brows knitted together. "Look, now. If I'm going to come out against this thing I've got to know who's supporting me and why. I don't want to look stupid and I don't want to be hanging out there all by myself."

"You won't be by yourself," Ransom said.

"Certainly not," Simmonds added. "All my people will be solidly behind you. We'll work for your reelection campaign."

"That's fine," Kindelberger said, his eyes never leaving Jesse's. "But I need to know why Dr. Marshak's going against his own brother on this."

Jesse said nothing. He tried to hide behind his coffee mug, his mind desperately churning. What should I tell him? Why should I open my guts for them? Simmonds should never have put me in this position.

"What the senator needs to know," Faber said in his soft, placating voice, "is whether or not your brother can actually regenerate organs in human beings."

"That's what the trial is supposed to determine," Jesse said.

"Oh, he'll be able to," Ransom said, his voice dripping contempt. "Give a scientist enough time and enough money and he can do anything. Anything at all. Without a thought about what it means to the rest of the world. They just don't care about anybody except themselves."

"That's bullshit," Jesse snapped.

"Is it?" asked Ransom. "If you let the scientists have their own way they'd be poisoning us with toxic chemicals, creating monsters with genetic mutations, giving us cancer with radiation. I know! I've fought all my life to stop them."

"Yeah, and all you did was delay developments that've given us better crop yields with smaller doses of pesticides. And cured victims of genetic diseases."

"If it weren't for me we'd all have cancer!" Ransom shrilled.

"Gentlemen!" Simmonds's deep powerful voice stopped them. "No matter how we feel about these issues, that's not what we're here to discuss. We are all agreed that this work on organ regeneration must be stopped, isn't that right?"

Jesse had to admit that Simmonds was right. *Arthur's work has to be stopped, and if I have to dance with the devil to do it, that's what I'll have to do.*

Simmonds went on, "I am unalterably opposed to using fetal tissue for this or any research. It encourages women to have abortions. It encourages them to create life and then deliberately commit murder."

"They never used fetal stem cells," Jesse said. "They only used adult stem cells, and that was just at the beginning of the work. They've moved past that; they don't need stem cells at all now."

"Then why are you against the research, Dr. Marshak?" Kindelberger asked again, with some irritation in his voice. "We've got to know."

Jesse took a deep breath, put the coffee mug back on the Lucite tray. Simmonds was eying him from beneath his shaggy brows. Ransom looked suspicious. Kindelberger was frowning impatiently. Even the normally placid Faber looked curious.

"My personal opinion," he said at last, "is that Arthur's got to be stopped."

"Why?" Kindelberger demanded.

"Because of the tremendous risks involved with this work."

"Risks?" echoed Simmonds.

"Arthur thinks he's got the tumor problem licked, but I'm not convinced of that. And then—"

"Tumor problem?" Kindelberger asked. "You mean it gives

you cancer, don't you? That's what you said at the trial yesterday."

Jesse answered, "In some cases the tumors have been malignant. They've been able to suppress them to some extent, but I don't think they've really solved the problem yet. The peptides they're using to initiate regrowth also stimulate tumor growth in just about all the experimental animals they've used."

"Cancer," Ransom said, as if he had invented the word.

"They think they can beat that problem," Jesse said. "I'm not so sure."

Ransom smiled. "Cancer is a scary word. We can use it like a club."

Kindelberger shot him an accusing stare. "Oh, yeah? Then why isn't yesterday's testimony on the front pages this morning?"

"Because the trial is being covered by science reporters," Ransom responded immediately, "not the first-team newshounds."

"It's buried on page sixteen of the *Post*," Kindelberger grumbled. "And the wire services barely mentioned it. None of the stories even say I was there."

"Don't worry about it," Ransom assured him. "When we want to make front-page news out of this, we'll have the material." He turned his cold gray eyes to Jesse. "Won't we?"

"What do you mean?" Simmonds asked.

"It's simple," Ransom said. Then he took a sip of his fruit juice, forcing them all to wait for his next words.

He put the glass down on the senator's desk, then resumed. "We stop treating this as a science story and turn it into a story about human conflict. Brother against brother."

Jesse started to object, but Ransom went on, "We can also go another route. The senator, here, calls for an investigation of this regeneration work. Gets his committee to look into the cancer-causing angle. That'll get headlines, believe me."

"There are other aspects to this," Jesse said.

"Cloning stem cells," Simmonds murmured darkly.

"But the threat of cancer is our ultimate weapon," Ransom

said, a nervous smile twitching the corners of his mouth. "We can use that one word to drown out everything else."

"That's not fair," Jesse said.

"All's fair in love and politics," said Kindelberger.

Faber spoke up. "Could we get you to testify in the trial, Mr. Ransom?"

His face clouded. "No, they won't let me. I don't have the scientific credentials to suit them, so they won't let me appear." Turning back to the senator, "But I could testify to a Senate committee, couldn't I?"

Simmonds saw the distress in Jesse's face. "There's something else bothering you, isn't there? Something you haven't mentioned to us."

Despite himself, Jesse nodded.

"You broke with your brother more than a year ago, didn't you?" Simmonds said. "Before this cancer thing came out. Why? What's your real reason for being against him?"

Because he blamed me for Julia's miscarriage, Jesse thought. Because he hates me for taking Julia from him.

But aloud he answered, "This regeneration process, even when it works, is only going to be available to the very rich. It'll cost millions."

"We've got health plans for the poor," Kindelberger pointed out.

"I work with the poor," Jesse snapped. "I see what your health plans do. You allow this into your health plan and it'll go bankrupt inside of a year."

Kindelberger stared at him.

"Think a minute," said Jesse. "Sooner or later Arthur's people will make the process work. They'll be able to regrow organs in your body without the threat of cancer. Then what? How many poor people need new hearts? How many alcoholics do I see every week who're dying of cirrhosis and need a new liver? Will your health plan be able to handle millions of regeneration cases each year? Each month? At a million bucks or so a shot?"

"A million millions per month," Faber mumbled.

"That's a trillion dollars," said Jesse.

"A trillion dollars?" Kindelberger gasped.

"Each month," Jesse said.

"Impossible!"

"The rich will do what they've always done," Jesse said, surprised at the heat in his own voice. "They'll buy their way into heaven. They'll live for hundreds of years once they can regenerate their failing organs. But the poor will still die like flies."

The office fell absolutely silent for long, long moments.

Finally Faber said softly, "Well, I don't know about you guys, but my health insurance sure won't cover anything that costs a million."

"It's got to be stopped," Simmonds said firmly. "It would be immoral to allow the rich to live longer and longer while the poor languish and die."

"You can't stop it," Jesse said. "Nobody can stop an idea."

"We can," said Ransom. "You've just given us the ammunition to do it. We play the poor against the rich." He laughed out loud. "By god, it's *beautiful*!"

Kindelberger leaned far back in his chair again and clasped his hands together, almost prayerfully. "If we can get the proper political support, we can outlaw it. We can make it illegal to use federal funds for such research. We can tie up the process in the FDA and the other regulatory agencies."

"I'll sue Omnitech Corporation and Arthur Marshak, both," said Ransom. "I'll tie them up in the courts for years."

"So Arthur goes overseas," Jesse countered. "Or some other scientists in foreign countries follow his lead."

"That's why it's so important," Simmonds said, fists clenched on his lap, "to make certain that this trial finds the process scientifically wrong."

"The trial's got to discredit the whole idea," Ransom said. "Paint it so black that nobody overseas will touch it."

"But that means they'll have to discredit Arthur," said Jesse.

Kindelberger nodded solemnly. "He's got to be stopped."

"No," said Reverend Simmonds. "He's got to be destroyed."

Ransom nodded eagerly. "And I think I know how to start moving things in that direction."

ARTHUR

The attack came a week after Reverend Simmonds's big rally in Central Park. A Sunday night. I was at the laboratory when it happened. They were fanatics, absolutely crazy. I think they would have killed me, if they had the chance. I know I would have killed as many of them as I could have, if I'd had the chance.

I'd been working all weekend on the idea of using Cassie Ianetta's tumor-killer in combination with the regentide, so we could lick the tumor problem and go ahead with the regeneration experiments. Not that I did any real lab work; it had been years since I'd gotten my hands wet. But I was carefully sifting through the reports Cassie had been sending up from Mexico and using my desktop computer to compare her results with the kinds of tumors that the regentide triggered in lab rats and the minihogs we had just started using.

Cassie's reports were far behind the schedule we had set, but I figured that she was having problems in Mexico that we hadn't anticipated. The results she had sent in looked good. Solid work. Encouraging. But something had slowed her down. I made a mental note to call her and see if there was anything I could do to help get her back on track.

The idea of using her enzyme to suppress the tumors that the regentide caused looked promising to me, but I had to be careful not to let my enthusiasm carry me away. I had to be certain that it really would work against the tumors, and I wasn't just convincing myself this was so because I wanted things to work out that way.

I remember I was pretty pissed off with Jesse. He had fallen in line with that evangelist minister and told him enough about my work to get the preacher to rail against me at the big rally he held in Central Park the weekend before.

I didn't attend the rally, of course. I had work to do. I hardly even heard about it. I think it was Phyllis, my secretary, who showed me a full-page advertisement for the rally in *News-day* or one of the other New York papers a few days before the event. Raising money for Jesse's hospital was a good idea, I remember thinking. I wrote a check and sent it to the box number in the ad.

That Sunday afternoon, though, Darrell Walters came sauntering into my office and plotzed himself in the chair in front of my desk.

"We're celebrities," he said, grinning. Darrell's got big, slightly protruding teeth. When he grins he looks more like a horse than usual.

I saw that he held the first section of the morning's *Times* in his hand. "Celebrities?" I asked.

Darrell showed me the front-page photo of the mammoth crowd in Central Park. The story under it was mostly about the entertainment stars and other celebrities who had appeared at the rally.

"Where does it mention us?" I asked.

Darrell turned to a back page, where there was a little box off to one side headlined, *Simmonds Blasts "Godless Scientists."* I scanned the story. It didn't mention the lab by name, or me, for that matter, but it was clear who and what Simmonds was complaining about. And I knew, of course, who had told him about us: Jesse. It couldn't have been anyone else.

Darrell was still grinning. "How's it feel to have the wrath of God called down on your head?"

I felt disgusted. "Why would Jesse do something like that? He's pandering to the wackos."

"Well," Darrell said, pushing himself up from the chair, "I just thought you'd like to know how famous we're getting."

"With the wrong people," I groused.

Darrell was chuckling as he walked out of my office. He left the newspaper on my desk.

I didn't think anything of it, except to feel pretty damned sore that Jesse would stoop to such tactics. Why? To raise money for his hospital? Or was he really so angry at me that he was trying to hurt me? What did I do to him to deserve that kind of treatment?

I thought that maybe I should call him and thrash this out, face-to-face. But then I figured that if I called him while I was angry it'd just lead to another argument. Cool down first. Let it rest for a few days.

A week passed.

Maybe I don't get into the labs and do any real work, but I was chewing into Cassie's reports and Zack O'Neill's latest analyses of the tumor problem so deeply that I forgot about dinner and just stayed there at my desk that Sunday evening. I got up a couple of times, once to the food dispensers for a granola bar and a cup of coffee (nowhere near as good as Phyllis's) and once to the toilet.

According to the police report, it was ten minutes before midnight when the attackers struck. They must have figured that on a Sunday night nobody would be at the lab except one or two security guards. Actually, we had two of the older men on duty, making their rounds, and one animal handler back in the pens: a grad student who worked the night shift so she could study in peace and quiet and attend her classes during the day.

The first inkling I got that something was wrong was when I heard the chimps start to howl. All the way in my office I could hear them. It made me look up from my computer screen, not scared but certainly startled.

My office door was open and so was the door to the corridor beyond the outer office. But still, what the hell could be going on at the animal pens to set the chimps off like that? It sounded as if the macaques were shrieking, too. I got up and headed for the rear of the building, feeling almost glad for an excuse to stretch my legs a little.

No alarm bells were ringing. The normal lights were on, although most of the offices and labs were empty and dark. But as I went down the corridor, hurrying a little because the chimps and the monkeys were all screaming now, I saw light spilling out from Zack O'Neill's lab. The place looked as if somebody'd set off a bomb in there. Shattered glassware all over the floor; all of Zack's apparatus smashed to pieces. The rat pens were all open and none of the animals were in sight.

Check that. I saw one of the lab rats scampering down the corridor. Like an idiot I chased after it.

Back toward the animal pens I ran, and when I passed the computer center I saw three people in there. In ski masks.

That's when my heart clutched in my chest. We're being raided! And if they trash the computer we'll lose every god-damned bit of data we've got.

They say heroism is a reflex action. I'm no hero, god knows, but I barreled in there yelling at the top of my voice, "What the hell do you think you're doing?"

The three of them almost jumped out of their skins. I could see whites all around their eyes, through their damned ski masks.

I'm not a big man, and I certainly didn't have anything on me that could serve as a weapon. But neither did they, thank god. They hadn't expected anyone to jump in on them.

I grabbed a metal ruler that was on one of the console desks and held it like a one-foot-long sword. "Get out of here!" I yelled. "Now!"

The biggest of the three said from behind his ski mask, "I'll take care of him. You go ahead and dump the machine."

He was wearing a light windbreaker and dark slacks, to-gether with the mask and gloves. Seemed pretty young to me, judging by his voice and his lightness on his feet. The other two were smaller, maybe women, for all I could tell.

"Better go away, old man," he said to me, coming straight at me.

Fencing blades are three feet long, my ruler was only twelve inches. But I was boiling with anger. He came at me and I feinted at his extended hand. When he made a grab for the ruler I disengaged and slashed him across his face. He yowled and backed away. I smacked him again, then kicked him in the shin as hard as I could, and when he was off bal-ance I jammed that metal ruler into his side hard enough to split his kidney, if only the ruler had a point.

He forgot his two pals and stumbled for the door. I screamed at the other two, "Get out of here before I kill you!"

They ran.

I picked up the phone. It was still working so I punched 911 and told the surprised woman at the county police headquarters that Grenford Laboratory was being attacked by terrorists.

"Is this some kind of joke?" she asked, half bored, half annoyed.

"This is Dr. Arthur Marshak. I am director of Grenford Laboratory and a band of people in ski masks are wrecking the place. Call the state police at once. We're under attack!"

"Yessir," she said. "Right away, sir."

I banged the phone down and wondered what I should do next. Suddenly I felt sort of ridiculous standing there with a ruler in my hand and my pulse throbbing so hard I could hear it in my ears. Should I remain here and guard the computer center? Or go out to the animal compound? The chimps and monkeys were still screeching madly and now I could hear the truculent squealing of the minihogs.

The computer or the animals? I hesitated. The computer held all our data, all the information we had gleaned so painstakingly. But the animals were irreplaceable, too. In their genes and their proteins were the results of years of careful breeding and experiments.

Max. I had promised Cassie I would look after Max. God knows what those bastards were doing out there in the animal pens. I bolted out of the computer center and ran toward the rear of the building, my ruler still firmly gripped in my hand.

I saw one of our uniformed guards as I raced down the corridor. He was sprawled on the floor like a sack of laundry. I stopped and knelt over him. He was breathing and his eyes were open, but unfocused. Pupils so dilated I could barely see his irises. Drugged, somehow.

The chimps and monkeys sounded as if a bloody war were going on outside. There were more than a dozen macaques in the cages, and four chimpanzees, three females and Max. They were making enough noise to wake Tarzan in Africa.

I saw more lab rats scurrying frantically as I ran down the corridor. And I could hear the stubborn angry squealing of our minihogs over the hoots and shrieks of the monkeys and chimps.

Pushing through the double doors into the animal compound, I saw a half dozen people, all in windbreakers and ski masks—except for one tousled blond youth who had a nasty gash on his cheek, just below his left eye.

"That's the sonofabitch who cut me," he yelled, pointing at me. I photographed his face with my mind. I wanted to remember what he looked like so the police could identify him.

Four of the youngsters were trying to push one of our minihogs into a van they had backed into the compound through the back gate, and the hog was resisting with all her stubborn strength. Inside the van, I saw our erstwhile caretaker wrestling with another hog. Her eye caught mine and she quickly looked away, but I recognized her easily enough. So that was how they'd gotten in. She was one of them, a plant, a spy in our midst.

The only chimp I could see was Max, who was way up in the topmost crotch of the taller tree in the compound, howling and screaming like mad, his lips pulled back to show his fangs. He looked ferocious, but I realized he was only scared out of his wits. It was he who had been making most of the noise, all by himself, although the macaques were doing their part, too. I found out later that the three female chimps had been easily drugged by their caretaker and put into the van. Just as she had shot the security guard when he made his rounds back there. Max had been too smart to stay there and watch the others fall to her dart gun. He had scampered up the tree and set up the terrible din that had scared the macaques and alerted me.

Max had also reverted to a time-honored tactic: I saw smears of brown on two of the raiders. He had thrown shit at them.

"Get that fucker!" said the blond youth. "He can identify me!"

The four who had been trying to haul the minihog into the van straightened up and came at me. Isn't there anybody else in the lab? I asked myself. There should have been one more security guard up in the front of the building, but god knows what had happened to him. I was alone against the gang of them.

Except for Max, who was hollering at them from the relative safety of his perch. And the minihog. Two hundred pounds of obdurate, angry muscle. Once the four kids turned their back to her, the hog put her head down and ran straight at their legs. She was like a pink bowling ball hitting eight pins. Down they all went in a tangle.

And I saw the dart gun they had used on the chimps, lying on the ground not more than ten feet from where I stood, by the door. I rushed for it while the hog bolted past me, squealing and running around the perimeter of the compound, as the terrorists scrambled to their feet.

I leveled the gun at them. "If these darts can tranquilize a chimp, think what they'll do to you," I said.

They stopped in their tracks. Until the caretaker, still in the van, yelled, "The gun's empty. I used up all the fuckin' darts."

They rushed me. I slugged with the gun butt and slashed with the ruler but they swarmed me under and beat the crap out of me. The last thing I remember was thinking that I was probably going to need a hell of a lot of dental work after this. I heard a siren wailing in the distance. And then I blacked out.

THE DENTAL work was minimal, but the damage to the lab was major. All of Zack's lab rats were gone by the time the state police arrived. We recovered a few, but his experimental apparatus was a shambles and the raiders had broken every jar or canister of chemicals they could find. They hadn't touched any of the other labs, though, and the computer was okay, but our three female chimps were gone, and one of our two minihogs. For some reason they hadn't touched the macaques; maybe they were smart enough to know that the monkeys bite. More likely they didn't have the time, once I sounded the alarm. I was stiff with bruises, both eyes blackened, ribs sore, but at least they hadn't broken any of my bones. And I still had all my teeth.

Max was a wreck. He just refused to come down out of his tree for days. His regular caretakers left food on the ground but Max wouldn't come down for it. They stuck it on poles and handed it up to him, but even so he hardly ate anything. He screamed and yowled, as if scolding us for letting the terrorists frighten him so badly.

The personnel files we had on the turncoat caretaker turned out to be worthless. She had given us a phony ID and background story. The university she claimed she was attending had no record of anyone by that name and no photo in their files of her. I called in the personnel chief and told her in no uncertain terms that from now on anybody we hire should be investigated thoroughly. She burst into tears and I had to spend half an hour convincing her that I didn't hold her to blame for what had happened.

The FBI sent over two crisp, clean-cut agents with a long file of known animal rights activists.

"Most of these people are honest, law-abiding citizens," said Agent Costello. "But some of them go off the deep end." He looked like the serious, hard-nosed, no-nonsense muscular type; the kind who goes through undergrad school on an athletic scholarship and then goes on to get himself a law degree.

"They've bombed laboratories," said the other one, Agent Harris. He was slimmer, lighter in build and coloring, although he wore the same kind of dark business suit as his partner. "They've caused a lot of damage and even killed a security guard in Kansas."

"By accident," said Agent Costello.

"Still," said the Harris, "there's a homicide charge out for them."

The dart gun that the caretaker had used was gone; they must have taken it with them, although the agents said the darts themselves might be a useful lead. The blond fellow I had slashed was not among the photos they showed me.

"Probably a new recruit," said Costello, looking grim.

"Might even be a foreigner they brought in for this job," Harris mused.

"You make it sound like an international conspiracy," I said. They nodded in unison.

"They weren't terrorists," I said. "Not like al-Qaeda or one of those groups."

"No sir, they're not," Costello reassured me. "They're just homegrown nuts."

"Fanatics," added Harris.

"But they can be dangerous, just the same."

Tell me about it, I thought, trying to breathe despite my aching ribs.

We downplayed the story to the news media as much as possible. Neither I nor Johnston and the corporate office wanted that kind of publicity. The local newspaper picked up the police report, of course, but I let Darrell handle the reporter they sent over. I kept my two black eyes out of sight and Darrell maneuvered the reporter past Zack's smashed-up lab and out to the animal compound, where there was nothing to be seen except some tire tracks in the grass and empty pens.

Max had settled down a little, but he still ran up the nearest tree whenever he saw a stranger. The reporter thought Max was cute; actually Max was terrified.

The damage the terrorists did was much more extensive than I had thought at first. We cleaned up Zack's lab soon enough, of course, and we hadn't lost any vital data from the computer center. But the rats were mostly gone and the minihog that they had stolen had already received a series of injections of regentide, and now we would have no way of knowing what was happening to the animal. And the chimps were gone; all of them except for Max. It was next to impossible to get more chimps; there was a strain of AIDS decimating the chimp population in Africa, and the UN had put a moratorium on buying chimpanzees for research experiments. Here in the States, NIH controlled chimp sales, and you had to wait months before they would approve your request.

That left us with only Max. And I had sort of promised Cassie that I wouldn't use Max in any more experiments.

It was going to be damned difficult to keep that promise, I knew.

The more I thought about it, the more I realized that Jesse was responsible for this atrocity. Not deliberately, I was sure. But he had told that preacher about the regeneration work, I knew, and the preacher had stirred up the yahoos against us.

Days went by, then weeks. Jesse never called to ask how I was, never indicated at all that he knew about the attack or cared about it. I began to realize how much Jesse had turned against me.

JESSE

I didn't hear about the raid on Arby's lab until two FBI agents showed up at the hospital to question me.

"They beat up my brother?"

The two of them nodded at me. They had told me their names when they had flashed their IDs at me, but I had already forgotten what they were. The two of them looked as identical as robots to me, in their dark suits and unsmiling faces. I took them into my cubbyhole of an office and told them I'd be happy to answer their questions. Had to drag in a chair from the office next door so they could both sit down.

It became obvious right away that they were trying to link the people who raided Arby's lab with Reverend Simmonds. I resented that. They had no right to make that assumption.

"Who put you on that track?" I asked them. "My brother?"

They glanced at one another before answering me. They weren't wearing mirrored sunglasses, or any glasses at all, but they acted as if they were. Stiff, grim, they were treating me more like a suspect than an innocent bystander. Right there in my own office.

"It seems clear that the terrorists did not raid your brother's laboratory until Simmonds attacked him verbally during the Central Park rally," said the bigger of the two agents. His lips hardly moved when he talked.

"That doesn't mean there's a connection between the two," I said.

"We're not saying there is," said the smaller of the robots. "We're simply investigating that possibility."

"Did you speak about your brother's work to anyone else?"

I had to think about that. "Not that I can remember," I said. "It's not exactly my number one topic of conversation."

"But you did mention it to Simmonds."

"Yeah. I did."

"On more than one occasion?" asked number two.

"I think so, yes."

"Who else was in the room with you when you discussed the subject?"

I thought back. "My wife. But she wouldn't do anything like that. She—she likes my brother a lot. And she thinks animal rights activists are nutty."

"Who else?"

"Faber. He's Simmonds's business manager."

"Elwood Faber," number one said, as if he had a complete file on the man.

"That's right."

Number two edged forward in his chair a little. "After the rally in Central Park you attended a party that Simmonds gave for his major supporters, didn't you?"

"What is this, am I a suspect?"

"No, not at all, sir," he said quickly. Too quickly for me to believe him. "But you were at the party in the Marriott that night, weren't you?"

"Yes."

"Were any animal rights activists there?"

"How should I know?"

"Did anyone speak to you about your brother's work?"

Before I could answer, number one added, "Anyone who gave you the impression that he was strongly against using animals in laboratory experiments?"

I half remembered some dotty old couple. "Maybe. I think so."

"Could you tell us who spoke to you about that?"

"Identify the person?"

I shook my head. "No, I don't think so."

Number one took an iPhone from his jacket pocket, opened it up, and ran a series of low-resolution photographs of people past me. Most of the pictures were in color, but poor, grainy, like they had been taken with hidden cameras.

"Any of these faces look familiar?" he asked.

None of them did. And even if I had recognized one of them I don't think I would've admitted it to them. Sure, that senile old couple at the party grumbled about animal experiments. But they weren't terrorists and I wasn't about to help the FBI stick their noses into the old folks' lives. I'm as much against those animal-rights kooks as anybody, but I was even more against making harmless old people miserable.

The agents left, but I had the feeling they thought I was holding out on them. Maybe I was. What the hell? It was over and done with. So some overzealous kids made a mess of Arby's lab and beat him up. He'll live through it, I told myself.

JULIA

I was determined to end the separation between Jesse and Arthur, but I didn't know how to do it. It hurt Jesse deeply, even though he tried not to show it. He simply stopped talking about Arthur; no mention of him at all. If I brought up his name in conversation, though, I could see the pain in his eyes. So I stopped mentioning Arthur, as well, even though I knew it was wrong of me to do so.

It was because of me, of course. Not that I saw myself as some femme fatale at the hypotenuse of a lovers' triangle.

But Arthur still cared about me, and it was my miscarriage that had driven this terrible wedge between the two brothers.

It was a shock when I learned that Arthur's laboratory had been attacked and he injured. Jesse didn't tell me about it; I read it in a magazine article about animal rights, a little sidebar about the excesses of the movement's radical fringe, several months after the attack had actually taken place.

I spent the entire day wondering what to do. When Jesse came home that night I asked him about it.

"That was months ago," he said.

"You knew about it?"

He looked pained, remorseful. "A couple of FBI agents asked me about a possible link between Simmonds's people and the terrorists."

I felt his pain. "Oh, dear," was all I managed to say. It was clear that Jesse believed there *was* a link between Reverend Simmonds's followers and the more rabid activists. And he felt guilty about it.

"Did you call Arthur? Speak to him?"

"No." Jesse looked away from me.

As gently as I could, I asked, "Don't you think you should?"

The sorrow in his eyes was enough to make me want to wrap my arms around him. "He's finished with me, hon. He hates me. Even more now, I bet. He'll blame me for everything, like he always does."

"I can't believe that Arthur hates you," I said.

"He does." And Jesse actually burst into tears and buried his head against my breast. I held him for a long time while he sobbed quietly. I stroked his hair and told him that I loved him and he mustn't be sad or upset.

Yet I knew that whatever pain Jesse was feeling, Arthur felt, too. He would never shed a tear, of course. Arthur kept his suffering entirely to himself. But the pain would be inside him, bottled up, hurting him just as much as it hurt Jesse.

So the following morning, as soon as I arrived in my office, I phoned Arthur. His secretary sounded surprised when I told her who it was.

"Just a moment," she said guardedly. "I'll see if he's in his office."

She put me on hold, and a bit of Vivaldi played in my ear.

"Julia?" Arthur's voice sounded brimming with wonder.

Without preamble, I said, "I just read something about your laboratory being attacked."

"Oh, that was months ago. We've recovered."

"And you were injured?"

He actually laughed. "I looked like a prizefighter. A losing prizefighter."

"Are you all right?"

"Yes, I'm fine now. And you?"

"I'm fine, too."

Suddenly we had nothing else to say. Nothing that wouldn't open up old wounds. The silence was embarrassing.

"And Jess?" Arthur asked at last.

"Busy as ever," I said. Then, before I could think twice about it, I added, "He rather blames himself for what happened to you."

"Does he." Arthur's voice became grim.

"It's nonsense, of course," I went on. "Jesse would never knowingly harm you, Arthur. You know that, don't you?"

It took him a long time to answer. "Yes," he said at last. "I suppose that's true."

"I really feel awful about the two of you."

"So do I."

"Then why don't you do something about it?"

Another long hesitation. Then, "Julia, I've tried. More than once. All I've gotten for my efforts is a lot of pain and misery. I think it's best if we stay apart, at least for a while longer."

"I don't agree," I said, although I wasn't being entirely truthful. Sometimes it actually is best to avoid the thing that hurts you. Or the person.

"Julia, dear," he said, "it was wonderful of you to call. I should have realized that you and Jess are just as agonized about all this as I am. Thanks for making me understand that."

"And that's all?" I asked.

"That's all for now," he said. "That's all I can manage to do right now. Give me time, Julia. I need more time."

"Very well, Arthur. I think I understand."

"Thanks for calling."

I didn't know what else to say.

Then Arthur said, very softly, "I love you, Julia."

And he hung up.

I felt miserable for weeks afterward.

And for weeks afterward, for months, actually, the Reverend Roy Averill Simmonds kept up his attacks on "the godless humanist scientists" who were "tampering with God's plan for mankind." He never mentioned Arthur by name, not publicly, but the news media began to pick up the trail and send reporters to almost any laboratory in the country that was working on stem cells or anything hinting of extending the human life span. They covered Grenford Laboratory extensively, and Arthur's work on organ regeneration became the center of intense media scrutiny.

Naturally, they got most of the scientific details wrong, or ignored them altogether. But the basic idea of growing a new organ within one's body, or regenerating a lost limb—that fundamental possibility became the focus of solemn round-table discussions on television and long, self-important, usually incorrect editorials in newspapers and magazines.

During all that time I was taking the best physical care of myself that I had ever taken. Ever since the miscarriage, I had decided that I would work myself up to tip-top physical condition before becoming pregnant again. I worked out at a "wellness center" near my midtown office. I had monthly checkups, not by my gynecologist (whom Jesse knew) but by an Indonesian internist who specialized in infectious diseases. I stayed on the pill.

My plan was to get pregnant once again only when I was absolutely certain that any possible infection that might have caused my miscarriage was completely gone from my system. I decided that I would wait a year; if twelve blood tests in a row showed that there were no exotic microbes lingering in my blood, then I could safely bear Jesse's baby.

My biological clock was ticking loudly; I knew that time was running fast, but I was determined not to go through another miscarriage. I wanted a baby, a healthy dear baby that Jesse and I could love and bring up together.

In the meantime I worked out, ate sensibly, drank little, and lost nearly ten pounds. Jesse never noticed, except now and then to comment on how terrific I looked. I smiled to myself and we made love whenever he wasn't too exhausted from the grueling hours he put in at the hospital and medical center.

I bided my time. And Jesse never knew what I was doing.

ARTHUR

The terrorists' attack on the lab wasn't as bad as the media's. Simmonds kept drumming away at us. He never mentioned me or the laboratory by name; we could have sued him for slander or gotten an injunction, the corporate lawyers told me. He was too clever to fall into that trap. But I watched one of his televised rallies one night, broadcast from Denver.

The baseball park was filled to capacity, and he was working himself up into a sweat beneath the bright lights. He had peeled off his Western-style suede jacket and pulled his string tie loose from his collar. One hand gripping a cordless microphone, he pranced and jittered across the stage, perspiration pouring down his reddened face, the picture of honest distress and righteous wrath. He looked like an overworked little gnome, with those bushy brows and his slightly hunched posture.

"This life is only a preparation for the paradise that God has created for us! And yet unholy scientists, godless atheists and Antichrists, they want to stretch out their lives, they want to make themselves immortal, they want to challenge God's plan!"

I thought he was very clever telling them that we want to

make ourselves immortal and ignoring the fact that we would make his audience immortal too, if we could.

"So they can keep themselves alive for ten or twenty or fifty-so years more with their devil's science," he went on. "How do you think God's going to feel about that? He's prepared paradise for us and they're telling him, 'No, thanks, Lord, we'd rather stay here in this vale of tears because we don't really trust You to give us paradise.'

"And that's what they're really saying, isn't it? They don't trust God and His goodness. They don't believe what the Lord Jesus Christ has told us out of His own mouth. They don't want paradise or any part of God's plan."

He hesitated, let his head droop and the hand holding the microphone drop to his side as if he were utterly exhausted. I couldn't hear a sound from the huge crowd surrounding him. Not a cough or a shuffle of feet.

Slowly, slowly, Simmonds brought the mike back to his lips. "Do you know what God thinks of people like that?" he asked softly. "Do you know what God's gonna do to those who don't trust Him?"

He turned slowly in a full circle, his question hanging in the air.

"He'll send them all to hell!" Simmonds roared. "And they'll deserve it! Those who have no faith in the Lord Jesus Christ will be condemned to spend eternity in hellfire! Don't let these fiendish scientists, these tools of Satan, lead you on the road to everlasting damnation! Accept God's plan, not the evil enticements of secular scientists. Save your souls, don't worry about your bodies. God will take care of you in this life and the next."

For a man who didn't worry about his body, I thought, Simmonds wears expensive shirts.

But he made me think about my own religious feelings. I really had none. I couldn't accept the idea of some supernatural being creating the universe for his entertainment. That's what most religions seemed to be saying: God created the universe and put us in it just to see if we would do what he tells us. Nonsense. It seemed to me that the only reason people turn to religion is because they're frightened of death. There are no atheists in foxholes, and many a dying man has suddenly seen the light. That's what Simmonds was playing on: stark fear. Fear of death.

For months he kept yapping about scientists interfering with God's plan, and he or somebody in his organization must certainly have tipped off the reporters about who he meant because it wasn't long before they started to descend on us like a plague of electronic locusts.

I'm a ham, I admit it. I don't mind in the least sitting in front of a TV camera and telling everybody what I think. But I didn't want to make the lab a target for more animal rights activists or religious kooks. We were doing very sensitive work and I didn't want the staff upset, either.

Johnston and the corporate board backed me all the way. A *little* publicity was fine, as far as they were concerned: just enough to keep up investors' interest in our work and keep the stock moving upward. That would even help blunt the European takeover bid. But tabloid stuff about Dr. Frankenstein creating monsters in his lab—whether in print or on TV—we all wanted to avoid that.

So I called a meeting of the whole staff, everybody, down to the cooks and security guards. Packed everybody into the cafeteria, standing room only. Rented a squad of security people to watch the building while I explained to my people what was going on and why. Held the meeting at the end of the nominal working day on a Friday, at five p.m.

The cafeteria was packed shoulder to shoulder, two hundred and fourteen people. I had our personnel chief take a count. I insisted that *everybody* be there.

I stood up on the only table left in the room; we had moved the others out into the halls. All their eyes were on me, from Darrell and Zack and Vince Andriotti down to the secretaries and stock clerks and our purchasing agent, who insisted on keeping a cigar between his teeth even though we didn't allow smoking anywhere inside the building.

"You're probably wondering why I called you here this

afternoon," I started out. It was a lame joke and it got more groans than laughs.

"I'm sure that all of you know about the research we're doing on organ regrowth," I said. "This is important work. Vital work. It's going to change history."

They shifted on their feet a little. Somebody coughed.

"We've tried to keep this work as quiet as possible as far as the media is concerned, but the terrorists' attack on the lab a few weeks ago has let the cat out of the bag. We're prime news now."

"Were they really terrorists?" a woman's voice asked from the back of the crowded room.

"I call them terrorists," I answered. "The FBI calls them terrorists. Working for animal rights is one thing. Destroying lab equipment, throwing genetically engineered rats out into the cold world, kidnapping experimental animals—that's terrorism and it's criminal."

"The rats can't survive on their own," Tina Andriotti called out. "Whoever broke them out of Zack's lab has killed them, one way or another."

"What happened to the chimps?" someone asked.

"Hold on. I don't want this meeting to become a debate about animal rights. We all treat our animals as humanely as we can, but we all know that without animal experiments we can't make any progress. Right?"

A few scattered voices answered, "Right." It was half-hearted, I thought, but enough. I went on.

"You probably know that an evangelist preacher has been bad-mouthing us all across the country. Other ministers and media commentators have taken up the same theme. Even a few politicians have spoken out against us."

"Only young ones," Zack O'Neill wisecracked. Everybody laughed at that.

"Some of you may have noticed," I went on, "that we're getting a lot of calls from news reporters. They've even been showing up at our doorstep unannounced. Perhaps you've received calls at home, or had reporters try to interview you."

I heard a few murmurs and saw heads nod.

"All right. From now on, I want you to refer any media contacts to me. If a reporter calls you or tries to talk to you, just tell them to call me about it. Then tell Phyllis. Get their names and their affiliations, if you can. We need to know who they are and where they're coming from."

More nods.

"Fine. One more thing," I added. "We've got to tighten up the lab's security. You probably know that the terrorists were let into the back compound by one of our own employees. That staggered me, I've got to admit."

I glanced at my personnel chief. I had warned her I'd be mentioning this, and assured her all over again that I didn't blame her for it.

"We've been studying the situation ever since the attack. I asked our personnel and security chiefs, together with the head of administrative services, to see what can be done about preventing another such attack. They've come up with several recommendations that I think are sensible."

I reached into my jacket pocket and pulled out a plastic badge.

"One of them is that we all start wearing security badges."

That brought out a collective groan. One wise guy in the back of the crowd yelled in a Hollywood Mexican accent, "Badges? We don' need no steenkin' badges!" That broke the unhappiness very nicely.

"I don't like them any more than you do," I said, clipping the badge to my jacket pocket. "But it makes sense. We want to be sure that everybody inside our building *belongs* here."

We were adding more security cameras, too, and tightening up our procedures for checking out new employees.

"Over the next week or so, each of you will be scheduled to have your photo taken," I told them. "If you like the picture you can order some for yourselves free of charge. Fair enough?"

"Whoever heard of an ID photo that comes out good?" Vince Andriotti grumbled.

The only full-time employee who was not at the meeting was Cassie Ianetta. Her field trials in Mexico had gotten even more seriously bogged down; what should have taken six months now looked as if it would drag on for more than a year. Of course, she had flown to the lab immediately as soon as she had heard about the terrorists' attack. She went straight from the front door to the animal compound. I found her there, rolling on the tiled floor with Max, the two of them hugging each other like long-lost siblings.

Once they untangled, I began to explain what had happened. Cassie certainly thought of the attackers as terrorists.

"Kidnap the chimps?" she raged, glaring at the empty cages. "Kidnap them? They'll kill them! They don't have the facilities or the people to take care of them! They've murdered them!"

Her voice was so shrill that Max let go of her hand and scampered back outside. Cassie's face looked as if she had crucified her own mother. She turned and ran after Max.

"I'm sorry," she called after him. Max had scampered up into his favorite tree. "I wasn't angry at you, Max, baby. I could never be angry at you."

From up in his perch, Max pointed his index finger at his mouth and twirled it around a few times.

"Candy?" Cassie asked, repeating the sign. "Come on down and we'll find some candy." She gestured for him to come down to her.

Cassie stayed for a weekend, spending just about the whole time with Max. She certainly coaxed Max out of his fright; in that one weekend she had him back to normal, just about.

Before Cassie left to return to Mexico, she dropped into my office.

"I'm sorry the trials are going so slow," she said, perching herself on the chair in front of my desk like a frail little sparrow. "It takes ten times longer to get anything done down there."

And ten times as much money as we had budgeted, I said to myself. But I didn't want to bother Cassie with that.

"You're making progress," I said. "You should be finishing up soon."

She nodded tiredly. "I'm going to try the enzyme on myself."

I could feel my eyebrows hike up. "Why?"

"It's come back," Cassie said. "I had a checkup and they found a spot."

That was what we had all feared: that her cancer wasn't gone, it was merely in remission. "Will you need more surgery?"

"They froze it with liquid nitrogen. I didn't want it removed. I want to see if the enzyme can destroy it."

She seemed very matter-of-fact about it. Very controlled.

"But once it's been frozen the cells are dead."

Again that tired nod, her head drooping and then slowly, painfully coming up again. "There'll be more."

It's hell knowing that your body is betraying you. Cassie looked as if she expected nothing less, as if she thought she somehow deserved to be put on the rack.

"Stay here, then," I said. "Get back to your own doctors and—"

"No." She pushed at that stubborn flop of hair. "The facilities in Querétaro are fine. So are the doctors. I'll be okay there."

"But if—"

She tried to smile. "I can inject myself with the enzyme down there without worrying about the FDA and all the other regulations. I'd be dead before we worked through the red tape here."

"Cassie, if there's anything I can do . . ."

"I'm not worried about it," she said. It looked like a patent lie to me. Then she leaned closer to my desk and said, "What I'm worried about is Max."

"He seems okay, now that you've been with him. That's another reason for you to stay, isn't it?"

"I'm going to finish these field trials," she insisted. I realized that she meant she wanted to remain in Mexico long enough to try the enzyme on herself. "I just want to make certain that you stick to your promise."

"What promise?" I asked.

"About Max."

"Oh. That."

"He's not to be used in any experiments," Cassie said firmly. "Just because you've lost the other chimps doesn't mean you can use Max again."

"We may need him."

"Get another chimp. Find human volunteers. Come on down to Mexico and I'll get hundreds for you."

Her eyes were burning as if she had a fever.

"You asked if there's anything you can do for me. That's what you can do. Leave Max alone. You promised."

I nodded reluctantly. "I did promise you, didn't I?"

THERE WAS no way we could keep the media totally out of the lab. The more Simmonds spoke, the more the word got around that Grenford Lab was the hotbed of godless scientists that he had been railing against. I'm certain he was giving our name—my name—to the reporters in private. Or Jesse was. At any rate, we were besieged with requests for interviews and camera coverage of the lab. It got so bad that Phyllis complained she was spending all her time trying to fend off reporters.

I went down to corporate headquarters to talk it over with Johnston and his public relations people. Nancy Dubois got herself invited to our impromptu conference: the marketing department had an interest in our public image, apparently. She greeted me coolly as she came into Johnston's office. It seemed clear that she was already running rings around her ostensible boss, Uhlenbeck.

We had a new corporate PR director, a tough-looking woman of fifty or so, Deborah King. She had let her hair go gray and wild, it looked almost like an Afro. She had a lantern jaw, narrow suspicious eyes, and a pugnacious nose. She looked as if she'd just as soon spit in your eye as say hello to you. And this was the head of our public relations department.

But her voice was silky and she knew her business. After listening to me complain about the media for ten minutes she said calmly, "What you need is a PR manager at the lab who can deal with this."

"I don't need a public relations assistant," I protested. "What I need is some peace and quiet. Can't I rout all these requests for interviews and whatnot to you?"

"Certainly you can, Dr. Marshak," she said softly. "But then I'd have to call you to find out if you wanted to talk to the reporter or not. And I'd have to come down to the lab to set up the areas that the camera crew would be allowed to photograph. It would be much simpler for all of us if you had a resident PR manager."

Johnston agreed. "You can't expect Deborah or one of her people to go running back and forth to your lab every day."

I looked at Nancy. She smiled thinly at me and said nothing.

"We've never had a public relations manager on the staff," I said.

"It needn't be permanent," Ms. King assured me. "Just until the present furor dies down."

"It'll save you a lot of grief," Johnston said.

A sudden thought struck me. "Are you thinking of sending one of your regular staff to the lab, or hiring someone from outside?"

Ms. King glanced at Johnston. "My staff is stretched pretty thin as it is . . ."

"Since we're thinking in terms of a temporary situation," said Johnston, "we ought to get a consultant to do it. No sense hiring anybody on a permanent basis."

I said, "All right. I know who could do a good job on this. She's worked here before; did that backgrounder on me last year."

"Oh, yeah." Johnston smiled. "The redhead."

"Pat Hayward," I said.

"I don't know her," said King, "but if you're happy with her, I'm happy."

I looked at Nancy. She was decidedly unhappy. In fact, she was glowering at me.

THE TRIAL:
DAY FOUR, MORNING

Arthur took his customary seat along the front row, then got to his feet as the three judges filed in and sat at their desks. Senator Kindelberger was nowhere in sight. Neither was Jesse. There were noticeably fewer reporters in the chamber, and only one TV camera remained.

Yesterday's testimony by Zapapas and the other experts had been a bore, although Arthur felt a sort of perverse admiration for the Greek. Zapapas had shamelessly tried to take the credit for everything that had happened in the field of biology since Watson and Crick discovered the structure of DNA. Arthur decided he wouldn't bother cross-examining him. At bottom, beneath his flow of words, Zapapas had confirmed that organ regeneration was possible. He even hinted that he had done successful regeneration work himself, although he never presented any evidence of it.

This morning they would hear from Quentin Phillips, the Nobel laureate from Oxford. Arthur looked forward to his testimony. Phillips was a man of uncommon good sense, one of the world's leading microbiologists, and he had never had any connection whatsoever with Grenford Laboratory or Omnitech Corporation. He'd talk sense to the jury, Arthur knew.

It was this afternoon's testimony that worried him. Rosen was going to play some DVDs that Cassie Ianetta had made before her suicide. Arthur had tried to block that, claiming that they would not be relevant to the trial, but Rosen had insisted and Graves had gone along with the examiner.

Arthur had no idea of what Cassie's disks would say. But since the first day of the trial Rosen and the judges had talked about her death as if somehow Arthur bore the responsibility for it. Omnitech's own lawyers had mentioned the possibility of a civil or even criminal action against Arthur once the science trial was over.

They're not only out to discredit the scientific work, Arthur told himself. They're out to get *me,* personally.

Arthur looked at the jury as the chamber settled down for the day's testimony. Graves had tried to make the jury as valid a cross section of working biologists as possible: someone from every major area in the field, someone from every section of the country, someone from every age group. Not an easy thing to do, with only twelve men and women to go with. Arthur had carefully read hundreds of curricula vitae before agreeing to these particular twelve.

Then Kindelberger came in and sat alongside the trio of judges. Why? Arthur asked himself. Does he think that Phillips and his Nobel will bring out the reporters? It certainly didn't look that way. There were only a handful of media people present.

Rosen looked more somber than usual in a dark blue suit and matching tie. From his seat at the end of the judges' table he riffled through some notes, then turned toward Graves and the others.

"I regret to announce to the court that Professor Phillips will not be able to testify here today."

The audience stirred. Arthur felt a flash of angry disappointment.

"Professor Phillips suffered a stroke at Gatwick Airport yesterday," Rosen went on mournfully, "as he was waiting to board the plane that would bring him here. He is in the hospital, in critical condition."

The crowd sighed. Arthur felt sad for the old man, but his irritation remained.

"In his place," Rosen went on, "we were fortunate to obtain the gracious consent of the retired chairman of the molecular biology department of Columbia University, Professor Emeritus Wilson K. Potter."

Arthur spun around in his seat and saw Potter, a frail and ancient wisp of his former self, limping up the central aisle, leaning heavily on a cane. Two students were walking a few steps behind him. When Potter caught Arthur's eye he smiled maliciously.

PATRICIA HAYWARD

The phone call from the new Omnitech PR director kind of surprised me. I mean, usually a new chief wants to bring her own people on board. I thought when the old guy retired I wouldn't hear much from Omnitech anymore. That's one of the hazards of the freelance business.

But she called me and explained what was happening and I knew without her telling me that Arthur had asked for me personally. I told her I was awfully busy—which was a whopper of a lie—but that I'd try to sort things out and see if I couldn't work her project in.

"This would be a full-time job for the next several months," she said. Her voice was kind of testy, like she was saying, *Who the hell do you think you are to turn your nose up at an opportunity like this?*

"I understand that," I said. "That's why I want to make sure I can clear my calendar of all other commitments."

"I see." Sniffy.

"Can I phone you back first thing tomorrow?"

"Certainly." And she hung up.

The only commitments on my calendar were attempts to find paying assignments. I had plenty of time to work on my novel, and it was actually starting to go somewhere, but that wasn't bringing in any money. My piggy bank was dangerously low and my mother's "career" as the neighborhood babysitter didn't bring in enough money to pay for her vodka.

Livvie was out at the supermarket just then, so I absent-mindedly fed the cats and then wandered back to my room, where my computer screen still flickered with my deathless prose. Arthur had asked for me to come and work for him. Only a temporary job, to be sure, but even if it lasted only a couple of months the money would be more than I'd made all year so far. That was on the plus side. Then there was Arthur himself, maybe a negative. Not that I didn't like him; I did. That was the problem. And he seemed to like me, at least we had a lovely night that time in Las Vegas. But–

"It's me!" Livvie shouted from the kitchen doorway. "I'm home."

I helped her tote the groceries in from the car and while we were putting them into the fridge and the cupboards I told her about the call from Omnitech.

"Terrific!" Livvie said. "Snap it up."

"I don't know," I said. "Maybe Arthur's got more on his mind than public relations."

Livvie gave me a lascivious grin. "Whatever kind of relations he's interested in, go for it."

"Mother!"

She raised both hands. "Only kidding. But, well, you said he was cute and you liked him. Looks as if he likes you, too."

"That could be a problem," I said.

"Patricia," she said, "there are times when you absolutely drive your poor old mother to drink." And she headed straight for the vodka bottle on the countertop beside the toaster.

I TOOK the job, of course. Showed up two days later at the laboratory and was ushered straight into Arthur's office. I wore a sea-green business suit with a tailored white blouse; no frills, no jewelry except a couple of rings. I was there to work, not to look alluring. Still, I didn't want to look like a clod.

Arthur seemed happy to see me, but he was all business. I listened carefully to his outline of the problem. It took him almost half an hour.

"What we need is three things," he finished, ticking points

off on his fingers. "First, to keep scare stories out of the media. Second, to keep the reporters off the necks of my researchers and me. And third, to take the workload off Phyllis."

"And something else," I added.

"Oh?"

"You don't want to give the reporters the idea that you're hiding something. Right? You want to appear to be open and aboveboard."

He thought about that a moment, nodded. "Yes, I suppose so. But I don't want any screaming headlines about mutant monsters and that sort of stuff."

"Then the best way to handle it is to be right up-front with the reporters. You're going to have to make yourself accessible to them. And some of the key players on your staff, too."

Arthur shook his head stubbornly. "I don't want them bothering my researchers. I'll talk to them all they want, but they've got to leave my staff people alone."

"I'm not sure that's going to work," I said.

"That's what I want."

No sense arguing with the boss the first day on the job. "Okay, we can try it that way and see how it works."

"Good." He reached for the intercom on his desk. "Phyllis has set up an office for you just down the hall."

"Wait," I said.

His hand stopped just over the intercom button.

All of a sudden I felt flustered. "I—I just wanted to thank you for getting me this assignment. I appreciate it."

He broke into one of those killer smiles of his. "I've got to admit, Pat, that you're the only person I could think of who has some experience in this area."

I smiled back and said something brilliant like, "Oh, sure," but inwardly I kicked myself for allowing girlish fantasies to seep into my brain. He had hired me because he didn't know anybody else, not because he had any ideas of romance. This is going to be strictly business, I told myself, and don't think for a minute that it's anything else.

As Phyllis showed me down the hall to the office I was going to use, I kept telling myself, Strictly business. Strictly business. It'll be better that way. Nothing but grief when you try to mix business and personal relationships. You've gone that route before and look what it's got you: nothing but grief.

IT WAS like doing a high-wire act. I had to convince the reporters that what Arthur and his people were doing was earthshaking, but not scary. Revolutionary, but not harmful. It'll save your life someday, but don't get upset about the changes it's going to cause.

We hit on an angle of approach right away. I juggled all the incoming requests for interviews and pictures and set up times for the reporters to see Arthur. They could interview him in his office and then take a walk through the working labs. We carefully set up an itinerary that took them through some impressive-looking labs with lots of glittering glassware and bubbling chemicals. Showed them lab rats and the minihogs and monkeys that Arthur's people were now using for experiments. And Max. The chimp was the star of our show. Camera crews spent more time on Max's antics than they did with Arthur or any of the scientific backgrounds.

We never let them see blood. We never let them close to any of the real working labs. And we *never,* ever mentioned stem cells or cloning. Not that we didn't get questions about them, but we tiptoed away from those subjects, telling anyone who asked that we don't need stem cells and we certainly don't clone cells. Not anymore, anyway. Some of the reporters smelled our evasions, some tried to dig up details that they could blow up into a big controversy. But most of them simply took what we said at face value and went away disappointed that they couldn't find any monsters or welfare mothers selling their fetuses.

I heard complaints, secondhand, that some of the lab people were upset about having a section of the building roped off for the media. They started to call it "Glamour Alley." But they cooperated, grudgingly. That was fine with me as long as they didn't contradict our party line.

The big problem, of course, was the tabloids. Whether print or TV, they all had the same goggle-eyed goal in mind:

show us the monsters. Show us how you kill unborn babies for their stem cells. Send in the clones. Here we were telling them that this research would someday help people to live forever and all they wanted was mutants and mad scientists. What they got was truculent minihogs and jabbering macaques and Max doing acrobatics in the trees out back. And Arthur, smiling patiently, the cool and confident silver fox telling each one of those nasty little bastards that sooner or later they're going to need a new heart, new liver, new legs.

Of course, we got some blatantly faked stories in the tabloid press about Frankenstein experiments on people and kids with two hearts—and even two heads—but they didn't seem to do much damage. I mean, the people who read those crap sheets aren't the movers and shakers of our society.

It was the so-called legitimate reporters that gave us the most trouble. The kind that can take a story about genetically enhanced food crops and write: *High-tech tomatoes. Mysterious milk. Super-squash. Are we supposed to eat this stuff? Or is it going to eat us?*

They were out for what Linda Ellerbee used to call "anxiety news." If they had been around when the Salk polio vaccine first appeared, they would've written sob stories about the poor guys who build iron lungs being thrown out of work.

They looked legit. They came from the big, authoritative news services and networks. But they were looking for bad news. They didn't trust science or scientists, probably because they'd been trained to look for the gloom and doom in every story.

A few of the jerks got confused about how regentide works and wrote that we were using fetal tissue. We weren't, of course. Regentide makes the cells it affects regress until they behave like stem cells, but we didn't use fetuses any more than we used hacksaws. Still, the fetal tissue story got all the antiabortion fanatics stirred up, but good. We had to spend a lot of time and effort doing damage control on the fetal tissue nonsense.

The reporters insisted on "balance." They would interview

Arthur and then go running to Joshua Ransom for a counter-point. It was all I could do to keep Arthur from refusing to see any more reporters, once he found his own quotes (somewhat garbled) side by side with Ransom's.

"That man's not a scientist!" Arthur growled. "He hasn't the faintest idea of what he's talking about!"

But Ransom could make headlines, and that's what the reporters wanted. It wasn't enough that Arthur promised them new hearts and spleens and whatever else they needed. Ransom warned of "man-made mutations" and "laboratory-built supermen."

And Reverend Simmonds kept up his drumbeat about atheistic scientists doing the devil's work. I had hoped that the more he yammered on that theme the less impact it would have. He'd get to be old news. I not-so-subtly hinted to a few key reporters that the reverend's problem was really anti-Semitism. Like Hitler, he didn't like "Jewish science." That backfired. Started a flurry of stories about Jews in science and anti-Semitism in general, but didn't take an ounce of pressure off us.

The most difficult reporters to handle were the smarter ones who weren't looking for scare stories but knew enough to ask about the side effects of the regeneration work and the long-term implications of helping people to live twice their normal life spans or more.

Arthur handled them pretty well. Gave them the official tour through Glamour Alley, brought them back to his office, and charmed them into thinking he was being completely open with them. I was always by his side during these sessions. It was an education for me.

"What's a normal life span?" he asked a gray-haired reporter from the New York Times. "The Bible's three score and ten? The actuarial averages that the insurance companies use? The official age of retirement at the Times?"

The reporter laughed at that one.

"Our generation lives twice as long as the average person did around the turn of the twentieth century," Arthur said. "Does that mean we're not supposed to live longer?"

The reporter said, "How will it affect Social Security if everybody lives to be two hundred?"

Arthur gave an elaborate shrug. "That's for the politicians to decide. And the people. I'll vote on the issue when it comes up."

"Isn't that a rather blasé attitude?"

Arthur leaned forward across his desk and clasped his hands together. "Listen. Let me explain to you the way the world works."

"I'd love to know." The reporter's smile was only slightly cynical.

"Scientists discover something new," Arthur said. "Atomic power, for instance. Or antibiotics. Lasers, computers, anything you can think of. It's new, a new capability. It allows you to do things you couldn't do before."

"Very well," said the reporter.

"Then engineers take this discovery out of the laboratory and make something useful out of it. A product, a tool, a weapon, a medical treatment."

"I see."

"Then businesspeople start to make money from it." I had never seen Arthur so intent. He looked like a priest reciting his liturgy. "Some people start to get rich from it. Others pay money to get it and complain that the price is too high and the sellers are making unreasonable profits. Commentators start to worry about how this is affecting our lives and our society. Philosophers hold debates on the ethics and morality of it. Lawyers sue people about it. And finally—absolutely last in the chain—politicians start to pass laws about it."

"And put a tax on it," the reporter added.

Arthur broke into a hearty laugh. "And put a tax on it! Yes, you're right," he agreed.

"So you seem to be saying that it's not your business how your work affects Social Security or any other aspect of our lives."

"It's not my business *as a scientist,*" Arthur answered immediately. "As a citizen, of course, I'll be just as concerned as anyone else. More so, I think, because I understand what's involved."

"Better than the average citizen?"

With a wave of his hand, Arthur replied, "That depends on how well you do your job. You're in the business of informing the public. They'll only know as much as you tell them."

"If that."

Arthur pointed to one of the mottos on his wall: Jefferson's *If a nation expects to be ignorant and free, in a state of civilization, it expects what never was and never will be.*

"Point taken," said the reporter. "You might also be interested to know that Jefferson once said that if he had to choose between newspapers and no government, or government and no newspapers, he'd take the former."

"Because the latter is a prelude either to a tragedy or a farce," Arthur added.

By the time the reporter left Arthur's office they were practically soul mates. The story that appeared in the *Times* the following Sunday was thoughtful and thought-provoking. A good, clean job with no hatchet work. Only a couple of references to "Joshua Ransom, the self-appointed public watchdog of science."

"Ask the *Times* if we can make copies of it and use it as a backgrounder," Arthur told me.

"They'll offer to sell you copies," I said.

"Good. Do it."

But despite all our efforts the basic story refused to die down. Simmonds—or whoever handled his publicity—was damned ingenious. He found a new way to get himself in the headlines and us in hot water at least once a week. The TV shows started calling for interviews with Arthur: *Meet the Press* and all those self-important Washington panel discussion shows. *Newsweek* did a cover story entitled *Biotechnology: Cure or Curse?* The phone kept jangling.

I had to go into Arthur's office and admit defeat.

"We haven't smothered the story," I told him. "It just won't die. If anything, it's getting bigger."

He didn't seem too concerned. "We're holding our own. I haven't seen any really bad horror stories in the responsible press lately. The TV interviews have been generally harmless."

Arthur came across terrific on television. Between his distinguished silver hair and his sexy smile, he looked great. And he was unflappable. I thought he'd be able to handle even *60 Minutes* if they came knocking at the door.

I took the padded chair at the side of his desk; it was closer to him, and the desk wasn't between us.

"I had thought," I confessed, "that by now we'd have soft-pedaled everything enough so that the media would have lost interest in the story. But it just seems to be rolling along with no end in sight."

"I'm not surprised," Arthur said. "This is a big story, no matter which way you look at it. We're offering the first step to immortality, Pat. What do you expect the media to do, forget about it?"

The truth was, I dreaded the moment when some news media heavy hitter took it into his or her head to crucify Arthur. So far they had all been easy on him, treating this more as a science story than as a blockbuster. But just let one of those egomaniacs understand that they could zoom their ratings by doing a story on cruelty to animals or tampering with human lives, and we'd be off to the races.

What I feared most was that Simmonds would challenge Arthur to a public debate. I knew that would be a circus, if Arthur accepted. And if he refused, it could be even worse.

"Maybe you ought to hire a first-class PR firm to handle this," I blurted. "Maybe I'm just out of my depth."

My own words surprised me. I hadn't really intended to say that. What the hell's going on inside my head? I asked myself. Do you really want to run away and hide?

He looked surprised, too. "You want to leave?"

I didn't, not really. But I was getting scared. Scared that this was getting too big for me. Scared that in the end Arthur would get terribly hurt and it'd be my fault.

"Don't go," he said before I could answer. "I need you. I think we work well together, don't you?"

My mind was racing, jumbling all sorts of thoughts together in a crazy hodgepodge. The money was good. And regular. But what if I screwed up and Arthur got blasted by the media? I was still hoping that he might ask me to dinner or invite me to a party he had to attend or fly me off to Samarkand. I was being stupid, I told myself. His affair with Nancy Dubois had ended, that much I knew from the gossip at the corporate office. But as far as I could tell, Arthur didn't get himself entangled with any of the women at the lab. Too smart for that. From what I had heard, Nancy was still steaming over him. He wouldn't want to get involved with me, I knew. He had hired me for business reasons only. Stop being a silly fool.

"If you need more help we can get you an assistant," Arthur offered. "Even if we hired a PR firm I'd like you to stay and be my liaison with them. I need you, Pat."

"Okay," I heard myself say. "I'll stay." And my stupid heart fluttered inside me.

Every evening when I came home, Livvie gave me that slaphappy vodka grin of hers. "So how's things at the office?" she'd ask.

It made me angry. Because it kept me dreaming, in spite of myself.

I kept wondering why Simmonds didn't challenge Arthur to a debate. Maybe he was afraid Arthur would mop the floor with him; after all, Arthur had all the scientific facts on his side, and he came across beautifully on TV. But I figured that Simmonds would go for the emotional appeal, you know, *There are some things man was not meant to know. Don't interfere with God's plan.* And then it hit me. If it came to emotional appeals, Arthur could clobber Simmonds but good. He was offering immortality! He could tell people that they could avoid death! No wonder Simmonds wouldn't want to be on the same stage with him.

Gradually I stopped worrying so much about my nightmare scenario.

And then the government people arrived at the lab.

ARTHUR

Simmonds was damned clever. When he saw that his public attacks weren't going to stop me, he turned to the government. No one will admit it, but I'm certain that's what happened. Either he got the government involved or Ransom did. Or maybe some bureaucrat somewhere in that tangle of Washington offices decided they'd better get involved before Ransom put public pressure on them.

Thanks to Pat Hayward's really professional handling of the media, we were weathering Simmonds's ravings with only a few blatantly hysterical headlines, and they were mostly in the tabloids that only the crazies read anyway. So there was no major public relations disaster, despite all the hoopla. In fact, the price of Omnitech stock kept creeping upward, in part because of our excellent handling of the media. The news was getting around that our research in organ regeneration was moving ahead nicely, and it would be worth megafortunes in the not-too-distant future.

It was the day of the first snowfall of the season, early in December. The lab buzzed with talk about a white Christmas. Zack O'Neill popped his head into my office and asked, "Got a minute?"

I waved him in. Funny how he had toned down his appearance; the more successful he became in his lab work, the less flamboyant his clothes and his hairdo. Of course, he still wore his earring, but it was down to a little jewel now, not a dangling iron cross.

He spread a handful of X-ray pictures across my desk. Macaques.

"Blocked the coronary arteries to induce cardiac insufficiency," he said, pointing to the first X-ray. I could see the dark shadows of the plugs they had inserted in the monkey's arteries.

"Injected regentide at this point." The second picture clearly showed necrosis of the heart tissue. It was dying from lack of blood, just as any muscle would if you cut off its nutrition supply.

Zack spread the other X-rays out and I could see the monkey's original heart dying while a new heart grew beside it, with new coronary arteries to feed it.

"The new heart took over thirty percent of the blood-pumping at this point," he said, tapping a finger on one of the pictures. "By here"—he tapped another—"it was doing eighty percent of normal and our patient started acting like a healthy macaque again."

I saw that tumors had appeared shortly after the first regentide injection, but then they shriveled and died.

"You used Cassie's enzyme on the tumors?" I asked.

Zack grinned and nodded. "Been talking to her every day on the phone."

"How is she?"

"Sounds okay. Says she'll be coming home in another few weeks or so. Everything's going well."

"But how is she? Healthwise?"

Zack looked surprised. "I dunno. We never talk about that, just the work."

I made a mental note to call her, find out how she felt.

Zack bit his lip for a moment, then said, "We've gone about as far with the macaques as we can. It's time to take the next step."

I knew what he was going to say.

And he said it. "We're ready to try this out on a chimp."

"But we don't have any chimps."

He gave me a sly grin. "Come on, boss. We've still got Max."

"I sort of promised Cassie that we wouldn't use Max."

"We need a chimp experiment. Genetically, they're the closest to humans."

"I'm trying to import some new ones. They'll be younger, probably better specimens for us."

"How soon can you get them?"

He had me there. Our application was already bogged down in red tape. "A few months, at best," I admitted.

"Max is our best bet, then. You don't want to let everything we've accomplished hang fire for months, do you?"

I wasn't even certain that it would be a matter of months. The way the various government agencies were processing our request for chimps, it might take a year or more.

"We could just do something simple, like a finger," Zack coaxed.

It was tempting. No sense slowing ourselves down because of an emotional girl. But still . . .

"Let me talk to Cassie first," I said.

Zack shrugged. "Too bad we can't try it on human volunteers."

I grunted as if he'd hit me in the pit of my stomach. "We don't have enough reporters prowling around looking for trouble. You want to start operating on people?"

Zack laughed. "Max is our best bet."

"I know," I admitted. "Talk it over with our medical team, get the protocols written up properly. I'll deal with Cassie."

Easily said. But that was my responsibility. Zack would do the experimental work, my task was to clear the way for him and then back him to the hilt.

No less than a week later we were visited by two NIH officials. I wondered if they had bugged my office.

They were both lawyers, not scientists. The senior of the two was a plumpish pink-faced woman with graying hair pulled back tightly into a ponytail. She wore a rather pretty flowered dress. She sort of looked like a TV commercial version of everybody's maiden aunt. The guy with her was also well fed, much younger but already paunchy. His face was pretty well covered by a heavy black beard, thick mustache, and beetling black brows. Put him in a doublet and he'd be your perfect pirate.

They had phoned from Washington to set up an appointment with me. NIH is not a regulatory agency, but when they told me they were from the legal division I called Johnston at his downtown office and asked him to provide a corporate lawyer. They sent a young man named, appropriately enough, Charles Eager. I also asked Pat Hayward to sit in on this meeting; it might have serious public relations repercussions, I thought. Besides, I've found it's always best to outnumber the enemy, even if it's nothing more than an informal visit by government representatives.

As if any visit from a government representative is informal.

So there we were, the five us, seated around the circular conference table in the corner of my office: three lawyers, a PR consultant, and me.

We exchanged pleasantries while Phyllis brought in a tray of coffee, tea, and soft drinks. The office smelled faintly of . . . nutmeg? Then I recalled that in Phyllis's mind, nutmeg reduces stress.

Once everyone had taken the drink they wanted, I asked the NIH people why they had asked for this meeting.

The woman started by saying, "We appreciate your granting us the time to talk with you, Dr. Marshak. We know you're a busy man these days."

I didn't like the sound of "these days."

"We've been monitoring your request for chimps," she went on. "And we've received several inquiries about the work you're doing on organ regrowth."

Before I could ask who the inquiries were from, the bearded pirate butted in, "Since your work is not being funded by NIH we don't have an official claim to oversight." He had a sweet tenor voice that didn't go with his fierce hairy face at all.

Our corporate Mr. Eager quickly said, "There has been no government funding whatsoever for the work in question."

"There's been quite a lot in the media about your work," said the woman, ignoring Eager. "From the nature of the stories, and the inquiries we've received, we thought it would be proper for us to have this little chat with you."

I glanced at Pat, sitting across the round table from me. Simmonds was responsible for this meeting, we both knew. Or Ransom. Directly or indirectly, one or both of them had stirred up the goddamned government.

I tried to smile and asked amiably, "What would you like to know?"

If they had been scientists, they would have been avid to get back into the labs and see what was going on, talk with the people actually doing the research, look over the hardware. But they were lawyers.

The pirate said, "Whether you're receiving government funding or not, there are still protocols to be followed in all animal experiments."

"I assure you we are following those protocols punctiliously."

He raised those heavy eyebrows almost to his shaggy hairline. I thought perhaps he didn't know the word "punctiliously."

The woman said sweetly, "I assume you have the proper documentation for your experiments?"

"We do indeed," I replied. "Tons of it."

"That's good."

"You've applied to obtain six chimpanzees," said the pirate.

"Most of the chimps we had were stolen by animal rights terrorists," I said.

"Yes, I read about that."

"You're planning to perform experiments on chimpanzees," the woman stated, a cheerless little frown on her buttercup face.

Why else would we want them? I silently retorted. Aloud, I explained, "Chimps are our closest relatives, genetically. Their DNA is only about two percent different from our own. Since this work involves genetic triggering, we'll need to test it on chimps."

"And eventually on human beings?" she asked.

I took a breath and then nodded. "Eventually on human beings. The entire purpose of this work is to help humans."

"Extend their lifespans, you mean."

"Grow new organs in their bodies when their original organs begin to fail," I said. "Think of it as a form of organ transplant, except that the patient is his own donor." I quickly added, "Or her own donor."

"And you don't need surgery," Pat added.

I smiled at her. "That's right. You won't need surgery."

We talked around the subject for the better part of an hour. Finally, the woman said, "Dr. Marshak, we have no real jurisdiction over you, since you are not being funded by NIH, but I think you should know that the government is taking this matter very seriously."

"The government?" I asked. "Who in the government?"

"The National Institutes of Health, for one," said the pirate. "The Justice Department might also become interested."

"The Justice Department?" yelped Eager. "What do they have to do with it?"

"It is their responsibility to investigate possible violations of federal code."

"We haven't broken any laws," I said. I felt certain he was bluffing, although Eager looked upset.

"If and when you go to human trials," said the woman, "you will need the consent of the NIH, regardless of your funding sources."

"And I wouldn't be surprised if one or more congressional committees wouldn't want to look into your program at that point," the pirate said.

"Perhaps sooner," the woman added.

Pat looked worried. Eager looked as if somebody had just put a gun to his head. I knew, there and then, that I would have to take steps to forestall an avalanche of government interference.

SO I went to Washington the following week. To the offices of the National Academy of Sciences, to see my old friend Milton Graves.

I had first met Graves when he'd been a visiting professor at Columbia. Back then, I thought for certain that one day I'd be elected to membership in the NAS.

The National Academy was founded by no less than Abraham Lincoln, right in the middle of the Civil War, to bring together the nation's best scientists to advise the government on technical matters. Being elected to it is just about the highest honor an American scientist can get in his own country.

But if you're an industrial scientist it's not so easy. And if you're a refugee from academia who's regarded as a pariah by somebody as vindictive as Wilson K. Potter—forget about it.

The academy's building had a great view of the Lincoln Memorial, but I wasn't in a sightseeing mood as I ducked out of the taxi from the airport. It was a raw wintry day in Washington, gray and overcast, with a cutting wind blowing in off the river. Pulling my trenchcoat around me, I hustled up the front steps.

Milton Graves had been president of the academy for more than five years. We had served on a handful of committees together, evaluating new procedures in molecular biology or generating a report to one government agency or another on where the taxpayers' money would be best spent. I always felt like an outsider on those committees, the token representative of industry and big business. The rest of the committee members were usually academics or government scientists.

But Graves had always been friendly to me. I got the impression that he didn't like Potter very much and he realized what a raw deal I had received at Potter's hands.

Graves's office was big but not pretentious. Warm and comfortable as an old shoe, dominated by an elaborately carved mahogany desk and beautiful glass-fronted bookcases. It was a corner office, with views that looked out on the classic white marble of the Lincoln Memorial and Berks's marvelous statue of Albert Einstein on the lawn below. The Vietnam Wall was out there across Constitution Avenue, too, but from Graves's windows I could barely see a corner of its low, dark, sinuous shape.

"You sounded distressed on the telephone, Arthur," Graves said as he gestured me to one of the heavy, upholstered wing chairs by the windows. He took the other one, across from the little rosewood sherry table.

"I am," I said, a feeling of relaxation easing over me. Graves had an air of the kindly old grandfather about him. He was spare, lean. There was nothing left of his hair but a white fringe around his bald dome. His face was pouchy, sagging around a hooked turtle's nose. But he exuded an air of quiet calm, of warm sensibility, that made me feel . . . I guess the best word is *safe*.

"You've been getting quite a bit of publicity lately. You'll be on the cover of *Time* soon, I expect." His eyes, magnified by his bifocals, told me he was amused by it all.

"Lord, I hope not," I replied.

Leaning forward slightly, Graves asked, "It's difficult to assess the work you're doing from these news accounts. How is it going? How far have you come?"

We spent the next hour or so discussing the regeneration work. He was surprisingly up on it, for a man who'd spent the past decade or so in administration rather than research. Slowly it dawned on me. He didn't have to say it, but I realized he was vitally interested in what we were doing because he was getting to the age where he could expect his organs to begin to wear out. As far as I knew he was spry and healthy, but still—the clock keeps ticking.

"My mother went blind from glaucoma," he said, his voice soft, almost musing. "Of course, we have better treatment for it now, but still it's something I have to worry about."

I had never thought about regenerating parts of the eye. "That's something we ought to look into," I said.

He broke into an amused grin. "Was that a pun, Arthur?"

We laughed together.

Then I started telling him about Ransom and Reverend Simmonds and all the pressures the news media were putting on us.

"And now I've been visited by two lawyers from NIH," I said. "It looks like the government's becoming very interested in our program."

"Can't say I blame them," he said.

"All they can do is get in the way," I said.

"Yes, you're undoubtedly right. But, Arthur, do you have any conception of the magnitude of your work? If you successfully grow new organs in people . . . why, it's earthshaking. Revolutionary."

"Some people want to stop the work."

"I have no doubt of it. Furthermore, I'm sure that they'll try to hedge you around with government restrictions. Perhaps they'll even get the Congress to pass laws to stop this kind of research altogether. Things like that have been done before, you know, with fetal tissue transplants, remember?"

I nodded gloomily. It had started to rain outside, gray and miserable and wet and cold. Just the way I felt inside.

"For what it's worth," Graves said, "no one has come to the academy to request a scientific assessment."

"They will, sooner or later."

He made a tiny little motion of his head, barely half a shake. "Don't be surprised if your enemies avoid the academy altogether. The last thing they want is a scientific study that says you're on the right track."

I sank back in the worn old plush chair. "Maybe I ought to ask for a study from the academy."

Graves nodded slightly, pressing his fingertips together before his lips. "Perhaps I have a better idea, Arthur."

"What is it?"

"It's an idea that's been around for some time, but it's never really been tried. Not in its full flower."

"What?"

"A science court."

I had heard something about that years ago. But nothing had ever come of it.

"A courtroom procedure," Graves said, "where we examine strictly the scientific aspect of a question of public policy. Strip away all the politics, all the emotional rhetoric and personal opinions. Stick strictly to the available scientific evidence. A jury of your scientific peers. You present your evidence and the jury makes an informed decision about whether or not your research is valid."

That could be an end run around all the bureaucrats and politicians who'd want to investigate my work and try to stop it for one reason or another. It could generate enough media attention—and the right kind of media attention—to finally get the truth through to the general public.

"I like it," I said. "A science court. Can we do it?"

Graves beamed like a happy grandfather. "I believe I can bring the necessary people together, if you're willing to go along with the idea."

"Certainly," I assured him. "I think it's a fine idea."

I really did. Then.

THE TRIAL:
DAY FOUR, MORNING

State your name, please, and your affiliation."

"Wilson K. Potter, professor emeritus, molecular biology department, Columbia University."

From his seat on the front row, Arthur saw Potter in profile as the old man sat at the witness table. He's had a stroke, Arthur realized. The half of Potter's face he could see was drawn, tense, the corner of his eye and mouth pulled slightly downward. His cane slipped from his fingers as he tried to rest it against the table and clattered to the floor. Potter glared at it momentarily, then left it there at his feet.

Rosen got up from his seat and walked slowly around the judges' desks as he said, "Professor Potter, it's fair to say that you are one of the pioneers in the field of molecular biology, is it not?"

"I suppose it is," said Potter.

"Dr. Marshak was one of your assistant professors, at one point in time?"

"He was, until he left for greener pastures."

Arthur's guts clenched. He could feel his face flame with anger.

Smiling at the old man, Rosen asked, "Professor Potter, are you still active in the field?"

"I am retired. But I still maintain an interest in the field. I read the journals. I write an occasional paper."

"You wrote a paper on the subject of organ regeneration, did you not?"

"Yes, I did."

Glancing at Arthur, then turning to face the jury, Rosen asked, "Could you give the jury a brief summation of that paper, please?"

"I assume they have all read it," said Potter.

"It was only entered into the file of testimony last night, when we learned that Professor Phillips would not be able to appear here."

"Anyone who wants to keep up in the field should have read my paper when it was first published," Potter said testily.

"Yes, sir, I'm sure," Rosen said smoothly, "but a brief summation would be very helpful, sir."

Potter huffed and turned painfully in his chair to look at the jury. "As you know, even if you read only the abstract, I proved that any attempts to grow new organs inside a human body are doomed to failure. There is no way on God's green earth that it can be done."

ZACK O'NEILL

Trouble is, Arthur said one thing when he meant something else. He told me to go ahead and set up the protocol for using Max, but I could see that all he was doing was putting off the decision to use the chimp.

He was hung up over Cassie. He knew she'd go ballistic and she was prone to cancer and her emotional condition was tied in to her autoimmune system so strong that he was afraid if she got cranked up about Max it'd knock her immune system down and she'd end up with another bout of cancer.

That wasn't my problem. My problem was that I had hit a dead end with regentide unless and until I could do some experiments on one or more chimps. Max was the only one we had and I couldn't see stooging around for a year or more waiting for another batch of 'em. I mean, who knows who else was working along the same lines we were? We had all this mother-loving publicity from that butthead evangelist, but sixteen dozen other labs could be working along the same lines I was and not say a peep about it. Just stay cool and quiet and beat us at our own game.

I had tried borrowing chimps from other labs, but no go. Everybody knew it took tons of red tape to bring new animals in from Africa or get newborns from a breeding facility. To make matters worse there was this strain of AIDS hitting the African chimp population and, believe me, *that* put a stop to importing, but good. And to borrowing, too. Nobody wanted to part with the animals they had.

So it was Max. Had to be. Nobody else in sight. I knew Arthur wanted to push ahead as fast as I did, but still he hemmed and hawed. Scared of Cassie. I don't think he gave a shit about the chimp itself. It was Cassie that was bothering him.

I had to have help. I went to Darrell Walters, the grand old man of the staff. If anybody could convince Arthur, it was Darrell.

"I don't know," he said when I bounced the idea off him. "Cassie's awfully attached to Max."

I wished I could use Cassie. It would cause less trouble. But I said to Darrell, "I won't hurt Max. We don't have to do anything major. Just regrow a finger, maybe. Just to show that we can produce a strain of regentide that works on chimps."

We were in Darrell's junk shop of an office. He was perched on his barstool, swiveling back and forth slightly like he was swaying in the wind. Looked like an older Howdy Doody, all arms and legs and that long horse face of his.

"Arthur's already thinking about how we can do human trials without having the government come down on us like an avalanche," Darrell said, trying to avoid making a decision.

"We won't get to human trials if we can't get good results from chimps," I pointed out. "Or one chimp, at least."

"We've got plenty of monkeys."

"We've got plenty of yeast molds, too," I snapped. "What the hell does that have to do with it? We can't move on to human trials without solid evidence from chimps. You know that!"

It was a no-brainer of a decision, yet still Darrell just sat there, swiveling back and forth, back and forth, like some brain-dead idiot who can't make up his mind.

"Tell you what," he said finally. "Let me make a few phone calls, pull a few strings, call in a few favors. Maybe I can get you a couple of chimps."

"If Arthur can't do it . . ."

"Let me see what I can do," Darrell said, and he winked at me. He actually closed one eye in what I guess he thought was a neat trick.

I was disgusted. But I went back to my office to think the whole problem through. One thing I learned as a kid: a little thinking can save a lot of blood, sweat, toil, and tears. Look before you leap, my stepfather always told me. Out on the streets in the neighborhood where I grew up, you looked both ways before you stepped out of the house. No telling who might be out there ready to give you a knuckle sandwich just for your lunch money.

I had been buddying up to Max for weeks, bringing him candy and treats, getting him used to seeing me. Okay, so it was a rat-fink thing to do. Better than having the chimp bite off one of *my* fingers, huh? Arthur said he would okay using Max, but I knew he'd try to figure out a way to keep Cassie from going into orbit.

If I could bring Darrell around I could get Arthur's okay to work on Max. The boss trusted Darrell, and besides, Darrell could godfather Cassie when she got back. But Darrell was sitting on the pot and I figured he'd stay there for weeks, maybe months. How to move Darrell? Vince Andriotti. Darrell and Vince had been two of Arthur's original staffers. Hired them when he started the lab. The rest of his researchers had been Arthur's grad students from Columbia, at first. But he had taken on Vince and Darrell at the beginning and regarded them as equals, almost, not former students.

Okay. How to get to Vince? And here I had to laugh. His daughter Tina, of course. What could be better? I liked her. This would give me an excuse to get as close to her as possible.

So I set out to win Tina Andriotti's heart and mind. It would even be fun, I thought.

ARTHUR

It took a surprising amount of politicking to get the science court out of the realm of dreamy ideas and into the real, workaday world. Even with Graves pushing for it, the first responses we got from the National Academy and most of the scientists I broached the idea to was—well, tepid, to say the least.

"It'll never work," was the kindest response I got.

"Arthur, you can't expect to keep a public trial restricted to nothing but the scientific facts," said the chancellor of the University of Texas, an old friend from back in the days when we were both students at Columbia.

"Of course we can," I insisted. He was in New York to meet with his university's financial advisors on Wall Street. I had invited him to have a quiet drink at a cocktail lounge in the Waldorf. I wanted his support for the science court; he could be very influential, either for or against.

His hair was still dark, and he had a fine tennis-player's tan. As chancellor of the university, he was involved far more with fund-raising and politics than with academic matters.

"I think the science court is an idea whose time has come," I said loftily.

He shook his head. "You might just as well simply mail

out all your reports to the people you want to serve on your jury and have them write their evaluations back to you."

"No, no!" I said. "If we set this up as a judicial procedure they can call countering witnesses, we can cross-examine each other."

"Strictly on the scientific merits of the question?" His voice dripped skepticism.

"Yes. The political, economic, and other issues can be discussed in other forums, once we have the scientific question settled."

He took a sip of his margarita and grimaced. "Nobody east of the Mississippi knows how to make a decent margarita," he grumbled.

I was drinking California chardonnay. Would you believe that the Waldorf didn't stock any Tavels? "We *need* a rational procedure for making decisions about science," I said. "The science court is the way to go, I'm convinced of it."

He wasn't. "You expect to have a courtroom-type of trial strictly on the scientific merits of your work—"

"And once that's settled, the politicians and priests and general public can argue about the economic impact or the morality or whatever else they want to bring up."

His expression was worse than dubious. It was positively sour.

But I went on, "The important thing is to settle the scientific facts first. The way the government makes scientific decisions today is crazy, absolutely irrational."

"I can agree to that, at least."

And it was. They mixed the science and the politics and economics and ethics and everything else all in a big jumble. You pick your side of the argument and go out and find scientists who agree with you and get them to make solemn pronouncements. That's how you get scientists on both sides of the issue; they're not speaking as scientists, they're speaking as regular citizens. They're not making scientific decisions, they're telling you their opinions. But to the public at large, it looks as if scientists are just as confused and ignorant as anybody else. The science court would separate out the scientific question from all the other facets. Scientists would have to stick to the facts, to the data, regardless of their opinions. Science would produce a definitive answer, one way or the other.

"The science court will make it easier for the general public to understand the scientific facts," I said.

"The general public." The chancellor sneered. "They don't know shit from ice cream." His margarita was starting to hit him.

"We've got to educate them," I said. "Otherwise—"

"Somebody's got to educate them," he agreed. "Did you see the survey the Chicago Academy of Sciences did a year or so ago? Eighty percent of the general public doesn't know what DNA is! Ninety percent haven't the foggiest notion of what bacteria are!"

"All the more reason for a science court," I insisted. "We can't let people who're that ignorant make decisions they're not equipped to make."

"The politicians make the decisions."

"And they're smarter?"

He scowled at me and gulped down the remains of his margarita.

THINGS AT the lab were getting tense. I was spending most of my time traipsing around the country to rally backing for the science court, but I was in the lab often enough to feel the growing tension.

Zack had gone as far as he could go without trying his regentide on a chimpanzee. We were trying to get him a few chimps to work on, but the red tape was titanic. And there was Max sitting out in the back yard, untouched. I had Zack do more work on macaques, and he got good results, but we both knew that we were just marking time. Wasting time, I should say.

More than that, Zack had started romancing Tina Andriotti pretty strongly, and her father apparently didn't like it. Vince had an Old World attitude about his one and only daughter: he didn't like to see her falling for a guy who wore an earring and never mentioned a word about marriage. Tina, from what

I could see, could handle herself without her father's glowering presence. Whether or not she was serious about Zack, I had no idea.

So I decided to use a spy.

"Pat," I said one chilly spring morning, "I need your help."

Pat Hayward had stayed at the lab all through our publicity ordeal. She had earned every penny of her consulting fee, screening us from the nutcases and orchestrating the serious reporters so that they saw enough to be impressed and write good stories about us. I had given her absolute control of Glamour Alley; she would lead the TV camera crews through that section of the lab and end the tour with Max. The chimp earned his bananas; he was on the tube more than I was. Which was fine with me.

"What is it?" she asked.

It had taken a certain amount of self-control to keep our relationship strictly on business. Patricia was a handsome woman, and intelligent. That night in Las Vegas could have turned into something extraordinary if either one of us had moved a centimeter closer toward the other. I got the feeling that she was struggling to keep her emotional distance from me, but that might have been nothing but my ego bragging to itself. She certainly made no overt moves; neither did I.

Yet, she was mighty attractive, sitting in front of my desk. Even in a tailored business suit with slacks that hid those long legs of hers, and her red hair neatly tied up, she looked awfully good.

"Have you ever done any espionage?" I asked, trying to make it sound light.

"Spying?"

I raised both my hands. "Let's call it intelligence gathering."

"Where?"

"Here in the lab."

Her expression went a little on the grim side. "Spying on one of your employees."

"Zack O'Neill seems to be spending a lot of time with Tina Andriotti."

"That's their business, isn't it?"

"I just want to know how serious Tina is about him."

Pat nodded briefly. "Her father. Vince."

"I'd like to avoid an explosion, if that's possible."

"Why don't you just bring the two men in here and ask them about it?"

"Too confrontational," I said. "I'm trying to avoid an explosion, remember."

"So you want me to go to Tina and ask her if she's shacking up with Zack?"

It took me a moment to realize that Pat was trying to shock me. I forced a smile. "Nothing so crude."

"Then what?"

With a shrug, I answered, "I don't know. Whatever it is that you women do, do it. You seem to be able to exchange complete life histories in thirty seconds when you want to."

She broke into a hearty laugh. "Is that what you think?"

"I've seen it happen," I said. "Two women meet, complete strangers, and thirty seconds later they know all about each other."

Pat shook her head. "Arthur, deep down inside, you're a male chauvinist."

I put on a hurt expression.

"I didn't say pig," Pat added.

"Well, that's something, at least," I said.

Her face became more serious. "You're really worried about this?"

"Wouldn't you be, if you were in my shoes?"

She thought about that for a moment. "Yes, I suppose I would be."

"I don't want to see Zack mess up what could be a fine career." Then I quickly added, "The same for Tina, too."

"But they're both adults . . ."

"Look," I said, leaning my elbows on the desk to hunch closer to her, "how many people do you know who've damaged themselves and their careers by making the wrong choices in their love lives?"

Even as I spoke the words their impact hit me. I was one of those people. And from the expression on Pat's face, she had been hit just as hard.

"We've all done it," I said, more softly. "I just don't want to see those two kids mess up their lives, if it can be avoided."

Pat looked straight at me with those marvelous green eyes of hers. "All right," she said. "I'll see what I can find out from Tina—on one condition."

"What's that?"

"You do the same with Zack."

I leaned back in my chair. "You want me to ask Zack about it?"

"Why not?"

"I'm his boss, his employer. He won't be completely frank with me."

Pat smiled slightly. "You think women always tell each other the whole truth and nothing but the truth?"

I mulled that one over. "Very well," I said. "It's a deal. You talk with Tina and I'll talk with Zack."

"Good."

"Under one condition."

Her brows rose questioningly.

"You have dinner with me tonight." I don't know what made me say that. I hadn't intended to. But there it was.

Pat seemed more puzzled than anything else. "I can't. Not tonight."

I mentally reviewed my calendar. "Friday night, then."

She nodded. "Friday. Okay."

Then she got up and left my office. Neither one of us was smiling.

TOWARD THE end of the day I wandered back to Vince's lab. He was bent over a display screen, tracing one finger across its green-glowing surface.

I stood in the doorway, not wanting to disturb him. As usual, Vince's lab was crammed with humming electronic equipment, dimly lit, hot, and intense.

"Come on in and grab a chair," he said, without turning from the screen. "Be with you in a minute."

There was only one chair to take: a spindly little typist's seat on wheels.

"Whatcha want, boss?" Andriotti asked as I sat down.

"How did you know it was me?"

I could sense his knowing grin. "I got mystical powers. And besides, you ain't no vampire."

It took me a moment to realize he had seen my reflection in the screen.

"What are you doing?" I asked. I knew that Vince could work and talk at the same time. Some people can't, but he could blithely hold a conversation and make the most delicate measurements without missing a beat on either.

"Tracing out this NGF map. Neurons follow the stuff like a bloodhound."

Nerve growth factor. Vince was still spending most of his time on the spinal neuron regeneration program. I had all but forgotten how we had started the regeneration work.

"We'll have paraplegics dancing like Gene Kelly one of these days," Vince said, still staring so intently at the screen that his snub nose almost touched it.

"That's good," I said.

"You didn't come here to check on my progress, though, didja?"

"Not exactly."

With one hand he pecked at the keyboard off to the side of the display unit. "Worried I'm gonna break Zack's skull?"

"It's crossed my mind," I admitted.

"Tina likes the jerk."

"Your daughter is a very intelligent young woman."

"Yeah, sure. But once those damn hormones start bubbling, their brains take a back seat. Guys ain't the only ones who think with their cojones, y'know."

"I don't see Tina doing anything irrational," I said.

"You're not her father."

"That's true."

"Arthur, I don't mind if the kids have some fun together. I

can't tell my daughter she's gotta keep her legs crossed at all times."

That was a relief.

But then Vince went on, "But if that punk little sonofabitch hurts her in any way, if I see just the glimmer of a tear in the corner of her eye, *then* I'll break his friggin' skull."

And he looked up from the screen with a fierce pirate's grin on his swarthy face.

CASSIE IANETTA

It all started out so wonderfully. I should have known it would end in a disaster.

"How would you like a week in Acapulco?" Bill asked me.

We were sitting in the living room, in the purple dark after sunset, sipping wine and just doing nothing. No lights. Just sitting in the shadows together on the sagging old sofa. Neither one of us had made a move to start dinner. I had just come back from my quick trip to Connecticut to see Max and make certain he was all right after the terrorists' attack on the lab. I was way behind on my work, and even though Arthur didn't push me much I swore to myself on the plane back to Mexico that I'd catch up and write the reports I should have done months earlier.

I hadn't told Bill about my cancer and my decision to inoculate myself. If the enzyme did its work on me I'd never have to tell him about the cancer. That's what I was praying for.

So now Bill was talking about a week in Acapulco.

"Can we afford it?" I asked him.

I never knew exactly what Bill's financial condition was. The little row house he rented sure wasn't in the expensive part of town, but it was a whole house and it was decently furnished and he even had a cleaning woman come in twice a week.

He shrugged. "My mother just sent me a check. Birthday present."

"It's your birthday? When?"

"Last month," he said carelessly. "Anyway, I want to see the tourist traps in Acapulco, make a nice contrast in my film to the reality of the poor people's living conditions."

That was another thing. Bill's idea of working on his film was to travel here and there soaking up atmosphere. I never saw him write anything down, although he had an old-fashioned manual typewriter set up in the bedroom. Whenever I asked him how his work was going he'd tap the side of his head and say, "It's all in here."

"You didn't tell me about your birthday," I said. "I would've gotten a present for you."

He smiled, bright enough to light the whole street. "Come with me to Acapulco. That'll be your birthday present to me."

A week. My work would slide even further behind. But one look at his smiling face and everything else faded away. We went to the glitziest, most expensive hotel in Acapulco and behaved like rich American tourists for a whole week. It was the height of the winter season and the place was crammed with Americans and Europeans and even a few busloads of Japanese tourists.

Bill was already deeply tanned, but I slathered sunblock all over myself the first day we went out to the beach. At this tropical latitude, even the winter sun could burn you to a crisp in minutes, I knew. Our second day, Bill took over the job of covering my skin with lotion and we never did get to the beach.

That was when I first mentioned children, while we were making slippery, slithery love on the big king-sized bed of our hotel suite.

"I want your baby," I murmured to Bill while we lay side by side, spent and sweaty.

He didn't respond.

I turned to look squarely at him. "I mean it. I love you and I want to have your baby."

Bill smiled gently at me. "I love you, too, Cassie."

He didn't say a word about babies, but I thought that it

didn't matter. He loved me and love means children, sooner or later.

We had our first argument two days later. Not an argument, really. A disagreement. A difference of opinion. But it hurt. While we were getting dressed for dinner he asked me if I was on the pill.

"No," I said. I almost told him that it's not recommended for women with a history of cancer, but I bit that back. I hadn't told him about the cancer and this wasn't the time to break that news to him.

"Are you using any protection at all?" he asked.

Pulling my dress on, I said vaguely, "Vaginal foam."

He looked very serious, more serious than I'd ever seen him. "I mean, when you said you wanted to get pregnant—you didn't mean right now, did you?"

"Why not?" I don't know why I said that. It surprised me to hear myself.

"Because I'm not ready to have kids, that's why not," he practically snapped at me.

"Men are never ready to have children, are they?" I snapped back.

He looked like he was ready to snarl. But instead he sat down on the edge of the bed and took a deep breath, a sigh, really. "I don't know," he said. "All I know is that I'm not ready. Not yet."

"But you will be someday?"

"I hope so," he said, almost in a whisper.

I went around the bed to him and sat on his lap and put my arms around his neck and kissed him. "I'll wait for you," I said. "It's all right, Bill, I'll wait until you're ready."

He tried to smile. It came out as a grimace.

By the end of the week I stopped using the sunblock, figuring I had built up enough of a tan. Stupid of me. Must have been something in my subconscious mind. Naturally, I had a good case of sunburn by the time we drove back to Querétaro. Red as a lobster. Not a smart thing to do for a woman who's prone to cancer. But I wasn't being smart where Bill was concerned. I was in love. I wanted to have his children.

For several days I was miserable and feverish from the sunburn. Every square inch of my arms and legs and even my face puffed up. It was agony to be touched or to feel warmth. I stayed in the house with the shutters all pulled down, telling myself over and over again what an idiot I was. Bill stayed away all day long, and slept on the ratty old sofa in the living room until I was back to normal—except for the peeling. By the time all my burned skin had flaked off, I was almost as white as when I had started.

But who cared? We could make love again.

Bill came home a couple of nights later with an enormous straw hat for me. He put it on my head while I was making dinner at the stove and pulled its leather thong tight under my chin.

"You don't go out in the sun without this on your head," he said, very serious. "I don't want you getting sick."

I still hadn't told him about the cancer. They had frozen the latest spot and I had started taking the enzyme injections. Physician, heal thyself, I thought. The first few weeks' results looked good. I did all the testing myself, even drawing my own blood. The enzyme was established in my cells. It ought to protect me against another outbreak.

So I decided that the time had come to be completely honest with Bill. I loved him and he loved me. I wanted his baby and I wasn't going to let cancer or anything else stop me. So over dinner that evening in our little candlelit dining room I finally told him.

"Cancer?" he said when I told him. "Jesus, that's a rough one."

"I'll be all right, though," I said with an assurance I didn't really feel. "I'm going to beat it."

"Yeah," he said. "I sure hope you do."

I explained to him that I had inoculated myself with the enzyme I had developed.

"Is that smart?" he asked. "I mean, it's still an experimental drug, isn't it?"

"It's not a drug and it works. I've seen it working in the volunteers we've been inoculating. It's working in me."

But even though Bill spoke all the right words, it was clear from the worried look on his face that he wasn't convinced. Not at all.

At work, I was watching for any possible side effects on our volunteers. So far the only noticeable quirk was that almost all those who received the real inoculations reported a sharp increase in their appetites. But they didn't seem to gain any weight. I noted it in my reports, guessing that the enzyme had some weird reaction on the subject's metabolic rate. It didn't seem to affect me that way, but maybe it was too early for the effect to show up in me.

It was in the middle of my series of inoculations that Bill told me he was thinking of returning to Los Angeles. We had just finished supper and were sitting on the sofa with a pair of half-empty wine glasses on the coffee table in front of us.

"I've gotten as much done here as I could," he said. "But I can't write here. It just isn't working."

The fear that I should have felt in the gynecologist's office I felt now, clutching at my heart.

"You're going to leave?"

"Yeah. Got to."

"Can't you write your script here?"

He shrugged. "I've tried, Cassie. It just isn't working out for me."

"What isn't? The script, or me?"

"You could come with me," he said.

"To Los Angeles? And what about my work here? What about my career back East?"

"I've got work to do, too, Cass."

I don't remember exactly what we said to each other after that. It's all pretty much of a jumble. I know I cried and Bill got more and more upset.

"But I love you!" I recall saying that, more than once.

He must have told me that he loved me, too. I'm sure he did. But the more we talked, the angrier he became. I knew he was really scared, frightened for me, frightened about cancer, about having children, about making a commitment. But it came out as anger, hot boiling rage. At me.

"I want to have a baby," I kept sobbing. "Your baby."

His face got so distorted with fury that I hardly recognized him. "I don't want a baby! I don't want any of this!"

"Any of what?" I pleaded.

"You! Dammit, I love you, but you're turning me inside out! I can't write, I can't even think straight anymore. I've got to get away. I've got to get free."

"But if you love me—"

He pushed his face so close to mine we were practically touching. "I can't have you hanging around my neck! I can't deal with it! With cancer and babies and the whole friggin' mess! I'm not going to let you tear my life apart!"

I sank back in the lumpy sofa, crying so hard that I couldn't see anything at all. Just the imprint of his red, twisted face burned into my retinas like the afterimage of the sun.

Then I heard the door slam and, outside, the MG cough to life. He roared away, out of my life. I had nothing left, nothing except my work. Nothing except what's inside me, the cancer and the antibodies, the good and the bad, the hope and the knowledge that there isn't a man in the entire universe who can be trusted.

THE TRIAL:
DAY FOUR, MORNING

Potter had come prepared. He had two assistants with him, graduate students. Young men, both of them; one black and one Oriental. Politically correct, even in retirement, Arthur grumbled to himself. The black student ran the old-fashioned overhead projector while the Oriental one sat beside Potter and turned the pages of his printed testimony, much as a concert pianist has someone turning the pages of the music.

His paper's a pile of crap, Arthur told himself. It's all based on statistics that make no sense. Arthur began to mentally assemble his cross-examination. Isn't it true, he saw himself asking Potter, that mathematicians in the past "proved" that bumblebees can't fly? That a heavier-than-air machine could never lift itself off the ground? That AIDS was going to kill half the human race in the next ten years?

Arthur began to smile to himself. Cross-examining Potter was going to be fun, a real pleasure. But then an inner voice warned, Don't dump on him too hard. Don't make him look like an object of sympathy. Make it cool and correct. Stick to the facts of his own presentation. I've got to read his paper before I face him. It was pretty shifty of Rosen to pull him out of his hat.

I'll get a copy of Potter's idiotic paper and read it thoroughly tonight, Arthur said to himself.

It took Potter only a few minutes to read the abstract of his paper to the jury. The slides he showed were all statistical graphs, Arthur saw. All nonsense, as far as he was concerned. The jury looked almost embarrassed; the judges uncomfortable. Arthur was surprised that Senator Kindelberger willingly sat through the entire presentation.

Once the old man had finished, Graves thanked him, then asked, "Will you be able to appear tomorrow morning for cross-examination, Professor? If not we can have the cross-examination now."

The Oriental student sitting beside Potter had retrieved his cane, which Potter leaned on heavily as he pushed himself up out of the witness chair.

"I'll be back tomorrow," he said. "You can depend on it."

As Potter turned to leave, with his student aides at his elbows, there was a stir in the back of the chamber. Someone came in and remained standing at the double doors. People turned to see him and whispers started floating through the spectators.

Graves rapped his gavel sharply, then said, "At the request of Senator Kindelberger, we will allow a slight deviation from our regular schedule."

Arthur glanced back at the little commotion, quickly dying away as Potter shuffled along the chamber's central aisle toward the doors to the corridor. Then he turned back to hear what Graves was saying.

"The senator has asked that we permit an interested citizen to read a statement to the court," the chief judge said, looking less than pleased, "and we have decided to allow this unusual procedure as a courtesy to Senator Kindelberger."

The man who had entered the chamber minutes before strode to the front and took the witness chair. Arthur recognized him: Joshua Ransom.

Arthur shot to his feet. "This man isn't a scientist! He can't make a valid statement to this court."

Graves looked pained. Before he could say anything, Kindelberger leaned into the microphone in front of his seat and said, "Dr. Marshak, I'm asking that we listen to Mr. Ransom's very brief statement. Even though he is not a professional scientist I believe that what he has to say is of importance to these proceedings."

Ransom sat hunched over in the witness chair, not looking at Arthur, but bent over his printed statement. Arthur realized he'd be handing out copies to all the reporters, if he hadn't done that already.

"Will I be allowed to cross-examine the witness?" Arthur asked.

"Mr. Ransom is not a witness," Kindelberger said, "merely an interested citizen."

Fuming inwardly, Arthur wondered what "interested citizen" they would call up next: Daffy Duck?

"I would still like the right to cross-examine him," he insisted.

The ghost of a smile flickered on Graves's lips. He looked down at Ransom. "Will you be able to appear for cross-examination tomorrow, Mr. Ransom?"

Ransom blinked several times. "Um, no. I'm afraid I have commitments elsewhere already on my calendar."

I'll bet you do, Arthur grumbled to himself. Aloud, he asked, "Well, then, may I cross-examine the wi—the interested citizen today, when he's finished reading his statement?"

Before Kindelberger could say anything, Graves nodded and replied, "I see nothing wrong with that. Do you, Senator?"

Ransom look startled. He began to shake his head negatively, but Kindelberger leaned back and shrugged. "Okay by me."

Arthur sat down. Ransom glowered at him over his shoulder.

"You may read your statement, Mr. Ransom," said Graves.

Ransom cleared his throat, pulled the slim microphone closer to his mouth, then began reading aloud:

"All concerned citizens protest the elitist procedure of this so-called court of science. Under the guise of impartial scientific judgment, a new and potentially devastating technical capability is being foisted on the American people and the world by a narrow group of self-serving white European-descent males.

"The ability to regrow human organs in vivo is the ability to create a super race. Just as the Nazis and other evil groups have attempted throughout history to impose a eugenic New Order on the human race, now we have a small band of elitist scientists proposing to do the same thing, cloaking their intentions with promises of helping the sick and impaired."

He went on in that vein for nearly half an hour. Arthur listened with growing fury. Are they all against me? Jesse, Kindelberger, Potter, even Graves? Aren't any of them on my side?

He heard movement among the spectators behind him. Turning in his seat, he saw that more reporters were coming in. Sharks drawn to blood. Well, if it's blood they want, Arthur told himself, I'll give them blood. Ransom's.

He turned back to stare at Ransom, still reading from his text:

"In just the past twenty years, science has given us Alar to poison our fruit crops, electromagnetic fields leaking from high-voltage wires to give us cancer, the ozone hole to allow deadly ultraviolet radiation to kill us, and radon in our homes to attack our children with radioactivity. And that's merely the tip of the iceberg."

Someone tugged at Arthur's jacket sleeve. Startled, he turned to see that Pat Hayward had moved into the seat beside him.

"Don't slaughter him," she whispered.

"What?" he whispered back.

"When you cross-examine him, don't make a martyr out of him. Don't bully him. That's what he'll be expecting and he'll turn it against you."

Before Arthur could reply, Ransom finished his statement, picked up his papers, and started to get up from his chair.

"Thank you," he said, already on his feet.

"One moment, Mr. Ransom," said Graves. "I believe Dr. Marshak would like to ask you a few questions."

"I would indeed," said Arthur. He stood up, gave Pat a quick wink, and walked to the front of the chamber.

Ransom sat back down and looked at Arthur sullenly.

"Mr. Ransom," Arthur said, thinking on his feet, "what is the average life span of the American male today?"

Ransom scowled. "I don't know. Something like seventy years. Something like that."

"Is this longer or shorter than the average life span of fifty years ago?"

"I don't know."

"What would you guess? Longer or shorter?"

With a huff, Ransom said, "Longer, I suppose."

"Does the average American woman live longer now than she did fifty years ago?"

"Yes, I suppose so."

"Despite all the disasters that you say science has brought down upon us?"

Ransom shrugged.

"Mr. Ransom, do you have a degree in science?"

"My degrees are in economics and history."

"What's the last science course you took in school?"

"I don't remember."

"A freshman survey course, perhaps?"

"I think so."

"Did you take a physics course in high school?"

"It wasn't required."

"But did you take it anyway?"

"No, I didn't."

"Chemistry?"

"No."

"Biology?"

"No."

"Who invented the microscope?"

Ransom looked disgusted now. "I don't know," he growled.

"Oh. I thought that with your degree in history you'd know." Arthur hesitated a moment, thinking. "How much of the United States' gross domestic product is spent on basic scientific research?"

"Billions."

"What percentage, roughly?"

Ransom shrugged. "Five, ten percent. Somewhere in there."

"It's actually less than one percent, Mr. Ransom."

"So what?"

"So what is the knowledge on which you base your views? You call me and other scientists Nazis. You equate us with mass murderers, and yet you know nothing about science, and damned little about history and economics!"

"I know more than you think!" Ransom shouted, his face reddening.

"I certainly hope so. But how can you say that science is killing us when we live longer than ever before? How can you say we're being poisoned when every medical statistic shows we are taller, healthier, stronger than any generation that preceded us? We set new Olympic records every four years, don't we?"

Ransom started to answer, thought better of it, and merely said, "I stand by the statement I made."

"Then how do you reconcile your statement with the facts? And how can you pervert scientists' attempts to improve our lives into some fantasy of mass murder?"

"Science hasn't improved our lives," Ransom insisted. "Science is dangerous."

"You are an ignorant man, Joshua Ransom," Arthur said.

"A petty ignorant man who'd be more at home in the Dark Ages or the Spanish Inquisition than in this world that modern science has made and which you obviously don't understand."

Quivering with rage, Ransom staggered to his feet, pointing an outstretched arm at Arthur. "You're just like all the rest of them, all you smug smiling bastards, laughing at me, laughing at everybody who isn't in your tight little club. You don't care about us! All you care about is your own power and your own privileges!"

Arthur stared at him for a moment. The spectators were stock-still. The TV cameras were staring. Out of the corner of his eye he saw Graves raising his gavel as if to end this session before it could go any further.

Softly, almost gently, Arthur said, "You're wrong, Mr. Ransom. When the day comes, as it inevitably will, when you need a new heart or a new kidney or other organ, we won't turn you away. We'll help you, just as we'll help anyone. Because we *do* care about the human race. Scientists work very hard and their work is aimed at making the world better. Never forget that, Mr. Ransom. That is our goal: a better world for you—and everyone."

Arthur turned his back on Ransom and went back to his seat. The audience remained absolutely silent. Even Graves seemed frozen, unable to move. Well, Arthur said to himself, they didn't applaud Lincoln's little speech at Gettysburg, either.

Graves stirred to life, rapped the gavel once. "We will adjourn for lunch."

Pat clutched at his arm, smiling approvingly. Reporters gathered around Arthur, shouting questions. Arthur beamed at them. I flattened the little twerp, he told himself. Flattened him good.

Then he remembered that after lunch Rosen was going to play Cassie's DVDs, and his elation sank into worried apprehension.

W. CHRISTIAN JOHNSTON

I liked Arthur, always did. He always tried to come across as a man of the business world, you know, all sharp and dedicated to making profits for the corporation. But he was really a scientist; underneath that slick shell of his he was like a little kid with a new toy to take apart.

Sure, his work had made plenty of profit for Omnitech. But that was then; this was now. Nakata made it perfectly clear where he stood.

"It would be very difficult for my board of directors to approve a merger when your most attractive research program is in danger of being outlawed by the United States government," he told me over the phone.

In my office at corporate headquarters I've got a video conferencing setup. I could see Nakata face-to-face on my desktop screen and he could see me. Not that it did much good: he kept his expression as stiff as a frozen mackerel.

I leaned back in my chair slightly. It was a little before seven a.m. in New York; nearly six in the evening in Tokyo. Nakata was in his office, tie neatly knotted, pearl gray jacket without a crease in it.

"I don't think the regeneration work is going to be banned altogether," I said.

"My experts have been following Dr. Marshak's trial. They conclude that your government will not permit human experiments."

"Dr. Marshak is much more optimistic than that," I said.

"Dr. Marshak may face legal charges in connection with the woman's death." Nakata wasn't asking a question; he was telling me.

I tried to keep my face from showing anything. "Look, even if human trials are forbidden here in the States, we could do them in Mexico or South America. Maybe even in Japan."

Nakata shook his head about half an inch in either direction. "If the United States forbids human experiments, it would be very difficult for me to permit my scientists to conduct such experiments."

Sure, I thought. Use the American ban on human trials as an excuse to drop the merger while you duplicate our work in your own labs, behind our backs.

Nakata just sat there, waiting for me to say something. He knew damned well the price of Omnitech stock was eroding; this damned trial in Washington was helping the goddamned Europeans to mount their takeover bid. The first wave of greenmail was already hitting our stockholders, and the lower the stock went on Wall Street, the more attractive the European offer looked.

"Well," I said, stumped for anything significant, "I think Dr. Marshak will come out of this trial in fine shape and we'll go ahead with human tests of the regeneration work pretty much on schedule."

Nakata pulled his lips back in what was supposed to be a smile. "I sincerely hope you are right. A merger then would benefit both of us."

I caught the slight but important emphasis on the word "then." Okay, so I said good-bye after a couple more minutes of polite jive. When the picture screen went dark I sank back in my chair and wondered how the hell I could keep this corporation together and out of the hands of those damned Europeans.

"Can I talk to you for a minute?"

I looked up, almost startled. It was Nancy Dubois, looking nice and sexy in a white silk blouse and navy blue skirt. She was a good-looking woman who knew how to use her looks. She had climbed over several bodies to move up the corporate ladder; I started to wonder if she had any ideas about mine. Me, when I need more than my wife can do, I go to professionals. No lawsuits and no repercussions.

I waved her into my office. "I thought I was the only one working this early."

She smiled as she sat primly on the chair in front of my desk. "I just got in. I have to go over the survey results on the Consumer Division's new product introductions."

"How's it look?"

She shrugged. Must have known it looked provocative, in that sheer blouse. "Only so-so, I'm afraid."

"That's what I was afraid of."

"I couldn't help overhearing part of your telephone conversation," Nancy said.

"It's not to be repeated," I warned her. "To anybody."

"Arthur's becoming a liability, isn't he?"

I had to blink at her. She and Arthur had been a twosome for a while. From what my personnel chief told me, he had helped her get into Uhlenbeck's department and then dumped her. She had been pretty pissed at him over that, but she got over it after a while. Or so we had thought.

"First time I've heard him called a liability," I said.

She was totally serious. "I know you like Arthur, but isn't it time we started to look at this problem squarely, without letting personalities get in the way?"

"What do you mean?" I asked, wondering what she meant by "we."

She looked at me as if I were some slow school kid. "What do you do when you recognize that part of the corporation has become a liability instead of an asset?"

I felt my eyebrows crawl upward. "You get rid of it. You sell it, if you can."

"And if you can't?"

"You dump it."

Nancy smiled warmly at me.

TINA ANDRIOTTI

It was amusing, at first. I mean, Zack was as obvious as a bulldozer at a picnic. He wanted me to help convince my father to let him use Max for experimentation. And Dad would influence Darrell, who had Arthur's confidence.

So Zack pursued me. And I let him. Why not? He was kind of good-looking, kind of cool. He knew the best restaurants in the area and he liked music, especially jazz. I had been more into hard rock, but Zack opened my eyes—my ears, really—to how great modern jazz can be. It was fun to be with him. But although I allowed Zack to pursue me, I had no intention of getting caught. This was strictly for laughs, a fling to be enjoyed while it lasted.

The really funny thing, though, was that instead of getting Dad on his side, Zack was making my father furious. Dad has *ancient* ideas about his only daughter; he still thinks a daughter should be a virgin on her wedding day. That possibility was kaput before my second year of college, but Dad didn't know it. So the more I saw of Zack, the *less* Dad thought of him and any ideas he may have had about anything.

Yet the more I saw of Zack, the more I liked him. Oh, sure, he was brash and full of himself. But underneath that veneer he was really kind of scared of being among the big boys. He was brilliant and he knew it, but he wasn't certain that he was brilliant enough to run with men of Arthur's caliber. Or even Darrell's. That's why he was constantly trying to prove to them how bright he really was. That's why he wanted to get into chimp experiments—so he could go on to human trials as soon as possible.

He tried to have lunch with me most days, in the cafeteria. Some days he was busy, though; some days I was. One particular Saturday I passed his lab around noontime and he wasn't there. I knew his car was in the parking lot and he couldn't be in the cafeteria, because it was closed on the weekends. Instead of driving over to one of the fast-food joints I went out back, looking for him.

Zack was there, all right, sitting on the concrete bench in the exercise area, feeding bananas to Max. The chimp was stuffing himself like a greedy little kid, hardly even bothering to peel one banana before he crammed it into his mouth and reached for another.

"You're going to make him fat," I teased.

He whirled around. I guess he hadn't heard me coming up to him.

"He'll be harder to operate on if he's layered with lard," I said, sitting next to Zack. Max hardly paid me any attention, he was so busy eating.

Zack gave me a funny look. "I don't know if I can go through with it," he said, sort of soft, sad.

"Go through with . . . you mean, using Max?"

He tried to force a grin. "I think I'm getting to like this dippy ape as much as Cassie does."

I looked hard at him. Zack seemed totally sincere.

"It's like, well, he trusts me."

"You feed him."

"Yeah, but it's not like a dog or a cat. He's more like a person." Again the forced grin. "Dumb, isn't it?"

I didn't think it was dumb at all. That's when I began to think that there was more to Zack than I had realized.

And there was. Nobody saw the real Zack except me. I got to know him really well, and as he let his defenses slide, as I got to see the anxious little boy who was hiding behind his bravado, I guess I started to fall in love with him.

And then one night, after we had driven all the way up to Boston for a lobster dinner at Anthony's Pier 4, Zack pulled the car into a side road off I-84 and parked on the shoulder beneath some huge old trees. It was after midnight, dark and raining. The only light I could see outside the car was the sign up the road, a motel, with a red VACANCY blinking underneath it.

Zack leaned across the console and kissed me. Very nicely.

He was a good kisser, although I hadn't let him get any further with me.

"I've got a confession to make," he said, kind of breathless.

"Oh?"

It was so dark inside the car I couldn't see his face, even though we were just about touching noses.

"I started dating you because I wanted you to get your father to help me convince Darrell and Arthur about—"

I broke into laughter. "You sure are going about it the wrong way," I told him. "You'd've been better off if you'd invited my dad to go bowling."

He laughed, too. At himself. "Yeah. I can see that now."

"So why don't you? He's the one you want to get close to; you don't need to impress me."

"But I want to impress you," Zack said in a low, low voice. "I love you."

That stopped me. For a long while neither of us said a word. No sound at all except the drumming of the rain on the car's fabric roof. I had never expected Zack to say anything serious. This was just supposed to be fun and games. Then I glimpsed the motel's sign again, just a smear of color in the rain-streaked windshield. He loves me. Sure.

And that's when I realized that I really loved him. It didn't matter a damn to me if all he wanted was to get into my pants. I loved Zack O'Neill and I wanted him.

"I mean it," he said, misunderstanding my silence. "I never thought it could happen to me, but I've fallen in love with you, Tina."

"And I love you, Zachary Taylor O'Neill," I said. It sort of sounded like plighting my troth, making a real commitment. I grabbed both his ears and kissed him so hard his teeth left bruises on my lips.

When I let go of him, I heard him gulp as if he'd been holding his breath for fifteen minutes. Then Zack revved up the car's engine, put it in gear, and swung up onto the road. Okay, I told myself, here we go to the motel.

But Zack made a careful U-turn and headed back for the highway.

"Where're we going?" I asked him.

With the dashboard lit I could see the big grin on his face. "I'm taking you home."

"Home?"

He pulled the car up onto the highway and put it on cruise control. Exactly at the legal speed limit. "I want to ask your father for your hand in marriage," he said.

I almost fainted from surprise. Zack was as old-fashioned as Dad, for crying out loud!

"Marriage?" I blurted. "We haven't said anything about marriage."

He looked stricken. "You will marry me, won't you?"

It was my turn to grin. "Not until I've found out whether you're any good in bed."

Zack actually looked embarrassed. But we found a motel just over the Connecticut line. He was terrific, actually.

ZACK O'NEILL

It was the wildest thing. I actually fell in love with Tina. She was beautiful, and intelligent, and the warmest, coolest woman I had ever met. Hey, I'm no celibate monk, you know. I've had my share of tosses in the sheets, back in college. But the truth is, all the way down deep inside I've always been kind of scared of women. They always get wonky, sooner or later. They're weird; I could never figure them out. Always saying one thing but meaning something else. Always giving you those spooky looks, like they expect you to say something or do something but they won't tell you what it is.

Tina was different. She was honest. Right up-front about everything. She said what she meant and she meant what she said. No game-playing. And she was smart, too. Never let her hormones get in the way of her thinking. Well, almost never.

I was doing a second series of experiments on the macaques, working with a couple of young surgeons from Yale–New Haven who were getting pretty good at amputating limbs. Damned monkeys were hell to work with, though. They howled their heads off whenever they saw one of us come into the cage area. Bit a couple of the handlers, almost chomped the thumb off one of the guys.

At first I was almost scared to talk anymore to Tina about chimp experiments. I didn't want her thinking that I was more interested in Max than in her. But she cut right to the chase.

"You really need Max, don't you?" she asked me one night in bed. She hadn't moved in with me, but we spent a lot of nights together.

I'd been having dreams about the frigging chimp. Guilt dreams, I guess. I mean, I was out in the exercise area with Max almost every day. I was getting to like the damned ape. And Max was getting friendly with me, almost as friendly as he'd been with Cassie. Of course, I was bringing him bananas and candy every time I went out back to see him, so he loved me the way a cat loves the guy who feeds it.

Still . . . I had to struggle to maintain my objectivity. Max was an experimental subject, nothing more. *If* I could get Arthur to okay using him before Cassie came back from Mexico.

I knew Arthur wanted to push ahead as fast as we could, yet he was hung up over Cassie. Scared of her, like she'd strike us all dead or something if we touched Max. I wished he'd make up his mind and tell Cassie to rug it.

"Yeah, I really need Max," I answered Tina. "Wish I didn't, though."

"I've been talking to Dad," she said.

"And?"

She smiled at me. "He'll come around."

I was out in the exercise yard a couple days later when Vince came looking for me.

I never learned sign language, but Max could make himself pretty clear anyway. Soon as I came through the double doors he swung down out of his tree like a kid happy to see his old man. Max gave his hello hoot as he knuckle-walked up to me. I sat on the stone bench by the jungle gym and he patted my shirt pockets just like a hairy detective.

He found the hard candies I had stuck in the left pocket and jumped up and down, screeching with excitement. Made me laugh. He was gesticulating like mad, saying something in sign language, I guess. I reached in and pulled out one of the candies. Max went stock-still, watching me with those big brown eyes of his, while I unwrapped the candy.

He grabbed it from me so fast his hand was a blur. I could hear the candy crunch between his teeth. Then he motioned his right hand back and forth, from his lips to about waist high, several times.

"That means thank you."

I turned and saw Vince Andriotti coming up the walk toward me. Talk about in-your-face! I guess a scowl was Vince's natural expression, but he always looked to me as if he'd just as soon slug me as say good morning.

Max backed away from Vince. For some reason the chimp was either afraid of him or just plain didn't like him.

Vince sat down on the bench beside me.

"You really going to marry my daughter, or do I have to go out and buy a shotgun?"

"Chill out," I said, "I really want to marry her."

"When?"

"We haven't talked about that yet."

"Talk about it," he said. Believe me, he was deadly serious.

"I will."

"Now, what about Max?"

The abrupt change of subject rattled me for a moment. "Max? It's not Max per se, Vince. I need a chimp—more than one, preferably."

"You'll be a married man with children before we can get our hands on another chimp."

I guess I nodded. "So it's got to be Max."

"Unless you want to wait."

"I wouldn't mind waiting, except that other labs are bound to hit on the same ideas we've developed. And I know Arthur wants to move ahead as fast as we can."

"He's applied for a patent on your regentide, y'know."

I had written the patent application. "Yeah, but with all the publicity we're getting, there must be dozens of teams working their butts off to duplicate what we're doing."

Vince nodded his head just once. Like he had already thought it over and come to an irrevocable conclusion. "Damn right. And some of those bastards have chimps that they won't sell to us. Won't even loan 'em."

"So it's got to be Max," I repeated.

"I'll tell Darrell. I think he already knows but he's still worried about Cassie."

"When will she be back?" I asked.

"Who the hell knows? Her reports are getting stretched out farther and farther. Instead of monthly, they're coming in now ten, twelve weeks apart. I think she's gone native."

"Cassie?"

"Either that or she's a lot sicker than she's letting us know."

"Any idea at all of when she'll be back?"

Vince grunted. "Can't be long now. Christ, she's been down there more than a year, now."

"Then we've got to make a decision about Max right away," I said.

"Yeah. Like I said, I'll talk to Darrell. And Arthur, too."

With that, Vince got up and strode back into the lab like a top sergeant heading off for a showdown with his officers. Max came scampering back to me, huffing and hooting. He wrapped his hairy arms around me and before I knew it we were tussling, rolling on the grass like a couple of kids. He only wants more candy, I kept telling myself. He's a frigging *animal,* he doesn't have emotions. He likes the candy, not the guy who brings it.

But I had a lot of fun wrestling with him.

PATRICIA HAYWARD

I don't think Arthur ever did have a man-to-man talk with Zack O'Neill. And I never confronted Tina, either. From the gossip in the ladies' room, Tina had really fallen in love with him and they were planning to get married. Vince Andriotti didn't seem overjoyed with the prospect, but the level of tension around the laboratory eased off palpably. There wasn't going to be an explosion, after all.

We were still getting a fair amount of media attention. But in a different way now. Reverend Simmonds was still thumping his drums about godless scientists, but the media had grown tired of his same old story and he faded from the headlines at last. Ransom had gone charging off after a government agency that was involved in getting rid of nuclear wastes.

Simmonds was still drawing big crowds at his revival meetings, though. That summer rally in Central Park had lifted him into the big time. I paid particular attention to his latest tour of the country; he was playing to packed stadiums wherever he went.

The news reporters now looked on our laboratory—Arthur's laboratory, that is—as a reliable source of copy whenever something happened in the biotechnology area. A university announces that its researchers have discovered a new gene that's involved in cancer, science reporters call Arthur to get his authoritative word on it. Activists go to court to stop an agribusiness firm from planting genetically improved tomatoes, the news media wants Arthur's "take" on the dangers of mutant tomatoes taking over the world.

I budgeted Arthur's time as efficiently as I could, but always made certain that he personally returned any calls from the news media within twenty-four hours. Usually the same day. I wanted the reporters to think of Arthur as a reliable source. I wanted them on his side.

Arthur and I had dinner together more than once during

those hectic months. Nothing very romantic about it; we usually talked business over the dinner table. I got to see behind the facade he presented to the world, at least a little bit. He was worried that the regeneration work couldn't go any farther until they did at least one experiment on a chimpanzee, but he was hesitating about using Max.

Arthur laughed ruefully. "Wouldn't it be ironic if we lost this race because we're too tenderhearted to experiment on a chimp?"

"Race?" I asked. "I didn't know anybody else—"

"Oh, we're in a race, all right." His face went tight. "Somewhere out there, maybe in Europe, maybe in Japan or Korea, other researchers are trying to duplicate what we've done and then move ahead of us."

"But no one's said anything."

"They wouldn't. We wouldn't have, if my fathead brother hadn't spilled his guts to Simmonds. This process will be worth billions of dollars, Pat. Thousands of billions. Of course others are trying to get there first."

That was the most passionate moment we shared. Yet even though Arthur framed it all in terms of money, I got the strong feeling that what he really was worked up about was being first, getting there before anyone else does, getting the recognition for making the big breakthrough.

He never made a move on me, and I never gave him a hint that I wouldn't object if he did. In fact, we spent one evening discussing sexual harassment and whether or not it was affecting the laboratory in any way.

"It hasn't bothered Tina," I told him.

Arthur didn't crack a smile. "Maybe," he said. "But doesn't it worry you that someone might bring up charges of harassment years after the fact?"

"Does it worry you?" I asked.

He raised both hands, palms out. "I've never mixed pleasure with business at the lab."

Was that his way of telling me that he was interested, but wouldn't hit on me as long as I worked for him? I wondered what he'd do if I resigned. Would he come calling, or would he forget about me altogether? And then I got a flash of the scene it would make, Arthur coming over to the house in Old Saybrook and meeting Livvie. The sophisticated scientist meets my mother, the vodka queen.

So I didn't resign.

I was in Arthur's office when they made the decision to use Max for experiments. He called me in specifically and sat me at his round conference table right beside him. Zack O'Neill, Darrell Walters, and Vince Andriotti were there.

"I've asked Pat to sit in on this," Arthur explained to them, "because what we're about to decide will have vast public relations implications, one way or the other."

"Cassie should be here," Darrell Walters said.

Arthur's face clouded slightly. "Phyllis has tried to reach Cassie by phone and e-mail. She's not answering. Fax, too, no answer."

Vince Andriotti shook his jowly head. "Maybe it's better if she's not involved in this. She's too damned emotional about Max. We gotta make a rational decision here."

"I don't want to use him," Zack O'Neill blurted. That surprised me, and the other men around the table looked shocked, too.

"This is no time for reverse psychology," Andriotti growled.

But Arthur knew better. "You've become attached to Max, too. Just like Cassie."

Looking unhappy, Zack admitted, "Yeah. Kind of."

"Saints preserve us," Walters muttered.

"I'd say we should wait until we get more chimps," Zack explained, "but there's a danger if we wait."

"Competition," said Arthur grimly. "I know."

"We've gone as far with the macaques and the minihogs as we can," Zack said. "It'd be a waste of time and effort to keep on with them. We know what we've got to know. Now we have to move on to chimps."

"Now, wait," said Walters. "We're still a *long* way from understanding how regentide is working at the molecular level. You can see the gross results, sure, but we don't know beans about what's really going on inside the cells."

"That doesn't matter," Arthur said.

"It doesn't?" Walters looked startled. "You mean you don't care if we just stumble along without a firm understanding of how these molecules interact with one another?"

Andriotti chimed in, "If we had a valid model of the molecular chemistry, maybe we could see why the tumors are growing and figure out how to prevent that."

But Arthur shook his head. "I don't want to get bogged down in heavy detail work. That's for universities."

"But—"

"I want to get results," Arthur insisted. "Let the academics figure out the details."

Walters shook his head disbelievingly.

"I want to be able to move into human trials as soon as possible."

"That means experiments on chimps," Zack said.

"One chimp," Arthur said.

"Max," said Zack.

Andriotti tilted his chair back and crossed his beefy arms over his chest. "Okay, then, who's running this lab, Arthur? You or Cassie?"

Arthur didn't dignify that with an answer. Instead he asked O'Neill, "Is the surgical team ready?"

Zack nodded. "I'd been thinking about just lopping off a finger, but the head surgeon says it'll be a much better test if we take the whole arm."

"That makes sense," Arthur said.

They all fell silent.

I heard myself ask, "When is Cassie due to return here?"

"She's got at least another month's worth of work in Mexico," Walters replied.

"But she could pop up here anytime she wants to," Andriotti added.

"Especially if she knows Max is going under the knife."

Arthur asked, "What about doing more than the arm?"

"What?"

He did not look happy, but he had made up his mind. "Do we want to do any of the internal organs? At the same time?"

"No," Zack said firmly.

"Might make sense to do a kidney," Walters mused. "While you've got the chimp on the table."

"No," Zack repeated. "I don't want Max opened up. The arm will be trauma enough."

But Arthur said, "In for a penny, in for a pound. What else can we do with Max?"

No one spoke for a long, long moment.

Then, very hesitantly, Zack said, "The head surgeon suggested . . ." He stopped in midsentence and swallowed hard. "She suggested that we take one of Max's eyes."

"One of his eyes!" Andriotti looked plainly disgusted.

Walters leaned back in his chair and stared at the ceiling.

But Arthur thought about it for a moment, then asked calmly, "What do you think, Zack?"

"I think I'm too emotionally close to the damned chimp to give a reasoned answer."

Walters ran a hand across his lantern jaw. "The eye is connected directly to the brain, of course."

"It's part of the brain," said Andriotti, "an extension of it."

"It'd make a helluva test," Walters admitted. "If you could regrow an eyeball."

"That's true," Arthur said.

"But it's kind of ghoulish," Walters said. "Gives me the willies."

"I don't want to do that to Max," Zack said. "But still—"

"But still he's the only chimp we've got," Arthur finished for him.

"If this leaks out to the media before the eye grows back," I said, "we'll have animal-rights commandos trying to blow up the whole laboratory."

"With us in it," said Andriotti.

"Maybe they'd be right," Walters muttered.

Again the table fell silent. All eyes turned to Arthur. It was his decision to make.

"All right, dammit," he snapped. "We use Max as soon as the surgical team is ready. Before the week is out. Take the arm, but not the one he uses for sign language."

"And the eye?" Zack whispered.

"Yes, the eye, too," Arthur said with an exasperated sigh. "What the hell."

Then he turned to me. "But not a word of this goes beyond the walls of this building. Understand that? This operation has got to be so secret it'll make the CIA look like a network news broadcast."

ARTHUR

I felt like a vampire. I wasn't as close to Max emotionally as Zack had become, and nowhere near as wrapped up in the chimp as Cassie. But still it felt—well, evil, almost, to be chopping off one of his arms and taking an eye, as well. What did Darrell call it? Ghoulish.

But what choice did I have? If we had other chimps, if we could have kept our work secret, then I could have gone slower, been more careful, kept my promise to Cassie to protect Max. But I wasn't going to let them stop me: not the competition, not the crazies like Ransom and Simmonds, not the government bureaucrats who'd smother us in red tape the instant we slowed our pace. Everything I've really wanted in life has been taken away from me. Columbia. Julia. Momma. Any chance of real recognition. Even Jesse had turned away from me.

Well, they weren't going to snatch this prize from my fingers. As long as I'm running the show we'll move as fast and as hard as we can, I decided. And damn the torpedoes.

I knew that Johnston was talking to at least two of the biggest pharmaceutical firms in Europe. Nancy Dubois wouldn't give me the time of day, but Johnston himself told me that more than one European corporation was interested in a merger with Omnitech.

"That could be our salvation, Arthur," the CEO told me.

Then he added, "But don't breathe a word of it outside this office, understand me?"

"Are the Japanese also interested?" I asked as casually as I could manage.

Johnston's brows popped up. "The Japs? I haven't talked to Nakata in weeks."

Which was an evasion, not an answer. I worried about that as I drove from corporate headquarters back to the lab. Is Johnston talking seriously to the Japanese? If he is, what conditions are they putting on a possible merger? Where does the lab fit in?

The only course I could see was to plow ahead. I still believed that the best thing we could do was to move forward with the regeneration work as fast as we could. That would make the lab too valuable to sell off. But would it make us so attractive that some overseas firm would buy the entire corporation?

We kept all the preparations for Max's surgery top secret. We swore the surgical team to secrecy, even made them sign confidentiality statements. Not that there was anything we could really do to them if they talked. This wasn't the government and they were consultants, not employees. About the worst we could threaten was to splash their names around the profession as unreliable.

Pat got a stroke of genius in that regard. She suggested sending the whole team off on a month's vacation after the operation on Max, just to get them away from the media.

"The Caribbean, Europe, anyplace where they won't be tempted to talk to reporters," she said.

"How about Australia?" I suggested.

"Or Tibet?"

We gave them their choices. I'm sure they knew the motivation behind our generosity but they went for it anyway. The chief of the surgery team opted for a month traveling through Italy. Most of the others picked the Caribbean, although one of the nurses wanted to visit her family in Taiwan. Fine by me. Sid Lowenstein got red in the face when I told him about it, but even he saw the wisdom of the plan once I explained it to him.

The day came. The team's anesthesiologist had mixed a powerful sedative into Max's evening meal. The chimp was sleeping like a baby when we went to his cage and started strapping him down and prepping him for surgery.

I went with them, every step of the way. This was my responsibility and I wasn't about to duck away from the messy part of it. I suppose Jesse would have said it's part of my god complex. As long as I'm there watching nothing will go wrong.

It was incredibly messy. Giving a sleeping chimp an enema is not easy, and the results are foul and stinking beyond belief. Then came the needles and the catheters. By the time they wheeled Max into our little surgical lab he was wired up like an astronaut. And firmly strapped to the table. The display screens off to one side of the room showed his pulse and respiration rates, blood pressure, brain wave patterns, everything. They beeped and hummed softly. The room was cold, tiled walls and floor, big ring of high-intensity lights over the surgical table. It smelled of antiseptics and strange, other odors. I wondered if we were catching whiffs of the anesthesiologist's gases from the metal cylinders up by the head of the table.

We were all dressed in hospital greens, complete with masks and hairnets and disposable booties over our shoes. Very antiseptic. They had put a breathing mask over Max's muzzle. I noticed that it was held tightly in place with leather straps. They were taking no chances on the chimp waking up and using his teeth. I thought it didn't show much confidence on the anesthesiologist's part.

Darrell stood beside me through the whole long, gruesome procedure. At the last minute Zack begged off. He looked almost as green as the surgical gowns. Sick with fear and guilt.

The chief surgeon was a little round butterball of a woman with the tiniest hands I had ever seen on an adult. She handled the laser scalpel without a flaw. Max's left arm came off just above the elbow, the laser beam cauterizing as it cut so there was relatively little blood. The whole procedure took less than ten minutes, once she started cutting. But the smell of burnt meat and hair made me queasy.

The eye was different, more delicate. She had to use knives for that. I had to look away. I was getting sick to my stomach from the smell and the blood.

I heard Max whimper.

"Watch it!" one of the assistant surgeons snapped.

I turned back and saw that Max was stirring slightly. The monitor displays were getting jagged instead of showing smooth curves and their audio signals whined to higher pitches. The anesthesiologist twirled knobs on his control console and Max calmed down. So did the displays. The chief surgeon glanced at the anesthesiologist. I could only see her eyes above the mask, but she radiated displeasure.

At last the eye came free. An assistant took it tenderly in her gloved fingers and deposited it in a freezer box. If the regeneration didn't work we would attempt to replace Max's original eye. I felt bile burning in my throat.

Then it was patching, suturing, bandaging, while I fought the urge to throw up. The homestretch. I looked up at the clock on the cold tile wall and realized with some surprise that we'd only been in there for a little more than two hours.

It was over. The chief surgeon peeled off her mask and hat. Her hair was matted down and glistening with perspiration. The tension dissolved. Everyone unmasked, relaxed, stretched tightened backs, and walked around a bit on stiff legs. The surgical team began to congratulate one another.

I looked down at Max, still strapped to the table and muzzled with the breathing mask. His left arm was only a bandaged stump now. More bandages covered the empty socket where his right eye used to be.

His other eye opened.

I felt a jolt, whether it was fear or surprise or guilt, I don't know. But in that instant I saw in Max's one remaining eye all the pain and shock and terror that a human being would have shown. I'm sure I was projecting my own emotions, yet I'll never forget the sight of that one eye going suddenly wide and then blinking and filling with tears. I knew, in that one startling moment, how I would have felt if I'd awakened one fine morning and found that my arm had been amputated and an eye put out.

Without a word I turned and walked out of the surgical lab as calmly as I could. Once outside I almost ran to the men's room and locked myself in a stall. I didn't want any of my people to see me vomiting.

I SENT a long e-mail to Cassie and then for good measure faxed the same letter to her, explaining as gently as possible what we had done to Max and trying to make it clear to her that we had no viable alternative. I thought that putting it all on paper would be easier—for both of us—than breaking the news on the telephone.

No response.

I tried phoning her in Mexico and got only an answering machine with her voice promising to call back as soon as she possibly could.

No call back. Nothing.

I asked Darrell what he thought about the situation.

"Let me go down there and get her," he said. "This must've hit her like an atomic bomb."

"All right," I said. "Bring her back here. I don't care what shape her program is in or what shape she's in. Bring her home."

"Right," said Darrell.

I tried to put Cassie out of my mind. I had work to do. Graves's idea of a science court was starting to get some support from key players in the field. I shuttled down to Washington several times and spent hours on the phone with scientists from some of the most prestigious schools in the nation.

Many of those academics were frankly skeptical of dealing with me. I was one of those big bad industrial guys who had turned his back on the purity of academic research. I was out to make a buck instead of pursuing pure research. It was an archaic attitude, ludicrous in the light of the modern scientific scene, but it was uncanny how quickly some of the academics could climb up on their white horses and pontificate.

Graves was an invaluable help. He had wanted to try out this idea of a science court for years, he told me, and now I had given him the opportunity to make it real. So he ran interference with the stuffier academics and began to line them up—not on my side, necessarily, but on the side of giving my work a fair and rigorous hearing before a court of my peers.

The more I thought about it, the more sense the court made to me. I wanted the regeneration work to be assessed rationally. I had no intention of allowing it to be tried in the media, or by mobs of six-pack-swilling know-nothings whipped into a frenzy by the likes of Joshua Ransom or Reverend Simmonds over nonsense like mutant monsters.

Simmonds. Every time I thought of him I thought of Jesse. That made me simmer with anger. Yet Julia had told me that Jesse never knowingly tried to hurt me. And I knew she was right. At least I tried to convince myself she was right. In all honesty, I couldn't picture Jesse deliberately getting Simmonds on my back. It's just that Jess is so damned blind to everything and everyone except himself. He wouldn't ask Simmonds to attack me, but he'd blithely tell Simmonds all about the work I was doing without even thinking for one moment that Simmonds would be smart enough to latch on to that idea and use it as a rallying cry to draw more attention and bigger crowds to himself.

Simmonds wouldn't be allowed to testify in the science court, of course. But Jesse could. He was in at the start of this work, and if the opposite side in the court procedure had any brains at all they'd call on Jess to testify.

Would he agree to appear? And would he testify against me? I had to find out.

Somehow, dealing with my brother had become like walking through a minefield. Ever since Julia had come into our lives.

No, that wasn't right, I told myself. Jesse had always been irresponsible, self-centered, even as a kid. It just never bothered me before Julia. We had never wanted the same exact thing before. He had never stolen anything away from me.

But no matter how much trouble or pain, I had to find out

what he'd do if he was asked to appear at the science court hearing. And, in the back of my mind, I could hear Momma telling me that it was wrong to be angry with my brother. And I heard Julia saying to me that I ought to take the first step in healing the breach between us.

I asked Phyllis to track him down on the phone. It took two days. Actually he called around midnight, just as I was getting ready for bed after a dinner out with Pat.

I was sitting on the edge of the bed when the phone rang. Somehow I knew it would be Jesse. Who else would call at this hour, unless it was Darrell with news about Cassie?

"Arby?" His voice sounded tired.

"Hello, Jess."

"I got a couple messages that you've been trying to reach me."

"Yes."

"What do you want?"

"How are you?" I asked. "How's Julia?"

"We're both fine. What're you up to?"

It felt both good and painful to hear his voice again. I wanted to love him the way a brother should, I really did.

"It's been a long time," I said.

He started to say something, then changed his mind and said simply, "Yeah."

"Do you have any time for lunch in the next few days? I could come down into the city."

"Breakfast would be easier," he said. "I never know when I'll get a chance to break for lunch."

"Okay. Breakfast." That meant I'd have to get up very early, or go into town the night before and stay over.

"Tomorrow?" he asked.

"How about the day after tomorrow?"

He hesitated. "No good. Got a fund-raising breakfast with some investors group on Wall Street."

"I could meet you afterward," I suggested. "Pick you up and drive you to the hospital. We could talk in the limo."

He laughed softly. "I don't think I ought to let those people see me get into a limo. I'm always poor-mouthing them."

"I'll come in a taxicab, then."

Suddenly his voice became suspicious. "What's so damned important?"

"I'll tell you when I see you."

He had to think about that for a moment. At last he agreed, and gave me the address and time when he would be finished with his breakfast meeting.

"I'll see you then," I said.

"Okay," he answered guardedly. Then he brightened and added, "Oh, by the way, Julia's pregnant again."

And he hung up.

THE TRIAL:

DAY FOUR, LUNCH RECESS

I wish I knew what's on those disks," Arthur said to Pat.

"The DVDs Cassie made?"

They were having lunch at one of the little restaurants just off Capitol Hill, leaning together conspiratorially over the tiny, wobbly table. Neither of them recognized anyone else from the trial in the restaurant, yet still they talked in near-whispers.

"Yes," Arthur said gloomily. "Cassie's legacy."

"I still think Rosen should have allowed you to see them before they're introduced as evidence in the trial," said Pat.

Arthur grimaced. "His position is that they're not scientific evidence. They're just a personal statement by a scientist who worked on the program."

"We've come a long way from restricting ourselves to the scientific facts, haven't we?"

Nodding, Arthur replied, "And Graves is letting him get away with it."

"She won't be helpful to you, will she?"

"Rosen wouldn't use the disks if they were helpful," Arthur grumbled. "The only question is, how much damage can they do?"

Pat tried to change the subject. "You really demolished Ransom."

"He had it coming."

"I didn't think he'd be so easy to knock off."

Arthur smiled grimly. "That sneaky little sonofabitch has never had to stand up to cross-examination before. Not in any way. He's always attacked through the media or through the courts, always arranged things so his victims are on the defensive and he's on the attack. Once he had to defend his own position, he crumbled."

"No," Pat said admiringly, "you crumbled him. And then you held out your hand to him, at the end. That was beautiful."

Arthur looked surprised. "Oh, you mean when I said he'd need regeneration one day?" He shrugged. "Well, we all will, won't we?"

"Potter needs it now," Pat said.

Arthur's face hardened. "I wonder what I'd do if we were ready for human trials and Potter came to me and asked for help."

"You'd help him."

"Would I? That man ruined my life."

Pat laughed. "I wouldn't say your life is exactly ruined, Arthur."

"No thanks to him."

She grew more serious. "His testimony was pretty damning, though."

Arthur huffed. "He made an ass of himself."

"He sounded very convincing to me."

"You're not a scientist. Anyone in the field who still has a few brain cells functioning will see that Potter's so-called scientific study is nothing but numerology."

"Really?"

"I'll tear him to shreds when I cross-examine him."

Pat smiled a bit. "Perry Mason attacks."

"You'll see." Arthur smiled back.

At least he's smiling, Pat thought as their waiter brought a pair of salads. Pat was drinking iced tea, Arthur a non-alcoholic beer.

"How much damage can Cassie do?" she asked.

Arthur's smile vanished. "Not much scientifically. But if her video is as emotional as I think it'll be, we're going to get lynched in the media."

"I don't think there'll be all that many reporters back for the afternoon session. They got their story when you and Ransom squared off."

"They'll be there," Arthur said. "Let Cassie break into tears just once on her videos and they'll swarm around us like piranhas. She'll be on the six o'clock news, not Ransom and me."

"Her and Max."

"And we'll look like monsters."

He picked listlessly at his salad, then looked up again. "I wanted this trial to go strictly on the scientific merits of our work. If we could just stick to the science we'd have no trouble whatsoever."

"But Rosen won't do that, and Graves is letting him get away with it."

"This isn't what Graves and I agreed to, at the beginning," Arthur said bitterly. "I've been betrayed."

"The trial hasn't been on the front page since the opening day," Pat said, trying to sound optimistic. "Even Reverend Simmonds's pickets have thinned out a lot."

"Senator Kindelberger tried to sabotage us," Arthur said. "He's out to get us."

"He's running for reelection," said Pat.

"And appealing to the crazies."

"I guess."

"But where's Jesse?" Arthur wondered. "Why wasn't he here?"

"I don't know. Do you want me to find out?"

"And what's on Cassie's disks? What's she going to say? How bad is it going to get?"

LAUREEN JARVIS skipped lunch. She went straight from the hearing chamber in the Rayburn Building to Senator Kindelberger's offices in the Dirkson Building, on the other side of the Capitol.

Inserting Ransom into the trial had been Kerry Tate's brilliant idea and it had backfired hideously. The little creep was totally outgunned by Marshak. As she headed for the senator's private office, Laureen saw that Kerry's door was closed tight.

He doesn't want any of us ragging him, she thought. Can't say that I blame him. But this next ploy is going to blow Marshak out of the water; it can't fail.

The senator was sitting at the conference table in his office, looking worried, one big hand wrapped around his luncheon glass of bourbon. Elwood Faber sat on the far side of the polished mahogany table, an attaché case opened on his lap. Laureen saw three plastic-covered DVDs inside the case; Faber seemed to be guarding them as if they were bars of solid gold. Reverend Simmonds stood over by the window, his head bowed over hands clasped in prayer.

Laureen complained, "The reporters won't be back after lunch. They got what they wanted from Marshak's takeout of Ransom."

Kindelberger shot her an annoyed glance. Faber looked up from the DVDs. "You're wrong, honey. I've phoned every reporter in town. They're all going to be there, watching these videos."

"You're certain of that?" Kindelberger asked.

"Depend on it," Faber said, smiling.

Simmonds lifted his face and said, "God is on our side. He will provide us with victory."

"He'd better," Laureen said. "Another fiasco like Ransom and we'll be wiped out."

Faber closed the attaché case tenderly, then patted its lid. "Listen, people: these videos are a godsend. Little Cassie's going to win this fight for us."

Simmonds sat down and leaned his arms on the polished conference table.

"But Marshak tore Ransom to shreds," Kindelberger grumbled. "That makes me look like a jackass."

"It doesn't matter what the scientists say," Faber said, putting both his loafer-clad feet on the tabletop. "Once little Cassie here starts blubbering on the TV screen about her monkey, the media's going to crucify Marshak but good."

Simmonds's eyes narrowed slightly at the word "crucify," but he said nothing.

"You stop Marshak and you're a national power, Reverend. A *national* political force. You'll get the senator here reelected. And then other politicians will come a-courting you. You'll see. They'll come to you with their hats in their hands and tell you that they've seen the light and they want your blessing on their campaigns. They'll beg you to let your followers work for 'em. And vote for 'em, of course."

"I'm not interested in political power," Simmonds rumbled.

"No, course not." Faber jabbed a finger at him. "But you want to put an end to creating fetuses just so's some scientists can kill 'em and use their stem cells, don't you? You want the schools to stop teaching about sex, don't you? And stop teaching about evolution, too. You want dirty books and smutty Web sites taken out of circulation, don't you? You want families to be families again, you want to stop all these welfare sluts from getting free abortions, you want to make these United States dedicated to the power and glory of the Lord, don't you?"

Simmonds said nothing. He did not have to.

"Well, then," Faber said, smiling broadly at him, "to get that done we've got to destroy Marshak. Not just beat him at this trial, not just stop his infernal scientific research. We've got to ruin the man, break him, crush him up so bad that nobody'll ever want to hire him even for janitor!"

Simmonds clasped and unclasped his hands for several long moments. His eyes shifted away from Faber, looked down at his clenching fingers.

At last he said, "God's will be done."

CASSIE IANETTA

Arthur's message about Max came while I was desperately trying to convince Bill he should stay in Querétaro. I had stopped checking my e-mail and hadn't even looked at my fax machine for days, just let the messages pile up. They weren't important. Nothing was important except to keep Bill from leaving me.

But he did leave. They all do. They break down your defenses and make you fall in love with them and then they go off and leave you alone, betrayed and sick and lonely and miserable.

I thought I couldn't feel any worse than I did the day Bill piled his stuff into his old MG and drove away. I couldn't work, couldn't sleep, couldn't eat. For days I just went through the motions. There were no more inoculations to be done, just follow-up examinations to see how the volunteers were doing, and the medical staff was taking care of that. I should have been spending my time analyzing their findings and writing a final report.

I should have been reading my e-mail and answering the messages on my phone machine and sorting through the faxes that had piled up.

I forced myself to start. I dragged myself to my office in the clinic after two sleepless nights and a whole day of doing nothing more than crying until I didn't have any more tears left in me.

I started reading through the mail while I listened to the phone messages. Mostly junk in the mail, bills forwarded from Connecticut, some of them several months old. A birthday card from Darrell, also several months old. The phone calls were routine, some of them in Spanish spoken so swiftly that I couldn't get a glimmer of it. I'd have to ask one of the Mexican medical staff to translate for me.

Arthur's secretary, Phyllis, called several times. And Darrell. No messages, just asking me to call back.

Then Arthur's own voice. It made me look up from the mail I was reading.

"Cassie, I'm sending you an e-mail and fax today. It's very important that you read it and get back to me as soon as you possibly can."

His voice sounded strained, urgent. The answering machine gave the date and time. Two days ago. I got up and riffled through the sheets that had piled up on the fax machine. There was a one-page message from Arthur:

> Cassie:
> We have been forced into a decision that you may object to. Since we can't obtain any other chimps, and our regeneration work desperately needs at least one chimpanzee experiment before we can go on to human trials, we have no alternative except to use Max. Please call me as soon as you have read this. We have to talk about it.
>
> Arthur

They wanted to experiment on Max! After all Arthur's promises, they were going to cut Max open and use him just like he was some lab animal. Even Arthur was betraying me, cutting me open. Why do people have to be so vicious? I wanted to scream. I wanted to tear the paper to shreds. I wanted to burn it.

But instead I just picked up the phone, cold as a glacier inside, and called the airline. It was like I was somebody else and the real me was someplace else and watching this woman calmly making a reservation for herself to fly to New York and rent a car to drive up to Connecticut and get to the murdering sons of bitches who were going to mutilate my Max.

I WAS too late, of course.

I should have phoned Arthur as soon as I read his fax, but what good would that have done? He had made his decision and nothing I could say on the telephone would change his mind. I knew that.

But his message didn't say how soon they were going to cut Max up. Maybe if I could get there fast enough I could rush in and stop them. How, I don't know. Maybe I could throw myself in front of Max and not let them take him or maybe I could get there before they were ready and sneak Max out of the lab and go live up in the woods or something or someplace. I didn't know what. All I knew was that I had to get there as fast as I could.

It wasn't fast enough.

I could tell from the startled look on Phyllis's face that I was too late. I came into the lab unannounced. Irene, the receptionist, recognized me, of course, but she wouldn't let me past the lobby until she wrote my name on a list and handed me an identification badge to clip onto my blouse.

"I'm sorry to hold you up," Irene said. "It's the new rules. You know, because of all the publicity."

I didn't know. "What publicity?"

"Oh, that's right. You've been away," said Irene. "You'll have to get your photo taken and get a permanent badge as soon as you can."

By the time she finished that sentence I was pushing through the doors into the lab's main corridor. I didn't go to my own office or stop at Arthur's. I just stuck my head through the open doorway of his outer office. One look at Phyllis's face told me that the worst had already happened. I practically ran to the back of the building, shoulder bag banging against my hip, out to the animal pens and the exercise area, without stopping to say hello to any of the people I saw in the corridors.

Max was nowhere in sight. Not out in the yard or in his cage. I thought, My god, they've killed him! My heart was hammering so loud I thought it was going to burst.

One of the kids who takes care of the animals came in with a bucket and mop in his hands.

"Hey, Cassie!" he said, surprised. "Long time—"

"Where is he? Where's Max?"

He got the same guilty look on his face that Phyllis did. "In the recoup pen," he muttered.

"Recoup?"

"We built him a special facility, just for him while he's recuperating—"

"Where is it?"

He pointed with a lanky arm, still holding the bucket. "Out behind the pharmaceutical storage area, y'know, down the hall from Dr. O'Neill's lab."

I ran. There were several small rooms back there, used for storage or temporary lab space, depending on what we needed at the moment. I opened one unmarked door. Nothing. Another. And another. Then the last one.

It was a prison cell. Max sat huddled in a corner. The room was brightly lit. Divided into two sections by a thick Plexiglas wall. Piles of straw on the floor. Toys and blocks scattered about. No windows. No fresh air.

And Max. His left arm ended in a stump just above where his elbow should have been. There was a soiled bandage over his right eye. A scream filled my throat but I forced it back, forced myself to stand on my two feet and not collapse, not scream, not do anything that would hurt poor Max more than the devils had already hurt him. I just stood there in the doorway and stared at Max, my legs rubbery, my insides burning like acid.

Max looked up at me with his one brown eye. He was torpid, drugged. I thought for a moment that he didn't recognize me.

"Max," I said, going to the Plexiglas wall and sinking to my knees. "Can you hear me, Max? It's me, Cassie."

He didn't move for a long, long time. He just stared at me like a child who's been punished for something he hadn't done, like a person who's been betrayed by the one who was closest to him.

My eyes went misty and I felt the tears running down my cheeks. "Oh, Max, I'm so sorry. I didn't know they would do this to you. I never thought they'd do this."

He struggled to his feet and knuckle-walked toward me, awkwardly, with only one hand to support him. He stopped in front of the transparent wall and reached out to me with his only hand. The Plexiglas wall stopped him.

I cried. For him. For me. For the cruelty that men can inflict on us so casually, without thinking, without caring.

"Oh, Max. Max," I kept blubbering. "Max, I'm so sorry."

He put his open hand to his face and moved it up and down several times. I saw that the stump of amputated arm was moving, too. The sign for sadness.

"Yes," I said, making the sign with both my hands. "I'm sad. You must be, too."

Then Max made a different sign. Only half of it, but I recognized the gesture. Hurts. He was in pain.

"Hi, Cassie!"

I jerked with surprise at the human voice. Turning my head, I saw it was Zack O'Neill. The butchering sonofabitch who had mutilated Max. Smiling at me. Smiling!

I scrambled to my feet. "You did this to him!"

His smile crumbled. "I didn't want to, Cass. Believe me—"

I'd believe him when hell froze over. I slipped my purse off my shoulder while he was blathering something about how he had no choice but to use Max and I swung it as hard as I could at his lying, deceiving, betraying face. He staggered back and I pounded him, kicked him, screamed at him until somebody was pinning my arms to my sides and Zack was staring at me, wide-eyed, a trickle of blood oozing from his nose.

One of the animal handlers and a security guard in a tan uniform dragged me away from Zack, took me screaming and cursing down to the security office and made me sit down and drink a glass of water. If I'd had a knife I would have sunk it in Zack's intestines and twisted it. Hard.

Another uniformed guard, an older man with a sergeant's stripes on his sleeves, eyed me carefully.

"You okay now?"

I wondered if he kept a gun in this cubbyhole of an office.

"Hey, Ms. Ianetta, can you hear me?"

I glared pure murder at him.

"I'll take care of her." It was Arthur. In his shirtsleeves, tie loosened from his collar, as usual. He looked grim. Silver-haired, sleek and handsome, and the biggest lying bastard of them all.

"Come on, Cassie," he said gently. "Come on back to my office. Phyllis will make you some tea."

I let him take me by the arm and lead me back to his office. Darrell came hustling up the corridor from the other direction, looking worried and startled and guilty all at the same time. Arthur waved him away and escorted me past Phyllis and into one of the big chairs in front of his desk. He sat on the one next to it.

"Max will be all right," he said.

I wanted to spit in his face.

"His system has accepted the regentide injections. His arm is already starting to form budding cells."

It was all I could do to just sit there and not claw out his eyes.

"I tried to tell you," he went on, just as smooth and soft as a lullaby. "I phoned and e-mailed and faxed you. You never answered. We couldn't sit here waiting."

"You promised," I said through gritted teeth.

"I said we wouldn't use Max unless there was no other alternative."

"No. You promised me you wouldn't use him."

Arthur sighed. "All right. If that's the way you remember it, then I promised. And now I've broken my promise. But Max will be all right. He'll come through this in fine shape."

"Why should I believe you?"

"Because you're going to be with Max and see how he regrows his arm."

"And his eye?"

Arthur looked slightly away from me. "His eye, too."

He was lying, I knew.

"Max needs you, Cassie. He's been through a severe trauma and he needs the one person he can trust to help him through his recuperation."

I heard myself say, "I want to take Max away."

"That can't be done. You know that. We've got to monitor his progress, adjust the treatment as we go along."

"I'll take care of all that. I want to move him to a different facility, away from here, away from all the frightening memories he has of this place."

"I don't think so," Arthur said slowly. "We do need to keep him under constant surveillance. Zack has to—"

"I don't want Zack to touch him!"

Arthur flinched visibly. He recovered immediately, though. "Cassie, I don't think you realize that Zack didn't want us to operate on Max."

"Yeah, sure."

"It's true. He grew almost as fond of the animal as you are. He couldn't even watch the procedure."

"But you did, didn't you?"

"Yes, I did."

I got to my feet. I felt strong, somehow, empowered. "I'll take care of Max," I told Arthur. "I'll do all the tests and treatments. I don't want anyone else touching him."

He gave me a patient, fatherly smile. "Are you going to sleep here, too?"

"Yes," I snapped. "Why not?"

WHAT ELSE on earth did I have? Why not stay close to Max day and night? Arthur was very conciliatory. He let me empty out the storage room next to Max's and bring in a cot, a microwave oven, a TV and DVD player, even a chest of drawers for a few of my clothes.

I took care of Max. It was his emotional pain that concerned me most. Just like me, he had been betrayed by someone he loved. I had to show him that I was at his side and I would protect him and I wouldn't allow anybody to hurt him ever again. I wished I could say the same about myself. It would be wonderful to have somebody who cared about me enough to shelter me from the rest of the world.

But I had something else now. I was going to get even with

them. With Arthur, with Zack, with all of them. I didn't know how, not just then, but I knew someday, sometime, I'd pay them back for what they did to Max and me. I'd pay them back with interest.

After several weeks Max started to show a little of his old playfulness. The first time he hugged me I almost fainted with happiness. He was starting to trust me again!

That's why I insisted that my oncologist come to the lab to test me. I wasn't going to leave Max for an overnight trip to Boston. No way.

Her tests confirmed what I had known from my own self-testing. The enzyme was working inside me just the way it was working in the volunteer test subjects in Mexico.

"You're in remission," she told me.

I didn't tell her that I had inoculated myself. I didn't want to influence her examination or her conclusions in any way. But I knew. I was cured. I'd never have to worry about cancer again.

"Still," the oncologist went on, "your general physical condition isn't good. You're run down, on the ragged edge of exhaustion. You've got to take it easier, gain a little weight, learn to relax and enjoy life a bit."

"But I am enjoying my life," I told her.

She glanced around at my spartan cell. "You actually live in here?"

"Temporarily," I said. "Until Max is well enough to go back to his regular quarters." That was a bit of a lie. I intended to stay with Max until his arm had grown back completely. And his eye.

When I wasn't with Max I was in my office, doing the work I should have done in Mexico. Every now and then I wondered where Bill was and if he ever thought about me. It still ached, deep down. And the wound wasn't healing; it was festering. Bill was just the same as the rest of them. I couldn't trust anyone, not a soul.

I began to wonder if I was going insane. All I could think of was revenge, some way to punish them all for what they'd done to Max. To me. I dreamed of tortures, I even found myself doodling pictures on notepads of men with their arms chopped off. Their eyes put out. Their cocks sliced into pieces.

I'm going crazy, I thought. And a voice inside my head answered, So what? They've made you crazy, the whole hateful bunch of them.

At least Max's arm was showing signs of budding and regenerating. The eye was a different matter, though. Max didn't like most of the tests I had to put him through, so when we had to do CAT scans I put him to sleep with a sedative in his evening meal and then ran him through the machine at night.

There were tumors growing where his eye had been. And spreading along the optic nerve into the frontal lobe of his brain.

Arthur, Darrell, Zack, and I held a conference about that. Zack sat across the table from me, making feeble wisecracks about my bashing his nose.

Go ahead and joke, I told him silently. One of these days you're going to pay for everything you've done. In spades. In blood.

"It's the same old problem," Darrell was saying. "The regentide isn't specific enough to regenerate only the cells we want to regrow. It starts other cells growing wild."

"We've got to use the enzyme treatment," I said. "Otherwise the tumors will kill him."

Darrell said, "That's compounding one experiment with another experiment. Not good practice, Cass."

But Zack spoke up. "We don't want Max to die on us, do we? That'd screw up the experiment terminally."

I'd like to take care of you terminally, I thought.

Arthur looked worried. He asked me, "Cassie, are you confident that the enzyme treatment can kill the tumors? After all, we don't have all the results in from your field tests, as yet."

"Confident enough," I announced, "that I've used the treatment on myself."

I had told Arthur that I was going to do it, but still his eyebrows went up. Darrell and Zack looked shocked.

"And it works," I added.

That kicked off a long discussion, with Arthur grumbling that it was a big risk for me to take, and Darrell worrying that I didn't have the proper scientific objectivity about either the enzyme treatment or Max, and Zack staying strangely silent, just eying me as if he were afraid I'd sock him again if he opened his mouth.

I would have, too.

In the end, they agreed to let me use the enzyme treatment on Max's tumors. I knew they would. They really didn't have any choice. If Max died, their precious experiment died with him. They couldn't move on to human trials without Max.

But they didn't have to worry. I wasn't going to let Max die. I was going to save him.

Don't think that I stayed in my little cell all the time. I didn't become a total hermit. And despite the crude jokes going around the lab, I didn't spend all my time with Max, either. I dug into the data from the Mexican fieldwork and started churning out the reports. I had one of the lab's visiting MDs do Pap smears for me, but I checked the results myself. The cancer was gone. Totally.

And I started catching up on the lab gossip and the news that I had missed while I'd been away. Like Zack's romance with Tina Andriotti. And Arthur's interest in his public relations consultant. "Maybe they're involved in some private relations," I heard more than once.

I also heard about Reverend Simmonds and his campaign against us. What a silly thing to do, to try to stop us from learning and growing.

I ran Max's enzyme treatments myself. Max went into hysterics when he saw me with a hypodermic syringe. He howled and ran around his pen throwing up handfuls of straw, peeling back his lips and snarling at me, flinging his toys at the Plexiglas wall between us. I put the syringe away and showed him that both my hands were empty. I wanted to go into his pen and calm him down, but for the first time in my life I was scared of Max. Even with only one arm he could've broken my bones, he was so frightened.

I had to give him the needles when he was asleep, snoring peacefully from the sedatives that I put into his evening meal. I watched his progress fretfully. The enzyme was tailored for human cells; I wasn't certain that it would work as well on a chimpanzee. If it didn't, we'd have to develop one specifically tailored for Max. And quickly. The tumors were starting to put pressure on his brain.

It wasn't affecting his behavior, so I thought we had enough time to make the treatment work. But I worried, worried every day and night. It was still too chilly to let Max stay outside for very long, and he looked so pathetic trying to climb the trees with only one hand. Even the jungle gym was a trial for him. More and more we just stayed indoors; in his pen, for the most part, but I walked him along the lab's corridors for exercise.

One night as I sat up sleeplessly clicking from one TV channel to another, I caught one of Reverend Simmonds's revival meetings. From some auditorium in Omaha or Fort Wayne or someplace out in the midwest.

"Don't be deceived by these godless men of science," he was yelling into a microphone, holding it up to his mouth the way rock singers do, his face beaded with perspiration, his shirt soaked through. "These secular scientists are evil incarnate."

It was nonsense, of course. But the more I listened, the more I realized that he was speaking to me. His eyes seemed to stare right out of the TV screen into mine. The words he was speaking faded from my consciousness almost entirely and I heard his *real* message, the message he meant for me:

Come to me and I will help you to avenge yourself on all those who have done you harm. Come to me and together we will work our vengeance on the men who have betrayed you.

It was weird. I was raised in the Catholic Church but had stopped believing in anything while I was still a teenager. I didn't for one minute believe that Reverend Simmonds was any closer to God than I was. But he wanted to stop Arthur and all those other men who could cut and maim you so casually. In the name of science. Just slice you open and leave you there to bleed inside forever. He wanted to punish them.

And so did I.

JESSE

So I sweet-talked these Wall Street people all through breakfast, telling them how important the medical center was to the city and how we needed their support to raise the fifteen mil that paid for the center's operating expenses.

"I'm not talking about bricks and mortar," I said to them, while we munched low-cholesterol muffins and sipped decaffeinated coffee. "The money pays for the research that the staff does. We're not building any monuments."

One of the women smiled guardedly at me. "I took the trouble to visit your medical center last week. It's certainly not a monument. It's shabby, in fact."

"On the outside," I countered. "The equipment inside is first-class. And so are the people."

"Yes, that's so," she agreed.

They were all in three-piece suits; even the women wore vests and tailored blouses. Grays and darker grays. The real sports among them wore navy blue. I came in a light brown suede jacket and darker corduroy slacks. Turtleneck shirt, so there'd be no problem about wearing a tie.

Arthur was waiting outside in a taxi, just as he said he'd be. I dashed the few feet from the building's doorway to the cab and ducked inside. The wind whistling down Wall Street was cold, driving litter and crumpled sheets of old newspapers through the air. It looked like real spring weather would never get here.

"Hello, Jess," Arthur said as I slammed the taxi door shut. He looked and sounded uptight.

"Hi, Arby."

"Where do you want to go?"

I tapped on the thick glass separating us from the driver. "Mendelssohn Hospital," I yelled.

"*Que?*" the driver hollered back.

I gave him the address in Spanish. He seemed to understand and got the taxi moving.

"I didn't know you spoke Spanish," Arthur said.

I could've grinned and told him there was so goddamned much he didn't know about me. Instead I just shrugged and said, "It helps."

"Yes, I suppose it does."

He just sat there, sunk into his cashmere topcoat, staring at me. I wondered what was going through his head.

"Why'd you want to see me?" I asked.

"How's Julia? You said she's pregnant again?"

"She's fine."

"When's the baby due?"

"Believe it or not, the target date is Christmas Day. It's going to be a boy, sonogram shows."

He didn't crack a smile, didn't say anything, just moved his head a little in what might have been a nod.

"So why do you want to see me? What's going down?"

"Do I need a reason?"

"Arby," I said, "you never do anything without a reason. We both know that. Don't try to pull the old brotherhood routine on me."

"You told Simmonds about our work," he said flatly.

So that was it. "It came up in conversation," I said. Which was the truth. "While we were setting up the rally last summer."

"You told him."

"So what? It wasn't a secret."

I can always tell when Arby's trying to control his temper. His face gets flushed, like he's embarrassed.

"It *was* a secret," he snapped. "At least, it should have been. Do you have any idea of the trouble you've caused? The difficulties we've had to deal with?"

"I heard about the raid on your lab," I said.

"Someone might have been killed."

Before he could get too far up on his high horse, I kidded him. "I heard you got a pair of black eyes out of it."

"Someone might have been killed," he repeated. He wasn't going to be jollied out of his mood.

The cab was inching up Riverside Drive, caught in the usual crush of cars and trucks and buses. The driver seemed perfectly relaxed. The meter was running faster than his speedometer.

"Okay," I said, trying to placate Arthur. "I happened to mention something about your work to Simmonds. Maybe some of his followers are kind of fanatic. Is it my fault they raided your lab?"

"Do you have any idea of how much effort it's taken to handle this problem?"

"Come on, Arby. I own some Omnitech stock, too, remember? I follow it in the *Wall Street Journal*. You're doing okay."

"No thanks to you," he muttered.

I couldn't get sore at him. He was angry enough for the two of us.

"So what do you want to do, Arby? Give me a lecture? I haven't seen Simmonds in almost a year, for chrissakes."

"I'm setting up a court trial."

"You're what?"

He waved one hand in the air. "Not a lawsuit, nothing like that. This is going to be a court of science. We're going to put our work on regeneration on trial, to see if a jury of scientists decides whether it's valid or not."

I felt puzzled. "A trial. By scientists? Why?"

Arby's eyes blazed at me. "Because your Reverend Simmonds is trying to crucify us in the media, that's why! We're going to have a sane, rational, disciplined trial that will involve some of the top scientists in the nation. *That* will provide the backing we need to show the world that our work is valid and should be pursued."

"Okay," I said. "Good for you."

"I want to know which side you'll be on."

"Me? Why should I get involved?"

"Because you helped to originate the idea. And you're my brother. One side or the other will ask you to testify, you can bet on it."

I shook my head. "I don't want to have anything to do with it. You took the ball and ran with it. I haven't done a thing on that subject for more than a year."

"Since you went to Africa," Arthur said.

"You're not going to bring that up again, are you?"

"Julia's really all right?"

"Couldn't be better," I said. And it was the truth. She looked radiant, her tests were all fine, and she hardly even had any morning sickness. It was going to be an easy pregnancy, from all the early indications.

Arthur fell silent. I knew there was more that he wanted to say; I just hoped he figured out how to say it before we got to the hospital. The traffic was easing up a little, now that we'd passed the George Washington Bridge.

A trial. A courtroom trial, about science. Leave it to Arby to come up with something like that. Maybe it wasn't a totally dimwit idea, at that. Get all the big hitters to testify, show the media and the politicians and anybody else who's interested that scientists can grow new organs for you. Might drown out Simmonds and his fundamentalist kooks.

But then I thought, would a trial like that really be fair? I mean, all the scientists will line up together like a battalion of Marines facing the enemy. Would they really bring out their doubts, really cross-examine one another? Not bloody likely, as Julia would say.

We swung off the Drive at long last and threaded through the streets leading to the hospital.

"I want you to come up to the lab," Arthur said all of a sudden. Like he'd been thinking about it for a long time. "I want you to see how far we've gotten."

"Arby, you don't need me—"

"No, I really want you to. If you're going to testify in the trial, at least you ought to see what we've been able to accomplish."

"I'm not going to testify in any trial," I insisted. "For one thing, I'm too damned busy to play games with you."

"Games?" His face went red again.

"And for another," I quickly added, "I'm not involved in this. There's no reason for you to call me to testify."

"The other side will."

"Other side?"

"This is going to be a real trial, Jess. An adversarial procedure. I want to get at the truth. I want people to feel that the decision of the science court is fair and impartial."

"And favorable."

"It will be," he said, "if we stick to the scientific facts."

"So you don't need me."

"But the other side is going to ask you to testify."

"What other side?"

"Our adversaries. Don't think that this is going to be a phony show-business operation. We're going to have to *prove* that our work is valid."

"And who's going to be your adversary?"

He shrugged slightly. "I don't know yet. But there'll be one."

And he expected me to be among them, that was clear.

"Will you come up to the lab and catch up on our progress?" Arby asked me. He was really sincere. He meant it.

"For god's sake, Arby, I'm so damned busy I don't know when I can take a piss, even."

He put on that stubborn superior look of his. "You ought to come up and see what we're doing, Jess. See the real world."

I almost laughed in his face. "The real world? Arby, you wouldn't recognize the real world if it sat on your chest." I pointed to the pathetic people hanging out on the street corners. "*That's* the real world, Arby. Not your nice clean lab. The real world hurts! The real world is poor and sick and more than half crazy. You live in a goddamned ivory tower!"

His nostrils flared like a bull about to charge. But he calmed himself down right away. "Will you come up to the lab or not?" Tight as a WASP at a bar mitzvah.

The taxi pulled up in front of the hospital's main entrance.

"Okay," I said. "I'll come up and look things over. Soon as I get a chance." What sense was there in fighting with him?

He nodded, satisfied.

As I got out of the cab I hoped that at least I had gotten Arby off my back. For a while. But as I hustled up the steps to the entrance, chilled by the wind coming off the Hudson, I thought, Maybe somebody ought to organize a real adversarial position for this trial. It shouldn't be a walk-through for Arby and his Omnitech pals. We ought to take a really close look at what he's doing and see if it actually works the way it should.

ARTHUR

I was getting more and more nervous as we came closer to the opening of the trial.

Max appeared to be recuperating well enough, although the tumor problem still plagued us. I started to wonder if I shouldn't have someone else looking after the chimp instead of Cassie. As if she'd leave his side. But Cassie was looking worse each day. She had always seemed like a sad little waif, but now she looked bedraggled, sick, and weary. She insisted that the enzyme treatment had eliminated her cancer, yet she was losing weight and her eyes looked hollow and black-ringed from lack of sleep.

"I want you to go to the Lahey Clinic for a complete physical," I told her.

She had refused even to come down to my office. I had to go back to Max's pen, back in the storage area where Cassie had set up an austere little cell for herself, next to the chimp's.

"I can't leave him," she said. Her face was gaunt, cheeks hollow, eyes rimmed with red and pouched with dark circles.

Max was sitting quietly in a corner of the pen, behind the bulletproof glass, pushing a few alphabet blocks with his one hand. His left arm was unbandaged. It had grown noticeably; you could see the tiny buds of fingers at the end of it, pink and new-looking. His eye was still bandaged, though.

"I'll arrange for the company helicopter to take you up and back. You'll be back the same day. You can have breakfast and dinner right here."

She started to shake her head.

"Cassie, I'm not asking you. The subject is not open to discussion. Either you go or you're fired."

Her eyes widened for a moment. Then she smiled weakly at me. "You fire me and I'll sue you for it."

I smiled back. "Go ahead and sue. But you'll have to do it from outside the lab. You won't be allowed to see Max at all."

"You wouldn't do that."

"I want you to get a checkup, Cassie. I want you to take care of yourself as well as you take care of Max, here."

Very reluctantly, she said, "Only one day?"

"One day. And afterward you've got to do what they tell you. I don't think you're eating right and I'm certain you're not sleeping well."

Her smile came back. "Yes, Daddy Arthur."

I got Phyllis to set it all up and before the end of the week the company chopper had landed in our parking lot and whisked Cassie off to Boston for the day. That gave Zack and his team a chance to examine Max thoroughly, without Cassie getting in their way.

"The eye isn't working out," Zack told me gloomily that evening.

He and Darrell and Vince had gathered in my office.

"What's wrong?" I asked.

Zack shook his head. "I don't know. It's not regenerating. It's just a jumble of tumors in the socket. A real mess."

Darrell said, "Maybe it was too much trauma for his body

to handle at once. Maybe we should've done the arm first and then the eye."

Zack nodded unhappily. Vince muttered, "Helluva time to think of that now."

All three of them were down. I tried to bring the problem into perspective a little. "Well, the arm's coming along, isn't it?"

They agreed that it was.

"That's the important thing," I said. "We just overreached ourselves with the eye."

Darrell ran a hand across his long jaw. "I suppose it's not really that important. If we're aiming at rejuvenating people, that is. Old age doesn't affect the eyes in ways that can't be handled conventionally."

"Cataracts can be taken care of surgically," Zack said.

Vince added, "They use laser surgery to bring your vision back to twenty-twenty. Instead of eyeglasses."

"Yeah, I see ads on TV for that," said Darrell. "The important thing is regrowing internal organs, not eyeballs. We don't need eyeballs."

"Limbs," Vince said.

They were whistling past the graveyard, I knew. Convincing themselves that the failure with Max's eye wasn't crucial, wouldn't stop our progress.

"Maybe we should put his original eye back in," Zack suggested. "Clean out the tumors before they get any worse and give him his eye back."

Darrell raised his brows questioningly.

"Let's wait another week or so," I said. "Give it a little more time."

We might be able to replace Max's eye, but reconnecting it so that he could see was a different story. I thought about how the news reporters would react to a chimp with a regrown arm but a blind eye. Max's usefulness with the media was finished, I knew. But I didn't say anything to them. That wasn't their problem, it was mine.

And Pat Hayward's.

More and more I was having my discussions with Pat over

dinner. There just didn't seem to be enough hours in the day to talk about PR problems, especially since I'd started shuttling down to Washington almost every week to set up the science court. So Pat and I usually met at the end of the day and drove out to one of the local restaurants. In our separate cars.

I explained about Max.

"You're right," Pat said. "The media would go into a feeding frenzy once they found out that you had deliberately taken his eye and it won't grow back."

"It will eventually," I heard myself say. It sounded awfully defensive, as if I were trying to absolve myself.

"Really?"

"I think so. Once his arm is fully regrown I think we can go back and do the eye successfully."

The restaurant was small and not terribly good. But it was quiet and nearly empty. We could sit at our table and talk without interruption; the owner and the two waiters knew how well I tipped and would have happily let us stay all night, if we wanted to. The owner had even bought a case of Tavel for me: "Dr. Marshak's special selection," he called it.

Pat took a sip of the wine, then asked me, "What about the tumors? Cassie's afraid they're going to kill Max."

That shocked me. "She told you that?"

"Yes."

"When did you . . . ?"

Pat grinned at me. "Arthur, you're not my only source of information. If I'm going to be useful to you, I've got to know what's going on in the lab. I don't sit at my word processor all day. I go out and talk to people."

I hadn't even thought about what Pat did when she wasn't in my sight.

"Do you have any idea of how tricky it's been to keep the reporters away from Max?"

"They want to see him?"

"Of course they do! They don't know about the surgery, they just remember that they got better footage out of Max than any of the humans they photographed."

"And they still want to see him."

"Whenever they come to the lab. They all ask to see Max. I tell them he's been quarantined; that seems to satisfy them."

"Good," I said, realizing for the first time that Pat had become invaluable to me. She was smart and resourceful. And loyal. That was important.

I must have been staring at her across the restaurant table. She was really good-looking, especially with the candle glow throwing highlights on her red hair.

Don't get involved with your employees, I warned myself.

She's only a consultant, I argued.

Same thing. You're her boss, her source of income. If she lets you come on to her, how do you know what her reasons are? If she doesn't, you're looking at a sexual harassment situation.

Well, I told myself, as soon as this trial is over I'm going to drop her as a consultant. Then we'll see what we've got going between us. If anything.

Pat seemed to understand what was running through my mind. Her smile seemed to turn a little sad.

"Arthur," she said softly, "someday, when this is all over and I'm freelancing again, you'll have to come up to my house in Old Saybrook and meet my mother."

"I'd like that," I said.

"No, you wouldn't," Pat answered, very seriously. "But she's the acid test. If you can stand her, then maybe there's a future to our relationship."

How did we get on the subject of relationships? It must have been mental telepathy.

"For now, though," Pat went on, "we ought to keep it strictly business."

I realized it had been months since I'd gotten laid. But I nodded and said, "For now."

And then we went back to the thorny problem of how we could use Max's arm to our benefit without showing his missing eye. We were forced to the decision that Max's days as a media darling were finished, unless and until we could regrow his eye.

I was less optimistic than I had let on with Pat. The tumors weren't succumbing to Cassie's enzyme treatment, they were getting into his brain. I was terribly afraid that they would kill Max even before his arm had completely regrown.

And what effect would that have on the trial?

CASSIE IANETTA

It wasn't murder. It was a mercy killing. I mean, they let doctors get away with "assisted suicide," so why shouldn't I put poor Max out of his misery?

The tumors were eating up his brain. Max didn't recognize me anymore. He just sat in his pen like a hopeless lump. He'd look at me with his one eye but he wouldn't show any sign of recognition.

I'd call to him and he wouldn't respond. I think he even forgot sign language, the tumors must've incapacitated that part of his brain.

And I couldn't go into his pen anymore. That was the worst shock of all. The night I came back from my visit to the Lahey Clinic up in Boston, I went straight to Max's room and opened the door in the Plexiglas wall and Max shrieked and ran away from me!

"It's me, Max," I said, keeping my voice soft and soothing. "It's all right. See, it's Cassie."

But Max cowered in the corner, covering his face with his one good arm.

"What did they do to you?" I asked him. He looked just the same as he had that morning, when I'd left on the helicopter. But Zack and the rest of them had had Max all to themselves for the whole day.

"What did they do, Max?" I asked again, hunching down and sort of duckwalking to be near him.

Max flailed out with his one arm and knocked me over

backward. Then he raced for the door in the Plexiglas wall. I had shut it, but hadn't bothered to lock it. Max knew how to use the door handle, but he fumbled with it and then gave up.

He whirled back at me, teeth bared, snarling at me. For the first time in my life I was scared of Max.

I backed into a corner and sat quietly, knees pulled up to my chin, avoiding direct eye contact. I could hear my heart racing. Where were the handlers? Couldn't they hear Max's screaming? Why didn't they come?

Max seemed to calm down a little. He edged slowly to the corner where he'd been when I first came into the pen. He kept watching me, though, so I didn't move. I hardly breathed. But my mind was spinning. Max, oh, Max, I thought. They've destroyed you and I let them do it. It hurt. All the way down inside me it hurt in a way that the cancer never did. It hurt the way Bill had hurt me. They had all betrayed me, even Max now, though it wasn't really his fault.

So we just sat there for hours, me in my corner, Max in his. Neither one of us moving. Finally Max stretched out on one side and closed his eye. I still didn't move. I waited and waited until he was breathing deep and regular, sound asleep. Even then I was afraid to stir, afraid that he'd wake up if I budged an inch and come at me with those ripping fangs and his powerful arm.

I must have dozed now and then, my head on my knees. My back ached, my legs tingled, but I didn't move. If they found that Max attacked me they'd destroy him. They'd shoot him like he was a wild animal when in truth they were the animals, the beasts. They had killed Max with their damned lies.

That was when I realized that Max was already as good as dead. He had nothing to look forward to now except pain and fear. The tumors would continue to grow, eat into his brain, destroy him. His body might remain but Max himself was already half gone. Why should I let him go on suffering like that? Why shouldn't I help him to escape all this pain and humiliation?

Then a new thought struck me. If Max dies now they'll never be able to say that they regenerated his arm. They'll have to admit that they failed. They're only keeping him alive long enough for the arm to regrow, I knew. Once they can show that, once they can take pictures and make all the tests and measurements and put it all in their reports, then they'll murder Max anyway so they can dissect him and see what went wrong with his eye.

I can stop them! I can beat them!

By the time the handler came to clean Max's pen and give him breakfast, every part of my body ached horribly. But I was smiling to myself.

"What the hell . . . ?"

The kid looked shocked to see me in there. Max woke up the instant he opened the door, and scrambled to his feet. But he didn't try to attack me or the handler; he didn't try to get out of the pen.

"I'm all right," I said, getting up slowly. Every muscle in me groaned as I slowly climbed to my feet, leaning heavily against the wall.

"You spent the night in here?"

I just nodded.

"All night?"

My legs were numb; it took a real effort to walk.

"Jeez." The kid grinned at me. "Does that mean you two are engaged?"

He started to laugh and I slapped his face. Max jumped back a little, frightened. I stumbled out of the pen, leaving the kid standing there with my finger marks white against his flushed red cheek.

THE WORD went through the lab like wildfire, of course. Cassie spent the night with Max. The two of them slept together in the chimp's pen. If it's a boy they'll name it Arthur. That kind of thing. They didn't say a word in front of me, of course, but I could hear them all snickering behind my back.

Arthur summoned me into his office almost as soon as he arrived that morning.

"What happened?" He wasn't laughing. He was completely serious.

"What did they do to Max while my back was turned?" I asked.

"Nothing that hasn't been done while you've been with him. Routine tests, that's all."

It was a lie, a damned lie. I knew it. Arthur could sit there behind his nice big desk and smile at me, all sincerity and polish, but I knew he was lying through his handsome teeth.

"Max didn't recognize me," I said. "He got terribly upset when I went to see him."

"Did he attack you?"

It was my turn to lie. "Do I look like he attacked me? He could've sliced me to ribbons if he'd wanted to." I didn't mention the ache in my ribs from where he'd hit me. I'd be bruised and sore for weeks, I knew.

"But he didn't recognize you," Arthur said.

"The tumors are destroying his brain functions."

"But you're all right."

"I'm fine."

"Good. I was worried."

Another lie. All he was worried about was the possibility that Max might have to be destroyed before the arm grew all the way back.

I spent most of the morning at the computer in my office, writing a long letter to the Reverend Roy Averill Simmonds. It took me even longer to find his address; half the afternoon on the telephone tracking down various organizations that had dealt with him. I finally telephoned Arthur's brother at Mendelssohn Hospital and got one of the secretaries there to give me his mailing address. It was in Wichita.

"That's where they send the donations," she told me. "Must be his home base."

"Or his bank," I said.

"They always have their offices close to their banks, honey."

That made sense, I supposed. So I sent my letter there. It was a complete report on what they'd done to Max, in nontechnical language. Five pages long. If Reverend Simmonds wanted to publicize how godless scientists were being cruel to animals, let him show the world what they'd done to Max. I even included two of the DVDs I'd been making over the past few weeks.

It was almost five o'clock when I slipped my package into the pile in the outgoing bin at the mailroom door. I had to hurry down to the pharmaceutical storeroom. Like the rest of the lab's service departments, it closed at five. The scientists might keep going all night long, but the support offices kept nine-to-five hours, unless somebody made special provisions to keep them open longer.

I had access to any of the drugs on stock, and plenty of times I had sent the lab's purchasing people scurrying after really exotic stuff. But for this task, all I needed was a bottle of tranquilizers. I already had enough cyanide.

Tears blurred my vision as I ground the tranquilizer capsules into Max's food, a paste of bananas and sugar that he always loved. Long after he had finished his regular dinner, I brought the stainless steel bowl to his pen.

The same kid I had smacked that morning was coming out of the cell as I walked down the hallway.

"I already gave him his dinner," he said guardedly.

His face was unmarked. I hadn't hit him that hard. Nowhere near as hard as Max had hit my ribs. Nowhere near as hard as he deserved.

"I'm giving him an extra treat," I said, struggling to keep my voice from trembling.

He started to grin, then thought better of it. "Uh-huh," was all he said.

"I'll stay with him tonight," I said. "You don't have to worry about him."

I could see that he was aching to make a wisecrack. But he restrained himself, probably afraid I'd bean him with Max's metal food bowl.

Still, he asked, "Uh, you're not goin' to stay inside again, are you?"

"No," I said, forcing a smile. "That was an accident. I'll keep an eye on him from outside his pen."

He nodded and walked off, probably dying to spread the word that Cassie was going to spend another night with her boyfriend.

Max watched me as I opened the food slot in the Plexiglas wall and slid the bowl inside. For long minutes he didn't move and I thought, If he doesn't take the drugged food he'll keep on living this miserable painful existence.

"It's your favorite, Max," I coaxed him gently. "You always loved it."

I was already speaking to him in the past tense.

After a long while he shuffled over to the bowl and sniffed it. Then he stuck a finger into the glop and tasted it. He looked up at me, his one brown eye showing none of the joy or excitement that he would've shown a few weeks earlier. None of the personality.

He's not Max anymore, I said to myself. Max is already gone. I wanted to cry, but I couldn't afford that luxury. Not yet.

I went to my room, next door, and got the camcorder so I could video Max's last moments.

He had dragged the bowl back to a far corner, squatted in front of it, and begun to dig his hand into it, clutching the bowl with his two feet. I videoed Max as he licked his fingers, just like a human child would, and then raised the bowl to his lips and licked it clean. It was hard to focus through the viewfinder, my eyes kept blurring with tears.

I kept recording, glancing at my wristwatch now and then to see how much time was elapsing. The dose took effect, finally. Max lay down on his back and fell deeply asleep.

I had to work fast. I ran back to Zack O'Neill's lab and rummaged through several of the drawers in his lab benches until I found his supply of hypodermic syringes. I took the biggest one he had. Let the instrument of death be his, I told myself. He's killed Max figuratively, it's only right that he bears the blame for the truth.

When I got back to Max's pen, he was still sleeping on his back like a big hairy baby. I closed the door to the room so no one could see me from outside. Then I opened the Plexiglas door and slipped into Max's pen, the syringe still hidden in the waistband of my jeans. Poor Max never stirred; the tranquilizers had done their job.

I took out the syringe and quickly pushed the needle straight into his heart. The syringe was empty, of course, except for air. Air bubbles would fill up his heart and prevent it from pumping blood. That would kill him.

Max twitched slightly as I pushed the syringe's plunger. I took the needle out of him, refilled the syringe with air, and stuck him again. I thought I saw his eyelid flutter, but I couldn't be sure. Otherwise he didn't move.

I left him lying there and went out to the trash bay by the loading dock in the back of the building and threw the hypo into the medical waste bin. By the time I got back to Max he was dead. He was lying exactly as I'd left him, but I couldn't see his chest moving. He wasn't breathing.

I had to wipe my eyes again. Then I went inside the pen and checked his pulse several times and finally worked up the nerve to peel his eyelid back. No response from the pupil. Max was dead.

I forced myself to stay calm. This was no time to dissolve into crying. Later. I would mourn for Max later. I went from Max's cell to my own room, down the corridor from his. I started thinking that Arthur would want an autopsy done on Max to see what killed him. It'd look superficially like a coronary, but if they did a chemical workup on his blood they'd find that he was full of tranquilizers.

I had to fight back the tears that wanted to flood through me. I had to think straight. Okay, Max is dead. He's safe now, there's nothing they can do to him anymore. I popped the video disk out of the camcorder and handwrote another letter to Reverend Simmonds. I didn't mention the cyanide in my letter; kind of foolish because here I am talking about it into this voice recorder.

I'm going to take out this audiocassette and put it in with the letter and the DVD that I've already addressed to Reverend Simmonds. Seal it and stamp it and take it down to the mailroom. Stuff it in under the pile of outgoing mail that's already in the bin, so it won't be noticed or stopped.

Then the cyanide. It hits quick; there'll be no chance of reviving me.

I wonder if Bill will ever find out what I've done. I wonder if he'll ever realize that he's one of Max's murderers. And mine, too.

THE TRIAL:
DAY FOUR, AFTERNOON

Pat had been wrong, Arthur saw. The hearing chamber was overflowing with reporters, all here to watch Cassie's disks. Someone must have tipped them off. The reporters' table was filled for the first time since the opening day and more media people lined the sides of the room. A third camera crew had set up during lunch. And Senator Kindelberger was back.

A fifty-two-inch projection-screen television set had been installed against the wall opposite the jury. Arthur could feel his insides clenching. This is going to be a circus, he told himself.

Rosen looked strangely pained as he sat at his place at the end of the row of desks in the front of the hearing room. He rose slowly to his feet and faced the jury, turning his back to Arthur.

"Several times during the course of this trial," the examiner said, "Dr. Marshak has objected to various questions or testimonies because they were not strictly on the narrow issue of scientific fact."

Arthur noticed that the reporters were focused on Rosen like hunting hounds who have sensed their prey.

"The videos you are about to see are highly emotional in their content, yet they are also highly relevant to these proceedings." Rosen turned to face Arthur. "Dr. Marshak himself introduced evidence from the animals on which his researchers experimented. These DVDs show the results of their experiments on a chimpanzee."

The examiner stood in silence for a long moment, then walked slowly back to his desk. Before sitting, though, he added, "Both the chimpanzee and the woman who made these DVDs are dead."

The jury stirred visibly and Arthur could hear a sigh, a murmur, sweep through the audience behind him. Then total silence, absolute stillness, as everyone waited for the TV to come to life.

Cassie's sallow, sorrowful face filled the big screen.

"My name is Catherine Ianetta. I am a principal research scientist at Grenford Laboratory. I'm making this video on my own, without the knowledge or assistance of anyone else."

Cassie did not quite have the forlorn look that Arthur knew so well. She looked gaunt, true enough, and there were black rings under her eyes. But those eyes burned with an inner fury. Her face was set in the expression of an avenging angel.

Cassie began a halting explanation of the lab's work on the regeneration program. Arthur watched her become tenser and tighter with each word. And he saw Senator Kindelberger leaning intently forward to hear Cassie's faltering voice, big rawboned hands clasped on the desk in front of him, his pale gray eyes roaming the hearing chamber while his face never moved. Neat trick, Arthur thought. Unless you watch him closely you get the impression he's totally absorbed in Cassie's testimony, when actually he's looking around for somebody. I wonder who.

Jesse was back in the chamber, too, sitting at his spot in the front row of benches, across the room from Arthur. He looked troubled. Not upset, actually, but not his usual relaxed smiling self, either.

"The laboratory director, Dr. Arthur Marshak, decided that the regeneration work needed a chimpanzee experiment," Cassie said, still staring straight into the camera. "This was Maximilian, the chimpanzee that they used."

Cassie had spliced in a few minutes of earlier footage she had taken of Max; it looked like home movies of herself and the chimp. As the screen showed Max cavorting across the jungle gym or scampering up his trees, Cassie spoke gravely: "Max was raised from infancy at Grenford Laboratories."

The screen showed Max and one of the handlers conversing in sign language.

Cassie, her voice beginning to tremble, explained, "Max had been taught American Sign Language, and could express himself quite well. He possessed a high degree of intelligence—and . . . a personality . . ." Her voice faltered, then came back to say, "He was almost like a human baby."

Arthur closed his eyes. *She might as well put a gun to my head and pull the trigger. She's trying to kill me.* Yet he could feel no anger for Cassie, not even a sense of betrayal. He simply felt sorry for her, and for himself for allowing her to put him into this position.

While the TV screen showed Max cheerfully peeling a banana, his lips pulled back in a big sloppy grin, Cassie's trembling voice said, "Max was used as an experimental subject for the regeneration program."

Suddenly the screen showed Max sitting sorrowfully in his pen, his left arm nothing but a stump, his right eye bandaged. The audience gasped. Even the jury seemed shaken.

"They've removed most of his left arm," Cassie said needlessly. "And his right eye in its entirety."

Max just sat there, forlorn. Arthur could almost feel the chimp's pain and bewilderment.

"They did this," Cassie said, in a little girl's tearful voice, "while I was out of the country and unable to protect Max."

Her voice obviously choking with tears, Cassie went on, "They wanted to see how the regentide would work on a chimpanzee. If it was successful, then they could go on to human trials."

The video ended with Max looking pitiful, hunched in a corner of his pen, obviously depressed, melancholy, pathetic. The audience buzzed with whispers as a clerk removed the first disk and put another one into the DVD player. Arthur could see that Max's arm was unbandaged now and the buds of new growth showed pink and hairless at the end of his stump. But that was not what the others were whispering about, he knew.

While the screen showed Max listless and dejected, Cassie explained that the Grenford experimenters had injected the chimp with an antitumor agent. Arthur noticed that she never mentioned that she had been the prime researcher who had developed the antitumor treatment.

"The treatment seemed to inhibit the tumors in Max's arm," she said, "but the ones in his eye socket continued to grow . . . along the optic nerve and into the forebrain."

Cassie stopped speaking. The screen showed different shots of Max sitting sadly in his pen. Arthur thought he could hear someone sobbing quietly in the audience behind him. The disk seemed to go on for hours. Finally it ended and the clerk put in the final DVD.

They saw Max stretched out on his back. It was impossible to tell if he was breathing or not because the camera was shaking so badly.

Suddenly Cassie's voice burst out, "They killed him! They killed Max! Arthur Marshak is the killer. He's a murderer! He killed my Max and he's killed me, too!"

The TV screen broke into a hissing, flickering jumble, then went black. Arthur felt all the eyes in the hearing chamber staring at him. And inside, he felt a cold fury. No, he answered Cassie silently. I didn't kill Max, you did. I could have saved him, but you made certain I'd never get that chance.

Graves banged his gavel and adjourned the session. Arthur hardly noticed until people started to get up and walk out of the chamber. The reporters converged on him, firing questions, while cameras flashed like an artillery barrage.

Arthur shook his head and held his hands up defensively. "I've got nothing to say—except that I feel terrible that Cassie was so emotionally unbalanced that she committed suicide."

"She says it was your fault," two of the reporters snapped in unison.

"She was obviously unbalanced," Arthur said, trying to

stay calm, seeing Pat off at the edge of the pack nodding encouragement to him.

"Do you feel responsible for her death?"

Arthur almost replied to the question. But a glance at Pat's face told him to duck it. "Look," he said, "we're supposed to be conducting a trial here, under strict rules of evidence. The other side has bent those rules almost completely out of shape, but I'm going to try to stick to them. I'll make my statement before the judges when my turn comes."

Past the crowd of reporters Arthur noticed Jesse getting slowly to his feet, looking grim. A messenger fought his way through the departing crowd to hand Jesse a note. Jesse scanned it, and his face went white. He crumpled the message and dropped it on the floor as he bolted up the aisle and through the crowd, pushing his way to the door with almost manic energy.

The reporters were still goading Arthur with questions, but he forced a smile and said, "That's all for now. I'll make my statement when the court reconvenes."

Reluctantly the reporters put their cameras and voice recorders away and left the hearing room. Pat Hayward struggled past them to get to his side. Arthur started up the emptying aisle, bent down to pick up the crumpled note his brother had discarded. It read:

I need you right away. Julia.

JULIA

Suddenly it didn't matter what Jesse was doing in Washington or how important this trial was to Arthur. I had to have my husband here with me. I simply didn't know what else to do. The second blood test was positive; my baby would be born with spina bifida, a hopeless cripple.

I hadn't mentioned my terrible fear to Jesse before; he'd

been so tied up with preparations for the hearings that I simply couldn't burden him with inconclusive test results. He would have dropped everything else to be with me. I didn't want that. After all, the first blood test wasn't absolute proof that the baby would be disabled.

I had undergone an amniocentesis test earlier, and when the obstetrician told me worriedly that she would like to take a tissue sample I hesitated.

"Why?" I asked. "Is something wrong?"

She was a gray-haired woman who had my complete confidence. Up until that moment. She never put a desk between herself and me; I always sat in the armchair in her cozy little office and she sat on the rocker next to me.

"The amniocentesis test doesn't necessarily detect everything," she said. "A tissue sample would give us much more information."

"About what?"

She spread her hands. "I don't want to alarm you, but we should make very certain that the fetus has no physical defects, now, while an abortion would be simple and relatively free of risk."

"Abortion?" I felt my pulse rate leap. "What's wrong? What have you found?"

"Nothing definite, but . . ."

"But what, for god's sake?" Her evasiveness was maddening.

"There may be a problem, and if there is, we ought to catch it while there's still time."

"What *kind* of a problem?"

She took a deep breath. "At best, nothing but an unusual ratio of blood factors that can easily be corrected. At worst—well, it could be spina bifida."

"I've heard of that."

"It's called open spine," she said. "The baby would be unable to walk, unable to stand. Often there are problems with the legs and bladder, as well."

Her stuffy little office began to swim. I felt dizzy, faint. No!

I railed at myself. You are *not* going to faint. You are going to face this thing and deal with it sensibly. We are talking about life and death here; you can't hide behind tears.

"That's the worst possibility," the obstetrician said. "It's probably nothing so severe as that."

"I see."

"That's why a tissue sample is necessary."

I was still trying to pull myself together. I heard myself asking questions, making comments, as if it were someone else speaking, as if I were watching these two women converse from somewhere far away.

Finally, I said, "You recall that I had a miscarriage earlier."

"Yes."

"Wouldn't this tissue sample you want be an invasive procedure? Would it increase the risk of another miscarriage?"

"Only slightly."

"Then I don't think I want to do it."

"But—"

"I don't want to risk another miscarriage."

She tried to smile reassuringly. "Your earlier miscarriage was the result of an infection. It won't happen again."

"Not for that reason."

She nodded.

"I still don't think I want to increase the risk of another miscarriage." Oh, I was so firm and logical!

"But the risk is minimal."

"Still."

The doctor looked disappointed.

"Isn't there some other test that doesn't have to poke around inside me?"

"Alpha-fetoprotein," she murmured.

"Alpha what?"

"It's a blood test. Completely noninvasive, as far as your pregnancy is concerned. We draw a blood sample from your arm."

"And that can tell if . . ." I couldn't speak the words.

"It's not as good as a tissue sample, but it should give us the information we need."

"Well, then," I said, full of a courage I did not truly feel, "let's do the blood test."

Except that this test was inconclusive. It took two weeks for the laboratory to mail the results back to my obstetrician and the results were so uncertain that we had to do it all over again.

"I'll get them to express-mail the results this time," the doctor said. It was getting late; I was already in my fourth month.

There was no doubt about it this time. Spina bifida. I was carrying a child who would be crippled all his life.

Jesse was in Washington when the phone call came. I simply couldn't bear it alone; I had to call him, had to ask him to come home to me.

It was late in the afternoon when he phoned.

"I got your message. What's the matter? Are you all right?"

How much should I tell him on the telephone? "Jesse, can you come home?"

"Now?"

"Right now. Tonight."

"What is it? Are you all right?" His voice went up half an octave.

"I'm fine, dear, but there's a problem with the baby. Please—I can't talk about it on the phone. I need you here with me."

He did not hesitate an instant. "I'll get the shuttle. I'll call you from Reagan Airport before I take off and from La Guardia when I land."

"Thank you, dear."

"It'll only take a couple of hours. You sit there. Don't worry about a thing, I'll be with you in a couple of hours."

"Wonderful."

He was as good as his word, although it was more like three hours before he burst into our apartment, jacket slung over his shoulder, shirt sweaty, eyes fearful. I ran to him and he folded me into his arms and held me for a long, safe, silent moment.

Then we went to the sofa and sat together and I told him, as calmly as I could.

"Spina bifida?" His voice was hollow, aching.

"Dr. Fieldman recommends an abortion," I said, trying to stay calm.

He looked into my eyes and I could see the agony in his. "Is that what you want?"

I said, "I don't know." Which was almost a lie. I knew what I wanted, but I didn't know what Jesse wanted and it had to be his decision as much as mine. But if I told him what I wanted he would automatically say he wanted that, too, because he loved me and would do whatever I wanted in this. This wasn't a decision I could make for myself; I loved Jesse too much to do it that way. And there was a third party to the decision, as well.

"The boy would be crippled from birth," Jesse muttered. "Spina bifida cases usually die before they're thirty unless you make extraordinary efforts to keep them going."

"Isn't spina bifida something like paraplegia?" The words just popped out of my mouth and suddenly I knew what had held me together since the doctor told me of the test results, the hope that had been so deep inside me that I didn't even recognize it until that instant.

Jesse gave me a strange look, pained, almost angry. "You think Arby will be able to save the kid? Make him normal?"

"Would that be possible?"

He looked away from me. "Maybe in twenty years, if they ever figure out how to regrow tissue without killing the patient first."

"Then there's *some* hope, at least."

I could see him struggling with himself. Then he took my hands in his, gently. "Julia, I wish I could say that it's true, that Arby or somebody could wave a magic wand and cure the baby and make his spine strong so he could walk."

"But you don't see it," I finished for him.

With a shake of his head, "Not for a long time, honey. So long that our baby would probably be dead."

"I can't have an abortion," I heard myself whisper.

"What?"

"I can't do it. I can't kill him."

"But—"

"He's alive, Jesse! I can feel him stirring inside me. He's alive and I can't kill him."

"He'll be a helpless cripple all his life. Is that what you want, to take care of a kid who can't even sit up? Who'll never be able to control his bowels? Who'll probably be mentally retarded, as well?"

He was shouting. I flinched and pulled my hands away from him.

Jesse instantly realized that he had let his temper show and he was instantly apologetic.

"Oh, god, I'm sorry, honey. I didn't mean to yell at you. It's just such a goddamned shock." His head sank to his chest.

I put my arms around him and we cried together for a long time, just sat there on our sofa bawling our hearts out, crying for the healthy baby that we would never have, sobbing for the son we had both hoped so much for.

But even as I cried I told myself that I would have to face the facts. I was going to raise a deformed baby. That was that. I could no more abort my baby than I could deliberately murder someone.

WASHINGTON, D.C.:

EVENING

Even though she was on a consultant's expense account, Pat Hayward stayed at the relatively inexpensive downtown Holiday Inn rather than the posh Jefferson Hotel, where Arthur was residing. There was more than frugality involved in her choice; she feared that if they were both in the same hotel sooner or later he would make a move on her, and she did not want to face making a decision about whether or not she would go to bed with him.

Maybe I'm fantasizing, she told herself. He hadn't come on to her at all. Far from it. As far as Pat could tell, Arthur seemed totally wrapped up in the trial. Romance, even a casual sexual encounter, was not on his agenda. She felt relieved and disappointed at the same time.

Yet she enjoyed his company. Even while she was reminding herself that it was foolish—no, stupid—to have fantasies about sleeping with the boss, she realized that she greatly enjoyed being with this handsome, urbane, complex man. And she certainly appreciated the elegant, expensive restaurants that he seemed to take for granted.

But today was different. Arthur looked shaken and grim after Cassie's videos. He had hardly said a word to her when they had left the hearing room. Arthur had simply led her out a back exit of the building, hailed a taxi, and brought Pat to the bar at the Jefferson, where they had downed several drinks in almost total silence before meandering into the plush, genteelly quiet dining room.

"Were you able to get a copy of Potter's paper?" Pat asked, to break the ice.

Arthur looked surprised. He was still brooding over Cassie's testimony, she thought.

"Professor Potter," Pat reminded him. "You said you'd have to read his paper before you cross-examine him."

He nodded. "Phyllis said she'd e-mail it to me. It's probably in among my cell phone text messages."

The waiter brought their menus, big oversized things in imitation leather bindings.

"Will one day be enough for all your cross-examinations?" Pat asked.

He shrugged. "I imagine Graves will call for a Saturday session if he has to. Or go into next week."

Finally she worked up the nerve to ask, "What do you want to do about Cassie's videos?"

Without glancing up from the jumbo menu, Arthur said, "Not a damned thing. There's nothing we can do."

"I thought not," said Pat. "She's done enough damage already, hasn't she?"

Tiredly, he replied, "I suppose she has, as far as the media are concerned."

"I'm dreading the eleven o'clock news."

"That's not important."

"It's not?"

The waiter approached their table and they ordered: striped bass for Pat, lamb chops for Arthur.

"Would you care to have wine with your dinner?" the waiter asked. He was a youngster, probably a local student trying to earn his tuition, Arthur thought.

"I'm red and you're white," he said to Pat.

"Tavel?" Pat suggested.

Arthur was pleased that she remembered. He asked for a Tavel. The waiter looked troubled and said he'd have to check to see if they had any.

"If not, then a glass of burgundy for me and a chardonnay for the lady."

Looking much relieved, the waiter hurried from their table.

The table was small and oval, niched into a curving high banquette upholstered in pastel, patterned moire. Similar banquettes lined the restaurant's walls like elegant hideaways where couples could dine and whisper secrets to one another.

Pat did not whisper, but she leaned toward Arthur and kept her voice low. "What do you mean, the media coverage of Cassie's testimony isn't important?"

"Not to the outcome of the trial, it isn't," Arthur replied. "The jury is looking at the scientific evidence, not the emotional state of the witnesses."

"But Cassie's testimony claims that Max died from the tumors."

"I'll show that we understand now that we induced too much trauma for Max's system to handle all at the same time, even with the tumor-suppressant treatment."

"So their conclusion will be that the regentide killed him."

Arthur suppressed a momentary flare of anger. "Max died of a heart attack. His blood was loaded with tranquilizers when we found the two of them like Romeo and Juliet in the last act of the play."

Pat hadn't heard that before. She didn't know which shocked her more, the idea that Cassie might have murdered Max before she committed suicide, or the idea that Arthur had kept that information from her.

Arthur saw the stunned look on her face. "There's no sense attacking Cassie posthumously. She killed Max, I'm fairly sure of that."

"And you never told me."

"You're only the fourth person to know. Darrell, the pathologist who did the autopsy, and me. Five, I suppose, if you count the lab technician who did the workup on Max's blood sample."

She didn't have to ask her next question. Arthur went right ahead, "I didn't want the story known. So I kept it as tight as I could. The best way to keep it quiet was not to tell anyone. It's the kind of publicity the lab doesn't need."

Pat felt more hurt than angry. "Couldn't you trust me to keep a lid on the story?"

"It wasn't a matter of trust. I didn't want to put you in the position of trying to cover up to the media. I didn't want to force you to lie to them."

"I see."

"That's why I don't want to respond to Cassie's video. I don't want to take any chances that it might leak out that she deliberately killed Max."

"But why not? You can defend yourself from—"

Impatiently, Arthur interrupted, "It's bad enough that Cassie committed suicide. Can you imagine the headlines if they find out she murdered Max, too? Scientist kills chimp, then herself?"

"Arthur, the media's going to have a field day with those disks! They'll be on everything from Larry King to *60 Minutes*. Don't you think it'll all come out sooner or later?"

"Not if we keep our cool."

Pat sighed wearily. "You don't know how persistent they can be. They'll hound you wherever you go."

Arthur shook his head.

"Believe it. Cassie's going to be on the tube more than

Oprah Winfrey, you'll see. The trial's become irrelevant, Arthur. You've been branded a killer."

He started to reply, but found that he had nothing to say. An icy cold gripped him. *Good god, maybe she's right. Maybe I should tell them how Max died. But what good would it do? It would just make things worse.*

The waiter arrived with their salads. And two glasses of wine, one white, one red.

Arthur picked up a fork, then put it down again. He had no appetite at all.

"The trial is not irrelevant," he insisted, more to convince himself than Pat. "And it's based on the *scientific* evidence and nothing else. The jury is composed of scientists, not people who read the *National Enquirer.*"

"They're human beings," Pat said. "And Cassie's going to be all over the *Washington Post* tomorrow morning."

Arthur pushed his salad away.

By the time they had finished picking at their entrées, Pat felt miserable with guilt. "I've ruined your dinner," she said.

Arthur forced a smile. "I notice you haven't done your own much good, either."

He called for the check and they left the restaurant. Without a word passing between them, Arthur led Pat to the elevators and took her up to his suite. He clicked on the TV set in the sitting room as Pat took in the accommodations with a swift glance: spacious, luxurious carpeting, tastefully furnished, bedroom through that door, a separate lavatory for the sitting room.

Arthur went straight to the phone; its message light was blinking red. He tapped the button for the built-in answering machine.

"Dr. Marshak? This is Ron Cohan of the *Washington Times.* I'm doing the story on today's testimony and I need to get your reaction—"

Arthur stabbed at the fast-forward button. The next message was from ABC News. Arthur kept hitting the button; there were nine messages, all of them from reporters who wanted his reaction to Cassie's testimony.

"I imagine they're also trying to reach you," he said to Pat grimly.

"Yes, I imagine they are."

Pat was supposed to deal with the reporters, screening Arthur from their urgent demands. No one was supposed to know where he was staying, but nine enterprising news reporters had tracked him to the Jefferson. God knows how many others are trying to reach Pat, he thought.

She excused herself and went to the toilet. Through the closed door she could hear him surfing through the TV channels, settling finally on CNN.

By the time she came out, Arthur was slumped on the sofa, jacket hanging from the bedroom door's knob, tie pulled loose. Pat took the easy chair next to the sofa; it rocked as she sat in it, startling her.

Better be careful, she told herself. This chair isn't the only thing here that's unsteady.

As the half hour approached, CNN did a brief story on the day's session, showing Cassie's blubbering testimony and the footage of Max. Then Cassie screaming, "Arthur Marshak is the killer. He's a murderer! He killed my Max and he's killed me, too!"

Arthur saw his own face on the screen, jaw clenched tight, eyes blazing unconcealed fury. He hadn't realized the TV cameras in the hearing room had been turned on him. His teeth clamped down so hard that his entire skull hurt.

Then the screen showed the commentator behind her antiseptic desk again. She said tonelessly, "The late Catherine Ianetta's shocking revelations will be the subject of the next *Larry King Live,* tomorrow at nine p.m. Eastern and Pacific time."

He turned off the TV and turned to Pat. She looked as miserable as he felt.

"But it doesn't matter," Arthur said stubbornly. "The jury has got to go by the scientific evidence and nothing else."

"Larry King isn't going to go by the scientific evidence."

"That's not important. It's the scientific evidence that counts, not all this hysteria."

Softly, Pat said, "But the scientific evidence shows that Max came down with brain tumors."

"We *understand* that," Arthur said, almost pleading. "We know what went wrong. When we get more chimps, we'll be able to prove that we can regenerate organs without causing tumor proliferation."

Pat said nothing, but her expression was clearly dubious.

"Look," Arthur said, jumping to his feet. "We've done several series of experiments, starting with the lab rats . . ."

And for nearly an hour he lectured, pacing up and down the spacious room. Pat sat in the rocker and followed him with her eyes. She realized what he was doing: rehearsing. He didn't need to convince her of anything and he wasn't even trying to. He was assembling his thoughts, marshaling his arguments, practicing the speech he wanted to make to the jury, to the judges, to the world.

But it was a cold, unfeeling kind of speech. More of a classroom lecture than the stirring oration that could sway someone's feelings. Arthur was reciting facts, making logical arguments, building an unassailable fortress of rational, analytical statements. It wouldn't convince anyone, Pat thought, who wasn't a scientist. Maybe it wouldn't even convince the scientists on the jury.

At last he wound down. Instead of a magnificent summation, he just stopped, looking slightly befuddled, almost embarrassed.

He blinked at her several times. "Does any of that make any sense to you?"

Pat looked up at him from her rocking chair. "Of course it makes sense, Arthur." Which was perfectly true. And entirely pointless.

It was almost eleven. Arthur shrugged, went back to the sofa and turned the TV on again, then fished around until he hit a local station.

"Let's see what the local news does to us," he muttered.

Pat was thinking that it was high time she left for her own hotel. Tomorrow was going to be a very rough day, and she knew there would be dozens of phone messages waiting for her. But she stayed in the chair, rocking gently as the news came on. Fires and murders, wars and terrorism, an inane clown spending four minutes to say that tomorrow's weather would be hot and humid, with a thirty percent chance of thundershowers in the late afternoon.

And then, "Here in the nation's capital a strange sort of trial is going on," said the female half of the anchor team.

"And today a charge of murder was made," said the male half, almost smirking. "But the victim was a chimpanzee, not a human being."

They showed a snippet of old footage of Max, before the surgery, then about twenty seconds of Cassie's footage, ending with her screaming accusation of Arthur.

And suddenly a commercial for an insecticide came on the screen.

"Well," said Arthur, "at least we got on the air before the sports results." He smiled weakly and clicked off the TV.

Pat studied his face. He was trying to keep it under control, but in his dark brown eyes she saw something that might have been pain. Might even have been fear.

"This means everything to you, doesn't it?" Pat asked.

"It means a lot to everyone," Arthur replied, "to the whole human race."

"But especially to you," she said.

"Yes," he admitted.

"Why is it so important to you?"

He al.nost flinched with surprise. "Why? It's my work. It's . . ." His voice died away momentarily, then he repeated, "It's my work."

"Would it be so terrible if the jury decides not to recommend that you go ahead with human trials?"

"Yes," he snapped.

"But why?" Pat probed. "You'd have to do more animal experiments, that's all. You'd get to human trials sooner or later."

Arthur felt almost nettled, until he realized that she was trying to soften the blows that were coming.

"Look," he said, "the corporation has a great deal tied up in this work. Not just money, that's the trivial part of it. But

Omnitech has been staked out by a European consortium for an unfriendly takeover. If I can make a success of this regeneration work, the corporation will be much too strong for anyone to take over. If we're delayed, sidetracked—we could be bought out by the Europeans. Or maybe the Japanese."

"But don't you see what they're trying to do to you?" Pat burst out. "Kindelberger and Simmonds and Ransom and all the others, they're trying to destroy you! You personally!"

"They can't—"

"Yes, they can!" Pat was almost shouting. "They want to take you down, Arthur. They want to blacken you so badly that your work goes down with you."

"But the trial doesn't deal with personalities," he said, but his voice was weak, uncertain.

"The trial doesn't, but the media does. And from here on in you're going to be tried in the media, no matter what happens in the hearing room."

Arthur sank into the sofa, his mind spinning. "They can't stop the work," he said, more to himself than to her. "Other groups will do it. Maybe not here in the States, but—Europe, Korea . . ."

"And then what?" Pat demanded.

It took him a moment to realize the answer. "I'd be left behind," he said, his voice hollow.

Pat said nothing, but the look on her face told him that she understood. Maybe.

"It's not just ego," he explained. "It's my life. I started this work, Jesse and I did. It's part of me, like a part of my mind, my brain. If they don't let me continue, if someone overseas steals it away from me—it'd be a form of intellectual mutilation. Maiming." He threw his hands up in the air. "They might as well kill me."

"Could the government stop this kind of work entirely?" Pat asked.

Arthur nodded glumly. "They've screwed up other lines of research with their regulations and red tape. They could stop anyone in the United States from engaging in this type of research if they want to."

"That's why this trial is so important, isn't it?"

Arthur leaned back tiredly in the sofa. "That's why this trial is so important. I want an unequivocal approval from that jury of my peers. I want the scientific establishment to proclaim that the work we're doing is valid and valuable and should proceed full-tilt. Then nobody could stop us."

"Really?"

"Rosen was right about that. If this trial gives me a positive recommendation the politicians won't be able to stand in our way, no matter what Jesse or that raving evangelist or any other nut group say."

Pat thought about that for a moment. But what if the trial comes out in some other way? she wondered. What if that jury of his peers says the work should *not* be continued?

Arthur tried to read the expression on her face. "How do you feel about this work? You've been close to it since we first began talking about it. Do you think we ought to go ahead?"

"Yes," Pat said. "Unequivocally."

Arthur felt almost surprised. "Really?"

"Absolutely. This is the most important thing since . . . since . . . who knows when?"

Arthur smiled and reached out for her hand. "I'm glad you think so."

Pat felt alarm bells tingling. And something else. Gently she pulled her hand away from his.

"Look at the time! I'd better get back . . ." She practically jumped to her feet.

Arthur got up, too. "Do you have to go?"

"Tomorrow's going to be a rough day," Pat said, her voice slightly shaky.

"Yes. You're right." Reluctantly.

She had to step around him to start for the door.

"I'll go downstairs with you," Arthur said.

"No need for that," said Pat. "The doorman can get me a cab."

"I don't mind."

"You've got to read Potter's paper."

"Tomorrow. Over breakfast."

"You need some rest," she insisted. "You've got to start cross-examining witnesses tomorrow."

He sighed. "Right. Tomorrow I put on my Perry Mason hat."

Pat forced a laugh. "You'll tear them to pieces."

"Sure I will."

She opened the door, hesitated, then turned and gave him a swift peck on the lips.

"Good night, Arthur." And she fled down the carpeted corridor.

"Good night, Pat," he called after her.

Then he shut the door, thinking, Sure I'll tear them to pieces. I don't even have the guts to make a pass at her and I'm going to be a vicious, take-no-prisoners interrogator tomorrow. Sure I am.

JESSE

When I got Julia's message, and then talked to her on the phone, I was scared that something had happened to her. Another miscarriage, I thought. Or maybe she's hemorrhaging or god knows what. All through the plane ride from Washington to New York my mind ran through the possible disasters that could happen to her. If a little knowledge is a dangerous thing, imagine how scary it is to know all the medical possibilities.

I was thinking about her, not the baby. When she told me it was spina bifida it caught me totally off guard. Jesus! The kid would be crippled from birth. And she didn't want to abort it. That was the real shock. She *wanted* the baby. She knew it was going to be nothing but pain and sorrow all the years of its life but she was not going to abort it.

She was so hurt and so brave it made me ashamed of myself. I didn't want to spend the next twenty, thirty years tending a helpless cripple. But I couldn't tell Julia that; she'd think I was some kind of coldhearted monster.

And then I started thinking that maybe that first miscarriage was a warning. Spina bifida is a genetic defect. Maybe it's my goddamned genes that're the cause of it. Maybe if we aborted this baby and tried again we'd run into the exact same problem. Or some other birth defect.

Christ! Maybe it's me, in my genes.

I didn't know what to do, where to turn. I couldn't let this poison my marriage. I loved Julia and if she wanted to have this baby—that was going to be a bitch and a half. Raising a helpless kid, knowing that it would never live a normal life, knowing that every day it existed it would need to be fed and washed and have its backside wiped and its diapers changed. God! I wanted a son, not some deformed helpless sack of shit!

And then she asked me if Arby'd be able to save the kid. That hit where it hurt. I realized that no matter what Julia said, down deep she had that little spark of hope that someday, somehow, my big brother would come riding to our fucking rescue, save us from a life of shame and heartache with a wave of his all-powerful hand. Yeah, I could see Arby doing that: showing me how much better he is than I, and taking Julia off with him as his reward.

Kindelberger's office called that evening. Where was I, why did I leave the hearing, when was I coming back?

I told them I didn't know. I had family problems and they'd have to get through the next couple of days without me.

Julia and I went through the motions of having dinner. She opened a couple of cans; I don't remember what it was and I didn't care at the time. I felt like drinking a bottle of wine or two but Julia wouldn't touch a drink, she just patted her belly gently and gave me a strange kind of smile.

We hardly said a word to each other all through dinner. I felt bone-tired, and so did she. We went to bed early.

As I turned out the lamp on the night table I said the toughest words I'd ever spoken. "Julia, if you want to keep the baby it's all right with me."

I didn't mean it, not from the heart, and she must have known that. But she turned toward me in the bed and kissed me lightly on the cheek.

"I love you, Jesse," she said.

"I love you, too."

"You're a good man."

Then why was I thinking that I had let myself in for a twenty-year sentence in purgatory?

"Thank you," Julia said.

"For what?"

"For understanding. For caring. For . . ." She choked up and started sobbing quietly in the darkness.

I slid an arm across her bare shoulders and pulled her close to me. "It's all right," I whispered, trying to make her feel better than I did. "It'll all work out all right, you'll see."

And then the phone rang.

It was Reverend Simmonds's deep voice. "I was told you're having some sort of family problem. Is there anything I can do to help?"

I started to say that I didn't think so, but before I knew it I was telling him the whole terrible story about Julia and the baby. He listened to me blabber on while Julia watched me from her pillow, her face set in an expression halfway between surprise and relief.

He listened to my nonstop unwinding of grief, then said simply, "I'll fly up first thing tomorrow. You shouldn't be alone at a time like this."

"Thanks," I said. I put the phone down and turned back to Julia. I felt kind of dazed. "He'll be here tomorrow morning."

She nodded as if she had been expecting that. "Get some sleep," Julia said. Good advice. I realized I was exhausted, physically, mentally, and emotionally washed out, drained. I thought I was too wound up to sleep, but my eyes must have closed the minute I put my head down on the pillow.

I had weird dreams. I couldn't remember all of them, but I do recall dreaming that we were kids again, Arby and me, playing in front of our apartment building on the street in Brooklyn Heights. It was a hot day, a real scorcher, and I wanted to go to Coney Island but Ma said we were too young to go by ourselves and I couldn't understand that because I was going to be a father but I was still just a kid myself. And then I couldn't walk! I just lay there in a heap on the sidewalk while people walked past me and around me and some even stepped over me. I was afraid they were going to squash me, they were real big and I was just a tiny little blob on the pavement and Arby was standing up at the top of the stone steps of our building's front stoop watching me but not doing a damned thing to help me and I was crying and calling to him to help me but he just stood there and did nothing.

I woke up soaked with cold sweat. In the dark I could hear Julia sobbing quietly to herself. I couldn't tell if she was awake or asleep.

"Julia?" I whispered, real soft, so that if she was sleeping I wouldn't awaken her.

She didn't move. But her crying stopped.

"Are you okay?" I whispered.

"Did I wake you?" she whispered back.

"Naw. I had a nightmare."

"I haven't slept at all."

I tried to make a laugh. "Then why the hell are we whispering?"

She turned over and I touched her cheek. It was wet. I reached for the lamp but she grasped my arm and stopped me.

"Don't turn on the light. I must look awful."

"You couldn't look awful if you tried," I said.

So we sat in bed together, my arms around her, while the window gradually brightened with the new day. In the dawning light I could see that Julia's eyes were red and filled with tears.

"I'd better shower and shave," I said. "I don't know how early he'll be here."

Reverend Simmonds arrived before nine o'clock. He must have had a private plane fly him up from Washington; he got here too soon for the commercial shuttle. He looked grave, like a shaggy concerned grandfather, when I opened our front door for him. He was wearing slacks and a navy blue blazer. No tie. I could see specks of dandruff on the jacket's shoulders.

We sat him on the living room sofa while Julia and I took the two cushioned chairs. She brought out a tray of tea things and put it on the coffee table between us.

"You have a difficult decision to make," he said, once the three of us had settled down.

"We've made our decision," I said.

"Yes, you told me on the phone last night." He peered at Julia, who had erased most of the signs of her grief with makeup.

"We've agreed on it," I said.

Simmonds nodded. "I think you'll find yourselves unmaking and remaking that decision a few hundred times over the next several days."

"Really?" asked Julia, very softly.

"That's been my experience in cases similar to yours. It's not an easy decision to make."

"No, it isn't," I said. Julia glanced at me, but said nothing.

Simmonds hunched forward, forearms on knees, hands clasped together. "Now, look. I could give you a whole morning's worth of religious talk about the sanctity of life. Make you cry and tear your hair out. But I know that neither of you believes in my kind of religion, so I won't bother you with that."

"We believe in the sanctity of life," Julia said, still in that small voice.

"Of course you do. Everybody does. But there's three lives here to consider, not just one. The two of you have to think about your own lives—which are just as sacred as the life of your unborn child."

"Which side are you on?" I blurted.

He grinned at me. "God's, of course. But sometimes the good Lord doesn't make it very clear as to which way He wants us to go."

"I can't kill the baby," Julia said firmly.

Simmonds nodded. "I understand how you feel. I agree with your decision. But I want you both to realize that there are going to be times when you'll regret that decision. You're going to wonder if you've done the right thing. You're going to hate yourselves and your baby for making your lives miserable."

"Never!"

He reached over and patted her knee. "Yes, you will. Even over the next few days you're both going to feel like you've martyred yourselves and thrown your lives away. That's natural. It's the devil tempting you."

I could believe him, all except that last line.

"Oh, I know you don't believe in the devil," he said good-naturedly, looking me in the eye. "Okay, call it self-interest or the instinct for self-preservation, whatever you want. But there will be times when you'll look at your child and ask yourselves why you ever let him ruin your lives."

Neither Julia nor I had anything to say to that.

"It's a natural reaction. Don't start hating yourselves or each other for it. Don't start hating the baby."

"I could never hate my baby," Julia said.

"Only the love that you two feel for each other can see you through this crisis. Only if you can share that love, enlarge it to include your baby, will you be able to make a happy life for him and for yourselves."

"I understand," I said.

"If you were religious, I'd tell you that God will strengthen you, that He has enough love to share His with you and your baby. But you don't have that kind of faith, so I'll just tell you that God will help you anyway. That's His way."

I wondered why, if god was such a nice helpful guy, he had given our baby spina bifida.

But Julia just smiled. "That's very comforting." She didn't mean it, I knew. And Simmonds knew it, too, but it didn't really seem to matter.

Then she asked, "Suppose—just hypothetically, now— suppose that scientists learned how to cure spina bifida. Suppose they could make my baby normal. What do you say to that?"

"It can't happen soon enough to help us," I snapped.

Julia gave me a pleading look. "But suppose it could."

Simmonds scratched at his thick mane of gray hair. "You

know I'm against tinkering with God's will. We don't know why God has sent you this cross to bear, but whatever the reason, it's part of His plan."

"Curing my baby could be part of His plan, too, couldn't it?" Julia asked.

Simmonds bowed his head. "Okay. We're going to get down into the details of this now." Looking up at Julia, he said, "Apparently the Lord has decided to test you. I don't know why, neither do you. He moves in mysterious ways. But someday you will stand before Him and He will judge you on the strength of how you accepted His test."

The same old religious hogwash, I thought. Julia kept her expression noncommittal, though, and continued to listen without interrupting.

"Now, suppose you circumvent His test. Suppose you latch on to some miraculous scientific cure for your baby. What does that mean for your relationship with God? What does it mean for your baby's relationship with his Creator?"

I couldn't take any more of it. "Do you honestly think that God doesn't want us to practice medicine?"

He turned to me. "I honestly don't pretend to know what God has in mind for us. Except for this—He sends His tests to us for His own reasons. And if we turn our backs on Him, we do it at our own peril."

"But curing my baby might be part of God's plan, mightn't it?" Julia insisted.

"I'm sorry, but I can't accept that," Simmonds said. "I think what those scientists are doing is the devil's work."

I must have huffed.

"You don't believe in Satan, I know. That's his strongest weapon against you."

It was incredible. One moment Simmonds was a kindly, thoughtful, helpful counselor to us. The next he was a religious zealot telling us to accept whatever plagues his god chooses to throw at us and warning us that Arby and his researchers are in league with the devil.

We talked back and forth for more than an hour with him, and I've got to admit that I felt a lot better for it. So did Julia,

I'm certain. By the time we finally got him out the door and had the apartment to ourselves again, I was almost smiling.

"It was awfully good of him to come and talk to us," Julia said, much brighter than she'd been at dawn.

I shook my head. "He's a nice guy, all right. But a meshuga."

"He has his beliefs," said Julia. "I almost wish I could be as convinced about it all as he is. It must be very reassuring."

We felt good enough to go out to a neighborhood restaurant for a late breakfast and we almost got through the whole meal without talking about the baby.

As we walked back home, Julia asked me, "Will you be going back to Washington this afternoon?"

I shrugged. "It's almost noon. I'll stay here, spend the weekend. I'll go back to the hearing Monday—if it's still going on by then."

"Do you think it might end sooner?"

"I think Arby's sinking faster than the *Titanic*," I said. "They've got him by the balls."

Julia looked shocked. "I can't imagine Arthur losing anything to anyone."

"Well, imagine it. It's going to happen, believe me."

Julia got real quiet the rest of the way from the restaurant to our building.

"Listen," I said to Julia as we approached our front door, "Even if the decision at the hearing goes in Arby's favor and he's allowed to start human trials, the work will never be done in time to help our child. Do you understand that? Don't think that my brother can save our baby, because he can't."

Julia smiled and patted me on the cheek. "Oh, Jesse, I love you. Don't you know that?"

I opened the front door and she went through. I followed her into the foyer, wondering what she meant by that.

Then she added, "I do think you ought to get back to the trial this afternoon, though."

THE TRIAL:
DAY FIVE, MORNING

Like an addict, Arthur turned on the morning news shows while he shaved, watching the little TV set sitting next to the bathroom sink with morbid fascination as its screen showed the same clips and footage as the late-night broadcasts had: Cassie branding Arthur as a murderer.

Both *Good Morning America* and *The Today Show* featured guest experts discussing not the possibilities of organ regeneration, but the ethics of using animals as experimental subjects. Two philosophers, a Jesuit priest, and a rabbi. Not a biologist in sight. In disgust, Arthur flicked to *CBS Morning News*.

A woman was being interviewed by a woman reporter. It took a few moments for Arthur to realize that the guest was an animal rights activist.

"And how did you feel when you saw the videos of Max, the chimpanzee who was used in those experiments?" the interviewer asked in a low, funereal tone.

The woman blinked back tears. "Actually, I almost felt relieved when the poor creature died. He had escaped. He's free now. They can't hurt him anymore."

Arthur wanted to ram his fist through the tube.

"Do you think he was in a lot of pain?"

Goddamned vampire, Arthur thought.

"Obviously," came the answer.

The interviewer shook her head sadly as she looked straight into the camera and said, "I'm afraid we've run out of time. Now this."

A commercial for a denture cleaner showed a frowning white-haired woman holding up a fizzing glass of water with her choppers in it.

* * *

PROFESSOR POTTER, please."

He came shuffling up to the witness table, his sparse fringe of dead-white hair catching the light like a filmy halo. He walked alone, leaning heavily on his cane. If his assistants were still in the chamber, Arthur did not see them.

There were even more reporters on hand than the previous afternoon, and five TV cameras now obstructed the side aisles of the hearing chamber. Reporters had clustered around Arthur when he arrived at the hearing room, their clamoring questions little short of accusations. Arthur had steadfastly refused to say anything except, "I'll make my statements on the floor of the hearing."

As Potter sat himself facing the judges, Arthur got up and walked toward the witness table. He took in his audience at a glance: Jesse's seat was still empty; Senator Kindelberger was up front with the judges, looking serious and concerned; Pat had moved to the media table, squeezing herself in among the reporters and photographers. He turned toward the jurors, sitting against the side wall: six men and six women, all of them from either academic or government laboratories. Political correctness went only so far, Arthur knew. No scientist from an industrial lab was asked to be on the jury; no one connected with a profit-making organization.

"Good morning, Professor," Arthur said, trying to make it sound friendly.

Potter said, "Morning, Arthur."

His stroke had pulled the left half of his face down into a grimace, his left eye almost completely closed. It made his habitual little smile into an ironic rictus, one corner of his mouth turned up, the other curled down.

"This is just a formality," Arthur said, "but I must remind you that you are still under oath."

"Of course, of course."

"I read the paper you presented to the jury."

"You'd better have."

Several of the jurors looked openly skeptical at the mention of Potter's paper. Arthur thought that was a good sign.

"Where was it published?"

Potter's right cheek ticked. "That information was in the reprint."

"For the record, where was your paper published?"

His eyes narrowed. "In *Counterpoint*."

"That's a British magazine, isn't it?" Arthur asked.

"British, yes. But it's not a magazine. It's a reputable scientific journal that publishes papers that the prevailing scientific establishment won't touch."

"Controversial papers?"

"That's right."

"Do you consider your paper to be controversial?"

"No," Potter said firmly. "My paper is self-evidently correct. You can't argue with mathematics."

"And yet you sent it to a journal that specializes in controversial papers. Why?"

"Because I knew the scientific establishment wouldn't publish it."

"Did you try to have it published in a more reputable journal?"

"There's nothing disreputable about *Counterpoint*!"

"Excuse me," Arthur said. Several of the jury members were grinning. "A more orthodox journal. Is that better?"

"Yes."

"Did you?"

"Did I what?"

"Did you try to get your paper published in a more orthodox journal? *Science*, for example. Or *Nature*. Or one of the refereed journals that specialize in the various branches of molecular biology."

"No."

"Why not?" Arthur knew the answer to his question. Papers submitted to scientific journals are reviewed by a panel of referees who read each paper, scientific peers who judge the merit of each paper submitted on its scientific quality. *Counterpoint* was a sensationalist magazine, nothing more.

"They wouldn't touch it."

"No refereed journal would publish it?"

Potter fidgeted in his chair. "It was too unconventional for them."

"Isn't it true," Arthur asked, "that you presented the basic material of your paper at the annual molecular biology conference in San Francisco more than six years ago?"

Frowning, Potter muttered, "I might have. I think so."

"I recall hearing your presentation," said Arthur. "As I remember it, the questions and comments from the floor afterward were less than flattering."

Potter said nothing; he just scowled at Arthur.

"Do you recall the comments?"

"No."

"Would you say that your paper was well received?"

Again the little twitching, squirming. "The general tone of the comments was negative. It often is when a new concept is broached for the first time. I was years ahead of them. Years ahead! Still am!"

"Did any of your questioners characterize your paper as 'numerology'?"

Potter bristled. "It's not numerology! It's mathematical fact!"

"What experimental corroboration do you have?" Arthur snapped.

Potter glared at him.

"You've written a paper that is entirely hypothetical. Have you tried to match your mathematical speculations with experiments?"

"They're not speculations!"

"They are until you get some experimental evidence to test them. What experiments have you done?"

"I—I'm not an experimenter." Potter turned slightly toward the jury. "Not anymore."

"Has anyone corroborated your ideas with experimental evidence?" Arthur demanded.

"Not that I know of."

"Not that you know of." Despite himself, Arthur could feel the heat rising within him. This doddering old fool thinks he can knock me down with a few pages of numbers, does he?

"Can you tell me *why* no one has tried to do experiments based on your work?"

"It's too far ahead of them!" Potter said. "They're not smart enough to understand what I've accomplished! None of them are."

Careful! Arthur warned himself. Don't appear to be bullying the old fart.

"Professor Potter," he said gently, "when Einstein published his theories of relativity, those papers were pretty much ahead of the rest of the field, wouldn't you say?"

Suspiciously, Potter said, "I suppose so. I'm a biologist, not a physicist."

"And yet, within a few years experiments were done that proved Einstein's theories were correct. Isn't that true?"

"I suppose so." Grudgingly.

"Yet six years have gone by since you first announced your ideas and no one has even tried to do an experiment to see if your mathematics correctly predict the real world?"

"I told you, no one has tried."

"Not one researcher has even tried to conduct an experiment based on your work?"

Rosen spoke up. "I think we've established that fact clearly enough, Dr. Marshak."

"I agree," said Graves.

Turning to the row of desks at the front of the chamber, Arthur said, "I merely want to show the jury that Professor Potter's mathematical treatment is not regarded as significant within the biological research community."

"But it is significant!" Potter screeched. "It's a fundamental concept, as fundamental as Heisenberg's uncertainty principle!"

Arthur almost laughed. From claiming he was no physicist, Potter was now equating himself with the heart of quantum physics.

"Is it truly?" he asked mildly.

"I have proved, mathematically, that it is impossible to alter the activity of the DNA in the cells of a functioning organism without incurring chaotic and unpredictable side effects."

"Which means, if you're correct, that any attempts at regenerating organs within the body of a living organism are doomed to failure."

"Certainly right."

Arthur stroked his chin, as if thinking. "According to your paper, *any* attempt to alter the activity of the DNA is foolhardy?"

"Any," said Potter firmly.

"Then gene therapy is a waste of time?"

"You mean inserting foreign genes into an organism? No, that's permissible."

"But gene therapy changes the activity of the organism's original DNA," Arthur said.

Potter began to shake his head.

"You're saying that gene therapy for treating, say, cystic fibrosis—such gene therapy will cause chaotic and unpredictable side effects?"

"If it alters the functioning DNA, yes."

"What side effects have been caused in cystic fibrosis patients?" Arthur asked.

"How should I know? I'm not involved in that research."

Arthur looked at the jury. Some of them were involved in gene therapy tests, he knew. "I searched the literature late last night," he said. "I could not find any cases of chaotic and unpredictable side effects."

"It's probably too early for them to manifest themselves," Potter said.

"It's been more than five years since the first tests on cystic fibrosis patients were started. How long should it take?"

Potter hesitated. "I don't know," he mumbled.

"If I read your paper correctly, the side effects should be immediately apparent."

"Well . . . perhaps not."

One of the women jurors was working on gene surgery, Arthur knew; replacing defective elements in a patient's gene so that it would function correctly.

"Are you aware, Professor Potter, of the work being done in the area of Tay-Sachs disease?"

"No." Grudgingly.

Of course not, Arthur thought. That's the last area you'd be interested in, you anti-Semitic piece of shit.

He turned from the jury to stand squarely facing Potter, ready to destroy this doddering old fool, the man who had hounded him out of academia, the nasty backbiting Jew-hating bastard who had tried to ruin his life. Now you get what you deserve, Arthur thought. Now I'm going to destroy you just as you tried to destroy me.

But what Arthur saw was the shattered shell of the man he hated. Potter sat at the witness table, shriveled, half dead, yet still glaring defiantly. And out of the corner of his eye Arthur saw Graves leaning forward, hands clasped on the desktop, staring at Potter the way a doctor might gaze at a patient who is beyond all help.

Arthur's anger evaporated. Briefly he tried to summon it up again, to fuel his moment of vengeance. But blasting Potter would be like kicking a cripple. He couldn't do it.

"Professor Potter," he asked softly. "Would you like to regain the use of the left side of your body?"

"Eh?" The question caught the old man completely off guard.

"If it was possible to repair the damage caused by your stroke, would you undergo such treatment?"

Now Potter glared pure hatred. "No," he snapped. "Never!"

Arthur shook his head sadly. "I have no further questions for this witness."

JULIA

It took all my strength to send Jesse back to Washington. More than almost anything I wanted him with me, I wanted him to hold me, I wanted us to face this terrible ordeal together.

But I couldn't let him avoid facing Arthur. He would never be able to stand himself if he backed out of their confrontation at the trial. He would always wonder if he'd been cowardly. Or, worse, if I thought that he wasn't strong enough to face Arthur.

And above all I didn't want Jesse to think that I harbored some wild hope in my heart that Arthur could save our baby. It's strange, the twists that our emotions lead us into. In a way, I was almost making a choice between Jesse and the baby, sending him out to do battle against his brother so that Arthur would have no chance of helping our baby, ever. The realization was crushing. Jesse or the baby. Already the baby was threatening to come between us.

So I gathered what little courage I could muster and sent Jesse off to Washington. He could fly there in an hour or so and be in time for the trial's afternoon session. He was reluctant, almost afraid, at first. But I insisted and soon enough he agreed that it would be best.

I watched from our apartment window as he trotted out to the taxi we had summoned. From my perch he looked almost like a schoolboy grudgingly heading off for his classes.

Jesse opened the taxi door, then looked up toward me. He waved, as he always did. But the expression on his face was absolutely grim.

I waved back and watched the taxi disappear around the corner. Then I sat in our living room, alone.

No, I'm not alone, I realized. The baby is with me. He'll always be with me, all the days of his life.

JESSE

I never felt so mixed up in my life.

Just before I ducked into the taxi I looked up at our window and waved to Julia. Her face was so damned pale, white as a ghost. Even her answering wave was weak, faltering.

I should have stayed with her and to hell with the trial and Arby and everything else. But to tell the truth, I was glad of the chance to get away, even if it was just for the few hours of the afternoon. I'd be back in time for supper. I needed a few hours of fresh air, some time to think this thing out.

There's no way that Arby's work would ever be able to help our kid. It'd take years and years of experiments and human trials before there'd be any chance of reversing the damage done in a spina bifida case. I knew that. No sense fooling myself, no sense getting up false hopes.

Unless—unless our boy became one of Arby's test subjects. Assuming the trial recommends going on to human tests, and the FDA and all those other government agencies don't slow things down to a crawl.

No, I couldn't do that. Use our kid as an experimental subject? Like that chimp? Julia would die first.

But what other chance did we have? We're going to be tied to a helpless, hopeless lump of protoplasm for years and years and then he'll die and Julia's heart will break, if it isn't broken already.

She's hoping Arby will be able to save the kid; I know she is. Maybe she doesn't even know it, but that's what she's hoping. It's the only hope we've got.

And it'll look great, won't it? Humanitarian of the Year elbows out everybody else to put his own son first in line for this experimental treatment developed by his brother. Million-dollar treatment saves doctor's son while poor people wait in vain. Great story. The media'll love it.

And so will Arby. Soon as he knows about the spina bifida

he's going to come at me all sincere and helpful and show me that *he* knows what to do, even if I don't.

By the time my plane landed at Reagan National I was so confused and shook up that I almost stayed aboard for the ride back to New York.

WASHINGTON, D.C.:
NOON

Arthur felt strangely let down after the morning's session was gaveled to a close. He had finished with Potter and chosen not to recall Zapapas. Graves looked somewhat surprised.

"The next witness scheduled is Dr. Jesse Marshak," said Graves. "But he is not present."

A clerk came up behind the chief judge and handed him a slip of paper. Graves adjusted his bifocals and scanned it swiftly.

"Dr. Marshak has sent a message stating that he will be present for the afternoon session," he announced. With a glance at the clock, he said, "We will break for lunch and resume at one-thirty."

Pat made her way through the departing crowd to Arthur. "Where's your brother?" she asked.

"I don't know," Arthur said. "Probably preparing for the cross-examination somewhere."

"With Simmonds's people?"

Arthur scowled. "Most likely."

Senator Kindelberger was a few feet away, chatting amiably with some of the reporters. He broke away from them and caught up with Arthur and Pat as they headed for the door. Arthur braced himself for a confrontation.

But the senator said, "Hope your brother can make it here

for the afternoon session. Surely wouldn't like to stretch this hearing into next week."

"Do you know where he is?" Arthur asked.

"He was back in New York last night," Kindelberger said, his leathery face looking slightly concerned. "Some problem with his wife's health, from what little he told my aide."

Arthur felt a flash of electricity surge through him. Julia! He reached for his cell phone as he said to Pat, "You go ahead to the restaurant and I'll catch up with you there."

Pat saw the stricken look on his face. "All right," she said, trying to hide the resentment that unexpectedly welled up inside her.

Arthur pulled up Jesse's number from the cell phone's data bank. Julia answered.

"Hello, Julia," he said, lowering his voice. "It's Arthur."

"Nothing's happened to Jesse, has it?" She sounded almost frantic.

"No, no," Arthur said. "I'm calling to find out how you are."

"Me? I'm . . . fine."

She didn't sound fine in Arthur's ears. Julia sounded frightened, almost terrified.

"Why would you think something's happened to Jesse?" he asked.

Julia looked out her apartment window. The summer sky was clear and bright, what little she could see of it.

"Jesse's flying down to Washington. I always get a bit testy when he's flying without me." It was a lie and she was certain that Arthur would recognize it as such but it was the best she could do.

He sounded suspicious. "Senator Kindelberger said you weren't feeling well. Is that why Jesse left the hearing?"

Don't tell him, Julia commanded herself. If he's got to know, let Jesse be the one to break the awful news to him.

"I'm fine, Arthur," she repeated, holding back the flood of tears and words that she wanted to pour out.

"Are you?"

"Yes," she insisted. Actually, she was. It was the baby who wasn't.

"What time will Jess be here, do you know?"

"He took the eleven o'clock shuttle; he should have landed already."

Arthur glanced at his wristwatch. Not quite twelve.

"I'll look for him," he said into the telephone.

"Yes. Do." Julia's voice sounded almost mechanical, as if she were deliberately holding back any hint of human warmth.

Arthur hung up, thinking, It's all over. Completely. Anything she might have felt for me is totally gone now. It's like talking to an answering machine.

In New York, Julia shuddered as she hung up the phone. I've got to get control of myself, she raged inwardly. I mustn't allow myself to go to pieces. If Arthur wants to help, he's got to do it through Jesse. I can't let Jesse think that I'm turning to Arthur instead of to him.

JESSE CRAWLED into the dilapidated taxi. The dispatcher slammed the door shut and banged on the cab's roof.

As the driver pulled away from the curb he asked, "Where to?"

Jesse barely heard him. The driver glanced over his shoulder and asked louder, "Where to, mister?"

"What's the difference?" Jesse muttered.

The driver was elderly, lean as a rake, two days of gray stubble on his face. "Man, you got woman troubles, don't you?"

Jesse stared at him. "You might say that."

"So do we all, friend. So do we all. But now I gotta know where you want to go."

"The Rayburn Building."

"Oh, man, you takin' your troubles to Congress, heh?"

With a sigh, Jesse repeated, "You might say that."

What a goddamned mess, Jesse thought. What a goddamned motherfucking no-good sonofabitch bastard mess. It's in my genes. It must be. The first baby miscarried and now we've got a boy with spina bifida. It's my fault. Got to be.

As the taxi crossed the Fourteenth Street Bridge and swept past the domed temple of the Jefferson Memorial, he asked himself, Could Arby really do the kid any good? The boy would be at least five, six years old by the time Arby could try his treatment on him. If he lives that long. If this hearing allows Arby to go forward to human trials.

I'm supposed to stop him. They're all looking at me to cut Arby's legs out from under him. Simmonds, Kindelberger— how the hell did I ever let myself get involved with them?

But he knew. Jesse knew exactly how and exactly why he had placed himself in opposition to his brother. Why spend billions of dollars to help rich people live longer when poor people are dying young? A ghetto teenager doesn't need a new heart, he needs decent nutrition and the kind of simple medical care that the average American takes for granted. A crack baby doesn't need a new spleen, it needs a mother who didn't take the shit. What good does it do to help the wealthy when the poor are dying in the fucking streets?

But my son is one of those wealthy ones. Why shouldn't I want to help my son? If I stop Arby I'm killing my boy. What will Julia think of me? What will I think of myself?

"We're here, friend."

With a start of surprise, Jesse realized that they had stopped. He got out of the cab, leaned into the front window to pay the driver. As he straightened up he saw, across Constitution Avenue, a few forlorn pickets tramping tiredly in front of the Capitol, their placards resting on their shoulders instead of being held high.

He turned and up at the top of the steps of the Rayburn Building, waiting for him, stood Arthur.

AFTER HIS chilling conversation with Julia, Arthur called the restaurant where Pat was waiting for him and told her to go ahead and eat her lunch without him.

"Something's terribly wrong between Jesse and Julia," he said. "I'm going to wait here and see if I can spot Jess before the hearing resumes."

He paced the corridor outside the hearing chamber for a few minutes, then went down to the main lobby and out to the stairs. It was blazing hot outside: Washington at its summer worst. A few pickets were trudging along cross the way but they could not see Arthur, the man their placards vilified. A taxi pulled up at the curb. Arthur stared at it, and sure enough, Jesse ducked through its rear door, paid the driver, and turned and looked straight at him.

Arthur's first instinct was to race down the steps to his brother. But he hesitated. Jesse saw Arthur up at the head of the stairs, standing there like some emperor waiting for his lowly subjects to come crawling up to him. With a shake of his head he started walking toward the corner, looking for another entrance into the building. It was broiling hot on the street but he could not face his brother. Not just yet. If Arby wants to see me, he knows I'll be heading for the hearing chamber, he decided.

Arthur went back inside, feeling nettled that Jesse was trying to avoid him. We've both got to be at the hearing chamber, he thought. But once the session starts I won't have a chance to talk to him.

He thought briefly about trying to guess which elevator bank Jesse would use, quickly decided that it was fruitless, and went back to the corridor outside the chamber itself. Hardly anyone else in sight. They're all out at lunch, Arthur told himself. He's got to show up here. Arthur glanced at his wristwatch again. Half an hour before the session begins.

The seconds crawled by so slowly that Arthur began to fear Jesse would stay away until the session actually opened. That would be just like him, he thought grimly. Avoiding me. But then he spotted Jesse coming up the corridor toward him. God, he looks as if he's been hit by a truck!

Arthur almost ran to his brother. "Jess! Are you all right?"

Jesse started to reply, but then just nodded.

"What's going on?" Arthur demanded. "Julia wouldn't tell me a thing."

"You talked to Julia?"

"Five minutes ago, maybe ten. What's happening with you two?"

Jesse ground his teeth together. He looked up and down the corridor, stalling for time as he thought, How much should I tell him? What should I do?

"In here," Arthur said, nudging him toward the doors to the hearing chamber. "Nobody's there now, we can talk in private."

The chamber was indeed empty. Long rows of seats, portraits on the walls, the bank of desks with their padded chairs at the front of the room. The TV cameras were cold, their lights off. No one else in the room.

The two brothers sat on the last row of benches, side by side, facing each other.

"What's happened?" Arthur demanded.

Jesse stared at his brother for long moments, saying nothing.

"Well?"

At last Jesse said, "You've got to promise me, Arby, that you won't mention any of this to anybody. And you can't use it in the hearing."

"Use what? What's going on?"

"Promise me that this is strictly between you and me; nobody else."

Puzzled, Arthur said, "All right, I promise."

"You won't use it in the hearing."

"I promised, didn't I?"

"Okay." Jesse took a deep breath, but then said nothing. Arthur could see the pain twisting his features.

"What is it?"

"The baby—"

"Not another miscarriage!"

Jesse shook his head. "Spina bifida."

Arthur felt as if someone had slammed a bowling ball into his gut. "Spina . . ." The words wouldn't come out.

"Julia won't abort the baby. She wants to keep it."

"I'm so sorry, Jess."

"Yeah. I know."

They sat in grief-racked silence for several moments,

heads bowed toward each other. Arthur wanted to take his brother in his arms, yet he could not bring himself to try. He sat there, thoughts spinning.

"Maybe," he began to say, "maybe we could—"

"Don't!" Jesse snapped. "Don't say it. Don't even think it."

"But if we can push ahead with the regeneration work, maybe in a few years, five or six at most—"

"The baby'll most likely be dead by then."

"They can be kept alive a lot longer than that, can't they?"

"I don't want him alive!" Jesse snarled. "I don't want him at all!"

"But if we could repair the damage to his spine, what then?"

"He'd still be a brain-damaged retarded child."

"But maybe—"

"I don't want you experimenting on him! I don't want you riding to Julia's rescue while I sit on the sidelines like a helpless idiot."

"But what other choice do we have?" Arthur demanded.

Jesse stared at his brother for a long moment. Then, "The same choice everybody else has, Arby," he said softly. "To raise a damaged child with as much love and as much patience as we can give him."

"That's stupid!" Arthur could feel the anger bubbling up inside him. "That's sentimental crap! That's what people try to tell themselves when they've got no other possibilities."

"That's what we're going to do, Arby."

"But I can save him. I *know* I can!"

"Jesus Christ, don't say that!" Jesse snapped. "You *can't* save him. Nobody can. Don't hold that up in front of us, Arby. You'll kill Julia with hopes that can't come true."

"They can come true! I'll make them come true."

"Not in time for our kid."

"No, you're wrong, Jesse. I can do it."

"You're still in love with Julia, aren't you?"

Thrown off balance by the sudden change of subject, Arthur snapped, "No. Not anymore."

"The hell you're not."

"I'm not," he insisted. "She loves you and that ended everything between us."

"Don't lie to me, Arby."

And suddenly Arthur realized what this was all about. "I'm not trying to get her away from you, Jess. You've got to believe me. I'm not. I'd never do that to you, even if she'd let me, and she won't. She loves you, Jess. She never really loved me. Not the way she loves you."

Jesse eyed him warily, wanting to believe, not daring to.

"And besides . . ." For the first time since his parents' accident Arthur felt tears welling up inside. "Jesse, I love you."

Jesse saw the look on his brother's face: hope and love and fear and pain, all mixed together.

He swallowed hard. "Christ, Arby, I love you, too."

The two men fell in each other's arms. For a while they simply sat, embracing, feeling the solid warmth of each other's arms gripping them.

Then Jesse pulled away. "But I'm still against you on this." He gestured vaguely around the hearing chamber.

Arthur nodded. "I know. I understand. But I don't agree with you. I'm going to do my damnedest to win."

"Yeah," said Jesse tiredly. "I know you will."

A voice from the front of the chamber called to them, "Say, you two are awfully eager to get started, aren't you?"

They looked up and saw it was one of the clerks, arranging an armful of papers on the judges' desks.

"Anxious to get it over with, I guess, huh?" the clerk said.

"Yes," Arthur said.

"Damned right," said Jesse.

THE TRIAL:

DAY FIVE, AFTERNOON

The audience was abuzz. They knew that this afternoon's session would be brother against brother. The reporters scribbled away and checked their voice recorders. The TV cameras swung to Jesse as he walked slowly to the witness chair and sat down.

"Jesse," said Arthur, striding from his own seat to the front of the room, "you stated in your testimony that you are against having the regeneration program move ahead to human trials."

"That's right."

Arthur saw Senator Kindelberger leaning forward slightly in his chair, as if he did not want to miss a syllable.

"Your chief reason, you said, was that in the animal experiments the test subjects developed tumors."

"That's what I gathered from the reports you submitted," said Jesse.

"And some of those tumors were malignant."

"That's what killed the chimp, wasn't it?"

Arthur hesitated a fraction of a second. "Actually, the chimpanzee died of a coronary thrombosis. A heart attack. It had nothing to do with the brain tumor."

"Tumors, plural," Jesse corrected.

"There was no connection between the two," said Arthur. Silently he added, Except Cassie's overwrought emotions.

"Several of the other lab animals died of cancer," Jesse said.

"But that was before we began to use the tumor suppressant treatment that we had developed."

"You can't use that treatment on human subjects until you get FDA approval," Jesse said.

"Which will come in a matter of months," Arthur countered. "Or so I'm told by the Food and Drug Administration."

Jesse raised an eyebrow. FDA approvals were never certain, and everyone on the jury knew it. Dealing with that agency had prompted Arthur to put up Yogi Berra's *It ain't over till it's over* on the wall of his office.

"Our reports also show that we are working on methods of narrowing the effective range of regentide, so that we can regress the cells we want to regenerate without inducing tumors."

"Your reports," Jesse countered, "show that such work has barely begun. You're a long way from achieving such a goal."

"Do you think we will achieve it?"

Jesse blinked with surprise.

Waving one hand in the air, Arthur added, "Let's forget about the time factor. Do you think it's possible that we will refine the regentide treatment to the point where tumor growth will no longer be a problem?"

Jesse could see where Arthur was trying to lead him. "Given enough time, I suppose virtually anything is possible. But it might take years. Decades, even."

"But it should be possible?"

"Given enough time," Jesse agreed reluctantly.

"And in the meantime, once FDA approval for the tumor-suppressant treatment comes through, we could go into human trials and deal with the tumor problem that way, couldn't we?"

"That would be adding one new and untried treatment to another new and untried treatment. That makes everything much more risky. You don't know what the long-term side effects might be."

Arthur paced a few steps closer to the witness table. He saw that the jury was watching him now, not Jesse.

"Have you ever been involved in a heart transplant procedure?"

"No," Jesse answered. "I'm an internist, not a surgeon. I've witnessed open-heart procedures, though."

"What was the major problem in the earliest heart transplant procedures?"

"Rejection."

"The recipient's immune system rejected the 'foreign' tissue of the donated heart, right?"

Oh, god, Jesse thought, he's going to snooker me again. "Right," he said.

"And how did the surgeons deal with the rejection problem?"

"With immunosuppressants."

"Drugs that suppress the activity of the body's immune system, so that the donated organ will not be rejected."

Jesse said nothing. He just stared at his brother, not knowing whether he was angrier at Arthur or himself. He's making me look like a damned fool.

"Wasn't that adding a new and untried treatment to a new and untried treatment?" Without waiting for an answer, Arthur went on, "And there are literally thousands of heart-transplant recipients alive and well today, as a result."

"And a lot of dead ones," Jesse snapped. "A lot of people were treated like experimental animals, back at the beginning of transplant procedures. A lot of people died before the technique was perfected."

Surprised at Jesse's vehemence, Arthur retorted, "But isn't that always the way it is with a new procedure? Isn't that the way we learn?"

"At the cost of peoples' lives."

"Those people were going to die anyway," said Arthur.

"So you want to give people cancer just to see if you can grow new organs in them."

"I want to give human beings the chance to grow new hearts, or livers, or arms, or spinal cords if and when they need them."

Jesse flared inwardly. He's going to throw the spina bifida in my face. Goddamn him, he's going to use it against me!

And Arthur was thinking, I shouldn't have said spinal cords. I mustn't make him think I'm trying to hurt him or take advantage of him. *Think* before you open your mouth, schmuck.

More carefully, he said, "If we have to deal with the threat of cancer we will deal with it. We will learn how to reduce the risk and eventually eliminate it. In the meantime we'll have given dying human beings the ability to regenerate themselves, to extend their lives—"

"Dr. Marshak!" Graves broke in. "You are supposed to be cross-examining the witness, not making your final summation."

Arthur felt startled. Then almost sheepish. He forced himself to smile at the chief judge and made a little bow. Then he turned back to Jesse.

And saw his brother. The little boy playing stickball in the schoolyard. The bewildered child terrified by the sudden loss of his father and the crippling of his mother. The handsome young man smiling his way through college and medical school. And now this intense, frightened, hurting brother who faced a lifetime of pain and sorrow.

With a shake of his head Arthur muttered, "I have no further questions for this witness." He went to his bench and sat down.

The hearing chamber was absolutely silent.

Jesse felt stunned. And relieved. It's over. He's not going to rake me over the coals, after all. Maybe he's afraid of badmouthing his own brother in front of the jury. Or maybe . . . He stared at Arthur. His brother's face was as blank as a marble statue.

Jesse started to get up from the witness chair. But Rosen rose to his feet.

"I have one more question for Dr. Jesse Marshak."

Arthur's brows knitted into a frown as he sat down. What the hell does Rosen want? He had his chance with Jesse three days ago. Jesse's his witness, after all.

Jesse sat back down, thinking, Won't it ever end? When can I get out of this and go back home to Julia?

Rosen did not move from his place at the judges' desks. He glanced over at Senator Kindelberger, then turned his attention to Jesse.

"Dr. Marshak, your objections to human trials for the regeneration work go beyond the technical details, do they not?"

"Yes, they do," said Jesse.

Arthur fumed. Technical details. He's trying to reduce the most significant scientific work in the past half century to "technical details."

"Can you tell the court what your other objections are?"

Jesse cleared his throat as he glanced back at Arthur. Christ, Arby let me off the hook but Rosen's putting me back on it again.

"Dr. Marshak?" Rosen prompted.

"Well," Jesse said slowly, "they're financial, chiefly. And moral. I guess, of the two, the moral reasons are most important."

Arthur shouted, "Objection! Those are not matters for this court to consider. They're not scientific issues."

Graves sighed wearily. "We have been over this territory earlier," he said.

Rosen said, "As the court ruled on the first day of this hearing, it is impossible to consider the scientific issues by themselves. Science does not happen in a vacuum. Financial and moral and many other factors influence the scientific issue."

"They don't change the scientific facts," Arthur snapped, his temper rising again. Why is Graves doing this to me? he wondered. This science court was his idea in the first place, and now he's wimping out on it. He's betrayed me. He's betrayed himself. He's just not strong enough to stick to his guns.

"I've already ruled on this issue," Graves said testily, peering over his bifocals at Arthur. "Your objection is overruled." Then he turned to Rosen. "Proceed."

Rosen asked Jesse, "Could you explain what you mean by financial and moral factors?"

I shouldn't do this to Arthur, Jesse thought. He keeps trying to isolate the science so he can ignore everything else. Like this is some kind of laboratory experiment where he can control the conditions. But what else can I do?

"Dr. Marshak?"

Jesse took a breath. "Even if the regeneration treatment can be made to work, even if it can someday regrow organs or limbs for human patients without causing cancer, the cost of the treatment is going to be enormous: I'd say on the order of a million dollars."

"A million dollars per treatment?"

"Yes," said Jesse.

Arthur sat in his place, seething. This kind of crap doesn't belong in this trial. Nobody's even started a cost analysis; Jesse's pulling numbers out of the air. And we shouldn't be talking about economics here in the first place!

Across the room, the reporters were devouring Jesse's testimony with glittering eyes.

"At a million dollars per treatment," Rosen was saying solemnly, "only the very rich could afford regeneration."

"Right," said Jesse. "But it's the very poor who'd need it most. Wealthy people are already healthier than the poor. They live longer; they have better nutrition and better health care. They can afford it. The poor can't."

"But couldn't the lower income groups apply to Medicaid or other government programs to pay for the regeneration treatments they need?"

Jesse shook his head. "At a million bucks a pop, the whole federal treasury would go bankrupt within a few years. It'd cost billions per month. Trillions!"

"Which means that the government could not afford to help the poor," said Rosen.

"Which brings up the moral issue," Jesse said. "Is it right for this treatment to be available only to the rich? That's what I object to most of all. There are hundreds of millions of poor, starving people all across the world—millions in the United States alone—and we're going to spend a ton of money to produce a treatment that'll allow the rich to live longer, a treatment that the poor can't afford."

Arthur saw that all the TV cameras were focused squarely on Jesse. He looked handsome and terribly, terribly righteous.

"Thank you, Dr. Marshak," said Rosen.

The examiner started back to his chair. Jesse got to his feet. Arthur struggled inwardly to keep himself from roaring with justifiable rage.

It's not Jesse's fault, Arthur tried to convince himself. He was willing to leave when I stopped questioning him. Rosen's done this. It's Rosen's fault, not Jesse's.

But Arthur knew that Jesse had agreed to testify at this trial specifically to bring out his objections. Financial and moral. I tried to make it easy for him and he throws that crap in my face.

Exerting every iota of self-control he possessed to keep his voice level, Arthur called out, "Just a minute. I have another question or two for this witness."

Jesse looked startled, almost afraid. He turned to Graves, who said softly, "Please be seated, Dr. Marshak."

"Which one?" Jesse asked.

"You, sir," said Graves. "Your brother has the right to cross-examine you further."

Jesse could feel his pulse thumping as he sat down in the witness chair again. Arthur looked grim, angry.

He asked, "Where were you born?"

Jesse gripped the arms of his chair, as if to hold himself steady.

"Where were you born?" Arthur repeated gently.

"Brooklyn."

A titter of laughter rippled through the audience. Why do they always laugh at the mention of Brooklyn? Arthur wondered.

"Did you grow up in Brooklyn?" he asked Jesse.

"Yes." Sullenly.

"Did you go to school in Brooklyn?"

"Public school. Then I went to Columbia and med school." Before Arthur could ask another question, Jesse added, "That's in Manhattan."

More laughter. Graves looked annoyed. Arthur scanned the jurors, then turned toward the head table. Kindelberger was smiling. Of course, Arthur thought, he's probably a lawyer; he can see where I'm heading.

"What did your parents do for a living?"

Jesse answered warily, "My father was a tailor. My mother helped him in his shop."

"Where they wealthy?"

"No."

"Middle class?"

"Lower middle class, I guess."

Turning to face Jesse squarely, Arthur asked, "If you or someone in your family needed a million-dollar medical procedure, could you afford it?"

Jesse's face went red. "Now, wait, that's an unfair question."

"Could you afford it?" Arthur thundered.

"That's not fair!"

"Then I'll answer the question for you," Arthur said, before Graves or Rosen or anyone could intervene. "Yes, you could. You have insurance and stock holdings and income from patents that we share. Don't you?"

"What's that got to do with anything?" Jesse snapped.

"You weren't born rich, but you could afford the most expensive medical treatment in the world if you or someone in your family needed it. Is that true or not?"

Seething, Jesse answered, "It's true. It's also irrelevant."

"Is it?" Arthur took a few steps away from the witness table, then asked, "When penicillin was first introduced to medical practice, it cost thousands of dollars per unit, didn't it?"

"Only until the pharmaceutical companies started to mass-produce it. Then the price dropped steeply."

"And now just about anyone can afford penicillin, can't they?"

"Yes, but—"

"When broad-spectrum antibiotics first were developed, their costs were so high that the federal government investigated the pharmaceutical industry, isn't that true?"

"The major companies were price-fixing," Jesse said.

"And now everyone can afford broad-spectrum antibiotics, right?"

Jesse did not bother to reply.

"Could it be," Arthur asked, "that a new procedure that costs a million dollars today will cost less in the future?"

"Regeneration doesn't involve just a new drug," Jesse replied. "It's going to require major hospital time and a long period of follow-up."

"Like a heart transplant?"

"Yes, very much like a heart transplant."

"Can poor people afford heart transplants?" Arthur asked.

"No, they can't."

"Poor people don't get heart transplants? Liver transplants? Kidney transplants?"

"Not all of those that need them."

"Ah!" Arthur almost pounced on his brother. "Then—morally—we ought to stop all the transplants. If they're too expensive for everyone, we shouldn't allow anyone to have them. Is that your moral position?"

"You're twisting my words," Jesse said.

"The hell I am! That's *exactly* your position, and it's morally wrong!"

The hearing chamber was so quiet Arthur's voice seemed to ring in the air, reverberate from the walls. Even the reporters were still, staring at the two brothers.

"If we have the ability to save a life—even if it's just one life—and we refuse to save it, that is as wrong morally as murder."

"You kill unborn babies!" yelled a woman in the audience.

Graves banged his gavel. But Arthur smiled at the woman. "We don't use fetal tissue. We don't need to."

The woman glared at Arthur, but said nothing more.

Arthur turned to the judges. "No further questions."

Jesse slumped back in his chair. Rosen stared at him for a moment, then looked away.

"You're excused," said Graves.

Gratefully, Jesse got up from the witness chair and hurried

down the aisle toward the double doors to the corridor. They think I'm running away from Arthur, he told himself. But I'm not. I'm running back to Julia. Then his heart constricted. Julia. And the baby.

Graves squinted at his wristwatch. "Dr. Rosen, Dr. Marshak, do you think you can give your final summations this afternoon? I wouldn't like to continue this hearing into next week, if we can avoid it."

Rosen said solemnly, "I'll need about half an hour."

Arthur said, "No more than fifteen or twenty minutes, I should think."

"Then we could be finished by roughly five o'clock," said Graves. "Very well. We'll take a half-hour recess and come back for the summations."

PATRICIA HAYWARD

There was something strange about Arthur's cross-examination of his brother. I mean, it was terrific, really. I thought Arthur dissected Jesse's objections like a surgeon. But it seemed to me that he was maybe *too* logical, too coldly analytical. Oh, there was passion there, anybody could see that. But Arthur kept it under control, you could see that, also. He reminded me of a hunting dog that's being kept on a leash, quivering to be turned loose and go chasing down its quarry. But the only leash on Arthur that afternoon was his own self-control. He could have demolished Jesse if he'd wanted to. Only he didn't want to.

The reporters sitting around me were kind of disappointed.

"I thought he was going to go for the jugular," one of them said to the reporter sitting next to him.

"Hey," she answered, "they're scientists, not lawyers. Be happy you got as much fireworks as you did."

"Not much." He got up and joined the crowd filing out into the corridor.

Assholes, I thought. Here Arthur took apart any and every objection against moving ahead with the regeneration program and they're grumbling because he didn't stage the last act of *Il Trovatore*.

I had planned to sit where I was, at the reporters' table, and not fight the crowd out in the corridor. I didn't have any deadline to meet, no story to file.

I looked over at Arthur. He was just standing there, in the front of the room, a kind of sad, dejected look on his face. I got up and went to him.

"I've lost him, Pat," Arthur said to me. "He'll never talk to me again after what I did to him this afternoon."

I had never seen Arthur show pain before.

"I thought you went easy on him," I said, trying to sound cheerful. "You could have sliced him up and served him as hors d'oeuvres."

He just sort of hung his head. "You don't know the half of it."

"The reporters thought you could have slaughtered him," I blathered on.

He turned and gave me the saddest look I had ever seen on his face. "He's my brother, Pat. I should never have allowed it to go this far."

"It's not your fault." I didn't even know what *it* really was.

"Yes, it is. All of it is my fault, just about. I've driven my brother away from me."

THE TRIAL:
DAY FIVE, AFTERNOON

One of the conditions that Arthur had insisted on, when he and Graves first started to put together the details of the trial, was that Arthur would give his final summation as the very last statement the jury would hear. Which meant that Rosen, the supposedly impartial examiner, gave his summation first.

He stood tall and grave before the jury in his usual dark blue suit and red tie. He looked utterly humorless, totally dedicated to getting his points across to the jurors.

"We have heard a week's worth of testimony," he began, "about a truly amazing breakthrough in the field of biomedicine. It is easy to become accustomed to new successes; what was miraculous yesterday becomes commonplace tomorrow."

Turning to look at Arthur, in the front row, Rosen went on, "But I believe that we should all keep foremost in our minds that what we are dealing with here is a breakthrough in biomedicine that has incredible implications for the future. For your future, ladies and gentlemen of the jury. For my future. For the future of each and every person on the face of this planet."

He hesitated, head drooping slightly. The chamber was completely still. The TV cameras were tightly focused on him.

"This is a court of science," Rosen resumed. "You have been asked to judge the scientific validity of the work done so far on tissue regeneration. You have been asked to make a recommendation about proceeding to human trials for this work."

Again he stopped, chin sinking almost to his chest, hands clasped almost prayerfully.

"You have heard me make the point that science cannot be judged in a vacuum. That other issues—social, economic, ethical—must be considered side by side with the scientific facts. I realize that this is a bending of the basic ground rules for this hearing. But there is a reason for my insisting on broadening the scope of your deliberations."

Rosen seemed to stand taller, as if he had just come though some inner struggle and irrevocably made up his mind.

"Whatever you decide will have the most profound effects on the entire balance of scientific research in this country, perhaps worldwide. If you decide that this regeneration work should proceed to human trials immediately, it will cause tremendous pressures to be put on government funding agencies."

Arthur wanted to object, despite the agreement that the summations would be uninterrupted.

"Yes, I know," said Rosen, glancing in Arthur's direction, "that this work has been done exclusively on private funding. That point was established in the first day's testimony." He stepped closer to the jurors. "But consider this: your approval of this work will mean that the federal government will be pressured to open its treasury to fund such research. No member of Congress could possibly refuse a constituent who demands that the government speed up research in organ regeneration—not once this work is 'officially' sanctioned by the science court. The pressures would be irresistible.

"Therefore," he went on, "you must decide whether or not this work is ready for a massive infusion of federal funding, and all the controls and regulations that inevitably come with federal funding. Are we ready for another version of the war against cancer? Or the biomedical equivalent of the war against poverty? Tens and hundreds of billions of dollars spent, to little avail. Thousands of careers interrupted or warped out of shape because funding for other research was usurped for the massive wars that Washington proclaimed. Is that what we want here?"

Arthur could see that he was scoring points. The jurors, all researchers themselves, had been scarred in the past by the twists and turns of federal funding priorities.

"And then consider the scientific evidence," Rosen said, changing gears once he saw that his point had been made.

"The researchers at Grenford Laboratory have made remarkable progress in little more than two years. But are they ready for human tests? Their one experiment on a primate resulted in the ape's death. Even their experiments on monkeys and rats have been plagued by tumor growth that's been controlled only by applications of an enzyme treatment that has not yet received FDA approval."

Several of the jurors were nodding. Arthur's insides were clenching. He suddenly wished that he had had the good sense to go to the toilet during the break.

"Those are the scientific facts," Rosen was saying. "Dr. Jesse Marshak, who helped to originate the very ideas that are on trial here, is himself against rushing into human tests. I won't say anything more about the ethics or morality issues that he brought up; those are for your individual consciences to decide."

Rosen hesitated for the span of a heartbeat, then said, "You are all scientists, but you have a responsibility that goes beyond your professional interests. You have the responsibility of judging the scientific merits of this work *in the context* of its social, economic, and ethical implications."

All eyes in the hearing chamber were riveted on him. Rosen fingered his mustache, as if searching for the exactly correct word. Then, "That concludes my remarks, ladies and gentlemen. Thank you for your attention."

The audience stirred as Rosen walked back to his seat at the front desks. Someone coughed. The TV cameras swung toward Arthur as Graves nodded at him.

Getting to his feet, Arthur thought, This is how Marc Antony must have felt when he went out to give his funeral oration for Caesar. Brutus has swung the crowd his way; now I've got to swing them back to me.

How to start? I can't say, *Friends, Romans and countrymen* . . .

Arthur glanced at Pat sitting at the reporters' table, as he stepped to the front of the chamber. She made a smile for him. He walked in silence as far as the empty witness table, touched the fingers of one hand against its green baize surface, as if to balance himself. He glanced at Graves and the other two judges, and realized with a start that Senator Kindelberger had not returned after the break. If he's not the center of attention he doesn't stay, Arthur thought.

Then he looked squarely at the jurors. Six men, six women. He took a deep breath, like a man about to plunge off a high platform.

"When I asked for this court of science to be convened," he began, "I did it because I did not want this work on organ regeneration to be tried in the media. You know as well as I that there are powerful forces aligned against us, against science in general and this work in particular."

Now the jurors were focused on Arthur. He took a few steps toward the judges' desks and their eyes tracked him closely. Good, he told himself.

"President Franklin Roosevelt said that the only thing we have to fear is fear itself. I agree. But behind that unreasoning fear lies ignorance. You've seen the scare headlines; you've seen the witless, fear-mongering demagogues whipping up the crowds against us. How many of you have had your own research interrupted or stopped altogether because some crackpot screamed to the media that your work might release mutated microbes into the environment or cause radiation that might increase the cancer rate a thousandth of a percent?"

Arthur knew that at least four of the jurors had suffered through legal battles brought on by self-styled activists who objected to their research.

"What we are fighting against here is nothing less than ignorance—colossal, cynical, egotistical ignorance that feeds the fears of the crowd against anything new, anything unknown."

He heard murmurs from the audience. Turning slightly toward them, Arthur went on, "Science has always had to fight against those fears and the ignorance behind them. In earlier ages scientists were burned at the stake or shut up in prisons because their ideas went against the prevailing opinions of the powers that be. Today they're hounded by lawyers and forced into court."

A couple of brittle laughs.

"By its very nature, science is always discovering new things. Science therefore is always causing changes: changes in our understanding of the world, changes in the way we think, changes—inevitably—in the way we live. Yet most of the other institutions of society resist change with every gram of energy they possess.

"Think of society's institutions," Arthur said. "Religion, law, social customs. All of them exist to preserve the status quo. They are all designed to make tomorrow exactly the same as yesterday. Societies seek stability and they have created these institutions to protect themselves against change.

"Yet here is science, always discovering new concepts, always forcing us to change our outlooks and even our behavior. No wonder so much of society fears and resists scientific advances. No wonder we are here in a court of science debating whether or not we want to help human beings to grow new organs and new limbs when they need them."

Arthur had never felt so strong. The entire chamber was concentrating on him, on his words. He felt like a knight on a white steed, holding up a banner and leading his people toward a shining castle on a hilltop.

"You have been told," he said to the jury, "that more than science is at stake here. You have been told that science does not take place in a vacuum, that you must consider the social and economic and ethical impact of the work under consideration.

"All right, consider this: a five-year-old girl is dying from a congenital heart defect. Do we hope that some other five-year-old dies so that we can take its heart and try a transplant procedure, or do we help this child to grow a new heart that is free of her defect?"

The jurors all nodded, almost in unison.

"Or suppose you're in an auto accident and you lose both your legs. Will you be content with a wheelchair for the rest of your life? Or prostheses? Or would you like to regrow your legs so that you can walk naturally again?"

Sweeping the room with his arm, Arthur said, "Every person

on earth could benefit from the work being considered here. If you must think of the social, economic, and ethical impact of organ regeneration, think of how we can change the world for the better! Yes, the changes will be significant. They will be deep, and wrenching. And they will make the world better! That's the important point. Not the pain of making these changes, but the benefits they will bring."

He had them now, he was certain of it.

"You've been told that you have a responsibility here that goes beyond your responsibility as scientists. I agree. You have the responsibility of being human. You have to make the choice between bowing to ignorance and fear or rising to the challenge of a new era of human capability. Science is the most human activity that human beings engage in; I know that as scientists and as human beings and as concerned citizens of our society you will make the right decision. Thank you."

As he turned and headed back to his seat, Arthur half expected a stirring round of applause. But the chamber remained absolutely still.

Graves waited until Arthur was seated, then turned to the jury. "Now it's up to you. You will retire to the room next door and deliberate your decision."

But instead of rising and filing out of the chamber, the jurors leaned together in a rough sort of huddle. The foreperson—a middle-aged woman—conversed briefly in whispers with the jurors closest to her, then got to her feet.

"Your Honor," she said, somewhat uncertainly, to Graves, "we arrived at our decision during the break earlier this afternoon. Nothing we've heard in the summations has changed our decision."

Arthur was thunderstruck. Nothing they heard has changed their decision! They didn't listen to a word I said!

The reporters all leaned forward avidly. They'd have their story in time for the evening news!

Even Graves looked surprised. And pleased that they wouldn't have to carry the hearing into the weekend.

"What is your decision?" he asked.

The forewoman looked directly at Arthur. "We've decided to recommend that Dr. Marshak's work should *not* go into human tests until the tumor problem is definitively understood and correctable."

Arthur sagged back in his chair as if he'd been shot through the heart.

WASHINGTON:
EVENING

Arthur felt a hollow chill of foreboding inside him as he rode alone in the limousine to dinner with W. Christian Johnston. The sudden invitation to have dinner with Omnitech's CEO, coming immediately after the jury's lethal decision, sounded more like a summons than a request.

The invitation had been waiting for him at his hotel when Arthur got there after a grueling, exhausting struggle to fight his way through the reporters crowding the courtroom at the end of the trial. Arthur still felt numb, dead inside, from the decision. The trial's killed me, he told himself. I've committed suicide, just like Cassie.

The Cosmos Club was quiet this midsummer evening, its big, genteelly elegant dining room almost empty. The maître d' brought Arthur straight to Johnston's corner table, well away from the few other diners. The CEO was already there, draining a tumbler of whiskey while a waiter placed a fresh one at his elbow. Johnston put his drink down and got to his feet, put out his big hand for Arthur to shake. But the expression on his dark face was grim, ominous.

"You're getting to be a famous man," said the CEO. "You're on the evening news again."

"I know," Arthur muttered as the waiter held his chair.

"They're watching you in Japan, too," Johnston added as

they both sat down. To the waiter he said, "Bring my friend here a glass of white wine."

"What brings you down to Washington?" Arthur heard himself ask. Stupid question, he thought.

"Oh, business," Johnston said vaguely, not looking directly at Arthur. "Lawyers, lobbyists, all that crap."

"Not the trial?"

"And the trial," Johnston admitted.

Arthur decided to go straight to the heart of things. "How will the jury's decision affect the merger talks?"

Johnston's eyes widened for a flash of a moment. Then he recovered and said dismally, "Just about kills the deal."

"That's what we were afraid of."

The waiter brought a tulip glass of chardonnay. Johnston waited for him to leave, then hunched closer to Arthur and muttered, "There's still a chance of putting the merger together. But it's gonna be tough—very damned tough."

His stomach knotting, Arthur mumbled, "If there's anything I can do . . ."

"This goddamned trial was a mistake, Arthur. A big mistake."

"You knew about it from the beginning. I kept you informed every step of the way."

Johnston huffed. "You made it sound like a scientific exercise. You didn't tell me you'd be on C-SPAN every damned day."

"I didn't know the trial was going to be subverted the way it's been. My idea was—"

"Your idea," Johnston snapped, "has turned into a goddamned booby trap. They sandbagged you, Arthur."

"But the scientific evidence is on our side. I'm still convinced of that."

"Yeah, maybe. That's what you keep telling me. But it doesn't make a rat's ass worth of difference as far as the Japs are concerned. Or the Europeans, either."

"Now that the trial is over—"

"The legal staff tells me you might be facing criminal charges, for chrissakes!"

"That's . . ." Arthur fished for a word. "Unlikely," he finished lamely.

"Likely enough to throw everything into the toilet, pal."

He's really angry, Arthur said to himself. He's sore as hell. At me.

The waiter brought menus. Johnston laid his on the table and took another slug of his whiskey. Arthur had no appetite at all, but found himself picking up his menu as if it could shield him from the CEO's anger.

"The stock price is gonna drop like a lead balloon," Johnston muttered. "The goddamned Europeans are licking their fuckin' chops."

"We could do human trials overseas."

Johnston scowled at him. "Not if you're in jail, Art."

"That's nonsense!"

"Yeah, maybe, but I've gotta face that possibility. You ought to be worrying about it, too."

"They can't possibly bring criminal charges against me. I'm not responsible for Cassie's suicide."

Johnston took another swallow of whiskey, then held the glass high and rattled the ice cubes in it. The waiter came over instantly, asking, "Another, sir?"

"Damned right," said Johnston.

Arthur had hardly touched his wine. He looked into Johnston's bloodshot eyes and said, "You know as well as I do that there's no way anyone can bring criminal charges against me. Why are you worrying about a problem that doesn't exist?"

"They can tie you up, Arthur. There's going to be a criminal investigation into that girl's suicide, did you know that? They're reopening the case up in Connecticut."

"That doesn't mean—"

"Kindelberger's people are already talking about a Senate investigation of the regeneration work. You'll be hearing from the NIH soon, I bet, and probably the goddamned FDA, too. Who knows who the hell else is going to stick their muddy boots into this?"

And he's blaming me for it, Arthur thought. He's convinced all this is my fault.

"Maybe you're right," Arthur said aloud.

"Huh?"

"It's all my fault. I wanted to bring this new capability to fruition; I wanted to show the world we could regenerate organs and limbs. And it's turned into a world-class mess."

The waiter arrived with Johnston's refill. He brought the glass to his lips, but instead of drinking he put it down gently on the table.

The CEO leaned back in his chair. "Take a look around the room," he said, more softly. "How many black men do you see? Outside the hired help, that is."

Puzzled, Arthur scanned the mostly empty dining room. Johnston was the only black seated at a table.

"You know how I got here, Arthur? By being as tough as anybody in the woods. And tougher than most of 'em. I'm not a token nigger, Arthur. I *worked* my way here. I make the tough decisions."

"I don't see—"

"We're selling the lab," Johnston said. "The executive committee's okayed the decision and the full board will rubber-stamp it at the next meeting."

For a moment Arthur thought his heart stopped. This was what he had been dreading, what he had feared was the reason behind Johnston's anger.

"I wanted you to hear it straight from me," the CEO said, his voice flat and murderously calm. "We can't afford to keep you, Arthur. You've become a liability to the corporation."

"Who's the buyer?" Arthur heard his own voice as if it came from a thousand miles away.

"A little outfit in Singapore. You never heard of 'em; they're not in the biomedical field yet. But they want to move in that direction and they're offering a good price for your lab."

"We'll stay in Connecticut?"

Johnston shrugged. "That's up to them. For the time being, I suppose."

"Most of my people won't want to go to Singapore."

Another shrug. "That's not my problem. Maybe it isn't even yours."

"What do you mean?"

"They don't want *you,* Arthur. They want your research staff and your facilities and all the data you've amassed so far on your ongoing programs. But they've got somebody else in mind to run the lab for them."

It hit Arthur like a high-power bullet. Shock and pain and an endless moment of rattled bewilderment. He thought he hadn't heard Johnston correctly. He thought it was all a joke, a mistake, a blunder.

"I'm sorry, Art," said Johnston, avoiding Arthur's eyes. "I don't like it any more than you do."

Arthur was about to ask who was going to replace him, but suddenly it didn't matter to him. Suddenly nothing at all mattered. Without another word he got up from the table, knocking his menu fluttering to the floor, and strode out of the dining room. Johnston stared at his departing back.

GRENFORD LABORATORY

Arthur spent the most miserable weekend of his life at the lab, alone, even though the lab was far from empty. But he would talk to no one, not Darrell Walters or Zack O'Neill or anyone. He sat for hour after hour in his office with the door shut and the phone on its answering machine.

He couldn't face any of them. Couldn't bring himself to tell them that the lab had been sold and he was fired. Couldn't admit to the men and women who had worked with him for so many years that he was out, finished, dead. They'll have a new boss soon. I'll be gone.

Everything I've ever really wanted has always been taken away from me, he told himself. Julia. My professorship at Columbia. My chance for a Nobel. And now this.

Phyllis was supposed to be off for the weekend, of course, but she showed up late Saturday afternoon and broke in briefly on Arthur's solitude with motherly advice to "get something to eat and a good night's sleep." Arthur had no appetite and he spent the night roaming the building's corridors and laboratories. If he slept at all it was in his big desk chair, fitfully.

Sunday morning, bleary-eyed, he drove home before anyone else showed up, before the sun rose, then shaved, showered, changed into a fresh shirt and slacks, and—after an hour or two of wandering through the empty house—got back in his Infiniti and returned to the lab.

At his office, the phone machine showed sixteen messages. He ignored them all and sank into his desk chair, uncertain of what to do next.

I've got to tell them, he said to himself. I've got to find the courage to tell my people what's happened. They should hear it from me, not from Sid Lowenstein or some other corporate official.

Lowenstein. Arthur thought of the comptroller's role in dumping the lab. He's happy about it, I'll bet. And Nancy. She must be ecstatic.

The phone rang. His private line. Only a handful of people knew that number. Maybe it's Jesse, he thought.

Arthur let it ring. Twice. Three times. Four.

Exasperated, he grabbed the phone. "Hello," he snapped.

"Arthur?" Pat Hayward's voice.

He took a shuddering breath. "Hello, Pat."

"Are you all right?"

"Yes. Of course."

She hesitated. "I was thinking—maybe you'd like to come over here to Old Saybrook. Unwind a little. We could rent a sailboat and then have dinner at dockside."

"I don't think so, Pat."

A longer hesitation. "There's a rumor . . . that Omnitech has sold your laboratory to some Pacific Rim company."

Christ! he thought. The news is out already.

"Arthur? Are you—"

"I've got to go, Pat. There's a mountain of work here for me to finish."

"Is it true?"

"Yes," he admitted. And hung up before she could ask another question.

IT WAS a bad weekend for Jesse and Julia, too.

As soon as his cross-examination had ended, Jesse had left the hearing and taken a shuttle flight back to New York. He and Julia spent the waning hours of the day in their apartment, trying to console one another, trying to make an adjustment in their thinking, in their lives, that would never be fully made. Trying to imagine what life was going to be like with a hopelessly crippled baby.

That evening, as they picked listlessly at the dinner they had prepared together, the phone rang. It was Elwood Faber with the news of the jury's verdict.

"Congratulations," Jesse said tonelessly.

"It's a victory for us, I guess," said Faber. "But not total victory. They're going to go ahead with more experiments on animals, you can bet. We'll have to work hard to stop them altogether."

"Leave me out of it," Jesse snapped.

For several moments Faber said nothing. Jesse could hear him breathing into the phone, like an obscene caller. Then, "I figured you'd drop out. The reverend thought you'd stay with us, but I figured you wouldn't."

"I've done enough," said Jesse. "I've got my own problems to deal with."

"Sure," Faber replied. "Well, you know how to reach us, if and when."

"Yep." Jesse hung up the phone.

In the dark of midnight, as they lay sleeplessly next to each other, Jesse whispered into the shadows, "Even if I hadn't opposed Arby, the jury would've voted the way they did. It didn't make sense to rush into human trials with so little evidence."

"Of course, darling," Julia whispered back.

"It's not my fault."

"No one has said that it is, dear."

"*He* blames it all on me. You can bet on that."

Julia turned slightly in the bed toward him. "Jesse, dearest, you are projecting. You blame yourself and you're telling yourself that it's Arthur who blames you."

He couldn't think of what to say.

Julia went on, "You did what you thought was right. It's not your fault that the trial went the way it did. It's not your fault that our baby is going to be handicapped."

Handicapped, Jesse thought. What a bloodless word. What a way of shifting the reality into a bland antiseptic compartment. That's what we do: when something's too horrible to think about we find more comfortable words to use. The baby won't be crippled, he'll be handicapped. He won't be a hydrocephalic mentally retarded kid, he'll be intellectually challenged.

"It's not your fault," Julia repeated, emphasizing each word in turn. "No more than it is mine."

"I know," he whispered. "But still . . ."

She waited, and when he didn't go on, she put one arm around him and leaned her head against his shoulder.

"Christ, it hurts," Jesse said. He broke into tears and Julia began to cry with him. They cried for a long, long time.

Saturday was gloomy and gray, but at least that night they both slept, exhausted physically as well as emotionally. Sunday morning broke bright and almost cheerful. When Jesse awoke he found that Julia was already up and about. He smelled coffee and bacon aromas coming from the kitchen.

By the time he had showered and pulled on a robe, she had breakfast on the table. Julia smiled at her husband as he came into the tiny alcove that served as their dining area. She was dressed in a loose-fitting sun suit.

"Are we going to the beach?" Jesse asked.

"Hardly," she said. "But the way I'm growing I won't be able to wear this outfit much longer, and it's a warm day, so I thought I'd throw it on."

The devils of the nights before seemed banished. Julia was as bright and perky as he had ever seen her. Yet he knew the darkness was still there, beneath it all. He felt it inside himself. It'll never go away, Jesse told himself. Never.

"Bacon and eggs," he said as he sat at their little glass-topped table. "The cholesterol special."

"The eggs have no yolks and the bacon is made of turkey meat," Julia said. "No cholesterol at all, practically."

He tried to kid with her, and she gave a good appearance of bantering back with him. But as he finished his decaffeinated coffee Julia grew serious again.

"You really should phone him, you know," she said.

"Who? Arby?"

"Of course."

His first instinct was, We don't need his help.

But before he could say a word, Julia went on, "He must be devastated by the results of the trial."

"You're feeling sorry for *him*?"

"He could use a friendly hand, I expect."

Jesse almost laughed at her. "He'd bite my hand, most likely."

"I rather doubt that."

He gave her a suspicious look.

"Jesse, darling," said Julia, coming around the table to sit on his lap, "we simply cannot go on forever with you being jealous of your brother. There is nothing for you to be jealous about."

"I'm not jealous of him!"

"Then why are you reluctant to phone him?"

"Because he'll be sore at me."

"So what is he going to do, say naughty words to you? He *needs* you, Jesse. Can't you see that?"

"And we need him, is that it?"

"No, we don't need him. We have each other. He has no one. No one except his brother."

"Arby's never needed anybody," Jesse grumbled. "He's always been at the top of the mountain, all by himself."

"He needs you now," Julia insisted, "and if you're going to let jealousy stand between you and your brother I shall nag you nigh unto shrewdom."

He sat there with her in his lap, his arms around her waist, their noses almost touching.

"There is no reason for you to be jealous of Arthur," Julia repeated firmly. "None whatsoever. There never was and there never will be. He's the one who needs you, right now."

"Maybe," Jesse conceded.

She kissed him on the lips and got up from his lap. Jesse, still feeling slightly uneasy, went to the phone on the kitchen wall and pecked out Arthur's number.

"No answer," he said after seven rings.

"He's probably at his laboratory."

Jesse tried the lab and got Arthur's answering machine. He left a brief message, feeling relieved that he had done his duty, as Julia conceived of it, and still hadn't had to face his brother.

PHYLLIS CAME in early Monday morning and immediately started coffee brewing. She peeked into Arthur's inner office and found him asleep in his desk chair, a day's growth of white stubble on his face, his sports shirt wrinkled and soggy with sweat.

She went back to her own desk, picked up the phone, and touched the intercom key. She heard the phone on Arthur's desk chirp once, twice . . .

"Yes?" His voice sounded groggy, thick with phlegm.

"Good morning," Phyllis said cheerfully. "Ready for some coffee?"

He cleared his throat. "Give me ten minutes."

"There's a couple of clean shirts in the top drawer to the right of the lavatory sink," said Phyllis.

"I know."

As he shaved, Arthur could smell the coffee. Staring at his image in the mirror, he thought, Okay, you've spent a weekend feeling sorry for yourself. Where do you go from here?

He called Walters, O'Neill, and Vince Andriotti to his office, bracing himself to tell them his news. They had already heard about the trial's outcome.

Before Arthur could work up the nerve to tell them, Darrell asked, "So what's the government going to do about this now?"

Andriotti grumbled, "They'll get involved, one way or the other."

"They could help get us more chimps," Zack O'Neill said hopefully. "NIH has a whole breeding colony set up out in California."

"That's a possibility."

"They're gonna want to set up protocols," Andriotti said, from his usual perch straddling one of the chairs from the conference table.

"Red tape." Darrell wrinkled his nose.

"They'll slow us down," said Zack.

"Wait a minute," Arthur said. "I've got something to tell you."

Andriotti cocked an eyebrow at him. "You mean, about the lab being sold?"

"We heard about it Saturday," said Darrell.

Arthur blinked with surprise.

"It doesn't make any difference," Zack O'Neill added.

"But the new owners don't want me to stay," Arthur said.

"Fuck them," Andriotti snapped.

"We're not staying, either," said Darrell. "We're forming our own company."

"We've been hashing it out all weekend," Zack said. "Got a luncheon appointment with some risk capital people."

Grinning toothily, Darrell said, "And I've got a cousin in the banking business who thinks he might be able to loan us enough to get us started."

Arthur sank back in his chair. "That's . . . great," he said, feeling breathless.

"Only if you come along with us," said Darrell.

"Now, wait," Arthur said. "I appreciate your loyalty, but—"

"None of us knows how to be a boss," said Andriotti.

"Or wants to be," Darrell added.

"It's not that simple," Arthur heard himself reply. "I've got an awful lot of baggage attached to me. You'd be better off without me."

"We need you," Zack said.

"They're talking about a criminal investigation into Cassie's suicide," Arthur pointed out.

"We need you," Darrell repeated. "The money people won't talk to us unless you're part of the deal."

Arthur stared at them. "You think the four of us—"

"What four of us?" Andriotti snapped. "We've got everybody in on this."

"Practically the whole lab."

"Including Phyllis," Darrell said, as if it were a trump card.

"Everybody?" Arthur felt almost giddy.

"Now, what we really need you for," Darrell said quite seriously, "is to go to Omnitech's corporate people and tell them we won't work for the company they want to sell us to."

"We'll buy the lab ourselves," Zack said. "Set up our own company."

"Do you think we really could?" Arthur asked, trembling inside.

"If you can sweet-talk the suits into selling the lab to us instead of the Orientals," Andriotti said.

Arthur took a deep breath. He sat up straighter in his desk chair. "I'll talk them into it. If they don't like it we can buy some space elsewhere and set up shop there. Let Lowenstein sell the empty buildings to Singapore."

"Want to come to lunch with us and talk to the money people?"

Arthur grinned at them. "Damned right I do!"

And he was thinking, We'll push ahead as hard and fast as we can with animal experiments. I'll get Graves at the National Academy to start leaning on NIH to loan us some of their chimps. Zack will have to get into the molecular structure of regentide and see what can be done about making it more specific so we can stop generating tumors.

The three men got to their feet and left Arthur's office. Alone, he pictured what the next weeks and months would bring. I'll have to deal with Kindelberger's committee and the investigation into Cassie's suicide and god knows what else. But they're not going to stop us. Slow us down a lot, okay, that can't be helped. But they're not going to stop us.

GRENFORD LABORATORY

After the three researchers filed out of Arthur's office, Phyllis popped her head through the doorway. "Your brother called yesterday, left a message to call him back."

Arthur felt his hackles rise.

"I've already phoned the hospital," she said, her face almost perfectly blank. "They're paging him."

"But . . ." Arthur wanted to say that he had no intention of speaking to Jesse, but Phyllis fixed him with her no-nonsense gaze.

He picked up the phone grudgingly. Phyllis nodded as if satisfied and left his office.

For a few moments all Arthur could hear was a background murmur, several people talking. Then a slight clatter and:

"Hello. Dr. Marshak here."

"Jesse, it's me. Arthur."

"Arby?"

"You left a message yesterday?" Arthur's throat felt tight, as if he could barely get the words out.

"Yeah. I, uh—I wanted to tell you I'm sorry things turned out the way they did."

"Sure." You helped them turn out that way, Arthur fumed silently.

Jesse's voice dropped a notch. "I really am sorry, Arby. I know how much you wanted to push ahead and—"

"How's Julia?" he asked, cutting off that line of conversation. It could only lead to a fight.

"She's fine."

"I mean emotionally. This must've hit her terribly hard. Both of you," he added.

"Yeah."

"I'm sorry that it happened."

"So am I."

"But you're going through with it? She's going to have the baby?"

"That's what she wants."

"And what do you want, Jess?"

A long pause. Then, "I guess I want what she wants, Arby."

"You love her that much?"

"Yeah, I do."

And Arthur realized that he didn't. He could never do what Jesse was going to do. Jesse really is ready to give his whole life to her, Arthur told himself. He's ready to make all the sacrifices that the baby will require. For her. For Julia.

"God," he said into the phone, "I could never do that."

"I don't know if I can," Jesse replied, his voice shaking slightly. "Not really."

"You can. You've got a lot more strength than I do, Jesse. A lot more strength."

"I wish I believed that."

"You'll see," Arthur said. And he knew it was true. "The two of you together can deal with anything that the world throws at you. You'll see."

"I hope so."

Jesse's voice sounded choked with tears, and Arthur's own vision was blurring slightly.

"Arby? Are you going ahead with the regeneration work?"

Arthur had to clear his throat again. "Yes. Certainly. As far and as fast as the goddamned government will allow."

"Could I—I mean, would it be all right if I stuck my nose in once in a while? Just sort of looked over what you're doing?"

Arthur straightened up in his chair. "Of course, Jess! I'd be happy to have you working with us again."

"I don't know how much time I can put into it."

Nodding, Arthur said, "Jesse, you know that it's going to take years before we'll be able to help your baby. Even if we could go as fast as we want to, I don't think . . ." He stopped, unable to say the words.

"I know," Jesse said. "But I'd still like to help, if I can."

Beaming, Arthur said, "I'll send a limo to drive you up here whenever you want."

Jesse said, "I can drive myself."

Arthur wondered if he'd have access to a limousine once the lab's staff owned the laboratory. But he said, "With somebody driving you, you can read our latest reports while you're on the way up here."

His brother laughed. "Christ, Arby, you're trying to make a plutocrat out of me."

"Just being efficient."

Another voice interrupted, muffled but sounding urgent.

"They need me upstairs," Jesse said. "I've got to run."

"Call me when you want to come up here," Arthur said.

"Julia sends her love."

"I'll come down and take you out to dinner later in the week. Got a lot to tell you."

"Great. 'Bye, now."

"Say hello to Julia for me."

The phone went dead. Arthur realized that "Julia sends her love" was nothing more than a polite conversational phrase. The words meant almost nothing. And they didn't hurt.

He took a deep breath, as if testing to see if he'd been injured. No broken bones, he said to himself. No internal bleeding.

Then he glanced at the digital clock on his desk. Darrell and the others expected him to go with them for their lunch with the investment brokers.

THEY WERE surprisingly young, Arthur thought, to be playing with tens of millions of dollars. The investment brokers turned out to be two men and a woman, none of them looking more than thirtyish. The men wore sports coats and casual slacks, the woman a tailored skirt suit.

They met in a less-than-elegant restaurant off the Saw Mill Parkway, roughly halfway between the laboratory and Wall Street. Darrell handled the introductions, but as their conversation lengthened, Arthur began to do most of the talking.

"So you want to push ahead anyway," the young woman said, the salad in front of her largely untouched, "despite the ruling at your hearing."

"Yes," said Arthur. "We've got to convince the world that we're ready for human trials." His salad of salmon and greens was almost gone.

"But what kind of restrictions will the government put on your work?" she asked.

Darrell Walters bobbed his head up and down. "That's the key question now."

Arthur put his fork back on its platter. "Let me give you an educated guess."

"I could use some education." She smiled.

"The first thing the government will do is appoint a committee. I think NIH will do that right away. The committee's task will be to investigate our regeneration work and any similar work going on anywhere in the country and then make a recommendation about how to proceed with it."

"I thought your trial already did that."

"It did." Arthur nodded. "But NIH will want to have its own committee and its own recommendation."

"Who'll be on the committee? Will you?"

"No. I'll be called to testify, certainly, but they won't want me on the committee. I'm too biased."

"Then who?"

"That's the really important question," said Arthur. "If they pick people who are truly impartial, they'll be picking people who don't know much about the field and have to be educated. We stand a good chance of convincing them to go our way, in that case."

"Otherwise?"

Arthur spread his hands. "They might pick people who already have strong opinions about this work. Potter, to cite an absurd example. Or Davila, over at Georgetown: she'd be on our side."

Darrell said, "The makeup of that committee will be crucial."

"It certainly will be," Arthur said. "In the meantime, of course, Congress will start its own investigation of the work."

"Senator Kindelberger," Zack O'Neill said.

"You can bet that Kindelberger's going to start one. Other

senators and congresspersons are undoubtedly being pressured already by the likes of Ransom and Simmonds and other know-nothings—as well as paraplegics and any other interest group that sees regeneration as benefiting them."

Andriotti made a low whistle. "AARP. And the motherlovin' Gray Panthers. I hadn't thought about them."

"Think about them," Arthur said, smiling.

The young woman frowned slightly. "And until all these committees and investigations come to some conclusions, the government won't formulate a policy about the work, is that right?"

"Right," said Arthur. "But sooner or later they'll come up with a set of regulations and make them apply to everyone, whether we take federal funding or not."

"You might as well take it, then."

"When that time comes, I suppose we should. If there aren't too many extra strings attached."

"And in the meantime?"

Arthur said, "We move as far and as fast as we can. We want to stay ahead of any possible competition and present the government regulators with as much of a fait accompli as we can."

One of the young men asked, "What do you do if the government decides to stop the work altogether? Makes it illegal to do this kind of research?"

Arthur felt a pang of alarm. But he tried to control it. "I doubt that they could do that even if they wanted to. The trial has at least generated enough publicity to make it virtually impossible to halt this work altogether. The worst they could do is refuse to fund it. But we're already planning to fund this research ourselves—with your help."

"Do you realize how many ways the government's got to lean on you?" the young man insisted. "Maybe they can't outlaw your work, but they could make it damned difficult for us or anybody else to support it, if they want to."

Arthur shrugged. "When the going gets tough . . ."

The woman smiled.

Then Andriotti said, "Remember the motto of the Navy's

Seabees: 'The impossible we do right away; the miraculous takes a little longer.' "

Everyone laughed.

ON THE drive back to the lab Darrell and the others bubbled with enthusiasm. Arthur thought that no one sinks ten million dollars into a high-risk investment so easily, but he didn't want to break up their cheerful mood.

They were still grinning and congratulating themselves as they piled out of Arthur's car and walked back into the lab building. Arthur was thinking about the call he had to make to Johnston. Got to get him to stop the Singapore deal before it's finalized, he told himself.

Then he smiled, thinking of the expression on the CEO's face when he told Johnston that the employees wanted to buy the lab and make it Grenford Laboratories, Inc.

He was walking down the main corridor, heading for his office. As he passed Pat Hayward's office, he saw she was cleaning out her desk.

"What are you doing?" he blurted, stepping through the open doorway.

Pat looked up, startled. Pushing back a strand of hair, she said, "Leaving."

"Who told you to leave?"

"Nobody. But the trial's over. You don't need a PR consultant anymore."

Her office was barely big enough for a desk and a visitor's chair in front of it, and the chair had a big filing carton on it. Arthur stood between the two and leaned on the desktop with both hands.

"Since when do you get paid to make personnel decisions about Grenford Labs?"

She stared at him for a moment, then realized he was trying to be witty. "I just thought . . ."

Arthur saw that she looked unhappy, harried. There was a big cardboard box on her desk chair, too, and she held a thick loose-leaf book in both hands, holding it almost like a protective shield. But even in a plain white blouse and baggy sea-green slacks she looked uncommonly beautiful to him.

"You can't leave," he said. "There's going to be an awful lot for you to do."

"I'm not sure that I ought to stay," Pat said.

"I need you."

"As a PR consultant."

"As a friend."

Pat pushed at the stubborn strand of hair falling across her forehead. "Arthur, your policy is not to mix business relationships with social ones. I think that's a good idea."

"Well, I don't."

"It's your policy," she said.

"I'm making an exception."

"What?"

Very seriously, Arthur said, "I'm making an exception to that policy, in your case."

"You can't do that!"

"Why not?"

"It'd set a bad example for the staff, wouldn't it? It'd be inconsistent—"

"A narrow consistency is the mark of a small mind," Arthur said, smiling.

Pat grinned back at him. "It's 'A foolish consistency is the hobgoblin of little minds.' Emerson."

He spread his hands in a gesture of helplessness. "See? I need you here to keep me straight on these things."

"Really?" Pat asked. "You really want to make an exception in my case?"

"Only for you," Arthur said, his smile widening. Inwardly, though, he was just as startled as she was. What the hell are you doing? he demanded of himself. And he answered, I'm not entirely sure, but it certainly feels good, whatever it is.

She put the loose-leaf book on the desk, pushed the cardboard box to the floor, and dropped onto her desk chair. "Arthur," she said, "I'm kind of scared."

He leaned across the desk and touched her cheek with his outstretched hand. "Don't think I'm not."

Pat looked up at him. "You're sure you want me to stay on here?"

"If you think it'd be better if you quit, then go ahead and quit. But I don't want you to go out of my life, Pat."

"I'll stay if you want me to."

Arthur sat on the edge of the desk. "God, we're like two trauma victims, frightened to take a deep breath."

Pat laughed. "Yes, I suppose so."

"Come to dinner with me tonight," he said. "There's a lot we have to talk about."

"My mother's expecting me home. I told her—"

"I'll come home with you."

Her eyes widened. "I don't know if you want to meet Livvie just yet."

"Why not?" Arthur asked. "What should I bring her? Flowers? Candy?"

Pat took a deep breath. "A half gallon of vodka would be more like it."

GRENFORD LABORATORY

In the months that it took to arrange the financing for their buyout from Omnitech, Arthur spent most of his time in Washington. The National Institutes of Health appointed a committee to study the research done in organ regeneration. Four separate subcommittees of the House of Representatives and two more in the Senate held hearings on the subject. Arthur testified to them all; so did Jesse. On several occasions they appeared together. Both the media and certain members of Congress were disappointed that the two brothers would not openly contradict one another. It was clear that Jesse was far more conservative in his opinions about the work, but he did not oppose his brother's enthusiasm; he merely tempered it.

It was two days before Christmas when the call from Jesse came. Arthur was as nervous as any expectant father would be. Phyllis had foreseen that he would be, and ordered a hired car for a boss she knew would be too distracted to drive. Not a limousine; a Mercedes sedan would have to do in the lab's new financial condition.

Pat came into his office, purse in hand, ready to go to the hospital with him. But just as Arthur was about to get up from his desk, Phyllis buzzed.

"Call from Tokyo."

"Switch it to Darrell," Arthur said brusquely.

"It's from Mr. Nakata, the head of Kyushu Industries." Even over the intercom Phyllis sounded slightly awed. "He wants to speak to you personally."

Frowning with exasperation, Arthur motioned for Pat to take a chair as he jabbed at the telephone console's speaker button.

"This is Dr. Marshak," he said.

"One moment, please," Pat heard a male voice reply in perfectly pronounced English.

"Dr. Marshak," came a deeper, rougher voice. "So kind of you to take my call without a previous appointment."

"It's very kind of you to call, Mr. Nakata," said Arthur. Pat saw that the expression on his face did not match at all his diplomatic tone of voice.

"I wanted to inform you personally that the merger of Omnitech and Kyushu Industries has been fully approved by both boards."

Arthur had known it would be, even though he had resigned from Omnitech's board of directors.

"Congratulations," Arthur said tonelessly. "I wish you both every success."

"I will be chairman of the board, and Mr. Johnston will remain as CEO of the Omnitech part of our company."

"You'll make a good team, I'm sure."

"I wish you to know that we have agreed to allow you to buy Grenford Laboratories. The deal with Singapore has been canceled."

Arthur felt a wave of relief wash over him. "That—that's very good of you. Thank you."

Nakata's voice changed tone slightly. "It seems very unfortunate that your own government is hindering your work."

"Yes, it is quite unfortunate," Arthur agreed. "But I believe that we will be able to move ahead anyway. They can slow our progress but they can't stop it."

"If you find yourself frustrated by your government's restrictions," Nakata said, as if reading a prepared script, "I can offer you all the facilities and staff that you require here in Japan. You can, of course, bring your own research people with you, as well."

Arthur leaned back in his swivel chair. "That's an extremely generous offer, Mr. Nakata."

"Your work is far too important to be stopped by political forces."

"I'm delighted that you think so."

"Remember my words in the weeks to come. I would be honored to have you continue your most extremely important work in Japan."

"I will remember," said Arthur. "And I thank you most sincerely."

"You are most welcome. Now, I have taken up enough of your valuable time. Thank you for receiving my call."

"Thank you for calling."

It took another three rounds of thank-yous before Nakata finally hung up.

"Come on," Arthur said, scrambling from behind his desk. "We're going to be late."

"How old is Nakata?" Pat asked.

Arthur hiked an eyebrow at her. "Old enough to know that he'll need organ regeneration sooner or later."

In the car, Pat asked, "Would you really move the work to Japan?"

Arthur shook his head. "Not unless I'm absolutely forced to. I'm still enough of a chauvinist to want to see this done in America."

MENDELSSOHN HOSPITAL

The traffic was impossibly heavy, and by the time they reached the hospital the cesarean had been done and little Bertram Marshak was in an incubator in the newborns' care center.

Julia was still heavily sedated and Jesse was sitting at her bedside, barely conscious of anyone except her. The attending physician asked Arthur and Pat if they would like to see the baby.

Glad that they had arrived too late to watch the surgery, Arthur let the doctor lead them down to the neonatal care center. Attendants helped them into pale blue smocks, complete with paper hats, masks, and booties. All he could see of Pat was her clear green eyes.

"I feel like we're being sent on a moon shot," Arthur quipped.

The neonatal care center was dimly lit and hushed, except for the faint beeping of monitoring equipment. Arthur saw preemies, some of them not much bigger than lab rats.

An attendant—he couldn't tell if it was a man or a woman underneath the shapeless gown—brought them to a glass-topped incubator that bore the name MARSHAK taped to its side.

The baby looked to Arthur like a tiny lump of reddish flesh, lying on its belly, mouth flapping like the gills of a fish, eyes closed, arms and legs unmoving. How frail and helpless! He saw that the baby's hands were clenching and unclenching slowly, the only motion it was making, except for the labored breathing that forced its tiny rib cage to expand and contract, expand and contract. Slowly, it seemed to Arthur. Painfully.

Someone stepped between him and Pat. One look into his eyes and Arthur knew it was Jesse.

This is Jesse's son, Arthur said to himself. His and Julia's.

"There he is," Jesse whispered, his voice shaking with hope and despair, wonderment and fear.

"We've got a lot of work to do," Arthur whispered back.

Jesse looked at his brother, then nodded. "We sure as hell do."

So I won't win the Nobel, Arthur said to himself. So what.

Yet he knew, at that precise moment, that he would go to Japan or Patagonia or the moon to carry on the work that this baby so desperately needed. For him, Arthur said to himself. For all of them. For the whole human race.

TOR

Award-winning authors
Compelling stories

Please join us at the website
below for more information
about this author and other great
Tor selections, and to sign up for
our monthly newsletter!

www.tor-forge.com